T0348183

Mandy Magro lives in the picturesque country township of
Grenfell, New South Wales, with her husband Clancy, and their
two girls, Chloe and Taylor. She loves writing about the Australian
outback and all the wonderful characters who live there, and her
own adventures on the land have made her the passionate country
woman she is today.

www.facebook.com/mandymagroauthor

www.mandymagro.com

THE
Wildwood
SISTERS

MANDY
MAGRO

mira

First Published 2015
Second Australian Paperback Edition 2018
ISBN 978 1 489 24132 0

Published by
Harlequin Mira
An imprint of Harlequin Enterprises (Australia) Pty Ltd.
Level 13, 201 Elizabeth St,
SYDNEY NSW 2000
AUSTRALIA

Printed and bound in Australia by McPherson's Printing Group

MIX
Paper from
responsible sources
FSC® C001695

For my soulmate and hubby Clancy,
and my beautiful forever friend, Tia.

Sisters we will forever be, our bond infinitely unbreakable, because even in death our souls will still be united for eternity…

An earthbound spirit…

One that has not yet crossed over into the spiritual realm, a spirit which is halfway between the living and the dead—a deceased person's soul, an energy that lingers in the physical world until their final message is heeded and acted upon. And only with the revelation of truth and justice, their spirit will be freed.

PROLOGUE

Nine years ago
Opals Ridge, Far North Queensland

Her laboured breath escaping her in short, painful gasps, the girl staggered through the engulfing darkness, the towering ghost gums she'd found so beautifully mesmerising in the daylight now seeming menacing and foreboding. With the frenzied drumbeat of her heart echoing in her ears, she frantically looked around, trying to decide which way to go, blindly following her first impulse. All around her the inhospitable landscape was eerily silent but for the scurries of night creatures.

Bile rose in her throat as she remembered his animal grunts and groans, relived the horrific sensation of his rough hands upon her, hands that had once been so gentle with their touch. He'd been playing her all along—the true reason for his infatuation now revealed in all its shocking truth. He'd never loved her. What a fool she had been, thinking her secret was going to make things perfect. She never should have told him. She should never have done any of it.

The icy breeze ruffled the leaves of the towering native trees surrounding her, prickling her skin and making her shiver to the core. A bush stone-curlew called out from the looming shadows, the bird's eerie song only heightening her anxiety. She had always hated their sound, usually pulling her doona up and over her head when she heard their nocturnal calls. But tonight she wasn't tucked up safely in her bed at the homestead. Instead she was out in the dead of night, fighting for her life.

Stumbling over a fallen tree branch, she collapsed to the ground, the impact stealing the air from her lungs. She rolled onto her side, screaming silently, horrified by the knowledge that he was somewhere behind her, searching her out in the dark. It was at this very moment she begged God for her life.

CHAPTER
1

Present day
Melbourne

Gazing across the table of the chic restaurant, Renee groaned inwardly. The softly lit room oozed romance, although she wasn't feeling the slightest bit amorous. Her date had not stopped talking about himself all evening—everything from how many hours he spent at the gym and how respected he was at his job as an accountant, to what brand of hair products he preferred to use—and it was driving her up the wall. She hadn't been able to get a word in edgeways and he hadn't shown one ounce of interest in who she was on the inside. She'd given up even trying to speak, instead smiling when necessary and nodding in agreement with everything he was saying. Whatever happened to the chivalrous men who opened doors and pulled out chairs and asked genuine questions so they could get to know you better? She drew in a breath and refrained from rolling her eyes. She'd made it through entree and main course—only dessert to go. Thank God.

As if on cue the waiter arrived at their table with two plates of sweet deliciousness and Renee had to stop herself from cheering. Not long now and she could get out of this restaurant and crawl into her warm and cosy bed—alone. Her mobile phone chiming in her bag stopped her from devouring her first mouthful of chocolate and macadamia tart. She pulled it out, her heart landing in her throat when she spotted the caller ID. It was close to ten so what would her pa be doing calling at this hour of the night?

She looked to her date and forced a smile. 'Excuse me, I have to take this.'

The bloke across from her nodded and started flicking through his phone before she'd even had a chance to answer hers.

'Hi, Pa, is everything okay?'

'Hi, Renee. Not really, love. Your nan has had a heart attack… but don't panic, she's going to be okay.'

Renee sucked in a sharp breath as tears prickled her eyes. She held them back, though, not wanting comfort from her date. 'Oh my God, Pa, where is she now?'

'She's recovering in the cardiac unit at the Opals Ridge hospital. The doctors are monitoring her very closely.'

'That's good. I'll try to organise a flight for tomorrow.'

'Oh Renee, no need to do that. You know how we feel about you coming back here after that letter. We don't want to risk losing you like we lost Scarlet. I think it would be best if you just stay where you are and I promise I'll keep you updated.'

Renee felt as dubious about returning to Opals Ridge as her pa did. And there was very good reason to, but this changed everything. 'I have to see her, Pa. I wouldn't forgive myself if…'

Her pa cut her off. 'That's not going to happen. Trust me. She's going to be alright.'

'I don't know, Pa. I just really feel like I need to see her.'

'It's late, Renee. I don't want you making a rash decision to come back here right now. I'll talk to you in the morning, okay?'

'Okay,' was all Renee could say, her throat so tight she could barely take a decent breath.

'Love you, Missy-Moo.'

'Love you too, Pa. And please tell Nan I love her too.'

It was just past midnight. Renee stood in front of her bathroom mirror, defeated, deflated and miserable. Peeling the spaghetti straps from her shoulders, her Swarovski-studded Louis Vuitton dress slid effortlessly from her body. Tia was certainly right, she had lost weight—the pressure of her job and the countless hours she spent doing it were taking a toll. Black rings circled her eyes, eyes that were bloodshot and glassy from crying—she hadn't been able to hold in the tears after she'd got off the phone to her pa, and mascara stained her cheeks from where they had fallen like a river.

As she'd predicted, her date had begged to come inside with her but she had declined, saying she was way too tired for company—besides, what kind of man would still press for sex after the heartbreaking phone call she'd received less than an hour ago?

The lack of depth of these city blokes was driving her round the bend. She'd always dreamt of finding the kind of love that would make her heart race and her toes curl, while leaving her blissfully breathless—the type of love she'd felt so briefly, yet poignantly, once before—but the last few guys she'd dated were making her doubt her faith in a happily ever after.

With her pa's words swirling around in her mind, her tears began to fall once more, her deep sobs breaking the silence of her one bedroom apartment.

Her beautiful nan, the woman that had always been there for her, now needed *her* to be there, and so did her pa. He had tried to reassure her that Nan was going to be okay, but Renee was finding it hard to believe him. What if he was just saying that to stop her coming home? What if she didn't go back and Nan died before she got to tell her to her face how much she loved her? Life could be really cruel—after what she had been through in her lifetime she knew just how damn cruel it could be. She couldn't bear the thought of losing her nan, not now, not ever. She needed to find the courage to return to Wildwood Acres, but even after nine years of being away, the note she'd found on her windscreen—the one that had made her skip town so suddenly—still haunted her, and the thought of the nightmares starting all over again overwhelmed her.

Smacking her open palm down on the marble vanity, she swore loudly. She was tired of letting fear run her life, and fed up with forever feeling as though she was treading dangerous waters with her lips just above the surface.

Pa was nearing seventy. With his long-time sidekick Mick recovering from a freak accident, and Nan in hospital, she knew he could use an extra hand around the place, be it in the saddle or around the homestead. Not that Stanley Wildwood was going to admit that to her. His fears about her returning home overshadowed any desire for her to ever go back.

But I have to.

Renee closed her eyes and breathed in deeply, turning back the clock in her mind to the days when her future seemed full of endless possibilities. She had spent the first seventeen years of her life at Wildwood Acres and there were many happy memories of her and her twin sister, Scarlet, growing up on the property, memories she had locked away after that devastating night almost ten years ago. It was about time she allowed herself to reminisce. Smiling sadly, she hugged her arms around herself as if trying to stop herself blowing away.

The world had been an enchanted place with Scarlet beside her, her sister always seeing everything through rose-coloured glasses. It had been one of her many beautiful qualities, one Renee treasured now more than ever.

Those who don't believe in magic will never find it, Reni.

Yes, sis, but those who live in an airy-fairy world will never be able to find their chosen reality because they're not living in the real world...

Oh come on, Reni, you have to learn to open your mind and trust in fate. Otherwise your life will be really boring.

I like boring. It means I know what's around the corner.

You're a stick in the mud.

No I'm not. I'm just a realist, that's all. There's no mud stuck on me.

Oh ha ha.

Even though they were born only minutes apart, Renee had always felt like the older sister—which technically she was as she had emerged from the birth canal first. But not being there to protect Scarlet from whatever had happened left her feeling guilty as hell.

With her turbulent emotions bringing back painful memories of that fateful night—the one that had changed all of their lives forever and left her with a gaping hole in her heart—Renee tried to focus on the handful of facts they knew for sure. Scarlet's bedroom window had been found wide open in the dead of winter, strange for someone who detested being out in the cold. The fact that her handbag and wallet were still there let them know she hadn't intended on going very far. Police had discovered blood deep in the woodlands that backed onto Wildwood Acres, and a week later, it was confirmed to be Scarlet's, meaning she was either very badly hurt or dead—Renee had known instinctively it was the latter.

But other than these few things there was nothing; no suspects, no fresh leads, no more evidence, and most devastating of all, no body to lay to rest. It couldn't remain this way. She'd been obsessed with finding Scarlet's killer back then, and she hadn't been afraid to say so—which had got her into a fair bit of hot water. Her desperation and lack of sleep had made her mind a muddled mess. She'd been way out of line, but there was still one person in particular she doubted was telling the truth. If only she'd had more time to do her own investigating, but the note left on her windscreen had changed everything. Now nine years later she was still none the wiser as to who had taken Scarlet from them, and neither were the police.

How was she ever going to free herself from the guilt, from the ache that scratched away at her soul every waking day? Finding Scarlet's killer and bringing him to justice would be a damn good start, and she'd yearned to do this every waking day for nine long years. But how?

Determination flooded her as ideas bloomed like buds in the spring. Maybe just being back where it had all happened and being able to view it all through fresh, more mature eyes, she might be lucky enough to finally unravel the truth. Maybe... She stared at her reflection, imagining it was her twin sister staring back at her. Reaching out, she stroked the mirror with her fingertips, smiling sadly, wishing with everything she had that Scarlet was still alive. Right now she'd do anything to be able to hold her hand or hear her voice. Just remembering Scarlet's addictive laughter gave her a little boost of courage. Renee's blood boiled as she thought about the killer still roaming free and the tremendous amount of strain that knowledge had put on her nan and pa over the years, as well as herself. The only reprieve she got from her deep-set heartache was that her dear sister was now with their mum and dad in heaven. If only angels could talk, she wondered what they'd tell her.

Over the past nine years she had tried to ignore her desperate aching need to find answers, but if she was to be brutally honest with herself, it was eating her from the inside out. And as much as the idea terrified her, she had to go back to Wildwood Acres. Because no matter how hard she tried to leave it all behind, the memories always shadowed her. Sometimes she would gain a comfortable lead in her daily life—lulled into believing she had put a comfortable distance between that night and the present day—but the fear of death always closed the gap. In the end, no matter how hard she tried to hide from it, that awful night always found her. And she was tired of running. It was time she put her demons to bed.

Dashing for the toilet, Renee fell to her knees, her stomach heaving. The thought of her twin sister's remains discarded like garbage, combined with the news of her beautiful nan, and the anxiety of going back was suddenly all too much.

At first, her dear nan, Pearl Wildwood, had told people she was sure Scarlet had just had some kind of freak accident and was still alive somewhere—maybe suffering from amnesia. She had forced herself to believe it, because the alternative was unthinkable, but as time passed and after the police confirmed the blood was Scarlet's, Nan finally came to understand that she was gone forever. Her pa, Stanley, being a realist, suspected all along that Scarlet had met with some sort of foul play.

Sadly, Renee had thought like her pa. She had felt the air go out of her very own lungs, as if someone had punched her in the stomach, the second Scarlet would have taken her very last breath, the intense sensation dragging her from a vivid nightmare where Scarlet was covered in blood and screaming for help. Her grandparents hadn't wanted to acknowledge the fact she had sensed something so horrifying.

And that same nightmare had haunted her every single night thereafter, for six agonising months, until she had hastily driven away from Wildwood Acres and the township of Opals Ridge in her beat-up old Suzuki Sierra. One morning she had found a note under the windscreen wiper of her car, telling her she was going to be killed next. After informing the police, her nan and pa had packed her bags and had sent her on her way, with strict orders to keep driving until she got to her aunt Fay's place in Melbourne—it would be over their dead bodies that they would allow this monster to hurt another of their grandchildren. She hadn't had the chance to say goodbye to anyone—not even to the boy who had stolen her heart. She still thought about him often, and wondered if he was married now, if he had children, and most importantly of all, if he had forgiven her for the way she left him. Meanwhile, the police, once again, came up with no leads from the note, and eventually came to the conclusion that it must have been a prank. The case went cold.

Walking with conviction from the bathroom, her long black silk robe floating out behind her and with her Blue Russian cat, Kat, hot on her heels, Renee went to her linen cupboard and began pulling out towels, sheets and tablecloths, tossing it all in chaotic fashion at her feet. Kat dodged the flying linen missiles—quickly deciding it was safer up on the white leather couch in the lounge room.

After emptying virtually the entire cupboard, Renee finally spotted it, buried deep at the back: the hand-carved box that had remained padlocked for nine long years. Her psychologist was right; now was as good a time as any to begin the final part of her journey into healing. She had procrastinated long enough. It was time she faced her anxieties so she could find a way to move forward. The call from her pa had been the kick up the butt she had needed. She believed she was ready to take the bull by the horns, hopefully…

The timber glory box now finally in her hands, Renee strode into the lounge room and placed it down on the floor, staring at it as she chewed her bottom lip. In need of a few moments to calm her racing heart, she gave a purring Kat a gentle stroke while admiring the view she had of the Melbourne skyline from her top-floor apartment. The city lights shone like beacons in the night, stealing the limelight from the seemingly invisible stars in the sky. It was as though the city itself was a living thing, pulsing with life twenty-four hours a day, three hundred and sixty-five days a year.

Unlike country life, the hustle and bustle never stopped here. It was tiring and invigorating all rolled into one. There were many parts of city living she just adored, such as her view of the pretty metropolitan hub, the wonderful fresh food markets, and being able to catch up with her amazing girlfriends at the trendy cafes and bars, but there were also some things she'd never got used to, no matter how hard she tried, like the fast-paced lifestyle, the constant noise and the dreary winters. Whenever the season turned cold, the country girl she had buried down deep within her all those years ago screamed to get out. As the saying went, you can take the girl out of the country but you can never take the country out of the girl. Although, she had grown to love the glitz and glamour of life in a place like Melbourne. Here, everything was at her fingertips and there was a multitude of events to choose from every single weekend. If only she could split herself in two…

Heading off to her bedroom to recover the key from her bedside drawer, and then grabbing a bottle of red wine and a glass from the kitchen, she returned and flopped herself down on the plush sheepskin rug in front of the couch. After pouring a glass of the red, she gulped the entirety of it down while staring at the box with wide eyes. How was she going to react to what was in there?

Kat took the opportunity to rub herself against the back of Renee's head. The feline's company calmed her a little. Kat had been her loyal companion ever since she had found her wandering the streets as a starving scruffy kitten four years ago. And she was certainly a puss unto her own. Kat ate her food with her paws, quite often had lengthy conversations with her in indecipherable cat lingo, and sat and watched the telly whenever it was on. Renee swore she was almost human. She couldn't imagine her life without her.

The glass now empty, Renee grabbed the key, brushed the dust from the timber top her father had so painstakingly carved for her for Christmas all those years ago, took a deep breath, and then began unlocking the box with quivering hands. Flicking open the lid, her heart broke when she spotted a small stack of photos with a rubber band around them. The top one was a picture of her and Scarlet with their mum and dad on their tenth birthday, the four of them with a five-metre python wrapped around their shoulders.

They'd spent the day at Cairns Tropical Zoo and Renee felt like it was only yesterday that she and Scarlet had been hand feeding the kangaroos, cuddling koalas and nursing baby crocodiles—it had been like a day at Disneyland for them. One day later, a horrendous car accident had stolen both her parents' lives—the bull her father had hit on the blind corner of the highway would have been impossible to see before it was too late. But here they were all so happy, their smiles outshining the sun, all of them without a care in the world. Little had they known the following day was going to change all of that, forever.

Renee began to look through the photos, smiling at one of her and her best friend from high school, Hayley Gregory. The pair of them were dressed in stonewash denim jeans and matching jackets. Good Lord, the fashion had been atrocious back then.

Continuing on through the pack, the next one made her heart squeeze tight. She was sitting bareback on her very first horse with her arms wrapped tightly around her dad's waist, her gappy five-year-old grin as enormous as her dad's. She smiled sadly as she ran a finger over her father's youthful face.

Throughout her early childhood years, he had been both her and Scarlet's hero. His passion for life and obsession with cattle and horses had been addictive. He had taught her so much in the short time she'd had with him on this earth, her undying love for horses all thanks to him. And her mum had been the typical country housewife, cooking, tending to the homestead and loving her girls and husband with everything she had. Renee closed her eyes and allowed the memories to flood her mind—she could still smell her mum's rose-scented perfume and feel her tender kisses on her cheeks. Why did God have to call them, and Scarlet, home so early? She missed them all so much.

Gently placing the photo in her lap as if it were made of the frailest glass, Renee finally got to the bottom of the pile—the last one making her belly do a backflip. Dylan Anderson's handsome chiselled face smiled back at her from where he was lying in the golden sunlight, the way his hands were tucked beneath his head making his muscular arms prominent. Her entire body tingled with the memory of his touch. With his dark hair and rugged looks, he really was the sexiest man she'd ever laid eyes on. And the intense look in his blue eyes, it swept her back to a time and place where love meant everything. She'd been the one who had taken the photo, and she recalled moments before this she and Dylan had been lying in the grass in each other's arms, cuddling and kissing for hours. Those were the days—if only she could get them back.

Placing the photographs down on the floor beside her, she slowly began to empty the box. She pulled out old birthday and Christmas cards, knick-knacks she and Scarlet had collected on their many adventures out on Wildwood Acres—including a lump of golden rock that they had at the time thought was a nugget of gold—high school yearbooks and snapshots of their years spent in Opals Ridge. Everything she touched sent waves of bittersweet emotions rushing through her.

When she pulled out a silver chain with a split heart pendant on it she broke down and wept. Scarlet had bought her this for her fourteenth birthday present, as a symbol of the way they were tied together through their twin bond. They both wore a half, and when put together the pendant read 'Sisters'. She'd taken it off a few months after Scarlet's disappearance, unable to bear the pain it brought every time she looked at it. But now she unclasped the latch, lifted the chain to her neck and fastened it, her desire to wear it once again outweighing the sadness. Bringing her fingers to the pendant, she pressed it against her chest, feeling a closeness to Scarlet that she hadn't experienced in many years.

Choking back sobs, she reached the bottom of the glory box, where some of her most treasured items had been kept buried—her diary, which matched the one of Scarlet's they'd never been able to find, along with a Queensland State of Origin scarf Scarlet had bought her for her sixteenth birthday present. Unknowingly, Renee had gone and bought the exact same thing for her sister—she and Scarlet had often unintentionally bought the same things for each other, like perfumes, CDs and books, their connection one that many identical twins shared—the only difference being that she had plaited the tassels on Scarlet's scarf before giving it to her. It had been their little thing—both of them always plaiting each other's hair while they had watched telly. Their whole family had been State of Origin addicts, their voices having enough decibels to carry for miles as they'd screamed encouragement at the mighty Maroons on the telly. Those were the good old days.

Renee smiled softly as more buried memories began to rise to the surface. Scarlet had been in the habit of wearing her scarf to bed every night, and she had apparently been wearing it when she'd disappeared as they'd never been able to find it since.

She hugged hers to her chest, deep in thought, her heart aching. Who had Scarlet met with that night? She remembered Billy Burton, Scarlet's boyfriend at the time she'd gone missing. Billy had always been a keen hunter, guns and knives his absolute passion, and his pride had been badly hurt when he and Scarlet had had a very public fight at a party the week before she'd disappeared. He used to always make Renee's skin crawl and she found it hard to understand what her sister saw in him. But like chalk and cheese, she and Scarlet had had very different ideas about what was attractive in a man. Billy swore black and blue he'd had nothing to do with Scarlet's disappearance, and had put forward a believable alibi—that he was home all night with his family. His parents had firmly backed him up, but wouldn't most parents protect their child, no matter what?

Renee had her doubts about him, and she had made the fact well-known around Opals Ridge. She still felt justified in doing so although she was very sorry about the unjustified accusations she'd made about a few others. She hadn't been in a very good state of mind at the time, desperately wanting to find who had taken her sister from her, and everyone had been a suspect.

She shook her head sadly. Nothing about that night added up—then or now—and it still infuriated her that the investigating police had met with dead ends every which way they had turned. Nearly ten years had passed, and Scarlet was now just another missing girl. She sighed despairingly. It was time she shone some light on the shadows of her past. Then she might be able to finally put it all behind her and move forward; for her sake, her grandparents', and for Scarlet's.

CHAPTER

2

The relentless Far North Queensland sunshine blazed down upon the rustic timber round yard of Ironbark Plains, and Dylan Anderson pulled his wide-brimmed hat down a little further as he fruitlessly swatted away the persistent flies. After discovering the pump that sent the water from the back creek to his paddocks tampered with this morning, as well as some fencing down at the back of his property and four of his yet-to-be-branded calves missing, he was seething.

It had taken a good part of the day to round up the cattle that had wandered off and another three hours to fix the damaged fence and pump. Along with everything else he needed to fit into his days, he didn't need this shit too. Everything seemed like it was going wrong in his life, as per bloody usual, and he felt as though he was balancing out on a branch that was about to break. It was about time things changed for the better. He had rung his long-time neighbour and true-to-the-core local, Craig Campbell—who was also the local copper and had been for the past ten years—but as usual there wasn't much the officer could do other than take a statement. There was no hard evidence, and not being aware of any enemies around the Opals Ridge township, neither he nor Craig had any idea as to who would want to do this to him—the trespassers were always fairly diligent in not leaving any clues behind. He suspected it might be some wayward teenagers, with nothing better to do than vandalise a local farmer's property—but why him?

Ignoring the beads of sweat running down his face, he spun the worn gold wedding band around on his finger, deep in thought as he weighed up his options. Not that he had many. No matter how much he tightened his belt, or cut corners, the bloody bills just kept rolling in, and with the cost of paying for water because he had no natural supplies on his property, as well as valued stock going missing, it was making him tighten the budget even more. The oversupply of cattle to the Far Northern market was pushing prices down, and with the local farmers feeling the pinch, the demand for his horse training expertise was dropping significantly.

Thankfully he had a small income from agisted horses, but between that and his thousand head of cattle it still wasn't enough to keep the place profitable. He'd begrudgingly remortgaged the property a few years back, to pay for an increase in livestock numbers and some much-needed repairs to the cottage and paddocks, but now that was adding pressure from every damn angle. Like a lot of Aussie farmers, between the running costs of the farm, living expenses and the mortgage repayments, he had less money coming in than going out—so something had to give. He needed to come up with a solution, fast, or he was going to be landing himself, and his family, in some deep shit.

If things were different he could go back and work at the mine as a heavy machinery operator, fly-in fly-out, but that was impossible.

He had to think of his little girl, Annabel Rose, who needed him around now more than ever. Annie loved it here so it was over his dead body that he was going to just sit back and let the farm go bankrupt. She had already lost enough in her young life to have to move from the only home she'd ever known.

And Dylan also had to consider his mum—she needed a place to live after what his low-life father had done to her. The bruises had long gone but the scars on his mother's heart would be there for eternity.

Peter Anderson had never been a loving husband—his drunken mood swings becoming more and more frequent over the years and his belittling words breaking his mother's heart into more and more tiny pieces—but smashing a fist into her face had been a first, and a last. If only he'd got a chance to get his hands on his useless father, he would have made him pay, but the coward had shot through before he'd got home from spending the night with his childhood sweetheart. And the day that had followed his father's disappearance had been filled with even more heartache, his father's aggressive behaviour raising suspicion with a girl that meant everything to him—and that had shattered his already crumbling world into a million pieces. It was almost ten years now and they hadn't heard a word from him—he'd never even met his granddaughter. Although that was probably for the best—Annie didn't need someone like that in her life, a man that would promise her the world and give her nothing, just as his father had done to his mother, and to him. Karma would get his father for what he'd done to Claire Anderson, Dylan was sure of it. Eventually, everyone paid for his or her sins, in one way or another.

Feeling as though the weight of the world sat upon his shoulders, Dylan groaned and closed his eyes, rubbing his throbbing temples. He was tired, beyond exhausted. Why did things have to be so damn hard all the time? His heart couldn't take much more sadness. He couldn't stand losing much more. But no matter how hard he tried, or how much he prayed, the aching black hole in his life just seemed to keep getting bigger and bigger, and he was afraid at any given moment he was going to fall in and never resurface. But he didn't have time to be defeated. He needed to stay strong for those around him. When was life going to give him the break he so desperately needed?

Dylan opened his eyes, took his sunglasses off and wiped the sweat and dust from his face. Squinting, he stared out across his horse-dotted paddocks, admiring the fresh green pasture that had shot up after last week's much-needed rain. Thank God for small mercies. Ironbark Plains was his dream property, and he and his wife Shelley had worked so hard to get it to where it was. It had been a two thousand-acre run-down farm when they had inherited it from his grandfather seven years ago, and even though it was still in need of some expensive TLC in certain places, he was proud of what they had achieved: well-fenced horse agistment paddocks now marked out neat sections of the fertile land; healthy Santa Gertrudis cattle wandered in the thousand-acre back paddock; and their three-bedroom cottage-style home had undergone impressive refurbishments, mainly thanks to his and Shelley's dedication to do-it-yourself handiwork. They'd even scrimped and saved enough to put a pool in, much to Annie's delight. It was all they had wanted, and more. If only life hadn't dealt them the low blow, their lives would have been close to perfect.

Now that the bank was on his back Dylan knew he really only had two choices: he could either sell off some of his land, or he could ask around town and see if someone was looking for a bit of casual hired help. He preferred the latter, as long as it didn't interfere with him being here for Annie. Opals Ridge was a fairly widespread township—expanding almost sixty-five kilometres, with plenty of cattle and fruit farmers, so surely there was a bit of work somewhere. Exhaling a frustrated sigh, he shook his head sadly, his throat constricting as he tried to block out the memory that had haunted him since that fateful day, and still had the power to bring him to his knees every time he allowed the horrific images to fill his mind. Things had been so much easier before...

With the heel of his timeworn R.M. Williams boot resting up on the rustic timber railings, he blinked back tears and instead turned his focus towards the job at hand. He couldn't fall in a heap right now—there was work to do. Taking a swig from his water bottle, his gentle gaze came back to rest on the buckskin stock horse he'd so aptly named Rascal, its buttermilk coat contrasting beautifully with its black mane, tail and legs. The saddled horse looked over at him and whickered, his tail curled and his ears pricked forward. Dylan smiled to himself. He'd definitely scored with this one— he was a bloody beauty. He'd always prided himself on having a knack to pick the good ones. He'd put so much blood, sweat, tears *and* money into the gelding this past month, he hoped the groundwork had paid off. It was about time to get in the saddle and find out.

He wasn't going to sell Rascal either, like he did with almost all of the horses he bought and trained. Annie had loved the gelding the second she'd laid eyes on him, and Rascal had equally loved Annie. To Dylan's amazement, when he had first brought him home from Emerald Station, the horse had stepped off the trailer and immediately walked over to his daughter, dropped his head, and put his nose to hers, blowing gently and also breathing her in. Their bond had been cemented in that very moment. Annie had spent a lot of time with Rascal since, grooming him, reading him her favourite books and simply loving him, and Rascal followed her around like a loyal puppy dog, no halter or rope needed. He was a completely different horse around her. She was going to be over the moon when she could finally ride him, and seeing his little girl smile made his problematic world feel so much better. His darling Annie was the only reason he dragged himself from bed every day. Without her, his life would be meaningless.

Walking over to the horse, he made sure to talk calmly as he ran his hand along his withers and neck, then carefully but confidently he placed his boot in the stirrups and planted himself firmly in the saddle. Rascal reacted instantly. Dylan gripped the reins as the gelding did what he was renowned for, and what had almost had him sent to the meatworks. Bucking, twisting and pig rooting like a trained bronco, Rascal did his best to throw Dylan off. But with Dylan's ability to ride the fiercest bucking broncos around, the gelding had Buckley's.

Always trying to see things from the horse's perspective, Dylan understood the bucking was just a defence mechanism, and once the horse figured out it was safe to have a rider on his back, Rascal would give up the buck, because just like a rocking horse, he wouldn't keep rocking unless Dylan kept him rocking. He believed horses were a mirror to your soul, feeling what you feel and fearing what you fear. If he showed them they were protected, and could trust him, he'd have a devoted friend for life.

With his body moving in rhythm with the horse, Dylan persevered, knowing that this wasn't fearful or panicked bucking, which was usually lightning fast and violent. He knew from experience that Rascal was instead being defiant, his bucking feeling somewhat premeditated, and in comparison to fearful bucking, lazy. Dylan just needed to show Rascal he was the boss, but in a way that wasn't dominating—he would never use whips or spurs on a horse. In the words of his horseman hero Guy McLean, knowledge, patience, compassion and imagination were what brought man and horse together, not heavy-handedness and domination.

With his heels down and one arm up in the air for balance, and his stomach and back soft, Dylan flowed with the horse's movements, rocking when Rascal rocked, ignoring his instinctive reflex to tug on the reins and instead focusing on the beautiful creature beneath him, allowing Rascal to have some freedom of movement. For if he tightened up, he would just become a spring that the horse's exaggerated movements would bounce right out of the saddle. And then the horse would think it had won. Just like a mother with her baby, this process was all about being gentle.

With the horse slowly beginning to wane in his fight-or-flight instincts, Dylan pushed Rascal forward by squeezing his legs, directing him into a trot and then a canter. Rascal responded to Dylan's gentle commands without too much of a fight, the trust between man and horse now becoming evident. He guided Rascal around the yard, concentrating on his body language, making sure to change direction every now and then so the horse remained focused on his cues. Then, pulling the reins a little tighter and sitting back in the saddle, Dylan silently instructed Rascal to stop, and the horse did.

He knew Rascal had it in him to be a good horse—until now he just hadn't had the right person in the saddle to prove it was safe to trust a human. Mindfully tugging the reins to one side and then the other, Dylan got Rascal to bring his head to each of his knees, and then pulling a little more firmly again, he got him to back up. Thrilled with the horse's progress, but not wanting to push him any further for today, Dylan let go of the tension on the reins and leant forward to give Rascal a rub on the neck. 'You're a good boy, Rascal. From the minute I laid my eyes on you I knew you had it in ya. You just needed someone to trust, didn't ya mate?'

Rascal's ears twitched as he turned his head to look at Dylan, his eyes bright and focused, his body language relaxed.

'Daddy!' Annie's angelic voice carried across the round yard, capturing Dylan's attention. 'You're finally riding him, yay!'

With Rascal turning towards the voice he loved, Dylan met eyes as dazzlingly blue as his own. Annie's waist-length sandy blonde hair was no longer neatly in a ponytail but was instead hanging haphazardly around her petite, dirt-smudged face as she skipped along the gravel driveway. She graced him with a big gap-toothed smile and Dylan's heart melted, as it did with so many beautifully innocent things Annie did.

'Hi, sweetheart, I sure am. And Rascal's being a very good boy…' His eyes travelled down to the splats of mud on Annie's school uniform. He couldn't help but grin. Annie rarely returned from anywhere without some kind of mess covering her and her clothes. His little angel was a tomboy through and through, much like her mother, although she did love playing around with her mum's make-up sometimes. 'What have you been up to between the bus stop and here, Annabel Rose Anderson?'

Annie looked down to where her dad was eyeballing, giggling as she tried unsuccessfully to tidy herself up. She sucked in her bottom lip and pointed to the left of her. 'You can blame Bossy for that. She was so excited to see me she bowled me over right in a big yucky puddle.' Their Great Dane, Bossy, tap danced happily beside her, her long legs proportionate to her massive head. The dog religiously met Annie at the bus stop every day and was never far from her side. They were the best of mates and it was comforting to know she had a fiercely loyal bodyguard in her canine pal.

Dylan chuckled and rolled his eyes. 'Poor Bossy, she always gets the blame. Even when you're the one sneakily feeding her your dinner.'

Trying not to laugh, Annie placed her hands on her hips. 'It's not my fault she pinches it from my fingers.'

'Well of course she's going to take it from your fingers when you're dangling your hand beneath the table, Annabel.' Dylan playfully shook his head as he spotted Annie's two pet ducks, Funky and Groovy, making a mad dash across the round yard just so they could side-track Bossy.

Annie grabbed Bossy's collar, the dog eagerly eyeing his feathered friends. 'Don't you dare, you big bully.' She gave her canine mate a small tap on the bum.

Dylan looked at Bossy, scowling. 'I'd listen to Annie if I were you…or you'll be sleeping outside for a month.' Bossy whined and then sat. Satisfied she wasn't going to give in to her yearning to play catch with the ducks, Dylan glanced at his watch. 'You're home a little early today. Everything okay?'

'Yep. Because it's my birthday on Sunday Mr Eddie dropped me off first as a treat.' Annie dumped her school bag on the ground and then climbed up to sit on the top barrier of the round yard, talking the entire time. Bossy eased herself down on a small patch of grass at her feet while snapping at the flies that kept landing on her nose. Annie continued. 'Ben Harrison was a big meanie on the bus again today. He poked his tongue at me and called me a girl.' Annie pouted as she defiantly folded her arms. 'But don't worry, I stuck up for myself. I'm not going to let a boy make fun of me, especially one that thinks he's better than everyone else, just because he's rich. What a loser!'

Ignoring his innate urge to defend his little girl by going and giving the toffee-nosed town mayor's teenage son Ben a stern talking to, Dylan stifled a smirk as he imagined how poised Annie would have been on the bus as she'd belittled her bully. Like her mother, Annie definitely had spunk. Directing an eager Rascal towards her, his heart both swelled with pride and ached at the same time, Annie's wisdom beyond her almost six young years endearing, but also heartbreaking. She had been through so much—too much— and he blamed himself for not being there to protect her from the unspeakable heartache she'd felt that day. 'That was nice of Mr Eddie. So what did you say to Ben, sweetheart?'

'I told him he's more of a girl than me, with his tight school shorts and his floppy hair hanging all over his face…and then the whole bus laughed at him.' Annie screwed her face up. 'I wanted to point out he had a massive pimple on his nose, too, but I didn't!' Throwing her hands up in the air she shook her head. 'I felt bad that everyone was laughing at him, but that'll teach him for picking on me in the first place.'

Dylan nodded. 'Ben Harrison needs to pull his head in a bit, or I'll pull it in for him. I'm tired of him being a bully to you kids all the time. His father needs to do something about it.'

'Dad, I really don't think it would be wise of you to pull Ben's head in. You'd probably get in loads of trouble off Mr and Mrs Harrison for that.'

Dylan couldn't help but chuckle at Annie's way of thinking. 'Yeah, you're probably right there, sweetheart. I better leave Ben's noggin alone.'

'Ben's noggin—you're funny, Daddy.' Annie tipped her head to the side.

'I'd be happy to have a chat to his dad about it, if you like.'

Annie defiantly shook her head, her eyes wide. 'Thanks, Dad, but no way José. It'll make me look like a tattletale, and a sissy. And besides, I don't think his snobby father would bother doing anything about it anyway. He thinks the sun shines out of Ben's butt.' Rascal whinnied his hello to Annie as she gave him a rub on the neck.

Dylan nodded in agreement. 'Okay, I won't say anything, for now. But if Ben picks on you again, I'm going to have to put my foot down and go and talk to his father, no ifs buts or maybes.' He gave Annie's hair a loving ruffle. 'And you're definitely no sissy, Annabel. You're actually a very strong little girl. Grammy and I are very proud of you, sweetheart—' he hesitated, '—and I know your mum would be too.'

Annie smiled sadly, her eyes watering. She sniffled and rubbed her tears away, smudging more dirt across her cheeks. 'Thanks, Daddy, I miss Mummy so much.' She placed her hand over her heart. 'I might not be able to see her anymore, but she'll always be in here.'

Dylan struggled to breathe, his emotions suddenly overwhelming him. Reaching out, he grabbed Annie from the railing as she wrapped her wiry arms and legs around him, squeezing him tight. He hugged her close to him, burying his head in her hair, wishing with everything he had that he could take his darling little girl's sorrow away. He felt terrible that a mere mention of her mother could send Annie into floods of tears. But he couldn't pretend Shelley had never been a part of their lives either. Annie's psychologist had hammered home the fact it was very important he and Annie talk about Shelley, as often as possible.

It was a fine line to walk, and one he and Annie had to balance on for the rest of their lives—but they would get through it together. He kissed his daughter on the cheek, holding his lips there for a few seconds as he closed his eyes and tried to push his own emotions away. 'I love you, Annie, with all my heart.'

Annie squeezed him tighter. 'I love you, too, Daddy, a million trillion bazillion.'

CHAPTER

3

Retreating from the icy chill of her panoramic balcony after watching dawn break over the crimson horizon, Renee stepped back into the embracing warmth of her heated apartment, her breath escaping her in little misty puffs. The Melbourne June temperature was sitting at a frosty five degrees. Closing the double-glazed door firmly behind her, Renee breathed a sigh of relief as the noise from the busy road twenty-six floors down disappeared along with the chill factor. Although she loved the hustle and bustle of the city, the hectic life outside of her apartment made her head spin this early in the morning.

Years of living in the city had transformed her from a rise-before-the-sun country girl to someone who was not usually out of bed before eight in the morning. Her realtor job allowed her the luxury of working her own hours, and also meant many over-dinner business deals with high profile clients at high class inner-city restaurants, one of the many perks of her job—albeit at times tiring. As a result she'd become a little nocturnal over the years. Watching the golden orb of the sun climb high into the powdery blue sky had been a pleasant distraction from her aching heart, but it hadn't been enough to alleviate the nerves that kept making her belly do backflips, forward rolls and somersaults. She seriously needed to get a grip, or she was going to end up making herself physically sick again, as she had last night.

Still shivering, she pulled her woolly robe tighter around her, while wishing she were instead somewhere hot and sunshiny with beads of sweat running down her cheeks and back. Even though it was the beginning of winter, she knew the Far North Queensland temperature would still be sitting in the luxurious high-twenties today, maybe even higher. The very thought made her smile dreamily. What she would give to be able to wander outside in a pair of shorts and a singlet in winter, with nothing to see for miles other than endless space, green paddocks, horses and cattle. It would certainly be a nice break from her usually hectic city lifestyle. And to be pulling on her old Blundstone boots again, and jumping in the saddle for the day to tend to the cattle, fix fences or whatever needed doing, without another soul in sight, would replenish her weary mind and body. If only she could click her fingers and get rid of her heartbreaking past, it would make going home a hell of a lot easier.

Her home. Wildwood Acres. A haunting past still lingered there, unanswered questions making it impossible for her to let that night go, but she had to find a way to do just that—let it go. Venturing back there would give her an opportunity to cut the ropes that bound her to her long-ago life. Not that she wanted to forget it all—there were many happy memories there too, ones she'd never get the chance to have again with her sister.

Come on Reni, don't be a party pooper. Let's climb up on the roof and pretend we can fly. You know, like they did on the Titanic.

We'll break our legs if we fall, sis!
Only if we miss the trampoline.
My God, Scarlet, Dad will kill us if he catches us.
He's not going to catch us, me and you are too clever for that...

Two hours later her dad was wrapping her sprained ankle up tightly with a bandage, and reminding both her and Scarlet, very sternly, how dangerous their little attempt at flying had been. Her mind floating away to another time and place, Renee jumped as Kat rubbed up against her ugg boots, purring softly. She leant over and picked her feline mate up, cuddling her as she massaged behind her ears. Kat pushed her head further into Renee's fingers and purred louder.

'I gather you're ready for breakfast?'

Kat meowed, her dark green eyes wide.

Renee smiled. 'Righto then, duck and barramundi in jus it is. You think you can handle that?'

Kat meowed once again.

Renee emptied the can of gourmet cat food into a ceramic bowl that Tia had given Kat for Christmas last year—which read 'world's most spoilt cat'—then placed it down on the laundry floor, shaking her head as she watched Kat pick the food up with her claws and then delicately put it in her mouth. It never ceased to amaze her how she ate. She certainly was a moggy unto her own.

Wandering back into the kitchen, Renee sculled the last of her fourth black coffee for the morning, screwing up her face because it was cold, and then tugged her unruly hair into a messy ponytail. She felt like death warmed up after spending the night chasing her pillow around the bed. She'd be lucky to have got an hour's sleep, and even when she had slept, she'd been tormented by dreams of a faceless person chasing her with a knife dripping with her sister's blood. She had awoken from the nightmare in a pool of sweat, her heart trying to bash its way out of her rib cage, but she was determined to not let her apprehension beat her. She'd had enough of living in fear. It was about time she stopped balancing on the edge of the cliff, and jumped. Who knew, maybe the cliff was only a few metres high, and not this menacing drop as she had always imagined it to be. There was only one way to find out. Grabbing her mobile from the kitchen bench, she dialled Tia's number. This was it. She was finally going to do it. No more procrastinating.

After six rings the call rang out and went to message bank. And she remembered it was Sunday morning. Damn it! In her mental haze she'd forgotten Tia would have only crawled into bed an hour ago after pulling back-to-back shifts at the hospital. As Tia had told her countless times, the emergency room was always rife with drug overdoses, bar fight casualties and car accident victims on a Saturday night. She hoped she hadn't woken Tia up. 'Hey honey, it's Renee. Call me back as soon as you get this message. It's really urgent. Sorry if I woke you…'

Renee hung up, wondering why she'd just whispered—seeing as Tia couldn't hear her leaving a message—and then began to pace the kitchen once more while chewing on the corner of an already short fingernail. She shouldn't have had that last cuppa, especially on an empty stomach; the caffeine was making her extra jittery. Grabbing a loaf of chia spelt bread from the freezer, she placed two pieces into the toaster and then pulled a jar of crunchy peanut butter from the cupboard. She had to eat something before her stomach ate itself.

Two minutes later her mobile began to play her favourite song of all time, 'Hungry Eyes', from the film *Dirty Dancing*. A bit lame, but she didn't care—she was a hopeless romantic at heart. She snatched it from the kitchen bench. 'Hey, Tia, I'm so sorry I woke you.' She sounded breathless. She needed to calm down.

'Hey, Reni, it's seven thirty on a Sunday morning...so I'm gathering you haven't even been to bed yet?' Tia said drowsily. 'And if you have been to bed, what in the hell are you doing up this early?'

'Oh, um, I just wanted to see the sun come up, that's all.'

'You got out of bed on a Sunday morning to watch the sun come up? Now I'm worried. What's up, babe? Is everything okay?'

Renee ignored the butterflies flapping furiously in her stomach as she pulled a plate from her overhead cupboards. 'Um, you know how you've been waiting for a place to come up for rent in my apartment block?'

'Oh my God, really? There's one for rent?' Tia was suddenly wide-awake as she almost leapt through the phone.

'Yeah, something like that. Um, well—'

'Reni, you're acting all weird. Just spit it out...' Tia dropped her voice. 'Is Mr Fancy-pants still there? Is that why you're acting strange? Has he upset you—because if he has I'll come round there and kick him in the balls with my spiky footy boots.'

Renee giggled through her nerviness. Tia was always so protective. Squeezing the phone between her shoulder and ear, she began buttering her toast. 'My God, draw a breath before you pass out. No, Mr Fancy-pants got sent on his merry way last night, much to his displeasure. And while we're on the subject, I can't believe you set me up with another bloke who cares more about his hair than I do.'

'Oh, Reni, you aren't going to find that hunky spunk manly man you always talk about here in the city—you should know that by now. Those rough and ready blokes that make you go all tingly and gaga tend to live in country habitat. You know, where there are tractors to be fixed while shirtless and covered in grease, and wild horses to be tamed with their bare hands while wearing nothing but leather chaps.'

Renee laughed. 'You've been reading too many bad novels. The men in the country are nothing like the ones on the cowboy calendar in your kitchen, Tia.' Although smirking at her best friend's endearing lack of country knowledge, Renee needed to stay focused on what she was about to say. 'Actually, this is a little more serious than my rotten love life.'

'Well in that case, I'm coming over. By the sounds of it you're in need of some girly company.'

'You're buggered from work, Tia, I don't want you to have to do that.'

'I'm already pulling on my ugg boots and about to head out the front door, so I'm not taking no for an answer. Hope you don't mind the fact I'll still be in my PJs.'

'Of course not.' Renee laughed at Tia's free spirit. Her best mate had never been one to care what anyone else ever thought of her. She reminded her so much of Scarlet. 'See you soon mate.'

Half an hour later, Renee opened the door to Tia, who true to her word was dressed in her Paul Frank flannelette pyjamas, her long blonde hair pulled up into a messy ponytail. 'Looking stylish there, girlfriend,' she said, smiling.

Tia grinned wickedly, then playfully modelled her outfit as she walked through the door. 'As always.'

Renee gave her a kiss on the cheek, then handed her a steaming cup of extra strong coffee. 'Wanna hang in the lounge room?'

'Sounds good to me,' Tia said as she followed Renee down the hallway. Positioning herself carefully on the couch so as to not spill her coffee, she stared at Renee who was busy puffing up the pillows beside her. 'Well, come on! Don't keep me hanging, Reni. You're making me nervous!'

Renee took a deep breath and prepared herself. *Spit it out Renee, you can do it.*

'I had a phone call from my pa late last night. My nan has had a massive heart attack.'

Tia gasped. 'Oh, honey, I'm so sorry. Is she going to be okay?'

'Pa reckons she's going to pull through, but I don't know if he's just telling me that to keep me from going home.'

'Oh, Reni. Have you had a chance to speak to her yet?'

'No, not yet. I'm going to give her a call at the hospital this morning. Pa said to call after nine.' Renee sucked in a breath. 'Tia, I've decided to go back to Wildwood Acres for a little while, to help take care of her, and to help Pa out around the place.'

Tia's manicured eyebrows shot up to almost level with her hairline. 'Oh my God, Reni, have you seriously stopped and thought about this? I know you love your nan, but what if the nightmares start again, or it spirals you right back to where you were all those years ago with your panic attacks, or God forbid, what if he's still there and he comes after you…'

Renee cut Tia off, determined to try and sound confident about her decision. She didn't need to be reminded about everything that could go wrong either—she had gone over the possible scenarios all night long. 'It's been nine years, honey. Surely it's safe to go back now—it just has to be. I can't sit here and do nothing. Mick, Pa's offsider, broke his fibula last week after flipping the four-wheeler motorbike on top of himself, so he's out of action for a while, and even though Pa's not letting on, I know he needs help. It'd be wrong of me not to go back at a time like this.'

Renee held her breath. Tia knew her background inside out and back to front, so Renee knew she was going to be as apprehensive about her going back to Wildwood Acres as her pa was. But right now, she needed someone to be encouraging about it.

Tia looked down at her coffee, sighed weightily, and then looked back at Renee. 'I understand, Reni, I really do, but it worries me, you going back there. I wouldn't be a very good friend if I said I didn't mind.'

'I know, Tia, but my nan and pa need me, and besides, I reckon it's time for me to go back. It's been years since I left... I can't avoid the place forever. As much as Melbourne is my base now, Wildwood Acres will always be my real home.'

There was a moment's silence before Tia nodded. 'You're right, Reni. As much as I hate the thought of you going back there, I will support whatever decision you make. No sense in me trying to talk you out of it because I know once you've made your mind up about something, there's no changing it. And to be honest, it's not really too much of a surprise. Since Fay passed away, you've been talking more and more about how much you miss Wildwood Acres and your nan and pa.'

'Have I really? I hadn't noticed. It's just, Fay's passing has left a huge hole in my life here, and I'm craving having family around me.' Renee smiled softly, willing herself not to cry. Tia was the most beautiful mate any girl could ask for. 'You know me too well, honey. Thanks for supporting me, it means the world.'

'You know I'll always be there for you, through anything, as you've always been there for me. It will be good for you to go home for a while. But I have to ask, are you going to go digging around in the past, you know, trying to find out who it was?'

Not wanting to worry Tia, but not wanting to lie either, Renee took her time to answer. 'Well, I'm not going to go there with guns blazing, but I am going to keep an open mind and if something or someone triggers a gut instinct I'm definitely going to look into it further.'

Tia reached out and took hold of Renee's hand, squeezing it gently. 'Oh mate, I understand your need to find out what happened to

Scarlet, I really do, but please promise me you'll be super careful...
Remember, you left there accusing quite a few innocent people of
her disappearance. You don't want to go doing that again.'

Renee swallowed and gave Tia's hand a loving squeeze back. 'I
know, and I promise I'll be very careful.'

'Good, that's what I need to hear.' Tia took a sip from her coffee
and then wriggled her eyebrows, smirking. 'So are you going to
look up that sexy bloke you always talk about and try to rekindle
the flame?'

Renee sucked in a breath. 'I don't always talk about him.'

Tia nodded fervently. 'Oh yes you do, you compare every single
guy you date to him!'

'It's been almost ten years. He's probably got a wife and five
kids and a cute little picket fence around his cosy family house
by now. So to answer your ludicrous question, no I'm not.' Renee
looked away, her mind in another place for a few brief moments
as she stared out at the high-rises. 'And besides, I doubt he'd want
anything to do with me after leaving him the way I did.'

'Hmm, you never know. Time can heal.' Tia placed her empty
cup on the coffee table in front of them. 'But enough talk about
hunky blokes. What are you going to do about work while you're
away? Is Grant going to be okay with you having time off?'

'Yeah, I rang him just before you got here, and he's being
surprisingly understanding—I think the fact I was a blubbering
mess at the time might have had something to do with it. I've got
almost six weeks of holidays up my sleeve, and Grant said to let him
know if I need any more time on top of that. I'm not really sure
exactly how long I'll be gone for, maybe a couple of months I'm
guessing. It will all depend on how Nan recovers, and how long it
takes Mick to be back in the saddle—and also how I feel when I'm
back there. Anyway, you're the nurse—how long do you reckon?'

Kat decided to join the two women on the couch and jumped up in between them. Tia reached out and gave her a loving rub.

'Well, if it's a fibula it's probably going to take Mick at least nine or ten weeks, possibly slightly more, to be fit for work again. And your nan, well, that all depends—everyone's different and it depends a lot on how fit a person was before their heart attack as to how long it takes to get better.'

'Well, Nan has always been pretty active, so I guess that's good news.'

'Yeah, she's a tough old country broad, your nan. She will probably be in hospital for a week, or maybe even two, before she's allowed home. And then she'll just have to take it easy and not go doing too much for a while.'

Renee chuckled. 'Nan, not doing much? This is definitely going to be a battle.'

Tia chuckled, too, before sighing. 'What about me? What am I going to do without my sidekick around? I'll be lost without you, Reni!'

'I know, I'm going to be lost without you too. But maybe you can come and visit me in the country and play cowgirl for a weekend. Maybe even find yourself that chaps-wearing cowboy. And while I'm away, you can play city apartment owner, rent-free. Just picture it: you can bring your dates home and you won't have anyone to answer to. They can even sleep over *and* you won't have to sneak them in and out of your bedroom window like you do now.'

'So basically, you'd like me to apartment-sit for an unknown amount of time, out from under my parents' roof for a while— away from my dad who still thinks I'm his little girl, bless him— and I can finally act my twenty-six years of age, rent-free?'

'You're spot on. There's just one catch.'

'Oh?'

'Would you mind looking after Kat for me?'

'Oh my God, you know you don't even have to ask me that, I love Kat. It's a deal!' Tia reached out and hugged Renee to her, the two women crying and laughing as they embraced each other.

Renee parked her black BMW convertible in the shade of a towering gum tree and then unhurriedly made her way to the back of the churchyard, the sweet scent from the freesias she was holding reminding her of many happy days gone by. Sometimes white or yellow, other times shades of pink and purple, never a day had passed without the beautifully fragrant flowers adorning the centre of her great-aunt Fay's antique French dining table. Although she'd been a lover of anything that bloomed, freesias had been Fay's favourite, and Renee always made sure to bring a bunch to her resting place whenever she visited.

It was the least she could do after the six years she'd spent living with Fay in her quirky two-bedroom cottage in Melbourne's swish suburb of Hawksburn—the same cottage Fay had left her in her will, with a firm request for Renee to sell it if it became a burden. But Renee couldn't bring herself to sell it. It was a piece of Fay that she just couldn't bring herself to part with. Instead she had decided to rent it out to an elderly retired couple, for now. Maybe one day it would feel right to put it on the market, if the need ever arose.

Fay had always made her feel welcome, the rarely complaining, often eccentric, always smiling sixty-six-year-old woman never making her feel as though she was in the way of her posh lifestyle. Although they were sisters, Fay was the polar opposite of Renee's country-loving nan, Pearl. Fay was a single free spirit with no children and no desire to ever settle down and get married. An urban-lover from early childhood, thanks to her childhood and teenage years growing up in the city, Fay had happily taken Renee under her diamond-studded wings, never batting an eyelid at Renee's initially laid-back, and sometimes unkempt, country ways. She had instead gently taught her about city life, and how to hold herself in the company of the swanky, her world-travelled wisdom always amazing and intriguing Renee.

It was Fay's own experience as a top-notch real estate agent and her connections to the real estate kingpins that had inspired Renee to follow the, at first, extremely challenging path of becoming a real estate agent in a very tight market, and it had eventually paid off, big time, when two years ago she had stepped up from being a suburban realtor to only selling the homes of the affluent—which meant much bigger commissions.

So much of who she was, was thanks to Fay, and she missed her exuberant go-get-'em personality immensely. Life in Melbourne was certainly less fascinating without her around, and the large void Fay had left was one of the big reasons Renee had found herself thinking more and more about Wildwood Acres and the life she had had there before Scarlet had gone missing.

Wiping the tears from her cheeks, she knelt down and popped the freesias in the vase embedded in Fay's grave, and then began to give the marble headstone a wipe with a cloth she always brought along, mouthing the inscribed words as she did every time:

In Loving Memory of
Fay Mary Elizabeth Johnston
A Devoted Daughter, Sister, Aunt and Friend
16/3/1947 – 18/4/2014
A smile for all, a heart of gold
One of the best this world could hold
Never selfish, always kind
A beautiful memory left behind

It had been just over a year since Fay had lost her battle with ovarian cancer, but the ache in Renee's heart was still as strong as it was the day she had passed away. Fay had fought long and hard, until the pain had got too much and she'd needed large doses of morphine to help her cope. She'd then refused to eat, the once vibrant woman fading away to skin and bones in a matter of weeks, her feisty spirit long gone before she was. Renee had sat and held her hand when she'd taken her final breath, and continued to sit by her side for hours, not wanting to say the ultimate heartbreaking goodbye. The only peace she got with Fay's passing was that her great-aunt was no longer in pain, her spirit now free to fly with all the rest of the angels Renee already knew were in heaven.

Sitting down on the grass, Renee pulled a tissue from her bag and wiped her eyes. 'Hi Fay. I got some big news to tell you. I'm finally going back to Wildwood Acres.' She sighed loudly, wishing she could hear Fay's reply, although, she knew it would be one filled with apprehension. 'You see, Nan has had a heart attack and I want to be there to help her and Pa. They've both been there for me my entire life, and now it's my turn to be there for them.

'And on top of that, I really need to try to find out what happened to Scarlet, because as much as I've tried to get on with my life down here, the fact we never found out who took her from us will haunt me every day until whoever it was is caught and brought to justice.' Renee's lips began to quiver. 'And I really need to try to find her, Fay, so we can give her the burial she deserves. I feel selfish going on about my days when Scarlet's body is lying out there somewhere. I'm going to make it a priority, besides taking care of Nan of course, to try and unravel the truth while I'm there. I don't know if I'll get all the answers I need, but I'm going to at least give it my best shot.'

Renee gently rested her hand on the grass that covered Fay's resting place, imagining she was in fact resting her hand over Fay's.

'I know if you were here you'd be worried sick about me going back, but I'm hoping that because you're in spirit now, you can be beside me while I'm there. You know, keeping me safe.'

Brushing her fingers over her lips and then placing her kiss upon Fay's headstone, Renee lay back on the impeccably manicured grass with her hands tucked behind her head, watching the clouds as they floated listlessly in the azure blue sky. The fruity scent of orange blossom floated in on the soft breeze, stirring vivid memories of her and Fay sitting in the garden with a cup of herbal tea, enjoying the morning sunshine as they caught up on their hectic lives. She imagined Fay, above the clouds, and smiled. It was a peaceful world up there, beyond the challenges, trials and tribulations of this earth. And knowing Fay, she'd be keeping all the souls in heaven on their toes, in a good way. She wondered if her mum and dad and Scarlet were up there with Fay, looking down upon her. She had to believe they were. It gave her the strength to take the big step she'd been avoiding for the past nine years.

She thought back to the second phone call she'd made this morning, after Tia had left to go home and sleep. Her pa had been extremely hesitant when she had called to tell him she was coming back. He had tried to talk her out of it once again, but she'd firmly told him he couldn't change her mind. And after telling him she'd hitchhike to Wildwood Acres if need be, he'd grouchily agreed to pick her up from Cairns airport, at the same time reminding her how stubborn she could be.

Pfft. He could talk. She didn't have a hope in hell of being anything else with him as her role model growing up. Stubbornness was a Wildwood trait.

Closing her eyes, Renee enjoyed the warm sunshine touching her skin as questions began to flood her mind once again. Would returning to Opals Ridge finally cure her, or would her long-buried fears emerge into a nightmarish reality? Did the man that had stolen her heart all those years ago still live there, and could she expect him to forgive her if he was? And would new information come to light that would expose her sister's killer and lead her to her sister's remains? There was only one way to find out, and tomorrow she would step onto a plane bound for Far North Queensland, with no chance of turning back.

CHAPTER

4

The flight attendant's robotic-sounding voice woke Renee from her light slumber, the young stewardess advising all passengers to close their tray tables, put their seats in the upright position, open all window shades, stow bags beneath the seat in front and make sure seatbelts were fastened, then finally announcing it was four pm and a balmy thirty degrees in Cairns.

Renee yawned, her mind lagging as she did what was requested. When the bloke behind her pushed his knee into the back of her seat yet again, she bit her tongue, determined not to make a scene. Normally she would shrug it off, but today her nerves were on tenterhooks. He'd being wriggling the entire flight, pulling her hair whenever he got up to go to the toilet, and burping loud enough to mimic a foghorn. The only reprieve from the constant jabs in the back and utter rudeness was to fall into a restless sleep. She understood that there was limited room on an aircraft, but this guy was pushing beyond the boundaries of acceptable. She couldn't wait to get off the plane and away from him before she lost her cool.

Sitting up in her seat, she stretched out her aching neck and then pushed open her window shade, momentarily blinded by the sunlight pouring through like a sea of molten gold. Allowing herself to be taken away by Mother Nature's beauty, she stared in awe as her focus came to rest on the crystal clear aqua-blue water beneath. The bird's eye view allowed her to grasp the Great Barrier Reef's unimaginable scale and beauty in a way that was impossible from the ground.

Tourist boats sped through the sea, on the way home from the reef or the islands, leaving white frothy trails in their wake. Exquisite palm-fringed golden-sand beaches hugged the lush green coastline, while towering mountains sat off in the distance, winding roads leading through the rainforest and up to the Atherton Tablelands where Wildwood Acres was. After so many years away she had forgotten just how amazingly beautiful Tropical North Queensland was. Her stomach did a backflip, and then another, the butterflies in her belly more like mammoth moths. She was finally here. Back to where it had all happened. Home. She pondered with equal measures of anxiety and curiosity what lay ahead for her.

The sultry heat hit her like a smack in the face as Renee stepped from the plane and onto the steps that led down to the tarmac. Removing her thick jacket, she looked towards the clear unpolluted blue sky and smiled. Even though this was technically winter, it was unquestionably shorts and singlet weather, her favourite. No more applying multiple layers of clothes before she headed out the door. She sucked in a deep breath of clean, salty sea air that carried just a hint of the frangipani trees that lined the edge of the airport's runway, the scents of the tropics tantalising her senses and distracting her from the nerves in her stomach.

Taking determined steps, her low-heeled shoes clomping on the pathway, she headed towards the arrivals hall where she knew her pa would already be waiting. Not one to condone tardiness, he was always early for everything, no matter what. Renee recalled the time he had taught her a valuable lesson in punctuality when he had driven off and left her stranded without a lift into town because she had refused his countless polite requests to hurry up in the bathroom. Never needing to raise his voice, or his hand, he had a certain way of teaching life lessons in a way that hit home hard, and now she was an adult, she adored him for it. It had been a different story when she was a hormonal teenager.

The security doors swung open and she instantly spotted her pa up the other end, leaning up against the barricade that separated the visitors from the people waiting. His commanding presence always made him stand out in a crowd, just like her dad used to. Like father like son. Stanley Wildwood wore what he always did, unless he was going to wedding, baptism or a funeral (to which he would wear a suit and tie): timeworn R.M. Williams boots, blue jeans, a brown leather belt, and a collared t-shirt, his cherished wide-brimmed hat old and tattered.

Renee waved madly through the crowd, feeling instantly at ease. No matter how old she was, her pa always made her feel safe and dearly loved, just by being near him. He blamed himself for Scarlet's disappearance, it being his inherent nature to fiercely protect the ones he loved. Back when it all happened he would say over and over how he should have been there to save Scarlet from whatever had happened to her. Hearing it had broken Renee's heart every time. Stanley was a good man, a loving grandfather—he needn't feel what he was feeling.

He looked towards her and then smiled, the weathered skin around his hazel eyes creasing as he waved back to her.

Renee's heart ached as she got a closer look at him. He looked so damn exhausted, and old beyond his years. She hadn't seen him since he and her nan had visited for Christmas almost six months ago, but he looked as though he'd aged twenty years in that time. The fright of almost losing his childhood love to a heart attack, and having to manage all the jobs around the station on his own this past week, had visibly taken a huge toll. He clearly needed her support, even though he had tried to convince her he didn't.

And he thinks I'm bloody stubborn!

As she stepped towards him with her arms outstretched, her pa pulled her close and embraced her, firm enough to make her feel as though any tighter and she wouldn't be able to breathe. She squeezed him back and then gave him a kiss on the cheek, while blinking back happy tears. 'It's so good to see you, Pa. I've missed you and Nan so much.'

'It's good to see you too, Missy-Moo, as always. Although you know I'm worried sick about you coming back here.' He shook his head and pinched the bridge of his sun-freckled nose. 'I know you're old enough to take care of yourself now. It just worries me, is all.'

'I know, Pa, but honestly, I can't hide away forever.' She gave him a reassuring smile as she held him at arms-length and gave his gnarled hands a squeeze. 'Everything's going to be fine. *I'm* going to be fine. So stop worrying about me. Okay?'

Stanley chuckled sarcastically. 'Me? Not worry? You got Buckley's of that.' He smirked and took his hat off to reveal his thinning grey hair. 'This is proof of how much bloody worrying I do, especially about you.'

Renee gave him a playful slap on the arm. 'Oh, Pa, lay off. I'm not that much of a headache for you.'

'I'll never lay off. You'll always be my little girl—you should know that by now.' Stanley half smiled and half frowned as he looked around, hands on hips. 'Now let's grab your luggage so we can get outta this joint—too many bloody people rushing aimlessly about for this old codger. And your nan can't wait to see you.'

Stepping through the doors of the disinfectant-smelling hospital room, Renee sucked in a sharp breath when she spotted her nan in the bed. An ECG machine beeped alongside her, monitoring her heart rhythms, and cords seemed to be attached to her everywhere. Usually so full of life, she wasn't used to seeing her like this. Nan looked so pale and drawn, her skin hanging from her bones, and for a painful few seconds Renee thought she might have been dead. Rushing to her bedside, she tenderly took her by the hand, being careful to avoid the drip that was taped to it. It was warm. *Thank God.*

Stanley sat down on the end of the bed and placed his hand on his wife's leg, rubbing it softly. 'Pearl, dear, Renee's here.'

Pearl Wildwood slowly opened her eyes, her sun-wrinkled face lighting up the minute she realised it was Renee holding her hand. 'Sweetheart, it's so nice to see you.' Her voice was almost a whisper. She rolled over stiffly to face her, acknowledging Stanley with a tender smile. Stanley leant in and placed a kiss on her lips, holding it a little longer than a peck, before sitting back and gazing lovingly towards his wife, his eyes glistening with unshed tears.

Renee smiled, her lips quivering as she blinked back tears of her own. The way her pa was regarding her nan with such adoration pulled at her heartstrings. These two amazing people had endured so much throughout their fifty-one years together; enough to break most, but yet here they were, clearly more in love than ever. Yes, both of them were as stubborn as old mules, quite often bickering over daily life and differences of opinions, but beneath the banter they were unquestionably soulmates. One day Renee hoped to experience a love like theirs.

'It's lovely to see you, too, Nan.' She leant in and gave her a kiss on the cheek. 'How are you feeling?'

'To be honest, I could be better. But don't worry yourself, the doctor reckons I'll be home and back to my old self in no time.' She reached out and patted Renee's arm. 'And then you can head back to the city, where you're safe, my love. I don't need you staying here and fussing over me.'

Renee shook her head. 'Sorry, Nan, but I'm not going anywhere anytime soon. You're stuck with me for a while, I'm afraid.'

Pearl raised her eyebrows at Renee, and then at Stanley. 'I think your pa might have something to say about that—and I must say, I'm not too comfortable with the thought of you being back in Opals Ridge either. You remember what the note said. It still scares me to death that whoever wrote it has never been found. What if…'

The heart monitor started to beep erratically and Stanley quickly rubbed his wife's arm. 'Don't you worry your pretty little head about anything right now dear—you just get better. We need you back at home to keep us all on our toes. I'll take good care of Renee. Don't you worry about that.'

'Yup, Pa will take good care of me, Nan, or should I say, I'll take good care of him.' Renee grinned cheekily at her pa and then winked at him, trying desperately to lighten the mood of the room. 'I'm a big girl now, Nan, and I can take care of myself. I would like to stay a little while to help take care of you, that's all.'

'Hmm. Let's just play it by ear then, love, okay? You know how much I hate people making a fuss of me,' Pearl said as her eyes drooped closed. She blinked them open, chuckling softly. 'I think this old duck needs some more beauty sleep.'

'Of course you do.' Renee gave her nan's fingers a light squeeze, her emotions welling once more with the frailness of her hand. Pearl had always been such a strong countrywoman with so much energy she'd bounce off the walls. 'I'll pop back with Pa tomorrow, okay? And I'll bring your favourites, Werther's Originals.'

Already asleep, Pearl didn't reply. Stan stood quietly, making sure to kiss Pearl one more time before he pointed to the door, whispering to Renee that they should head home. She nodded, her pulse quickening with the anticipation of driving through the front gates of Wildwood Acres. She couldn't wait to see what had changed, or if it was still the same as she remembered. The last memory she had of the place she'd spent the first seventeen years of her life was watching through heavy tears as it disappeared into a trail of dust in her rear-view mirror.

Crawling from beneath the comfort of her feather doona, Renee sat up and turned her bedside lamp on, relieved she'd slept through till morning nightmare-free. It was definitely a good sign. Soft light filled the cosy bedroom of the almost one-hundred-year-old home and her gaze flicked over the furniture she'd had as a teenager—a rosewood dressing table, cupboard, drawers and stand-alone mirror.

All her nan and pa's furniture was still the same as when she'd left, except for a few of the whitegoods, notably a you-beaut new double-door ice-making fridge that her pa was extremely proud of. He was flabbergasted by the discovery that a fridge could make ice, and he'd been quick to tell her how when he was a young anklebiter they didn't even have fridges. Renee loved the way he always referred to his childhood when he was speaking about the wonders of the modern day—it was endearing.

In the corner of the room her overstuffed suitcase—which had annoyingly cost her excess at the airport—lay opened on the floor. It would be impossible to close it now—sitting on it had been the only way she had zipped it up in the first place. Her once neatly packed clothes were now in complete disarray after her late night hunt for pyjamas, the two glasses of rum she'd had with her pa while stargazing from the swing chair on the back verandah not aiding her search for sleepwear.

She chuckled to herself, remembering how wobbly she'd been as she'd said goodnight. Not being a big drinker, the rum had gone straight to her head, and her legs. She would pack everything into the cupboard and drawers later, making sure to hide the school yearbooks and scarf she'd brought along. She didn't want her grandparents catching onto the fact she was determined to discover the truth... Otherwise her pa would drag her by the ear and force her onto a plane headed back to Melbourne, with no chance of ever returning.

Pulling her eyes from the suitcase, Renee continued to gaze over her old room. Long gone were the posters of Christina Aguilera, the Dixie Chicks, Shania Twain and Alan Jackson, and instead two of Nan's watercolours hung in pride of place. One was of her pa's old stockhorse Gus, and the other was of the glorious views from the sprawling front verandah of the homestead—the land seeming to drop off the edge of the earth in the distance of the painting. A vase with fresh lavender sat on the dresser—her pa had sweetly remembered they were her favourite—and a large framed photo of her and Scarlet taken when they were sixteen sat beside it.

She hugged her knees to her chest and rested her chin on them, her eyes watering as she took in all of Scarlet's now fading features. The two of them had been identical back then, even down to the way they wore their hair—short, shaggy and very bleached blonde. Scarlet looked so happy it made her heart sink. She wondered what her sister would be doing now if she were still alive.

'I'll find whoever did this to you, sis, I promise. And then you can finally rest in peace,' she whispered, a lone tear escaping and rolling down her cheek. She sniffled and wiped it away with the back of her hand just as the fragrance of frankincense filled the room, so very fleetingly that Renee wondered if she'd imagined it. She sniffed deeply, trying to catch a hint of it again. But she couldn't. Her skin prickled with goosebumps and the hair stood up on the back of her neck. Frankincense had been Scarlet's favourite. She had worn the essential oil as a perfume all the time.

'Are you here, sis?' Renee murmured as her fingers gripped the pendant around her neck, almost afraid she was going to get a reply. But of course, there was none. She suddenly felt stupid for even asking. The mind was a powerful thing, so it was very possible she had imagined it. Being back in the homestead was obviously triggering memories she'd long ago buried. That made a heck of a lot more sense than believing Scarlet's spirit was still floating around.

Shaking off the weird sensation, Renee turned her attention to the doorway, where there were different coloured pencil marks with either her or Scarlet's names up one side of the doorjamb. Her dad had started the height chart when they were only two years old, and her pa had continued the tradition after their parents had passed away, etching the progress of their growth from toddlers to young women into the homestead's history forever. It was a beautiful thing.

Renee's heart pinched with the memories of her and Scarlet standing up against the wall, most of the time the pair of them giggling madly as either their dad or pa begged them to stand still.

You may technically be the eldest, Reni, but I'm the tallest.

You are not, sis. You're standing on your tippy-toes!

No I'm not, that's just a figment of your imagination.

But you don't reckon I have an imagination, so how could that be?

Ha ha, always the serious one, Reni, that's why I love you.

I love you too, sis. Even when you're standing on your tippy-toes.

Renee sighed despairingly. She wasn't going to allow herself to feel weighed down with the anguish. For if she did, she would send herself spiralling down that awful pain-filled path once again and possibly bring on a return of the debilitating panic attacks she'd experienced all those years ago. As her therapist had told her over and over, she needed to focus on the positives, remember the good times, and rejoice in the lives of those she loved and had lost. She was now home with the two people she loved most in this world, back where she had longed to return to for years, so she was going to try her hardest to focus on that.

Checking the time on her watch, a wisp of a smile tugged at her lips. It was just before six in the morning—almost daybreak. Pa would already be out at work on the station with his six-year-old trusty border collie, Henry, beside him—Renee had met the dog last night and had adored him instantly. Pa had mentioned that he had to fix one of the windmills in the bottom paddock. She had offered to help but he had told her to take some time today to settle in, so she'd organised to join him for smoko. She was delighted she had a few hours to herself to potter around the house and venture outside for a good squiz around.

Four generations of Wildwoods had lived under this roof and made a living off the land and there were so many memories of her own precious time here. A buzz of excitement rushed through her. Having got home in the dark, she'd only caught fleeting glimpses of Wildwood Acres in the headlights of Pa's dependable old Land Cruiser. She couldn't wait for dawn to break so she could finally lay her eyes on the countryside that had stolen her heart all those years ago.

Jumping from the bed, Renee tugged her robe over her pyjamas. Back in the city, she'd hated early mornings, but out here in the country, it was a whole different story. With no traffic noise, pollution or loud neighbours to dull her into being blasé about the undeniable beauty of a sunrise, she got to witness the birth of a brand new day. Padding down the hallway, the old timber floorboards creaking beneath her bare feet, she admired the family photographs hanging on the walls, some colour, and some black and white. She would take time to look at them in more depth later, but for now, she longed to feel the grass and dew between her toes while enjoying her morning cuppa.

Stopping off at the heart of the home—the large galley-style kitchen—Renee switched on the lights and got to making herself a cup of tea, halting to admire her nan's pride and joy, a classic AGA oven. So many mouth-watering meals and gloriously moreish cakes, scones and biscuits had been baked within its cast-iron doors. At the centre of the kitchen sat a lengthy island bench with bar stools lined down one side of it, the timber top worn beautifully over the years from her nan's passion for cooking. Near the huge double window, with a scenic view to die for, was an eight-seater dining table, the same table she and Scarlet used to sit at with Mum and Dad. In a book stand, open to a page with a recipe for raspberry white chocolate cheesecake, sat a Country Women's Association cookbook. Above this, a myriad of well-used copper pots hung from a reclaimed-timber pot hanger, and off to the side of the kitchen was shelving that housed at least a hundred other cookbooks. Her nan loved getting cookbooks for presents, and they had added up over the years—Renee religiously buying her one every birthday and Christmas.

While waiting for the kettle to boil, she wandered into the walk-in pantry, her mouth watering at the sight of the endless delectable goodies on its shelves. Jams, relishes and every type of pickled vegetable sat waiting to be devoured, and the herb and spice rack was something to be envious of. Licking her lips, she spotted her nan's old biscuit tin in the exact same place it had always been.

She smiled to herself. Not a lot had changed around here, and that in itself was extremely comforting—she needed familiar comforts to ease her through her first few days. Grabbing the tin, she popped open the lid, her face lighting up like a Christmas tree upon discovering it was filled with her favourites—homemade macadamia shortbreads. She eagerly took two to enjoy with her tea. Not the healthiest of breakfasts, but yummy all the same.

Cuppa and bickies in hand, Renee wandered through the warm and welcoming lounge room which smelt a little of leather from the laundry-cum-tack-room beside it, and towards the back door, admiring the big open fireplace along the way. It didn't get used much, the weather on the Atherton Tablelands usually warm enough without it, but when they did have the occasional cold snap her pa was always keen to stoke it up. She and Scarlet had spent many a night by the fire with their grandparents over the years, toasting marshmallows, sharing yarns and telling jokes. Those were the kind of memories she would be forever grateful for.

Stepping outside, the view stole her breath instantly. She paused as the screen door closed softly behind her, unable to move, her eyes filling with happy tears, the beauty of Wildwood Acres somehow otherworldly. Her hand fluttered to her chest and she shook her head in wonder. How had she survived staying away from such a heavenly place so long?

She wandered dreamily to the swing chair and eased herself down, completely captured by what was unfolding before her. The atmosphere felt acutely alive, the energy around her filling her spirit with the kind of vitality she'd been craving. A slight mist lingered above the lush green grass, the sky partly cloudy with patches of powdery blue peeking teasingly through. Off in the distance, a stand of ghost gums and a slowly revolving windmill stood like towering shadows contrasted against the first rays of light as, like a chivalrous bow, night began to give way to day. Like the burning red and orange embers of a fire, the sun rose slowly amongst the coal grey clouds, sending hues of pink and auburn throughout the blue. It was like watching a well-choreographed dance as the elements of the earth came together in a spectacular show worthy of a standing ovation. And stand she did.

The horses in the paddock opposite the homestead whinnied and snorted as they, too, welcomed the new day. Renee's heart sang at the sight of her old chestnut stockhorse, Jackson. He was close to seventeen now, and retired from station duties, happily living his days out grazing and sleeping. Her pa said he and Mick took him out occasionally, just to keep him on his toes, but he preferred to use his own horse, Gus. She couldn't wait to go and give Jackson a good brush down while breathing in his glorious horsy scent. Jackson had always been extra keen on being groomed. She wondered if he'd remember her.

With the landscape now bathed in golden sunlight, she stood and made her way down the five front steps and towards the horses, the earth beneath her bare feet pulsing with life and filling her with the kind of peace that she'd found impossible to ever feel within the grip of the city. Until now, she really hadn't realised how much she had missed the sensation of being at one with the earth. After all the years of stress over coming back here, the sense of feeling at home took her by surprise. Wherever she gazed, she was completely captured by the beauty surrounding her. It just felt so good to be able to walk out the front door and feel grass beneath her feet, instead of cement, and to see glorious rolling land instead of building after building. Here, in the heart of the country, she couldn't help but look forward to her day.

First, she was going to go say hello to her horsey mates, and then after a shower she was going to pop over to the workers' quarters and say a quick g'day to Mick before she met her pa for smoko.

Pa had warned her that Mick was a little on the grumpy side at the moment—a result of the sixty-two-year-old stockman finding himself cooped up all day long when being used to working the land day in day out—but she didn't mind. After forty-four years of loyal service at Wildwood Acres, Mick was like an uncle to her. The old bushy was as tough as nails on the outside, but a big softy on the inside. It was such a shame he'd never got married, but he was happy that way.

After nine years away, she was looking forward to giving him a hug—he'd always been a champ at bear hugs. Drawing in a lungful of fresh air, she smiled broadly as she bounced across the dew-covered front lawn and towards Jackson, feeling like today she was ready to face whatever the universe wanted to throw her way.

CHAPTER
5

Admiring the blanket of flickering stars in the velvet-black sky while noticing they all looked way brighter and bigger than he'd ever seen before, Dylan strolled from where he'd just parked his Land Cruiser in the machinery shed and made his way up to the front door, being careful to remove his boots before he stepped inside. It had rained for half the afternoon, leaving him grottier than usual. Shelley would kick his butt if he walked mud in on her freshly cleaned floors. He grinned as he imagined her giving him a serve. She was so adorable when she was angry.

He gave Bossy a scratch behind the ears, then pointed to her blanket on the verandah. Bossy happily obeyed, walking around in circles before settling herself down for the night, her eyes shut in seconds. Wearily, Dylan removed his wide-brimmed hat as he stepped through the flyscreen door, yawning as he hung it on the horseshoe hook Shelley and Annie had handmade especially for it. He couldn't wait to have a hot shower and then sit down at the table to enjoy a Sunday night roast with his two favourite girls. After spending a full day out in the saddle and then having to run in to town to grab a few things and check on Shelley's uncle Ted, he was absolutely buggered. Ted had insisted upon going to the pub for a quick one, and he couldn't say no to a recently widowed seventy-eight-year-old man. The poor old bugger was so heartbroken at losing his one and only love he didn't know what to do with himself. Dylan could only imagine the loss he was feeling. His life would be hollow without Shelley.

The house was unusually quiet and dark. The smell of something burning in the oven wafted through, a mixture of rosemary and charred meat. It was very unlike Shelley to forget about dinner cooking. Unease kicked in.

'Anyone home?' His voice was a whisper, fear ridding him of vigour.

There was no reply.

His skin prickling, Dylan sensed something wrong. Why hadn't Annie run out to greet him, like she usually did? Taking hurried steps, he rushed down the dark hallway.

'Shelley? Annie? Where are you two?' He half expected them to jump out and scare him, giggling.

A loud sob reached him from the bathroom, and then a cry for help. 'Daddy! Hurry! Please! Mummy's fallen and hurt herself, and I can't wake her up!'

His feet pounding the timber floorboards, Dylan bolted for the bathroom. Time slowed down, the world stopped spinning, his heart was in his throat. Annie's sobbing got louder. He opened the bathroom door and his eyes came to rest on a sight that brought him crashing to his knees. He reached out for Annie and pulled her into him protectively, his hand resting on the back of her head as he gently pushed her face into his chest. Annie clutched him, weeping, crying out for her mummy. Shelley was motionless on the floor, deathly pale and lying in a pool of blood.

In a daze he cried out Shelley's name, over and over, but there was no reply. He reached out and touched her hand, recoiling from the sensation. She was stone cold. Her eyes were open and soulless, and her beautiful face lifeless. His instincts told him she was gone, but he didn't want to believe it. He couldn't. This wasn't happening.

No, please God; you can't take her from us.

This was his wife, Annie's mother, the woman they both loved so deeply, the woman he'd planned to grow old with. She couldn't be dead. And his poor darling Annie, how long had she been lying on the floor beside her mother, holding her hand, trying to wake her up?

Nausea washed over him with the thought of her being a witness to something so devastatingly heartbreaking. This was all his fault. He should have been home earlier.

Something wet pressed against his palm and he yanked it out in front of him. His fingers were covered with blood, the blood that had soaked Annie's hair. He quickly checked her over, making sure she wasn't injured. Although her eyes were wide with fear, and her face stained from crying, Annie told him she wasn't hurt. Her pyjamas were covered in her mother's blood too. He closed his eyes, not wanting to see what was in front of him—hardly believing it— involuntary sobs escaping him as his reality shattered into shards around him. Being the man of the house, he was meant to protect the ones he loved. He'd failed.

Finally he got to his feet, still clutching Annie, and carried her into the lounge room. Gently placing her down on the couch, his arm still wrapped around her, he pulled his mobile from his pocket and called an ambulance. He knew it was too late, but part of him prayed to God for a miracle. The operator tried to keep him on the line, but he told her he had to go and take care of his daughter. Annie needed him like she'd never needed him before. And by hell he was going to try and shield her from what was about to unfold.

He cupped Annie's cheeks, his eyes gripping hers. 'Sweetheart, I have to go and check on Mummy. How about I let Bossy in and you can sit with her and watch cartoons while I do, okay? And I'll ring Grammy and ask her to come over too.' Every word cut like a knife. How was he going to explain to a little girl that she was never going to see her mummy again? His already broken heart squeezed painfully with the thought of it.

Sobs wracking her, Annie nodded, tears spilling down her cheeks. 'Please make Mummy better, Daddy. Maybe put a Band-aid on her sore head and then she'll be okay again.'

His throat constricted so much that Dylan found it almost impossible to answer. 'I'll do my best, sweetheart.'

Ripping himself away from her, Dylan ran for the front door, called Bossy in, and made her sit beside Annie on the couch before switching on the telly. *The Muppet Show* was on, Annie's favourite, but the distraction did nothing. Annie wrapped her arms around her pooch, burying her head into Bossy's neck as she wept. Dylan fought to keep it together. He wanted to stay here and hold Annie to him, but he needed to cover his wife's naked body before the ambulance officers turned up. Even in death she deserved some dignity. He didn't want strangers seeing her exposed.

Heading back towards the bathroom, Dylan rang his mother's granny flat down the back of the cottage, the words that spilled from him sounding like they were coming from another's lips. After breaking down and quickly recomposing herself, his mum assured him she'd be there in two minutes.

Dylan sucked in a few deep breaths. Surely this was all just a bad dream, and he was going to wake up any minute now. This, right here, wasn't his real life. It couldn't be. Things like this didn't happen to him.

Stepping through the bathroom door, reality punched him in the chest once again and his legs gave way. He crumpled to the floor beside Shelley. Tenderly pushing the hair from her face, he leant in and kissed her cheeks repeatedly as he slipped his arms around her limp body. Blood stained her beautiful blonde hair and soaked through his shirt, the sensation of it against his skin crushing his soul. It was then he spotted what had killed her; the entirety of the back of her head was caved in. It looked like she had stepped from the bath, and while reaching for the towel she had slipped and hit her head on the bathroom sink. A simple accident, a devastating outcome, three lives changed in an instant, forever. He could now hear his mum consoling Annie in the lounge room, his little girl's sobs crushing him even more. How were they going to survive this?

Sobbing to the point he could barely breathe, Dylan placed a towel over his wife, lay back down beside her and hugged her to him, telling her over and over how much he loved her, and how he couldn't imagine his life without her. This was it. She was gone. He was never going to get to kiss her lips, laugh with her, cuddle her or make love to her, ever again. His earthly angel was now flying with the angels in heaven.

Gasping for air, Dylan sat bolt upright, his sheets in disarray around him and his doona in a pile on the floor. Although it was cool with the ceiling fan going, sweat covered his body and his cotton boxers stuck uncomfortably to his skin. He took a few wheezy breaths, trying to stop his heart from bolting like a startled horse. Calmly grabbing his inhaler from the bedside table, he drew in the lifesaving medicine, his constricted airways opening up in seconds.

Having suffered with it for most of his life, asthma didn't faze him—he'd learnt to live with it. What did scare him, though, was that Annie suffered from it too, at times quite badly, especially if she was anywhere near tobacco smoke, cats or musty mouldy places. By using a specially designed spacer along with her daily preventer they'd at least got it under control, but it didn't lessen the risk of a bad attack if something set her asthma off.

It was a never-ending job reminding her to take her inhaler with her wherever she went—a major reason he'd decided to buy her a locator watch for her upcoming birthday, along with the inflatable bouncing house and backyard waterslide she'd been begging him for. The watch looked pretty as a picture with a pink band and a fairy themed face—so Annie would love wearing it. It worked off GPS—and thankfully Opals Ridge had great coverage in most areas other than the showgrounds and the national park, so if she ever found herself in trouble, all she had to do was push a button on the side and it would notify him by text so then he could use the locator's special map application on his iPhone to get to her. It at least gave him a little reprieve from his worry. If only he could get her to wear something like that when she became a teenager—he imagined that would make his life a hell of a lot easier.

Now able to draw a decent lungful of oxygen, he willed his heart to relax by taking a few deep breaths. Then, when his breathing was back to normal, he threw his legs over the side of the bed and hung his head in his hands.

When were the nightmares going to stop? He had relived Shelley's death over and over, at least once a week since she had passed almost three years ago, and still it shattered him every time. He couldn't go on like this. It made him dread going to sleep, for fear of having to go through it all again. He couldn't remember the last time he had slept through the night and woken refreshed. Maybe he should listen to his mum's advice and go to the shrink in town. He had to do something. He needed peace. This wasn't living—it was barely surviving. He wanted his life back, his happiness back. Shelley would forever live in his heart, but he needed to get on with his life, especially for Annie's sake.

The bedroom door flew open and Annie stood in the doorway with a plate in her hands, her Minnie Mouse pyjamas covered in spots of what looked like Vegemite, and with purple mulberry juice stains on her hands, lips and face. She had obviously been feasting from the laden mulberry tree in the backyard.

'Morning, Daddy. Grammy and I made you some toast.' She walked over and placed the plate on the end of the bed, beaming proudly. Two bits of toast were thickly spread with Vegemite, and a few squashed mulberries sat beside them.

Dylan smiled from the heart as he stood and strolled over to her, kissing her on the cheek as he ruffled her dishevelled hair. 'Oh, sweetheart, you and Grammy are so thoughtful. Thanks.' Taking the piece of toast with almost half a jar of Vegemite smeared on it, Dylan took a bite, making sure to leave traces of it around his mouth. He beamed a tooth-filled grin, his teeth also covered in the Aussie staple. 'Mmm, yummy!'

Annie giggled, her missing front tooth making her even cuter, if that was possible. 'Daddy! It's all over your face, you grommit.'

'Hey, what do you mean *I'm* a grommit? That's your nickname when it comes to getting food all over the place.' Dylan playfully tried to lick it from the corner of his mouth, while pulling a stupid face. 'Did I get it?'

Annie shook her head, still giggling, her eyes twinkling with mischief. 'No, silly. I think you might need Grammy to wipe your face with the dishcloth, like she wipes mine. But I gotta warn you, it's a little annoying.'

Dylan wriggled his eyebrows. 'Nah, I reckon I know what I can do.' He scooped his daughter up from the floor and buried his face in her already Vegemite-stained pyjama top as he tickled her ribs. Annie's raucous laughter was contagious, and his aching heart momentarily mended.

Annie snorted with merriment while trying to wriggle from his grasp. 'Daddy, stop it. Your prickly face is tickling me.' She could barely talk through her giggling.

A curvy figure appeared at the door, a heartfelt smile on her face, her veiny weathered hands holding a steaming cup of coffee. 'What are you two scoundrels doing in here? I can hear you laughing all the way from the kitchen.'

Dylan turned to face his mum, grinning like a mischievous schoolboy. 'I'm using Annie as a dishcloth. Apparently I'm a grommit because I got Vegemite all over my face. Go figure!'

Claire Anderson smiled fondly as she fleetingly assessed Dylan's face, and then peered at Annie's top with raised eyebrows. 'Well, it looks like it worked.' Wandering over to the dressing table, she placed the cuppa down beside the dusty bottles of perfume and jars of face creams.

Dylan spotted her brief frown as she scanned Shelley's personal effects still neatly arranged on the dresser before bringing her gaze back to him and Annie. She smiled sadly at him, so much passing between them without a word being said. She had told him on a number of occasions that it was time they put Shelley's things away, wholeheartedly believing it would help him heal. He knew, deep down, that she was right. He had tried a few times to pack it up, but had failed every time. It was his way of pretending Shelley was away on holidays somewhere, and would one day come walking through the front door, announcing she was back. In his eyes, packing up her things would be a final goodbye. And that would hurt. Tremendously. But he knew he had to find a way to finally let her go.

'Annie and I are going into town to grab a few things for her birthday party tomorrow afternoon. I need to drop the decorations and cake off to the pub so Lorraine and Rex can set up the kids' play area in the morning. They've even managed to organise a clown.' Claire winked at Annie, her kind face lined with the many years of hardship she'd suffered at the hands of Dylan's alcoholic father. 'Do you need anything while we're in there, love?'

Annie squealed, clapping her hands. 'Oh my goodness, a clown! I can't wait, it's going to be so much fun.'

Dylan smiled at Annie's enthusiasm. It was beautifully addictive. 'You know what? I think I might come with you both. I need to grab a few things from the hardware store. And if Rex is about I want to ask if he's heard of anyone looking for some casual hired help. Maybe we could all have a counter meal for lunch while we're in there too. Sound good?'

Annie's face lit up even more brightly. 'That would be fantabulous, Daddy! Yay!' She jumped from Dylan's arms and ran off down the hallway, shouting back to them excitedly. 'I'm going to pick a pretty dress for lunch, and I'm going to wear my shiny clip-clop shoes too.'

Claire placed her hand on Dylan's cheek. 'We'd love for you to join us. But before we go, I reckon you need to tidy yourself up a bit—you know, have a shave and maybe give that hair of yours a brush. You're looking a little worse for wear.' She tipped her head to the side, holding his gaze, as though reading his thoughts. 'I'm worried about you, love. You're constantly tired, and under so much pressure with the farm. I wish you'd let me go and get a job in town so I could help out more financially, and I wish I could take away your sorrow. It breaks my heart to see you suffer so much and not be able to do anything about it.'

Dylan's emotions welled, but he swallowed them down. He had to stay strong for the women in his life. He was the only man they could rely on. 'Mum, you do more than your fair share around here with cooking and cleaning and looking after Annie when I'm working. I don't know what I'd do without you. But I do have some pride left and I'm not going to let you go and work for a measly couple of hundred bucks in town, when I can just get a second job somewhere.' Claire went to protest but he shushed her. 'And as for my sorrow, I'm finally going to follow your advice and make an appointment to see the shrink in town. It won't hurt to give it a go, I suppose.'

A broad smile softened Claire's features, and her eyes filled with tears as she reached out and wrapped her arms around him. Her lack of height was made even more obvious alongside Dylan's six-foot frame. 'Oh, Dylan, you don't know how happy that makes me. Good on you, son. It helped me so much, talking to someone, and I know it's going to help you too.'

Dylan squeezed her back. 'Thanks, Mum, I reckon it's about time I moved on with my life. And who knows, maybe if I make the first move, life will grant me some miracles. Lord knows I need some—we all bloody well do.'

'Amen to that,' she said, smiling. 'Now let's go have ourselves a lovely day.'

CHAPTER

6

The following day was a perfectly relaxed Sunday afternoon for a birthday party. Adam Harvey and Troy Cassar-Daley's version of the classic song 'Lights On The Hill' played unobtrusively on the jukebox at the corner of the dance floor, the atmosphere of the Opals Ridge Hotel bright and friendly.

Well over a hundred years old and with publicans who loved anyone with a story to tell, the two-storey colonial style pub dripped with history. Warm sunlight dappled through the many leadlight windows, sending a scattering of multicoloured beams bouncing across the antique timber dining tables. Plush dark-red carpet lined the dining room floor and soft lighting glowed from strategically placed lamps. Refurbished train bench-style seats gave the eating area a romantically cosy feel. Reclaimed timber floorboards—saved from a few of the timeworn cattlemen's huts around the area—took pride of place around an equally impressive horseshoe-shaped bar, and a guitar signed by the country music legend Slim Dusty hung proudly as the centrepiece. Old boots, hats, whips, spurs, belts, halters and horseshoes—in fact almost anything a stockie wanted to leave behind to make his mark on the pub—hung around the walls amongst many new and old photographs, all of it thoughtfully put together and creating a distinct country atmosphere.

It was an atmosphere Dylan felt right at home in. As a younger man he had frequented the pub quite often before he met Shelley, trying to drown his sorrows after losing his first true love so abruptly and unexpectedly when she skipped town—the horrible fight they'd had when she'd accused his father of the unthinkable marking the beginning of his bad drinking habit. But thankfully Shelley's unconditional love had helped heal his broken heart, and taught him that true love can happen more than once in a lifetime. He'd known he was lucky for a deep love like that to have struck him a second time round, but a third time would be an absolute bloody miracle. He had Buckley's of ever feeling it again. Now, he rarely drank at all—a glass of wine here and there, and the odd stubby when it was roasting hot and he wanted to quench his thirst, or if he was at a party just a few to get his dancing groove on. Long gone were his days of being a wild boy. Getting married and having a child had certainly got him on the straight and narrow, and he was thankful for that. There was no way in hell he ever wanted to end up like his drunken low-life father. 'Like father, like son' was a saying Dylan took great offence to, and also one he worked hard at proving very wrong to the sometimes-suspicious elderly locals.

The iconic pub was unusually busy for Sunday lunchtime—the fact the owners, Lorraine and Rex Thompson, had been advertising a spruced up new gastro-style menu probably having something to do with it. Dylan was sad to see most of the normal pub grub off the menu—although they had kept the reef and beef and good old-fashioned battered fish and chips—but like almost everything in life, the pub had to move with the times. Numerous tourists stopped off at the pub en route to the many attractions on the Atherton Tablelands, and the call for a more modern menu had finally won over the usual chicken parmigiana—'chicken in pyjamas' as Dylan liked to call it, much to Annie's amusement—and the almighty seafood basket. Lorraine and Rex were still going to do their famous Sunday roast dinners that brought families from far and wide, but today it was the mouth-watering steak and Guinness pies, salt and pepper calamari, crispy pork belly with orange sauce, and mussels cooked in white wine and garlic doing the job, and rightly so. Dylan had indulged himself with the mussels yesterday when he had come in for lunch with his mum and Annie, and today he'd ordered the crispy pork belly with caramelised brussels sprouts and crunchy sweet potato chips. His tastebuds were still thanking him for it.

Leaning up against the handcrafted mango wood bar, Dylan smiled to himself. His family-friendly local pub was full of squealing kids so sky-high on sugar they were having a wow of a time. And with one child on each hip and the others swarming around her like bees around a flower, his mum was clearly enjoying every second of being in the thick of it. It was both entertaining and heartening to watch. Over near the indoor play area, young Waylon Markesan was spinning round in circles, making himself stupidly dizzy so he'd fall over while seeing stars, as a few of the girls watched on in utter hysterics. And the newly assembled indoor slippery slide was proving popular—with the majority of the kids deciding it was more fun to slide down backwards. Most of the children who had been invited to Annie's sixth birthday party had turned up in the requested cowgirls and Indians costumes—the boys being the Indians. Annie hadn't stopped smiling since they'd got to the pub mid-morning, and it was a beautiful thing to see her so happy.

A tap on his shoulder pulled Dylan's attention behind him and he was met with his neighbour's unsmiling face. But he didn't take it personally, Craig Campbell's last few years involved a fair bit of heartache, and his time spent working with the law made him appear ten years older than his thirty years and always a little on the cantankerous side. He held out his hand and Craig shook it, his grip vice-like. 'Hi Craig, glad you made it mate.' He eyed Craig's police uniform, smirking. 'The invitation said cowgirls and Indians though, nothing about coppers.'

Craig chuckled, his laughter deep and throaty, and a little too loud as though it was forced. 'Oi, fair play, I'm on duty today. Just thought I'd pop in to wish birthday girl a happy one.'

'Appreciate it, Craig.' Dylan's smile faded. Craig looked like absolute shit. He really felt for the bloke with his wife leaving him the way she did, and with his son too. 'I know how hard things have been for you lately…always here if you need to talk.'

Craig held his hands up as if stopping traffic. 'Not one for deep and meaningfuls, Dylan, that's for sheilas.' He glanced around the pub. 'Anyways, where is the little anklebiter?'

Dylan pointed to where Annie was doing somersaults across the play area with one of her friends. 'She's over yonder, and may the force be with you wading through the kids—they're all a little cray-cray thanks to the sugar.'

'I'm sure I'll be able to handle them.' Craig smirked suggestively as he tapped his handcuffs. 'The uniform tends to make them behave.' He wandered towards where Dylan had pointed. 'I'll catch ya later on.'

'Yup, catch ya.'

He watched as Craig crouched down to Annie and wished her a happy birthday, and Annie responded by giving him a firm hug, along with four other kids at the same time. Dylan laughed at how

Craig was *handling* the kids—it appeared more like he was being mauled.

Pulling up a bar stool, Dylan sat down beside 'Freaky' Frank Watterson, nodding his head in greeting. Frank nodded back, his crooked grin, scarred left cheek and tiny beady eyes a little unnerving. Although the pad of the seat was basically moulded to the shape of his butt from the amount of time he spent at the pub, Frank was known for not being one to indulge in idle chitchat. And Dylan was fine with that. He and Frank were of similar age, but didn't have much in common. Frank was what he'd call a little peculiar, actually his entire family were. Dylan had once gone into Frank's house as a young teenager with his dad, and it had terrified him when Frank and his father had been extra keen to show off their interest in taxidermy, the countless stuffed dead animals reminding Dylan of the many horror films he'd watched. He'd wanted to run from the house screaming, but had instead stood firm, not wanting to tarnish his hard-as-nails reputation. It had mortified him for weeks.

That's when he'd nicknamed Frank 'Freaky', and the nickname had stuck amongst his friends at high school. It had never seemed to bother Frank; in fact one day after school he'd actually thanked Dylan for his cool nickname. Dylan was sure there were more dead animals in Frank's house than alive at the zoo. It probably explained why Frank had never married—no decent woman would be caught dead in a house like that. There was just something about the man that made Dylan's hair stand up on the back of his neck, but it took all sorts in this world, and he just tried his best to act nonchalant around him.

Turning his attention back to the kids, Dylan smiled. Watching the overly excited group be entertained by the clown was just what the doc had ordered, the children's laughter containing something magical. Dylan loved kids. He and Shelley had been trying for a brother or sister for Annie before she had passed away. He wondered if he would be able to grant Annie a sibling one day. An only child himself, it broke his heart to think she could grow up like he did, pining for the special best mate that only a sibling could be.

Another tap on his shoulder broke his train of thought, and he turned to see a lobster-faced Rex grinning back at him, the stocky man's weekend out fishing in the northern sun clearly evident in his beetroot-coloured skin and the glowing white marks where his sunglasses had been. He looked like he'd been shoved in the oven and left to cook to a crisp while wearing goggles.

Dylan turned on his stool, resting his forearms on the bar while trying not to laugh at the state of Rex's face. 'Hey, Rex, how'd you go mate? Catch any bigguns?'

Rex grinned and clapped his hands together, his wiry copper hair reminding Dylan of a rusty scourer. 'Yup, I sure did. I caught a bloody shark, this big!' Rex proudly stretched his arms as wide as they'd go, giving Dylan an image of the size of his catch while he whistled through his teeth. 'I reckon we might have flake and chips on the menu for a month, thanks to my handiwork.'

'Shit hey! That would've been a bit of a hairy moment for you, pulling the bugger into your little tinny.'

'It sure was. The bastard tried to bite my bloody arm clean off. Talk about crap my pants! Thank God Trev was there to give me a hand, otherwise I woulda been in deep shit—' Rex chuckled, '—literally!'

Dylan laughed, raising his glass of Coke. 'You're a bloody legend, mate. Here's to ya.'

Rex puffed his chest out, smirking stupidly. 'That I am, Dylan, that I am.' He leant on the bar and took a swig from his freshly poured beer, still grinning. 'Listen to this. I got a ripper joke for ya... A man and his wife are sitting in the living room and he says to her, "Just so you know, I never want to live in a vegetative state, dependent on some machine and fluids from a bottle. If that ever happens, just pull the plug." So what happens? His wife gets up, unplugs the TV and throws out all of his beer.'

Rex burst into uncontrollable snorting laughter, making Dylan do the same. His laughter was contagious. Rex was the king of jokes round these parts, his good-hearted nature one of the big reasons the Opals Ridge Hotel was so popular amongst the locals and returning travellers. Being a publican was certainly Rex's calling, and Lorraine's too for that matter.

Their laughter finally subsiding, Dylan remembered what he had come into the pub for yesterday, only to find out from a slightly annoyed Lorraine that Rex had taken the weekend off to go fishing. 'Hey, Rex, you don't know of any farmers looking for some hired help, do you? I really could do with some extra dosh at the moment.'

Rex's bushy copper eyebrows met in the middle as he rubbed his stubbly chin in thought. 'Hmm, there's not a lot of work about, Dylan, with the cattle market the way it is. Somebody mentioned the other day that a cocky was looking for someone, but I can't for the life of me remember who it was...' His eyebrows parted and shot up in recollection. 'Ahh, that's right, it was old Stanley Wildwood. I bumped into him at the supermarket and he mentioned he was looking for a bloke to help out a few days a week.'

Dylan almost fell backwards off his stool in shock. Stanley Wildwood. Renee Wildwood's grandfather—how bloody ironic. 'I'll give Stanley a call. Do you have his number?'

'Nope, but you could look him up in the phone book.' Rex gave him a friendly shove. 'Although, if I were you, I'd just call out there. Stan strikes me as the kind of bloke that would rather do business in person. You might have a better chance of snapping the job if you turn up ready for work and raring to go.'

'Yeah, good idea, I'll pop out there first thing tomorrow morning. It's right over the other side of town from me, and I was hoping to get something a little closer to home, but beggars can't be choosers hey.'

'Exactly. You gotta take what you can get at the moment, buddy. It's lean times for everyone in Opals Ridge, the worst I've ever seen it in my twenty-five years as publican here. That's why Lorraine and me had to—' Rex drew quotes in the air, '—*la dee dah* the menu up a bit, to pull in more of the tourists. Sadly, we just can't survive off the locals alone, like we used to. Times are a-changing, and you gotta roll with them or you'll get left behind in this dog-eat-dog world.'

Dylan nodded solemnly. 'You got that right, mate. I'm feeling the pinch pretty bad myself, and if I don't do something soon, I could lose my property to the bloody bank. I've worked too damn hard for that to happen, and over my dead body am I gonna let Annie, or my mum, go through any more shit in their lives.'

Rex sculled the last of his beer, frowning. 'Well, asking Stan for the job's a bloody good start. And if there is anything Lorraine and I can do to help out, you let us know. You're kinda like the son we never had, Dylan. I hope you know we're here anytime you need us, okay?'

'Yup, thanks Rex, I know you guys are, and I really appreciate it.'

Rex gave him a nod and a smile. 'I better go do the rounds, but let me know how you go with Stanley.'

'Will do.'

Watching Rex strolling over to the other side of the bar to chat to some of the other patrons, Dylan took a sip from his Coke as he wondered what had ever happened to his first love, the beautifully spirited and always enchanting Renee Wildwood.

The woman had stolen his heart and then vanished without a trace, without even a goodbye, crushing his soul in the process. If she hadn't left her mark so deeply on his heart, he would have doubted she'd even existed. How hard would it have been for her to pick up the phone to tell him she was leaving, or where she was going, to at least put his mind at ease? It still saddened him when he thought about how easily she had discarded him. Had she really been that mad at him for telling her how wrong it was to accuse people of Scarlet's disappearance without proof, or was it that she had been too ashamed of herself after what she had so wrongly assumed about his father?

Maybe she just hadn't loved him as much as he'd thought she had. Or maybe he'd been young and naive, and she'd taken advantage of him. He'd probably never know. The only thing he knew, from the word around town, was that her grandparents had believed it best for her to leave town. No explanations, no clues as to where she'd gone. End of story. It was as if she'd vanished like her sister, Scarlet.

Although the big difference was that Renee was living her life somewhere whereas Scarlet would never be coming home. The amount of blood the investigating officers had discovered in the wilderness beyond the family property was enough to prove Scarlet had most certainly met with foul play. He remembered the horrific day the detective had informed Renee and her family of the discovery like it was only yesterday. Renee had turned up on his doorstep, her body wracked with sobs, and he had lain with her in his arms all night, soothing her as she'd wept. It had torn him to pieces, seeing her like that, and knowing that Scarlet had very possibly been murdered. Poor Scarlet, she'd been a light in everyone's life—he still found it hard to believe someone would want to harm her. And the fact that her body had never been found and her killer was still roaming free was all kinds of wrong. Life could be so fucking unfair.

Trying to make sense of the thoughts and long-ago feelings now rolling around inside him, he pictured Renee's pretty face. It had torn him to pieces for the first year, not knowing where she was— his love for her at the time was so intense he was completely lost without her. For months he couldn't take a decent breath because his chest was so tight with the grief of losing her. He'd once googled her name before he'd got with Shelley, but nothing had come up other than the stuff about Scarlet's disappearance.

Sighing from the weight of his past, he sculled the last of his Coke, and then ordered another from the overly flirtatious, and very attractive, barmaid. He wished he had it in him to take her blatant advances on board, but he needed much more than outward appearances to turn him on. There had to be a sizzling spark for him to be interested. He'd always been that way, and nothing was going to change him. He hadn't been with another woman since Shelley.

True to form in always being late to anything and everything, his best mate, Ralph, suddenly appeared beside him, his shaggy hair as frazzled as he looked.

Ralph gave him a friendly slap on the back. 'Hey there buddy, sorry I'm late.' He pointed to the splatters of mud on his clothes. 'I decided to cut through the neighbour's paddock and got myself a little bogged.'

'How many times is that now?' Dylan pretended to count on his fingers as he chuckled.

'It's the third time,' Ralph replied stoutly, as if he was proud of the fact. 'And each and every time I've got myself out with only a little bit of effort.'

'And a little bit of mud, too.' Dylan pointed to Ralph's clothes and shook his head, smiling. 'You'll never learn, will you?'

Ralph grinned like a naughty child. 'Nope.'

A squeal halted their banter and they turned to see Annie running full pelt for them, her arms wide. 'Uncle Ralph! You came!'

Ralph swept her up into his arms, showering kisses all over her cheeks as he did so. 'Of course I came. I wouldn't miss your party for the world! Happy birthday, sweetheart.' He hugged her closely. Annie tightly wrapped her legs and arms around him as he dug into his shirt pocket and pulled out a beautifully wrapped little box. 'I got a little something for you. Hope you like it.'

Annie grinned, showing her lack of front teeth as Ralph placed her back down and handed her the package. Annie tore it open with excitement, her eyes and mouth wide as she flicked open the box and spotted the gold necklace inside, a tiny cross hanging from it.

'Wow, this is so pretty. Thank you so much. I love it.' She reached up on her tippy-toes, motioning to give Ralph a kiss.

'My pleasure, sweetheart.' Ralph leant over and pecked her cheek.

'Do you want me to put it on you now?' Dylan asked as Annie handed him the box.

'Yes please, Daddy. I want to go and show all my friends.'

Kneeling down then clasping the necklace, making sure the cross was positioned properly, Dylan smiled from the inside out. Everyone who meant something in their lives had made an effort for Annie's special day and it warmed his heart no end to see her so happy.

Ralph placed his hand on Dylan's shoulder and gave it a squeeze. 'I'm going to grab a beer, mate. You need a top up?'

Dylan stood, watching Annie race back towards her friends. 'Nah, I'm right for now. Still got half a glass of Coke left.'

'On the hard stuff, hey,' Ralph said lightheartedly.

'As always,' Dylan replied, grinning.

'Righto, I'll say a quick g'day to Rex and Lorraine and then you can fill me in a bit more on this bloody fence debacle.'

'I don't want to put my shit on you today, Ralph. I've complained enough and you need some chill time too.'

'You're looking stressed, Dylan, like you might need to unload a bit, mate, so I'm all ears.'

'Yeah, tell me about it, between my money worries and now this, I feel like I'm going to drive myself around the bend.'

Ralph grinned playfully. 'Well, if that's the case, I'll drive around the bend with you…can't be letting you do it alone.'

Dylan chuckled. 'Thanks, mate.'

Ralph gave him a slap on the back. 'That's what mates are for.'

Carrying an exhausted Annie in his arms, Dylan quietly padded into the cottage with a pirouetting Bossy at his feet. Grinning at his doggy mate, he let her in with him, closing the door softly behind them all. After a few quick licks to Dylan's leg, Bossy took off towards the lounge room, clearly excited she was being upgraded to her doggy penthouse for the night—her 'inside' dog bed. Whirling round in circles, then chasing her tail for a few more spins, Bossy then thumped down on her bed in the cosy corner, her tongue lolling out to the side and her long legs sprawled out at angles other dogs would find impossible. Life was a ball of fun to her, each day an adventure to be had. Dylan chuckled at Bossy's enthusiasm— the cottage wouldn't have been the same without her.

Silently, he crept off down the hallway. It was only just past five in the afternoon but Annie had crashed in the car on the way home, and he didn't want to wake her. He was expecting her to sleep until tomorrow morning, given the full day she'd had at her birthday party. His mum had retired to her granny flat out the back too, the children having exhausted her. He had to admit, though, his two special girls—Claire and Annie—had been the happiest he'd seen them in months today, and it was wonderful to witness. Things might be tough financially, but after a nice weekend spent together, life was looking a little brighter. It was as though he'd been wandering through a dark tunnel and could now see a fraction of light at the end of it, still very far away, and very dim, but light all the same. It made him feel a little more optimistic for the future, his decision to go and see the psychologist in town lifting some of the weight from his burdened shoulders already. The first step was normally the hardest to take.

Placing Annie down on her bed, Dylan began gently changing her out of her pink cowgirl outfit and into her pyjamas. He felt as bushed as she looked. It was a hard job being a single parent, even though he had his mum there to help, but he wasn't complaining. He loved being a dad, especially to such a big-hearted adorable little girl. Being biased didn't even come into it. Looking down at her he smiled. If only Shelley could see how beautiful their little girl was. Tears filled his eyes but he blinked them away.

Tomorrow, he was going to call the shrink and make his first appointment, and then he was going to drive out to Wildwood Acres and get himself a job. As far as he knew, Stanley Wildwood wasn't even aware he'd dated Renee, and that was probably a good thing, because he didn't want that to have any bearing on his chances of getting the job. Renee's grandfather had been strict with the girls as teenagers—especially when it came to *not* having boyfriends. Hopefully Stanley had forgotten about the time he'd chased him off the property all those years ago when he'd turned up desperate to find out where Renee had vanished to—nine years had changed his appearance somewhat. This was his lifeline, his way out of financial hardship, so he didn't want anything ruining that chance. The extra money to help put food on the table and pay for the household bills was going to make a huge difference. God, he hoped nobody had gotten to Stanley first and taken the job.

Lightly tugging Annie's sticky hair into a shambolic bun on her head—he'd get her to wash out whatever foodstuff was pasting her hair together in the morning—a jolt of positivity rushed through him. The fact he was doing something to aid his plight felt empowering, like he'd finally taken the reins of his life again. Tenderly, he brushed the hair from Annie's face, and then tucked her beneath her *Dora the Explorer* covers, at the same time checking that her asthma puffer was on her bedside table.

Annie had loved the GPS locator watch—when she'd first put it on this morning she'd made him promise to never make her take it off. Planting one last loving kiss on her cheek, he headed off to have a shower, watch a bit of telly and then hit the sack himself. Tomorrow was a brand new day, with brand new experiences and the possibility of big life changes. His instincts were telling him there was something magical just around the corner, and he couldn't wait to find out what it was.

CHAPTER

7

His breathing a little shallow and his hands a little shaky, Dylan sat down at his desk and picked up the phone, dialling the number from the business card his mum had given him almost a year ago. Quickly hanging up before it started to ring, he drummed his fingers on the desk, his stomach feeling as though a swarm of angry bees were at war with one another.

I can do this—I have to.

He snatched the phone up and pressed redial, fighting the intense urge to hang up again. Even though he knew this was a step in the right direction, it still made him extremely anxious. He'd been raised to believe that tough country men weren't meant to talk about their feelings, especially to some stranger. But he had to do something, and what did he have to lose by at least giving it a go?

'Good morning, Wise Psychology, Jaycee speaking.'

Shit, Jaycee was an ex-barmaid from the pub, and known to be one of the biggest gossips in town. What in the hell was she doing working there? He almost hung up, and then stopped himself. Who cares if she told people he was seeing a shrink—not that she should, as it would be very unprofessional. It took guts to admit he needed help. So fuck anyone that tried to hang shit on him for it. 'Yeah, um, morning… I'd like to make an appointment with the doc please.'

'Sure, I've actually just had a cancellation for eleven tomorrow morning. Would you like to take it? Otherwise it's a two week wait, I'm afraid.' Her voice was so cheery it was almost annoying.

So there you go. The doc was booked out for weeks. So he wasn't the only one in Opals Ridge needing help. It made him feel better about going. 'Yup, I'll take it for now, but can I get back to you later if I need to change it? I'm not sure if I'm working tomorrow.'

'That should be okay, as long as you let me know by mid-afternoon today.'

'Oh, yup, no problems. Will do.' Dylan's right leg was bouncing like the clappers. He placed his hand on it to stop it. *Bloody nerves.*

'Okey-dokey then, what's your name so I can book you in?' she sang down the phone.

He wanted some of what she was on. 'Dylan Anderson.' He waited for her to say something like, *Oh my goodness, you need to see a shrink, really? I never would have guessed.*

But she didn't. She just very professionally booked him in without even a mention of knowing him from the pub.

'Okay then, Dylan, all booked in. We'll see you tomorrow if I don't hear back from you this afternoon.'

'Great, thanks, see you then.' Dylan was relieved to hang up and he took a few deep breaths. He'd finally done it.

Staring out his office window to the paddock Rascal called home, he grinned. The gelding had his head up in the air, lips back and teeth bared while snapping at the flies. Rascal certainly was a character and a half. Over the past two months he'd really bonded with the horse, as had Annie, and he was glad he'd followed his gut instincts and brought the horse home. It hadn't taken long for Rascal to trust him, and all the hard work he'd put into him had certainly paid off. He'd deliberately put him in the closest paddock to the cottage as a pal for his stockhorse, Turbo, and also so Annie could hang out with her new buddy whenever she liked, which was quite often. Not long now and she'd be able to ride him in the round yard, under strict supervision of course. Sculling the last of his coffee, he stood and pulled on his wide-brimmed hat. One huge accomplishment down and one to go. Time to hit the road and get himself that job at Wildwood Acres.

***

Rinsing the last of the cutlery in the sink and then popping it into the dishwasher, Renee took off her flour-covered apron while bopping along to the Brad Paisley song playing loudly on the local radio station. It was a rare treat to turn the wireless on and have country music playing. Staring out at the spectacular pastoral views from the kitchen bay window, she sang the words out loud and *way* out of tune, but she didn't care. Nobody could hear her here.

For the first time in as long as she could remember, she felt free of worries, as though she was somehow lighter just by being back at Wildwood Acres. Something magical in the country air was cleansing her from the inside out, making her feel more invigorated and alive than she had in years. And she loved it. Immensely. It was the complete opposite of what she thought she'd feel, her panic attacks and nightmares not rearing their ugly heads at all.

Packing her nan's legendary homemade strawberry-and-rhubarb jam and a container of freshly whipped cream alongside the flask of tea and pannikins, Renee then wrapped some of her freshly made date-and-walnut scones into a clean tea towel. She made sure to keep two of the delicious golden mounds aside for Nan, wanting to take some homemade treats to her at the hospital this afternoon. The AGA stove had worked a treat, the scones the best she'd ever made. Even the demerara sugar she'd sprinkled on top had gone nice and golden.

She'd made sure to save some for Mick, too—the poor bugger was going stir-crazy being confined to his lounge chair. When she'd walked in yesterday he was entertaining himself by whacking flies with his fly swat then writing down his tally as he successfully belted them—he'd been up to twenty-eight, and still counting. At least her scones might cheer him up a bit, along with the stack of old western movies she'd found in the TV cabinet. She'd drop the care package over to him later this arvo, before heading into the hospital with Pa to see her nan.

A lamb-and-pumpkin stew she'd prepared after an early brekkie this morning simmered away slowly on the stovetop, the yummy aromas wafting from the cast-iron pot making her mouth water. The pumpkin was her little trick for thickening the stew without the need for cornflour—and it made it so much more delicious too. She would pop it in the heart of the oven before she left for smoko. Her pa was going to be mighty proud of her.

She'd only been here three days, and she was already settling back into country life—albeit at times a little reluctantly. Although there were countless things to love about Wildwood Acres, there were also many things she missed about her life back in the city—Tia for one, and especially the fact that she lived on her own and could wander around in her knickers and not have to shut the door when she went to the loo. And she missed Kat too, big time. But, in the scheme of things she could live with this for a few months, because after years of fearing returning home, it was a weight off her shoulders to feel so relaxed and at peace here.

When she went into town for the first time it might be a different story. The thought of Scarlet's killer possibly wandering past her in the street was more than a little daunting, especially given the fact that he—or she—had wanted her dead too. Pa had suggested not venturing into town on her own for now, just until she felt comfortable, and most certainly to curb his own worries too—not that he'd admit that. She thought it to be a good suggestion.

Her basket of goodies now packed, Renee headed out of the kitchen, stopping momentarily to look at herself in the full-length mirror near the front door. After returning from the hospital last night, Pa had recovered a few boxes of her old clothes and things from the loft, and it had been like Christmas sorting through it all. She'd even found an old bottle of her favourite perfume, J'adore Dior, still in its box. It had been a welcome surprise as in her haste to pack, she'd forgotten to bring any perfume along with her from Melbourne.

It was disappointing that Nan's doctor wanted to keep her in for another week or so, just to monitor her, but at least she was where she needed to be if she took another turn for the worse. He'd explained that her heart was still being a little erratic, so it was for the best she stayed in a bit longer. Renee was looking forward to getting her home, but until then, she was happy to be out helping her pa around the station.

Today was her first full day of work, and she couldn't wait to get her butt in the saddle for a while as they checked the fences, and then get her hands dirty helping with treating the cattle for ticks. She felt blessed to be stepping through the front door and into her 'office' for the day, unlike the urban dwellers who had to drive for hours in peak hour traffic, or jam themselves into public transport like sardines just to get to work. Although it had plenty of perks, urban living could be tough to manage day in day out. And even though being in the country had its challenges, it came with so many blessings too.

Turning to the side, she smiled while trying to suck in her very slight podge around the waist. She couldn't believe her old Wrangler jeans still fit after all these years, and her timeworn Bonds singlets were a little tighter around her boobs than she'd like, but they fit all the same. Tugging on her button-up long-sleeved shirt, she did it halfway up—covering up as much as possible when working out in the harshness of the North Queensland sun was imperative.

It felt wonderful to be heading out the door make-up free, with her long hair pulled into a ponytail and wearing boots instead of a suit and heels. She'd always felt a little fake when dressed up to the nines in Melbourne. She'd certainly enjoyed the buzz of wearing high-end suits and Gucci heels, but this, right here, the reflection staring back at her, was the real Renee Wildwood. If only her sister was alive, she'd look exactly like she did now; at least through her own appearance she could imagine what Scarlet would have looked like as she'd aged.

'I miss you so much, Scarlet,' she whispered as she brushed her long fringe from wet eyes.

A strange sensation pulled her focus from the mirror, as though someone was secretly watching her. The hair on the back of her neck stood up and she spun around, her heart thudding and her breath held. 'Hello? Pa? Mick?' Her voice was merely a squeak. 'Henry?'

There was no reply, not that she should really expect one from a dog—Henry being her pa's faithful pooch. And then there it was again. Frankincense. The big difference was, this time Renee knew she wasn't imagining it. It was pungent, the aroma lingering in the air so strongly she felt as though she could reach out and touch it.

Gradually placing the basket down on the floor, she reached out while slowly turning around in circles, trying to feel something, anything. 'Scarlet? Please, if you're here, do something to make me believe. I'm begging you.'

She stopped, frozen to the spot, eyes wide, heart galloping, waiting, hoping and praying, all her senses on high alert. But nothing happened. And then, as quickly as the scent had arrived, it was gone. Her mind spinning like a whirlwind and her legs as wobbly as jelly, Renee eased herself back against the wall and slid down to the floor.

Was it true? Was Scarlet trying to reach out to her from the other side? Was her spirit still roaming the homestead, stuck between this life and the next until somebody discovered her body and she could finally be laid to rest? The very thought horrified her. Renee had never believed in ghosts, but now, with one simple scent, she was second-guessing her strong beliefs. Not that she would be openly admitting that any time soon. If she told anyone about this—even her nan and pa—they'd think she'd lost her bloody marbles.

As her breathing returned to normal, she took stock of the situation. She had to try and stay calm, as much as part of her wanted to run from the house, screaming like a mad woman. But freaking out was not going to achieve anything. Something beyond this world was beseeching her to unravel the secrets of Scarlet's disappearance, but where was she meant to start? It was like someone throwing a coin into the ocean, and then asking her to find it. Nine years was a long time after the event.

Whatever else, she was looking forward to getting out amongst the beauty of Wildwood Acres, revisiting places she and Scarlet used to hang out all the time: the caves, the secret place they used to go skinny-dipping, and the old hunter's shack where they'd shared so many happy memories with their friends—and snuck their boyfriends too. But that would have to wait, because today Pa needed her to help with a few jobs around the place and she was really looking forward to getting her hands dirty.

When the majestic old grandfather clock in the hallway loudly announced it was ten am, Renee snapped back to the present moment and jumped up from the floor. She was supposed to be meeting Pa for smoko and he'd be wondering where she'd got to. Where had the time gone? Her planned leisurely twenty-minute ride would now be more of a wild gallop. Thank goodness she'd kept her horseriding abilities alive by going for regular trail rides out on the Mornington Peninsula with Tia, otherwise she might have been struggling to keep her butt in the saddle. Her old horse Jackson had always been a goer when asked to give it all he had.

Grabbing her nan's wide-brimmed hat from the hook near the door, Renee pulled it on, picked up the basket and then hurriedly made her way down the steps, across the front lawn and towards the stables, where Jackson was already saddled up and waiting. He'd seemed as keen as her to go out for a ride this morning, the bugger almost unable to stand still while she was trying to saddle him up earlier. She'd had to lunge him for twenty minutes just so she could get his girth strap tight enough so the saddle didn't slip sideways.

Just as she went to step through the stable doors, the sight of a modern trayback Land Cruiser coming up the long dirt driveway made her stop and curse under her breath. It wasn't like the city out here, where she could say a quick hello and get back to what she was doing. Here, people liked a casual chat, and normally weren't in a major rush to get where they were going. Now she was going to be stuck talking to whoever this was for God knows how long—she didn't want to seem rude by rushing off.

She wished her pa carried a mobile phone so she could call him and tell him she was on her way, but the old-fashioned codger didn't believe in them. In fact, he didn't believe in modern-day technology whatsoever, reckoning it poisoned people's minds and made them lazy. She'd had a hard enough time trying to talk him into upgrading his video player to a DVD player a few years back, Pa refusing to believe that videos were going to eventually be obsolete. The first time he and Nan had watched a DVD, he'd rung and asked her how he was meant to rewind it. The recollection still cracked her up.

Smiling the biggest smile she could muster, she gave the Land Cruiser driver a wave to catch their attention before they drove off towards the now unoccupied homestead. They instantly spotted her, giving her a wave out the window to let her know, and then slowly drove towards her. Because of the glare bouncing off the windscreen, she was struggling to make out the driver, but something about his chiselled features was familiar. Then, as he got closer, their eyes met and it all came flooding back. And for the second time that morning, her legs threatened to give way.

CHAPTER
8

Trying to make out the silhouette up ahead, Dylan squinted into the morning sunshine, his Ray-Ban sunglasses not doing much to shield his eyes from the glare bouncing off the windscreen. From the curves he could tell it was a woman, but he couldn't make out her face. It couldn't be Pearl, as Rex had told him yesterday she was still in hospital. Whoever it was, her clothing made it pretty obvious she was off to work for the day, though he didn't think old-fashioned Stanley Wildwood would be one to hire a woman. Maybe the old bloke had got desperate. Had this woman already beaten him to the job? Damn it! Like a sinking ship, his positive vibe nose-dived.

Finally coming to a stop under an old Bowen mango tree, Dylan once again eyed the woman and his heart almost catapulted out of his chest.

No bloody way. It couldn't be her, could it? She was blonde last time he saw her...

After squeezing his eyes shut for a few seconds, he opened them again, feeling as though he was seeing a ghost. The gorgeous woman stared back at him, looking as shell-shocked as he felt, her unforgettable beautiful brown eyes wide and her desirable lips quivering. Time stood still. Neither of them said a word. And although they were only like this for a moment, their eyes stayed locked for what felt like an eternity, until Dylan tore his away from hers and subtly drank her in.

With her long silky dark hair pulled loosely back, curvaceous figure and womanly looks, she was even more exquisite than he remembered. Gone was the blonde bombshell teenager he'd fallen deeply in love with all those years ago, only to be replaced by a creature more captivating than he'd ever be able to envisage. It seemed like a lifetime ago that he and Renee had been together.

The last time they'd spoken had been extremely heated, so how was he meant to act around her now? And how was she going to react seeing him? For a few seconds his mind whirled back to that fateful afternoon when they had both said things that never should have been said. He could recall it like it was only yesterday, the amount of times he'd run it through his mind making the memory very easy to evoke.

How do you know he's not capable of murder? He's just skipped town, or just vanished into the scrub round here for all we know, to avoid the consequences of doing what he did to your mum. So please explain how can you be so damn sure, Dylan?

Renee, please stop.

No, Dylan, you need to hear this… Maybe his guilty conscience has finally got the better of him, which is why he snapped and bashed your mother, and now he knows if he is caught by the police for that they will somehow discover he was the reason Scarlet went missing.

For Christ's sake, Renee, he's my dad. I can't believe you could even think such a thing, let alone say it out loud...

Well what do you expect me to think?

I expect you to stop pointing the finger at every Tom, Dick and Harry! You're pulling at straws, Renee, and hurting innocent people in the process, including me.

Maybe you should take off your rose-coloured glasses and see it's a huge possibility, Dylan.

I have taken them off, Renee, and to be honest, I don't know if I can be with you now that I know what you think.

Fine. Leave then.

Fine, I will.

Dragging himself back to the here and now, Dylan turned the ignition off. 'Renee?' His voice was husky, a potent mixture of nostalgia, nerves and resentment swirling within him as he opened the door and stepped from the Land Cruiser. He cleared his throat, trying to get a grip, wanting to act nonchalant. No way on this earth did he want her to know she had hurt him so badly. He was shocked at his emotions running so high. He thought he'd got over her years ago.

'Dylan, is that you?' She cautiously took a step towards him, and then another, while her hand fluttered to her chest. He couldn't pull his eyes away from her. She. Was. Stunning.

'Yup, that's me.' He smiled as he removed his hat and gave her a nod, at the same time wishing his stomach would stop flipping. How could she still have this effect on him after all this time? He tightened his jaw, and willed his bolting heart to slow down.

She shook her head as if dazed. 'Oh my God, Dylan Anderson.' She just stood and stared at him, as if she didn't know what else to say.

He gazed back at her, speechless. The way she said his name, so tender, so soft, it had the power to caress his soul—but damned if he was going to let it. She'd always had that knack with him, her words as seductive as her touch. Happy memories of their time together flooded his mind and he struggled to stop himself from opening his arms wide and inviting her into them. He quickly reminded himself that many years had passed, and a lot had changed, *and* she had discarded him so easily after throwing such hurtful accusations his way. They weren't lovesick teenagers anymore. They were adults with pasts, and undoubtedly with completely different futures. And even though Shelley was never coming back, part of him felt guilty for even feeling such things towards Renee. Like he was somehow being unfaithful.

Now only metres away from him, he watched as her hesitancy began to give way and she lifted her hands to shade her eyes from the sun, smiling dazzlingly back at him. 'I can't believe you're the first person I've run into here.' She placed the basket she was carrying down on the ground and popped her hands in her pockets as she walked towards him. 'Life must be treating you well, you're looking great.'

She obviously didn't know how shittily life had treated him, and she clearly didn't know about Shelley. And in a way he was relieved about that, because it meant she didn't have to feel sorry for him, like ninety-nine per cent of the people he talked to around Opals Ridge.

Renee stood in front of him now, her movements a little awkward as she reached out to hug him. 'It's so good to see you.'

Dylan hugged her back, enjoying the sensation of her body against his a little too much as her familiar citrus and floral-scented fragrance lingered around him, enticing him back into their past. *My God, she's still wearing the same perfume.*

In the blink of an eye he was transported straight back to his adolescent years, back to when she was his and he was hers. Two teenagers, standing in the paddock at dusk, their arms wrapped around one another, the passion between them intensifying by the second. But along with the sentimental flashback, his resentment towards her for leaving him high and dry so unexpectedly returned too, alongside the immense hurt she'd caused him by accusing his father the day before she'd left town. It all resurfaced from where he'd long ago buried it, like a buoy rising rapidly from the depths of the ocean. And, once again, he felt as though he was cheating on Shelley. Abruptly pulling back, he tried to hide his discomfort by fiddling with his belt buckle.

Renee stepped back too, grinning a little too broadly. 'Oh my God, it's been like—' she threw her hands up in the air, '—forever!'

'It's been a little over nine years to be exact.' His voice was a little stern, and he tried to soften it by taking a breath. 'You basically vanished without a trace, Renee. Where have you been all these years, hiding under a bloody rock?' Shit, now he sounded like he cared. His throat suddenly felt as dry as the Simpson Desert and his mouth felt like it was full of cotton. He would almost kill right now for a drink of water.

Renee's smile faded and her shoulders stiffened. 'I'm so sorry I left without saying goodbye. I never meant to hurt you. If it's any consolation, it broke my heart leaving you like that too, especially with how things were between us.'

Silence fell, the sounds of the cockatoos in the treetops a welcome distraction. She bit her bottom lip, unable to hold his gaze any longer, instead looking down at her boots.

So unexpected was his reaction, and her apology, Dylan also found himself stunned into muteness. What a dickhead he was, bringing up what should have been left in the past. What was wrong with him? And what in the hell was he meant to say now? Thank God he'd made the appointment with the shrink. He obviously needed help to mend unhealed wounds—ones he didn't even know existed anymore, not to this depth anyway. And they were treading very dangerous waters here. He had come for a job, and that was that. Stanley Wildwood wouldn't take kindly to some bloke turning up for a job and then reminiscing with his granddaughter, no matter what the history was between them.

Dylan shook his head and looked to the skies, his hands on his hips. 'Sorry, Renee, it doesn't really matter what happened back then. I'm just being a dickhead.' He brought his gaze to meet hers once again, this time with his emotions firmly under control. 'It's all water under the bridge as far as I'm concerned. I've moved on with my life, as I'm guessing you probably have too.' There. Even though it was a white lie he felt much better, like he had gained some of his power back.

Renee's gaze travelled from his face, slowly down the tattoo on the side of his neck, and then to his left hand, something indecipherable flashing across her eyes as she spotted his wedding ring. He almost told her right then and there that he was a widower, but it didn't feel right to do so. This wasn't the time and place, and really, it wasn't any of her damn business. It would do her good to think he was completely out of her reach.

'Yeah, life goes on, hey? Mine certainly has, too.' Renee laughed a little too loudly. 'Any mini Andersons?'

'I have a six-year-old little girl, Annie. Love her to bits. You?'

'Me? Kids?' Renee blew air through her lips like a horse. 'Nope, I haven't had time. I'm too busy with work.'

'The good old *I've been too busy*, hey,' Dylan said, fighting to remove the disdain from his voice.

Renee looked at her watch. 'Speaking of time… I'm sorry, Dylan, I really have to get going. I was meant to be down the paddock with smoko by now. Pa's going to be worried sick. I'd love to meet your little girl some time.'

'It's a small town, you'll run into her one of these days, I'm sure.' His tone was a little cold. He felt like kicking himself for letting Renee's presence shake him up so much.

The galloping of a horse's hooves grabbed their attention before Renee had a chance to respond, and in seconds, Stanley Wildwood was upon them. By the stony look on his face, he wasn't happy at all. 'Renee, I've been waiting for you for the past half hour, wondering if something had happened to you. By Christ, girl, you're going to give me a heart attack and you've only been back home for a few days. Not a good start, I must say.' Still in the saddle, and not waiting for Renee to answer, he turned to face Dylan, his eyebrows raised and his nostrils flaring. 'And who in the hell are you, boy?'

'I'm Dylan. Dylan Anderson.' He pulled his hat back on and stepped forward, his hand raised in offering for a handshake. He prayed to God Stanley didn't remember the last time they'd crossed paths—it'd be getting off on the wrong foot for sure.

Stanley gripped Dylan's hand like a vice, his eyes piercing through Dylan's as he held the handshake longer than necessary. 'You're Peter Anderson's son?' The question held so much disdain that Dylan almost crouched down from the weight of it—his father was notorious around Opals Ridge for his many pub brawls and fiery short temper.

Dylan wished he could deny it, but he couldn't. 'Sadly, I am.' He hung his head in shame. 'Not that I'm anywhere near proud of the fact.'

A moment of silence passed before Stanley exhaled, a shadow of understanding in his blue-grey eyes. 'Well, you can't pick your family, hey boy.' He let go of his vice-like grip. 'And to what do we owe this visit, Dylan Anderson?' Stanley's stern tone of voice was softening, but still laced with caution.

His hand finally free, Dylan regrouped and stepped back to look Stanley in the eyes. He wanted to show he was nothing like his father. Stanley Wildwood was well-known for his intimidation skills, and the last time Dylan had been here Stanley had certainly intimidated him—chasing him off the property with a shotgun. But this time round, and with due respect, he wanted Stanley to see him as more of an equal. It was the only way he was going to get the job, especially with his father's bad reputation. 'Rex Thompson mentioned you were looking for someone to help out around the place, so I thought instead of phoning you, I'd just pop out and ask.'

'Is that so?' Stanley's scowl began to ease. 'And what did Rex say exactly?'

'Oh, not much really, just that he'd run into you and that you might be looking at hiring someone for a few days a week.'

'Yeah, well, as long as you know it's not a permanent thing. Once my usual offsider, Mick, is fit to work again, I won't be needing extra help.' Stanley removed his hat and wiped the sweat from his brow with his sleeve, his steely gaze never leaving Dylan. 'You had much experience with cattle and horses?'

'Know them like the back of my hand, Mr Wildwood. I got cattle of my own and I train horses for a living.'

Stanley looked impressed. 'Well why do you want work somewhere else then, if you have your own property?'

'Times are tough, and I just need a few days a week at the moment to tide me over.'

'Fair enough. So I can ring Rex and get a character reference from him?'

Dylan nodded, still wondering whether Stanley recognised him from all those years ago. If he did, he was hiding it well. 'Sure can.

Rex has known me for years. And I can give you the name of my last employer too, at the Rutherford mine, if that helps.'

Stanley shook his head. 'No help to me getting a reference off someone I don't know from a bar of soap. I don't trust any bugger I don't know. But I trust Rex. We've been acquaintances for years and he's a good bloke, so I'll give him a call tonight and let you know tomorrow. Okay?'

Dylan wanted to jump for joy, but instead remained cool and calm on the outside. 'Yeah, that'd be great. I'd really appreciate it. Thanks Mr Wildwood.'

'Right then, that's settled.' Tugging his hat down, Stanley turned his attention to Renee. 'Come on then, Missy-Moo, we got us some cattle to tend to.'

Renee grabbed the basket at her feet, looking slightly embarrassed to hear her pa using her pet name in front of Dylan. 'I'll just go grab Jackson, and I'll be with you.' She glanced at Dylan, her cheeks glowing red. 'Will catch you another time. Was good seeing you again.'

'Yup, it was good to see you too, Renee.' His voice was still a little steely.

Silence fell as Stanley looked from Dylan to Renee, and then back at Dylan. 'You two know each other?'

'Oh, yeah, we were friends before I left... We used to go to high school together,' Renee added a little too quickly.

'Is that so,' Stanley said, his brows furrowing once again. 'I thought your face looked a little familiar, Dylan.'

'I'll be hitting the road then,' Dylan said as he turned on his heel, wanting to escape before there was a barrage of unanswerable questions. He sauntered off, waving casually over his shoulder. 'Speak to you tomorrow, Mr Wildwood.'

It took every bit of his reserve not to turn around and have one last look at Renee, the lingering scent of her perfume making his imagination run wild. Scolding himself for being so weak, he climbed back into his Land Cruiser and headed off, feeling Renee's eyes on him the entire time.

Why now, after all these years, had fate brought them back together? Was it so he could finally get over her, or was there another reason? He didn't know. But one thing he was damn sure of was that she better not think she could woo him into her world again, because after how badly she had broken his heart the last time, that was never going to happen.

***

With her heart in her mouth, Renee secretly watched Dylan turn and walk back to his Land Cruiser as she headed towards the stables. Her eyes travelled over where his shirt pulled taut against his back muscles and diverted once she reached his well-curved tight arse. She had no right to be perving at him the way she was, and what if her pa caught her out? It would most certainly ruin Dylan's chances of getting the job—and also be highly embarrassing. But she was fighting to keep her eyes off him.

With his rugged, tall dark and handsome looks, strong physique, and confident gait, he reminded her a little of her all-time favourite actor, Patrick Swayze. She'd thought Dylan was all the man she'd ever need as a teenager, but he'd certainly matured into one hell of a manly man these past nine years. Wow! And that eagle tattoo at the side of his neck, the tips of the soaring wings showing above his neckline then the rest of it snaking its way down beneath his collar and onto his chest and stomach. She knew from experience just how far down it went, and oh how she wished she could trace her tongue all the way down it, right down to where it stopped, and beyond...

Stop it, Renee! Control yourself! She trembled with the very thought. Dylan Anderson was just so much…*man.*

Sighing at her misfortune of losing such a gorgeous hunky bloke, Renee stepped into the shade of the stables. For years she had daydreamed about running into him again, and now that it had happened, she felt utterly miserable. Her prediction had been right. He was a happily married family man and therefore unavailable. If only she hadn't said what she had, and then run for the hills the next day, maybe she'd be the lucky Mrs Anderson. In a matter of minutes, her nine-year-long fairytale had been shattered, leaving her feeling crushed. Damn it all!

Maybe you don't, but I truly think he's capable of murder, Dylan.

How about maybe you've lost your fucking mind, Renee…

Maybe I have, and maybe I should just bugger off so everyone can pretend Scarlet never went missing and get on with their fake little lives.

Maybe you should!

After carefully packing the basket of goodies into the saddlebag, Renee placed her boot in the stirrup and pulled herself into the saddle. Her pa had headed off before her, with strict orders to get her butt down the paddock—ASAP.

Directing Jackson out of the stables and into the magnificent sunshine, she enticed him into a canter, relishing the feeling of the wind whooshing past her, her mind's eye filled with images of the gorgeous man who had stolen her heart. Dylan Anderson, working here, with her pa? How did she really feel about that? She wasn't sure, but the shock of running into him so unexpectedly had left her mind in a spin.

She could tell from his tone of voice and tense body language that he deeply resented her, and she really couldn't blame him. At least she'd be tending to her nan most of the time, so she didn't need to be spending loads of time with him, if any. If he did get the job, it would be tough knowing he was here a few days a week, but she would find a way to let go.

CHAPTER
9

The wail of a siren slicing through the Opals Ridge main street traffic hum grabbed Dylan's attention, the piercing noise getting exceptionally loud before drifting off into the distance. He tried to figure out whether it was a police, ambulance or fire siren—finally coming to the conclusion it was a fire truck when he saw a flash of red outside the office window. He hoped it was just a practice run for the local fire fighters, and that no-one he knew was in trouble. He'd pop down and see if by chance Ralph was at the station on his way home, just to make sure. Ralph was only a volunteer fire fighter, so he wasn't always there, but if he had a day off from his usual business of dozer contracting he would quite often be found making himself useful around the station. Dylan admired his mate's commitment. He was not one to sit still, always remaining active within the community.

Pulling his attention from the window and back to the shrink, he fought to focus on what she was saying. He had been doing his very best to listen and to answer all her questions, but it was as if his unconscious mind was fighting any chance of healing—it kept wandering off in different directions like an ill-disciplined child. Damned if he was going to let it win, though. He needed this, more than anything right now, to help him cope. And he was determined to beat the feeling of powerlessness that had haunted him for the past three years.

Discreetly looking over the woman's shoulder, Dylan eyed the clock on the wall—the second hand seemed like it was moving in slow motion. His hour was almost up, and he was glad of the fact. The aqua-themed room was very tranquil, with its cosy couch and daydream-enticing paintings, but it was hard to talk about his deepest darkest feelings, even harder than he'd expected. Although the therapist wasn't as scary as he'd envisioned; she reminded him more of someone's nanna than a psychologist, and had instantly put him at ease. She had a sincere air about her that he liked, and a very gentle way of getting him to open up.

'I feel, from what you've told me, Dylan, that you are suffering with immense guilt over what happened to Shelley. Which is very normal given your situation. What we need to work on, in your next sessions, are some ways to help you let go of the blame. You have to come to understand that it wasn't your fault, and there was nothing you could have done differently.' Her voice was soft, soothing. 'And you also need to believe that it is okay for you to move on with your life.'

Dylan looked down at his tightly folded hands, his knuckles white, and the lump in his throat making it almost impossible to speak. 'I know what you're saying is right. I just can't find a way to make myself believe it enough to move on. And the nightmares— they're torture. I just wish they'd stop.'

Theresa Wise smiled compassionately. 'I promise you—the nightmares will stop once you stop judging yourself for her death.

The unconscious mind can be a very tricky thing. It's going to take a little time and some determined work, but together we'll get you there.'

Dylan bit the inside of his lip, nodding. He. Was. Not. Going. To. Cry. 'I really hope so. I want to be the man I was before she died, especially for my little girl's sake…' He looked up, blinking fast, begging himself to hold it together. 'I just want to find my happy place again.'

'Anything in life is achievable, if you want it badly enough. So just believe in yourself, and before you know it, you'll be that optimistic happy man you spoke of once again.' Looking at her watch, Theresa put her pen down on her notepad, her brightly coloured kaftan top suiting her friendly demeanour. 'Well, that's our time up today. I think you need to come regularly for a month or two at least, to get the results we're after, so would you like to make weekly or fortnightly appointments, Dylan?'

'Um, I'd like to say I'll come weekly, but it's hard with work and all. I might be starting a new job soon and I'm not really sure of the hours.'

'Well, I do have the odd after-hours appointment for clients like yourself who work during the day, so that's not a problem at all.'

Dylan smiled for the first time throughout his session. It was a slight smile, but a smile all the same. 'Great, well, I'd like to come weekly then. I'm willing to give this everything I have.'

Theresa's kindly face broke into a broad grin. 'Wonderful. That's what I want to hear—a man who's determined. Because you know what? That's the very first *huge* step into healing.' She wandered over and opened the office door for him. 'I'll see you next week then. Just make an after-hours appointment with Jaycee on the way out.'

Dylan stood to leave. 'Okay, will do.' He turned to face her before he stepped away. 'Thank you, you know, for listening.'

Theresa chuckled lightly. 'My pleasure, Dylan. That's what I'm here for.'

With the next appointment made, Dylan walked outside into the glorious sunshine, feeling like the heavy burden he'd been carrying had lifted a little bit, putting a bit more of a spring in his step and a taste of happiness in his heart. Before seeing Theresa Wise, he'd tried to avoid certain people in town, just so he didn't have to observe their pity for him, but today he felt like smiling and waving to absolutely everyone, skipping down the street while singing 'Happy' by Pharrell Williams.

Shoving his hands in his pockets, he tried to curb his sudden enthusiasm to dance down the sidewalk, for fear of looking like a lunatic. It was a strange yet welcome sensation to feel bubbles of life within him. Instead of forcing himself to smile, he was smiling from within, and it felt great. If he could feel like this after his very first appointment, imagine what he'd accomplish working with Theresa for a couple of months. It was heart-wrenching talking about everything, but he had a feeling it was going to be well worth it. Now that he knew what could be gained by going to a shrink, he couldn't believe he'd been stupid enough to put it off for so long. Why did men—and some women for that matter—make life so hard for themselves sometimes, just to keep up the 'I'm tough, I can handle anything' facade? His mother had been right all along; as it had been for her after what his father had done to her, this would be his saving grace.

The ringing of his mobile phone stopped him in his tracks. Pulling it from his pocket he noticed it was a private number. He hated private numbers. Why did people feel the need to hide their identity when they called? It was probably some damn salesperson trying to sell him something he didn't need. 'Hello.' His tone was laced with annoyance as he waited for the sales pitch.

'G'day, Dylan. Stanley Wildwood here. Have I caught you at a bad time?'

'Oh, hi, Mr Wildwood, not at all. How are you?' His pulse rate picked up. This was it, his chance at making their lives more comfortable, dangling in front of him like a carrot in front of a horse.

'I'm not too bad, thanks, no use complaining. I'm not going to beat around the bush, Dylan. Before I tell you whether you got the job or not, you have to answer one question for me.'

Nerves danced in Dylan's stomach. 'Okay, sure. What would you like to know?'

'Were you the boy that came looking for Renee? You know, the one I chased off my property with my shotgun all those years ago?'

Time stood still as Dylan held his breath, the details all coming back. It had been a week since Renee had skipped town and in desperation after way too many drinks at the pub he'd made the long trek out to Wildwood Acres to beg Stanley and Pearl to tell him where she had gone. Stanley hadn't been one bit welcoming— and how could he blame him, seeing as he hadn't even known he'd been dating his granddaughter.

Shit! What was he meant to say? If he said yes, it would probably blow any chance he had of getting the job. Veering off the footpath, Dylan stood in the shade of a bottlebrush tree for some privacy. 'Um...'

'Well, come on, boy, it's a yes or no answer.' Stanley's firm tone of voice set off warning bells. He was not playing around. This was deadly serious.

His shoulders slumping, Dylan replied the only way he knew how. 'Yes, Mr Wildwood, that was me. I'm sorry—'

Stanley cut him off. 'Okay then, good, that's settled. I'd already jogged my memory and remembered it was you—I was just trying to find out if you were going to be honest about it. From what Renee told me last night, you two were good friends back when she was a teenager.'

'Yeah, we were. That's why I came out looking for her that time, because I didn't know where she'd gone.' Dylan bit his lip in a bid to stop himself being any more honest than he needed to be. He didn't want to push his luck too far. He held his breath, waiting for Stanley's response. Did he have the job, or not?

'Good, she needs a decent friend she can trust around here. I can't watch her all the time, but from what Rex tells me, I reckon I can trust you to help keep an eye on her. You can start tomorrow morning—I'll need you a couple of days a week to help me around the place with odd jobs, and collecting supplies in town from time to time. You can use one of my horses or bring your own, up to you. There's room in the paddock for another if you prefer to bring your own ride.'

Dylan punched the air. If getting the job meant he had to babysit Renee sometimes too, then he'd do it without question. Not that he was entirely comfortable with it; surely she was old enough and determined enough to take care of herself. 'Oh, thank you Mr Wildwood. You have no idea how much this means to me.'

'You're welcome. Just don't make me regret my decision, okay?'

'You won't, you have my word.' Dylan started pacing the sidewalk, his elation making it impossible for him to stand still.

Stanley chuckled. 'I'll hold you to that. And one more thing, Dylan.'

'Yup, anything, Mr Wildwood.'

'Will you stop calling me "Mr Wildwood"? Just Stan will do nicely. I don't like formalities, makes me uncomfortable.'

'Okay then, Stan it is.'

'Good, glad that's settled. See you bright and early tomorrow.'

'You sure will, Mist— I mean, Stan.'

In a daze, Dylan shoved his phone back in his pocket and strolled off towards the fire station. He hoped Ralph was there—he couldn't wait to tell him he'd just scored a job. Best buddies since primary school, Ralph was like the brother he'd never had. He told him everything, and knew he could rely on him for anything, as Ralph could him.

Deciding to walk instead of driving the kilometre down the street, Dylan followed the footpath, the textbook northern winter's day perfect for a stroll. Passing the bank, he stopped off at the local bakery, famous for its floating pies—a meat pie sitting in a pool of rich gravy with mushy peas and mashed potato on top. Grabbing one for him and one for Ralph—he'd easily eat them both if Ralph weren't at the station—he turned to walk out of the store, bumping straight into his neighbour, Craig Campbell. As usual, Craig's police uniform was ironed to a crisp, his black boots devoid of any scuff marks. Even with his wife having left him almost two years ago, Craig still kept himself and his house as neat as a pin. His meticulousness amazed Dylan.

'G'day, Craig.'

'Howdy, Dylan, how's things?'

'Yeah, not too bad. Any closer to figuring out who the bastard is that is letting all my cattle out?'

Craig shook his head. 'Sorry to say, I'm not. I haven't got much evidence to go off really. But that's not to say I won't eventually find the mongrel, or mongrels, responsible.'

'Well, keep me posted if anything pops up.'

Craig nodded. 'Will do, mate.'

'Thanks, appreciate it.' Dylan went to say goodbye but halted. 'Hey, you'll never guess who I ran into yesterday.'

'Do tell.'

'Renee Wildwood.' Dylan's heart picked up pace with the mere mention of her name.

'Shit hey, I thought she'd vanished with the wind and was never coming back.' The two-way attached to Craig's belt buzzed to life but he turned it down. 'How'd she look?'

Dylan huffed. 'Pretty damn good, actually.'

Craig chuckled. 'Yeah, she was always a looker.'

The woman behind the counter looked to Craig for his order. He gave her a quick nod to acknowledge her then brought his gaze back to Dylan. 'I better grab my lunch.'

'Okay, catch ya.'

'Yup, catch ya,' Craig said before turning his attention back to the girl at the counter.

Wandering into the fire station, Dylan heard his name being called. He looked left and right and up and down, but couldn't for the life of him work out where Ralph's voice was coming from. 'Where in the bloody hell are ya?'

'I'm down here, ya moron.' With a swoosh Ralph emerged on a mechanic's creeper from underneath the fire truck, his eyeballs glowing white and his face covered in black grime. He grinned cheekily, his teeth almost iridescent against his sooty black face.

Dylan shook his head at the state of his mate, laughing. 'What have you been doing under there—trying out for land rights or something?'

'I've been *trying* to fix a damn oil leak.'

Dylan pointed to Ralph's face. 'Well, it kinda looks like you're not really succeeding with that, buddy.'

'I know, I know, don't judge. I'm meant to know what I'm doing, seeing as I'm a heavy equipment operator and all, but this beast can be a complete bitch when it wants to be,' Ralph said with a grin as he unsuccessfully tried to wipe the blackness off with the rag in his hand. He stood up, pointing at the pies in Dylan's hands. 'And it appears to me that you've brought sustenance. Good on ya! I'm Hank Marvin!'

Dylan waited for Ralph to stand up and then handed him the styrofoam container.

Ralph opened the lid, the gravy oozing out of the opening. He licked the tasty morsels from his fingers. 'You're a legend, mate. I bloody love these things!'

Dylan chuckled. 'Yeah, me too. I can't walk past the bakery without grabbing one.' He pulled one of the plastic forks from his jeans pocket and handed it to Ralph.

Ralph pointed to the smoko area in the corner, his shaggy blonde hair flopping around his head. 'Wanna coffee or tea to go with it... or something stronger?'

Dylan chuckled. 'It's too early in the day for something stronger. A coffee would be good, thanks.'

Ralph began to try and eat the pie without his fork by using his lips like a horse eating bread. 'Sure thing, you party pooper.'

'Yeah, whatever,' Dylan said lightheartedly.

Ralph pulled a seat from the smoko table and pushed it towards Dylan, before grabbing one for himself. 'So anything exciting happening in your world? I hope so, because mine's been pretty fucking boring.'

'Yup, I got me a job. Oh, and I ran into Renee Wildwood.' Dylan shoved a mouthful of pie in, groaning in pleasure with the taste of it while trying to act offhand about running into Renee.

Ralph's mouth dropped open. 'Holy shit, times two! That's great you picked up some work so quickly—whereabouts? And how the fuck do you feel about running into Renee after all these years? I thought she'd disappeared forever.'

'I've scored a job working with Stanley Wildwood over at Wildwood Acres, just a few days a week. Hence the reason I ran into Renee. To be honest, I don't know how I feel about running into her.'

'Can't blame you really, after what she said about your dad. And then taking off like that, well, what can I say.' Ralph forked a mouthful of pie in, his eyebrows raised while he chewed. 'How'd she look?'

'Oh, trust you to ask something like that, Ralph,' Dylan said, laughing.

'Well?' Ralph said, shoving another forkful in.

'She looks—' Dylan smirked, '—bloody amazing.'

Ralph nodded. 'I thought she would have, she was always a good sort. You reckon you'll both be able to let sleeping dogs lie, so you can at least be mates?'

Dylan chuckled cynically. 'Dunno. Time will tell, I s'pose.'

'It won't look good if you're arguing with the boss's daughter, so watch your step.'

'I know, I know, I'll be civil at least.'

'Good.' Ralph scraped the last of the tasty lunch from his container. 'I'm glad you picked up some work, buddy. It might take the pressure off you a bit.'

Dylan fought the urge to lick his container clean, instead lobbing it towards the bin and cheering along with Ralph when he got it in. 'It will certainly ease the pressure a bit, but I still need to try and tighten the belt a little on the farm. God knows where though.'

Ralph grinned and leant forward in his seat. 'Well, I've been thinking about ways I could help you out, and you know what I reckon?'

Dylan licked the last of the gravy from his fingers. 'We should rob a bank?'

Ralph swiped the air indifferently. 'That was my idea last week.' He smiled wickedly. 'This week I'm thinking we should build a dam on the border of your property, down on the lower part. You know, where there is a bit of a natural valley, so you can catch the water running off from Craig's property—which means free water and drastically lower water bills. One good storm and you'd fill the bugger. I don't reckon Craig would mind, seeing as it's not taking away from his water or costing him anything.'

Dylan grinned, nodding eagerly. 'You're a fucking genius, Ralph. I can't believe I never thought of that myself.'

Ralph pretended to blow smoke from his fingers as he sat back all puffy-chested, his confident joviality and surfer dude looks a big part of what attracted women to him like bees to honey. 'In tribute to my favourite movie of all time…I like to think of myself as a bit of an ideas man.'

Dylan laughed at the old line, the movie *The Castle* being his and Ralph's all-time favourite. 'How big would we build it?'

'I'm thinking about three to four metres deep and about thirty across, which means it would hold about thirty megs—roughly. We can't go any deeper than five metres because then you'd need permits and shit from the council, and it'll take forever to organise. But the size I'm suggesting should be plenty. It'll only take about three or four days in the dozer and the job will be done.'

Dylan thought for a few moments, rolling the idea around. A dam was a great idea, but he would have to find some money to do it, and he just didn't have the funds right now. There was no way in hell he was going to ask Ralph to do it for free. 'How much will it cost to build it? I mean, I have to pay you for the time you spend in your dozer. Times are tough for everyone right now and I ain't going to accept handouts from my best mate.'

Ralph leant forward, smiling. 'For you, my friend, nothing.'

'No way, Ralph. You got to pay the bills too. It's gonna take almost a week to build the thing, which means you won't be making money somewhere else in the meantime.'

'Dylan, I'm not taking no for an answer. You've done loads of favours for me in the past, including breaking in a few of my horses for free—which wasn't an easy task with the latest temperamental bugger—so let me do this for you, please.'

Dylan drummed his fingers on the smoko table, thinking. 'Are you sure, mate?'

'Positive. When I've got a couple of days to spare I'll be out at your place with bells on. I've got a full week next week so I'm guessing I can make a start on it the week after that.'

Dylan reached out and squeezed Ralph's shoulder. 'Thanks, mate, I really appreciate it. I'll owe ya big time for this.'

'Oh no you won't. Just have a few cold ones on hand at the end of each day and we'll call it square. Deal?' Ralph held out his hand.

Dylan shook it, beaming. 'It's a deal.'

CHAPTER
10

It had been a few days since she'd first run into Dylan, and it still hadn't got any easier—they hadn't even spoken a word, just nodding or waving a quick hello if they crossed paths on the property. She was sure he was just being nice to her to put on a show for her pa. Oh well—she'd play along with it to keep the peace. Pa didn't need any more drama in his life, especially because of her fuck-ups.

Shaking her head at the memory of Dylan spotting her at her worst while sitting out on the front verandah this morning—in her faithful pink-and-purple polka-dot flannelette pyjamas *and* with bed hair from hell—Renee popped the lid on the slow cooker. She was mighty proud of her effort at concocting a hearty stew out of what was left in the fridge, which wasn't much—she really needed to do some food shopping tomorrow. The smells wafting from the comfort food were making her mouth water. Satisfied she had dinner under control, she padded into her bedroom to get changed, her thoughts seized by Dylan's ruggedly handsome face. By God he looked good in a pair of jeans. And those manly hands...

Watching him stroking his horse so fondly as he'd saddled him up this morning, she had imagined him instead stroking her naked skin. He didn't know that after absconding to the house she had watched him from behind the curtains in the lounge room, each and every move he made making her want to caress his lips with hers. She completely respected the fact that he was married, and she would never even consider going near a married man—and not that he'd want her within ten feet anyway given how he'd reacted to running into her last week—but it was okay to dream. Nonetheless, she had to find a way to rid herself of the feelings she harboured for him, and the only way she saw that happening was to allow herself to fall for someone else.

How the hell she was going to do that she hadn't a clue, but she at least had to open herself up to the idea. She knew deep down that she had unconsciously stopped herself from falling for another man these past nine years, in the hope that she and Dylan would someday get back together. But now she knew he was spoken for, and that he felt nothing for her other than resentment, she had to finally let him go. It broke her heart to do so, but she just had to.

Grabbing her togs from the bottom drawer, Renee shoved them into her already jammed-full backpack. She was basically going to have to sit on it to do it up—a bit like her suitcase when she'd left Melbourne. Her pa had always taught her that when she was going out adventuring around Wildwood Acres, she should be prepared for anything, and with everything from her fully charged mobile phone, insect repellent, a torch, a bandage if she got bitten by a snake—yes she was being overcautious—warm clothes if the weather took a turn for the worst, to enough snacks and water to keep two people alive for days in the bush, that's exactly what she was doing. A bit of overkill, but it was better to be safe than sorry. She'd told Pa she was going to have a look around the place today, choosing to leave out the fact she was venturing as far as the Opals Ridge National Park. She didn't want to worry him, and if he knew she was going as far as that he'd be worried sick. From her calculations of how long it would take, she expected to be home well before dark anyway, and certainly before her pa. So, like the saying went, what he didn't know wouldn't hurt him.

After the backbreaking work of treating the cattle for paralysis ticks and then spending the last few days fixing the fencing around the horse paddocks on her own—Pa had been busy doing other jobs with Dylan—she was secretly relieved to have time off. Although she'd been careful to cover up and use sunscreen, she was still a little sunburnt, her entire body ached, and her hands were covered in blisters, much to her mortification. She used to be much more resilient when it came to hard work—when she was a teenager being out for days on end in the saddle was a breeze. Now, after years of working her city job, it was clearly going to take her a little while to get used to the strenuous physical work required at Wildwood Acres again. Murphy's Law—she'd probably just get used to it and then return home to Melbourne the next day. Not that Pa was going to need her too often now he had Dylan, it was more the fact that she *wanted* to help when she could. Farm work was damn tough, and she had to toughen up to handle it, but she loved it, and that was the most important thing. She adored getting outside and being at one with Mother Nature. And she wanted to use the time she had here to get outside as often as possible so she could return to her job as a realtor in Melbourne refreshed and renewed.

Nervous excitement filled her as she pulled on her jeans and then began brushing her teeth. She was going to revisit some of her and Scarlet's childhood places today and she couldn't wait—knowing it would make her feel close to her sister. Mapping Wildwood Acres out in her mind, she thought about her movements for the day, hoping to God she didn't get lost seeing as she hadn't ventured around the countryside here for years. First she was going to head down to the back of the property, to the caves, and then work her way back to the hunter's shack, stopping off in between the two places for lunch and a swim at the bottom dam where she and Scarlet used to have loads of fun.

Come on, Reni, I'll race ya! Last one in has to do the other's washing for a month.

You're on. Oh my God, sis, are you taking your bra and knickers off too?

Yup, why not? Get those clothes off, Reni, and let yourself feel free for once!

You really are crazy…

I might be, but crazy people have way more fun!

Renee smiled as she recalled the first time Scarlet dared her to skinny dip at fourteen—and then how it had become a tradition. It was such good old-fashioned country fun. They would both strip off and run squealing to the dam's edge before diving beneath the goosebump-enticing water, the risk of being caught making it much more exciting. Now she thought of it, who in the heck was going to catch them out in the sticks anyway? She shook her head, laughing, the workings of a teenage mind something an adult would never understand.

The thought of female company made her feel homesick for Melbourne. It would have been nice to have some girly company for the day, but she had no-one to ask. It made her miss Tia even more than she already was. They'd sent the occasional text, but hadn't spoken since the day she arrived. Tia had let her know that Kat was doing fine and also filled her in on the comings and goings of the odd guy in her apartment block that they both swore was involved in something shady, but it wasn't the same as having a good old chinwag. If only Tia could jump on a plane and come visit for a weekend, but it wasn't that easy with her high-pressure job at the hospital. She made a mental note to call her tonight.

Spitting her toothpaste down the plughole, and then rinsing her mouth out with cheek-blasting Listerine, Renee tugged on her favourite t-shirt and sat down on the end of the bed to pull on her socks. She found it hard to believe she'd been back almost a week. Having been confined to the station other than during her and Pa's nightly visits to the hospital, it felt more like a month. Even though she was enjoying being back home, she was also feeling lonely and she found herself missing her social life and the independence she had in Melbourne. She was hoping to get back in touch with Hayley Gregory, her best friend from high school, but still hadn't gathered enough courage to call her, afraid she'd get the same cold welcome she'd had from Dylan.

She really had to bite the bullet and call—it would be good to catch up for old times' sake. Maybe she could organise a night out at the pub, as long as it didn't send Pa into a worried panic. Renee rolled her eyes. She loved how protective Pa was of her, and understood his reasons completely, but the complete loss of her usual adult freedom was making her feel a little like a teenager again.

Grabbing her loaded backpack from the floor, Renee threw it over her shoulder and headed outside, keen to get the day started. She just had to drop a basket of goodies down to Mick, and then she'd be on her merry way. Jumping on the four-wheeler parked out the front, she revved it to life and skidded off down the dirt track, a cloud of dust trailing in her wake, grinning broadly while the wind whipped her ponytail around her face. Coming a close second to horse riding, she loved being on a motorbike, especially a four-wheeler, although Mick's accident had certainly made her very aware of what could go wrong on them.

Passing the machinery shed and then the stables, she turned down the track that led to Mick's cottage, slowing down to admire the horses grazing in their paddocks along the way. She loved the saying that horses made the landscape more beautiful—it was so very true. With their grace, strength and amazing spirit, horses were such beautiful creatures, and ones that would be your friend for life if treated properly. It angered her beyond words when people mistreated them, some individuals believing that a heavy hand was the way to train a horse. In her experience, it was actually the opposite, and she admired anyone who trained a horse with the love and respect they deserved. From memory, Dylan had a magical way with horses—not once did she ever see him raise his hand to one when they were teenagers. Just another damn thing she loved about him.

Pulling up in front of the workers' quarters, Dylan was pushed to the back of Renee's mind as she broke into fits of laughter at the sight before her. Mick was out on his front porch, trying to chase off several clucking chickens while wobbling precariously on his crutches. The swear words flying from his lips would have made an old-fashioned mother shove a bar of soap in his mouth. It was absolute chaos, chickens running in all directions, two of the feathered foes making a mad dash for freedom by escaping between Mick's legs and into his cottage.

'Oi, you little bastards! Get outta my house! If you even think about crapping on anything in there you're gonna be my roast dinner tonight!' He went to disappear through the cottage door.

'Are you in need of some help there, Mick?' Renee called out as she got off the bike. He hadn't even realised she was there he was so preoccupied.

Sticking his head back out, Mick grinned his notoriously mischievous grin. 'Hey there, Reni, didn't see you there… I wouldn't say no. The bloody mongrels are shitting all over my porch and I'm sick of having to hose it off every day. I'll give them bloody something to shit their dacks about if they don't bugger off—I got me a big gun in here which I'd be more than happy to introduce to them too.'

Racing over to give Mick a hand before he fell over and hurt himself more, Renee busied herself shooing the chooks off Mick's kitchen bench and out the back door. Mick wobbled after them as best he could, cursing when his crutches hampered him. In a flurry of feathers, the chickens joined their partners in crime out on the back lawn and took off down the dirt track and into the old shed across the track—and well out of harm's way.

'I'd be bloody running too, if I were you lot!' Mick shouted out after them.

'You tell 'em, Mick!' Job done, Renee pointed to the basket, still chuckling at the hullabaloo. 'I brought you some corned beef and mustard pickle sandwiches, and some sponge cake I made last night. Thought you might be in some need of some more good old-fashioned tucker.'

Mick smiled while rubbing his rotund belly, clearly having forgotten to put his false teeth in. 'You're a star, Renee, just like your dear old nan. Pearl always makes sure I'm fed up to me eyeballs too.' Shaking his head, he sighed. 'So sad the poor old bugger's holed up in that hospital. She'd be going insane, and driving the hospital staff equally insane while she's at it.' He chuckled with the thought. 'I just thank God she's gonna be okay.'

Renee nodded, her smile fading. 'Bloody oath, I couldn't bear the thought of anything happening to her. I'm really looking forward to her coming home next week, so I can have some girly chitchat.

All this blokey stuff is fun, but a gal needs another gal to liven her spirits at times.'

'Yeah, you women have this weird thing about yas that only other women can understand. That's why I never got married.' Mick smiled a gummy smile. 'She's a tough old broad, your nan. So don't worry, she'll be right.' Nicking a strawberry off the top of the sponge, Mick threw it in his mouth, then realised he had no teeth in. 'Shit. Hang five, I just gotta find me chompers. I think I left them on the coffee table.'

Renee chuckled at him as he wandered back inside, returning with his teeth now in his mouth.

He tried to suck his plump stomach in. 'Look at me—I'd fade away to a shadow without you around.'

Renee giggled. With his little ears and bald head he reminded her a bit of a gummy bear. 'Yeah right, I reckon you're pretty capable of looking after yourself after all these years as a bachelor, Mick.'

'True, but a man gets sick of opening cans of baked beans and spaghetti after a while.' He gave her a cheeky wink.

'Oh come on, I've tasted your lamb roasts and that famous beef and dumpling stew you cook in the camp oven—you're a man who knows how to cook.'

'You got me there, I suppose.' Sitting down on his camp chair, Mick broke off a bit of the sponge and shoved it in his mouth, grinning. 'Now that there is marrying material. When are you going to get yourself a husband you can cook for, Reni?'

'Oh don't start on me again, Mick. You've been asking me that question since I was about fifteen.' Giggling, Renee shook her finger at him, mimicking a girl from the hood with an over-pronounced headshake. 'I'll get me a husband when I'm good and ready. I got to find a decent man first, and one I could bloody put up with for the rest of my life.'

'Well, there's plenty of them round these parts. You just got to know where to look.'

'I wouldn't know where to start.'

Mick raised his eyebrows. 'I reckon I know. There's a Studs and Fuds ball on over at the showgrounds this weekend. The CWA women cater for dinner inside the hall, and outside they set a stage up on a semi-trailer for the band and everyone dances on the grass in front of it. There're a few bonfires scattered around the place too, to sit around if you feel like chillaxing. It'll be a top night. You should go if your pa will let you out of his sight.'

Renee sat down beside him, excited by the prospect of a night out, especially one where she could dance out under the stars—she hadn't done that since she was a teenager. 'Hmm, sounds like fun. But I have to ask, what the hell is a Studs and Fuds ball?'

Mick looked at her with one eyebrow raised almost to his hairline, like she was from another planet. 'Really? You've never heard of one? What have you been doing all these years in the big smoke?' He grabbed another piece of the cake and stuffed it in his mouth. 'The studs are all you youngsters, and the fuds are all the old fuddy-duddies.' He gave her a nudge with his elbow, a cheeky grin curling his lips. 'I'm still trying to figure out which one I am—a fud or a stud. I like to think I still got it in me to impress the ladies, but I must admit I like hanging out in the hall with all the other fuds for the night. Dancing's just not my thing anymore.' He wriggled his eyebrows, chuckling as he tried to flex his flabby arms. 'Maybe I can score me a fuddy-duddy hey.' He shrugged. 'But all jokes aside, the age differences make for a really good night.'

'Oh Mick, I reckon you're definitely still a stud.' Renee laughed, shaking her head at his wicked sense of humour. She stared out over the eastern paddocks, bubbles of anticipation filling her. 'A Stud and Fuds ball, hey? Sounds like it could be loads of fun.'

Mick grinned proudly. 'Yup, we sure know how to have a decent hoedown out here in the sticks. The one last year was a hoot. I remember a couple of the local lads being covered in tar and chicken feathers by the end of the night. How in the hell that came about I haven't a clue, but it was bloody hilarious!' Mick pointed to his cast. 'Not sure if I'll be able to make it too easily with this bloody thing on though—driving's a bit of a challenge.'

Renee clapped her hands together excitedly. 'I'll make you a deal, Mick. If you tell Pa you're going to chaperone me, I'll drive you there *and* I'll get you back home the next morning, once I've slept off the few drinks I'll be having of course. I reckon Pa will relax about me going if you're there to keep an eye on me. I don't want to have him up worrying about me all night.'

'It's a bloody deal.' Mick held out his hand, grinning like he'd just won the lottery, and Renee shook it. 'But don't get up to too much mischief or your pa will kick my butt.'

'My days of mischief are long gone, Mick, so you'll have no worries about that.'

'Oh come on now, you're still a spring chicken.' Mick waved his hands in the air. 'That city lifestyle has made you old and boring—where's your sense of adventure?'

Without warning, Mick's words hit home. Yes, she had a very active social life in Melbourne, but if she was going to be brutally honest with herself, she was never truly at ease in the classy restaurants and bars—never feeling as though she could really let her hair down and have fun like she used to with Scarlet leading the way. Being back here gave her the opportunity to regain that old piece of herself once again, and even though she no longer had Scarlet to encourage her, she was eager to give it a damn good try on her own. 'You know what, Mick? You're right. I need to get out and have some fun, and that's what I'm going to do. I'm going to stop worrying, catch up with old friends and dance until the sun comes up.'

Mick gave her the thumbs up, his toothless grin almost comical. 'That's the spirit, Reni!'

Standing, Renee gave him a quick hug. 'Thanks for the pep talk. I got to head off, but I might pop back in later. Enjoy your basket of treats.'

'Oh, I will, trust me,' Mick replied appreciatively, and then pointed to her bulging backpack on the back of the bike. 'Where you heading for the day anyway? Looks like you've packed enough for a week.'

Hesitating, Renee considered whether to let Mick in on her plans. Pa hadn't asked her where she was going today when she'd said she was going to go for a bit of a mosey around, so she avoided having to tell him, but she wasn't going to outright lie when directly asked. 'Umm, I reckon I might head down the back, check out the caves and the old hunter's shack for old times' sakes, and have a swim at the bottom dam in between.'

'You be bloody careful out there girl. It's unforgiving countryside if you get yourself lost, or God forbid, hurt.' His scrunched eyebrows shot up in question. 'Does your pa know where you're heading?'

'Kinda sort of...' Renee screwed up her face, knowing Mick's response was going to include a bit of a lecture.

'I take it that's a no then.' Mick shook his head. 'I'd rather you not go venturing over that way on your own, but you've always been a determined little bugger when you set your mind on something, so I'm not going to tell you not to go because I know you'll go anyway. I'd come with you but I'd just slow you down all day in the state I'm in. Just promise me you'll be careful...and let me know when you're back so I can stop worrying, okay?'

Renee crossed her heart. 'I promise I'll let you know the second I get back.' She looked at her watch. 'And I reckon it'll be around fourish, if not before.'

'I'll hold you to that,' Mick said, giving her a wink.

'I won't let you down,' Renee said, giving him a quick wave before heading back to the four-wheeler.

CHAPTER

11

The morning sun blazed radiantly in the clear blue sky, its luxurious warmth erasing any lingering dawn chill. The gathering cloud of grit and dust hovering over the drove of Brangus cattle glimmered within its rays, a rural scene that had inspired many works of Australian art. Dylan smiled to himself. How blessed was he to land a job like this? Was Lady Luck finally smiling down on him?

With a gentle breeze and no chance of rain, it was picture-perfect weather for a muster. Feeling at peace in the saddle, Dylan looked past the relaxed ambling mob and out over the horizon, the endless sweeping views of Wildwood Acres mesmerising. He always found the way the Opals Ridge National Park rolled seamlessly onto the borders of the properties surrounding it visually absorbing, the hundreds of towering ghost gums dotted in every direction giving Wildwood Acres an otherworldly feel. It was hard to believe his property was on the opposite side of the vast national park, the drive over here probably taking about the same amount of time as it would to gallop through the park on horseback—not that he was going to make Turbo gallop here and back every day to get to work. He quite enjoyed the casual twenty-five minute drive as it gave him time to think.

Gazing out over the small herd, Dylan kept a keen eye on the wayward stragglers from the sideline, making every effort to keep the mob quiet and calm as he and Turbo gently pushed them onwards. With their size, speed, strength and potential for aggression, cattle needed to be handled thoughtfully and with confidence, and agitating them with aggressive movements was a certain recipe for chaos. Other than a young bull stirring the mob up occasionally with his playful pushing and shoving, and a dogged older bull that had made a few half-hearted attempts at freedom, the muster was going fairly smoothly, not that it couldn't all go belly-up in the blink of an eye if he wasn't careful.

Dylan had experienced his fair share of musters in the wilds of the Australian outback, and had a lengthy scar on his back from a micky bull's deadly horn to prove it. At the tender age of fifteen, he'd been lucky to survive the frenzied attack when he'd fallen off his horse and found himself face to face with the belligerent beast, the quick actions of the Waratah Station staff and the Royal Flying Doctor Service the only reason he was still alive today. It had taught him a valuable lesson at a very young age—to always keep on his toes when he was working with cattle, wild or not—and it had definitely come in handy over the years. To this day he had never blamed the bull, or the horse that had bucked him off.

Pulling his hat down a little further to shade his eyes and then taking a swig from his water bottle, Dylan's belly rumbled, the two Weetbix he had gobbled down at five thirty this morning not curbing his hunger. He was guessing another two hours or so and they'd have all the cattle at the drafting yards, just in time for a late smoko while they let the cattle settle after their walk. When he'd arrived almost half an hour early for work today, Dylan had been stoked to find out he and Stanley would be mustering the cattle to be drafted, the ones ready to be sold at the meatworks being trucked out early tomorrow morning, while the rest would be put back out onto pasture to fatten up. Mustering was his favourite kind of station work, fencing his least favourite. He looked at his watch—it was now nearing eight o'clock. Annie would be getting on the bus headed for school right about now. Thank God he had his mum there to help. He wouldn't be able to cope without her.

Allowing the peace of the countryside to fill him, Dylan hummed one of Alan Jackson's new bluegrass tunes to himself—the CD had been on repeat in his Land Cruiser for over a week now. Beneath him, Turbo did his job with precision. The eleven-year-old gelding was an old hand with stock work, and he loved it. He'd been like a frog in a sock when Dylan had got him off the float at daybreak this morning, knowing from experience that he was being put to work for the day.

Ahead, Stanley rode at the lead, guiding the cattle towards the yards over at the far eastern paddock. Dylan admired the way Stanley worked his stock with a gentle hand, the cattleman only using his stockwhip once when a bull had tried to break ranks. There was a lot to be said for a man whose cattle and horses trusted and respected him.

Moseying along peacefully, the sound of Turbo's hooves clip-clopping on the earth and the soft bellows of the cattle carrying with the breeze, Dylan's mind wandered back to earlier this morning—to when he had pulled up and spotted Renee sitting on the front verandah in her pyjamas, cuppa in her hands and a dreamy look in her eyes as she'd watched the day break.

Even though he wanted to deny it, she still looked damn amazing, bed hair and all. Her pretty face gave the sun something worth shining on, and he'd found it hard to drag his eyes away. She had given him a quick wave before retreating into the homestead, her blushing cheeks and slight coyness making her even more captivating.

He'd never liked women that were loud-mouthed and 'look at me', finding them overbearing and fairly shallow-minded. Renee Wildwood was certainly not one of them. Her laid-back country attitude was one of the many attributes that had attracted him to her all those years ago, and from what he could tell after running into her the other morning, although she was a little more sophisticated on the outside, she was still that gentle and soft-spirited country girl he remembered on the inside. Part of him had been relieved when she had escaped into the house and he didn't have to talk to her, but another part of him wished he could retreat into the house and make love to her like he'd done once before. The very thought had sent a warm rush throughout him, the memory of her touch enough to send his heart bolting.

Sighing loudly, Dylan shook his head. He couldn't deny it. The woman was drop-dead gorgeous, and past experience told him she knew exactly how and where to touch him to send him beyond cloud nine. He imagined what it would be like to feel that with her again, that deep soul love, a hunger that was so intense it was almost unquenchable. He had loved Shelley with all his heart and more, and had loved being intimate with her, but, he'd never experienced that feeling of delving inside her and touching her soul like he had with Renee.

Squeezing his eyes shut for a few brief seconds, Dylan tried to clear his mind. He was angry with himself for making a comparison between his wife and his first love. His shoulders slumped as guilt weighed heavily upon him. Shelley may have left this earth, but in his heart he was still committed to her, which is why he refused to take his wedding ring off. Just thinking about Renee in such intimate ways felt wrong, very, *very* wrong. He wished he had an off switch for his brain because being back here at Wildwood Acres was reviving memories he'd long ago buried, including one he'd rather forget.

For it was here, on this station, cuddled up in his swag under the roof of the old hunter's shack, that he and Renee had lost their virginity to one another. It had been a powerfully poignant moment, when their bodies had become one, both of them clinging to one another as they'd stated their undying love for one another. Renee had told him she could never live without him, that he was all she had wanted, and more, swearing to him over and over that she'd never leave him. And he had told her the same. The only difference was, he had meant it, and she obviously hadn't. How could a woman say they loved you, and then go and say what she did the very next day? How naive he had been, believing it was going to last forever, because as he had so harshly learnt on his journey through life, nothing really did.

***

Carefully heading up the steep rise towards where Wildwood Acres backed onto the Opals Ridge National Park, the sheer vastness of the countryside came into full view. Reaching the top of the summit, Renee gasped in splendour. Overawed by the sight, but trying to keep her focus on the job at hand, she manoeuvred the four-wheeler over some rough terrain, the opening of the cave at the bottom of Shadow Mountain now visible in the jutting red rock face dotted generously with lush green vegetation. There was something about this vast, untamed, ancient landscape that drew her like nothing else on Wildwood Acres, a certain kind of magic making her feel as though she was stepping back in time, as if the sound of the breeze was the whispers of her ancestors and the sun upon her skin their warm touch. The land spoke to her out here in a way where words weren't necessary, every inch of the earth a living pulsing entity unto its own. The untouched countryside definitely owned whoever stepped foot out here, not the other way around, its power something that needed to be experienced first-hand to be understood. Renee felt sorry for those souls that never ventured into Australia's rural heartlands—they were missing out on so much.

Coming to a stop now that she was safely on the flats again, and with the bike engine still rumbling, Renee took in the panoramic view, and the raw beauty of Wildwood Acres stole her breath away. Above, a wedge-tailed eagle circled in the cloudless cobalt sky, its birdsong capturing her attention as it disappeared over the mountaintop, a dead snake within its lethal grasp. She wondered where its partner was—eagles one of the few animals that mated for life. How she would love to find her mate for life. Her desire to love and be loved was becoming stronger as each day passed her. The very thought of having a man who came home to her every day, and loved her like he'd loved no other, warmed her heart. Would she ever be lucky enough to cross paths with her soulmate? Or had she already, and ruined it?

Just ahead, a surprised mob of kangaroos bounded out of the thick scrub, giving her a fright and snapping her out of her train of thought. The biggest of the group stopped momentarily to observe her before thump-thumping off to safety. She shook her head at her jumpiness, the knowledge that this was a sacred Aboriginal site putting her a little on edge. She held high regard for Aboriginal beliefs, it being the oldest living culture still in existence. When she was a child the local elders had given her family their blessing to visit the cave as they wished, and she had explored it with Scarlet a number of times, but their blessing did nothing to alleviate her nervousness. Unlike Scarlet, who was an adventurer at heart, she'd always felt as though she was trespassing. But she had to do it—the place was one of Scarlet's favourite spots to visit together.

Parking in the shade of a towering paperbark tree, she switched off the bike and silence met her, the absence of man-made noises beautiful. The scent of lemon myrtle lingered in the air, the aroma reminding her of Nan's yummy lemon myrtle and wattle seed muffins she used to eat as a kid. All around her, Mother Nature thrived, the earth untouched by human hands. Goosebumps prickled her skin. There was something mystical about standing amongst such natural beauty, as though she could feel roots coming up from the dirt beneath her feet, ridding her of society's expectations and grounding her back to pure innocence—a spiritual sensation she could never experience in the city. It was no wonder some city-siders escaped to the country whenever they got the chance.

Taking steady steps, she climbed up the rocky embankment that led to the cave, ducking just in time as a flock of fruit bats swooped out of the hollow blackness. Drawing in a few deep breaths, she tried to calm her racing pulse, her hand clutching her chest as if to stop her heart jumping out. Standing at the mouth of the cave, where the roots of an ancient gum tree had slowly, over many years, worked through the rock, she peered into the eerie darkness, her imagination running riot as to what she may find inside—spiders, snakes, rats, or maybe even the bogeyman? She laughed nervously to herself—although typically a realist, she certainly had a very creative mind at times.

Oh, Reni, there's no such thing as the bogeyman.

I know that, Scarlet. I just don't like the fact this is a sacred place.

I love the fact it is… It makes it so dark and mysterious, don't you think?

No, it makes it dark and scary.

Oh, come on, Reni, be adventurous. Come inside the cave with me, you big scaredy-cat!

I am no scaredy-cat, Scarlet Wildwood, and I'll prove it to you by going in first.

That's the spirit, Reni. You show that bogeyman who's the boss.

Pulling the torch from her pocket, Renee switched it on and shone the beam over the Aboriginal rock art on the walls while slowly stepping inside. Gradually, she worked her way around the small space, avoiding the massive cobwebs. While admiring the drawings that immortalised the creatures the Aboriginal ancestors had seen and hunted, she finally smiled. She swore she could feel the auras of the traditional owners still lingering in the rock art.

On the stony ceiling was the largest dreamtime painting of them all—the rainbow serpent that created all things. It was ethereally beautiful. But although there was so much to admire, there were also a few things that made her skin crawl. She could hear the scurrying of small marsupials over in the corner. Water dripped down the sides of the cave, and murky puddles pooled at her feet. Although it was warm in here, she shivered. The putrid stench of the bats that had made the cave their home filled her nostrils, driving her back towards the entrance, where she escaped back into the glorious sunshine. Gasping in lungfuls of fresh air, she headed back to the four-wheeler to continue on with her exploration, the rising temperature making her crave a plunge in the dam. Her belly rumbled and she looked at her watch—close to lunchtime. So, a stop off at the dam for a quick dip and some scrumptious nourishment from her lunchbox full of goodies. Just what the doctor ordered.

**

When his mobile phone rang for the third time, Dylan motioned across the rails to Stanley, letting him know he had to answer it. If this was Ralph ringing to ask him to go to the pub tonight for the darts tournament he was going to give him a friendly serve. He'd already said no about ten million times and he wasn't going to change his mind. Darts bored him to tears—unlike a good game of pool, which he was always up for. But pulling the mobile from his pocket, he noticed it was his mum—she wouldn't be calling him at work if it weren't important. His thoughts instantly went to Annie and his stomach somersaulted. He hoped to God nothing was wrong. 'Hey Mum, what's up?'

'Hi Dylan, sorry to ring you at work and I don't want to stress you out, but on my way home from town I spotted some of our cattle out on the road.'

'Again! Fuck me dead, whoever's doing this has a lot to bloody answer for.'

Dylan began to pace, his grip tightening around his phone.

Claire sighed. 'Dylan Anderson, language, but yes, they do. I just don't understand why someone would be doing this to you, to us… It's not like we have any enemies around Opals Ridge—not that I know of anyway.'

'I know, I'm as confused as you are.' Dylan drew in a breath, and then exhaled forcefully. 'Look, I can't do anything about it right now, Mum, and you can't get on a horse with your hip the way it is. I'll have to sort it out when I get home, and just hope the cattle don't cause a bloody accident in the meantime. Otherwise I'll be in deep shit.'

'Dylan Anderson. Language.' Claire's tone was lighthearted.

'Sorry, Mum. I'm just so damn tired of this.'

'I know and I can't blame you. Look, I'll give Ralph a ring and if he's not busy I'll see if he has time to come over and round them up. And while he's doing that, I'll go for a drive and see if I can find where they've got out—Ralph might be able to do something about fixing it, even temporarily, just until you get home tonight.'

'Yeah, good idea. Thanks Mum. Just look for where the fence has been cut. The buggers do a good job of it so you won't be able to miss it.'

'Will do. You get back to work and I'll send you a text later letting you know how I got on, okay?'

'Okay. Thanks, I'll give Craig Campbell a ring too, let him know the bastards have done it again. I just wish he'd hurry up and find out who's doing this to us.'

'He'll be doing his best, Dylan. You know how diligent he is.'

'I know, my patience is just beginning to wear very thin, that's all. This really has to stop.'

'Yes, I couldn't agree more. We'll find out who's doing this, Dylan, I have every faith.'

'I hope so, Mum, before they get bored with what they're doing now and maybe start doing something more serious.'

'Try and stay positive, son. Chat later.'

The phone call now ended, Dylan bit his tongue as he walked around in circles, not wanting to lose his temper in front of Stanley. His blood was boiling and he felt like hitting something. He wished there was some way he could catch whoever it was out—or even better, if Craig could catch whoever it was and give them a damn good dose of justice. There just had to be a way.

Stanley gave him a nod, motioning towards the phone grasped in Dylan's fisted hand. 'Everything okay?'

'Not really, some bastard is determined to make my life a living hell by letting my cattle out and cutting my fences in the process—it's a never-ending battle to keep my stock in, and it's costing me a lot of time and money.'

Stanley nodded, scowling. 'What a low act, messing with a farmer's livelihood. Scum of the bloody earth people are that do that. You need to go home and sort it out, lad?'

'Nah, my mum's ringing my best mate to see if he can handle it for me. Should all be good, hopefully.'

'You reported it to Craig down at the cop station?' Stanley poured himself a pannikin of tea from his flask, motioning to Dylan to ask if he wanted some.

'No thanks, got my water here… Yeah I have, not that it's got me anywhere. It's really bloody frustrating.'

Stanley's brows furrowed as he shook his head. 'Hopefully the culprits don't get away with it—the victims always seem to get the short end of the stick these days. So much for our so-called justice system. Sometimes I reckon we should go back to the good old days and sort things out without the law getting involved.'

Dylan smirked. 'I'd have to agree.'

Leaning on the rails, Stanley shoved a piece of hay between his teeth, silent for a few moments before smiling. 'You know what I reckon you should do?'

'I'm open to suggestions.'

'Go get yourself some of them spy cameras, and set them up around your place, but make sure you hide them well. You might be able to catch whoever's doing this red-handed—they won't be able to deny it when you got evidence like that.'

Dylan slapped the rail in front of him. 'You're a genius, Stanley, thanks. I'll order some off eBay tonight.'

'More than happy to help,' Stanley replied as he opened a gate and began drafting the cattle again. 'And I wanna hear all about it when you catch the bugger too.'

'You'll be one of the first I tell.'

***

After a half-hour ride through dense bushland—her belly now full and her skin fresh from her swim in the dam—Renee reached a small clearing where the little early 1900s hunter's shack had sadly been left to perish. The shack was just as she remembered it, although a little more unkempt now that she and Scarlet weren't here to give it occasional doses of TLC. The corrugated iron roof had rusted beyond repair and drooped in the middle, and the three timber walls left standing were clinging onto each adjoining slab for dear life. Sunlight filtered through the cracks of the weathered boards, illuminating the historic structure with dusty streams of light. There was no front door, or wall for that matter, the remnants of the front of the shack now decaying on the ground in front of it, leaving it completely open to the elements from the western side. The inside was unadorned, other than an ancient potbelly stove, a rickety fold-out table—which she and Scarlet had put here—and an army-style stretcher bed that Renee was sure would collapse if she even blew on it.

Renee wondered about the people that had once called the hunter's shack their home. Its untold stories would be ones of terrible hardship, but also of sheer grit and determination. History had always intrigued her.

When she stepped inside the hut, the floorboards creaked wearily beneath her weight. An unexpected rush of emotions hit her, and her eyes filled with tears. She blinked them away, smiling. There were so many happy memories within this humble abode. She and Scarlet had made it their little getaway as teenagers, camping out here most weekends with their close girlfriends so they could enjoy the star-studded night sky by a bonfire. There was only one rule they had to stick to: that no boys were allowed here.

Scarlet had broken that rule quite a number of times with Billy Burton, but Renee had broken it only once, late one rainy Sunday afternoon almost six months after Scarlet had disappeared. It was here, with the rain hammering on the old tin roof, she had lost her virginity to Dylan Anderson on her seventeenth birthday. Sadly, the magic had been short-lived.

Closing her eyes, Renee tried to forget the bad stuff and instead piece together her fragmented memories of that beautiful night: Dylan's lips gently brushing her skin, his hands caressing her so tenderly, his whispers of love, their gasps of pure pleasure as they'd slowly removed each other's clothes, their shared nervous smiles as they'd pushed beyond the boundaries. They'd climbed into his swag, their bodies entwined as Dylan had kissed her for what had felt like hours, his tongue still exploring hers as he'd slowly slid inside her, the mixture of pain and pleasure sending her to places she'd never been before, and since that night, had never been again.

They'd made love all night long, only stopping to fall into a contented sleep in each other's arms for a few hours before waking to hungry kisses and touches once more. Dawn had been the only thing that could drag them from each other's arms, Renee having to head home before her pa came looking for her and Dylan wanting to get home to check in on his mum, and lucky he had because he'd found her lying on the kitchen floor unconscious after being bashed by his father.

The next afternoon, when Dylan had sought her out for comfort and to also explain what had happened, she'd accused Peter Anderson of having something to do with Scarlet's disappearance—the fact he'd bashed his wife to within an inch of her life making him a prime suspect in her eyes. Of course, Dylan had thought otherwise. Then the terrible fight had started, with both of them saying things that had broken each other's hearts. Less than twenty-four hours later she was forced by her grandparents to skip town because of the threatening note left under her windscreen. At the time she couldn't help but wonder if Dylan's father had had anything to do with the note, thinking he'd somehow found out about what she'd said to Dylan, but with rationality on her side she now knew she'd been clutching at straws.

Although they'd parted on bad terms, that beautiful night together had still left her craving for more of him, her desire for Dylan only getting stronger as time went on. The experience had been burnt into her heart, leaving a fire within her soul for him that she'd never been able to extinguish. Would she ever be able to? She hoped so. It was obvious Dylan had not forgiven her, and probably never would. And she couldn't move on in her life completely with him still alive in her heart.

The recollections almost too much to bear, Renee stepped back outside, her skin tingling as the sunlight touched her skin. The sound of running water pulled her attention behind her, to where a stand of native trees shaded a trickling creek from the worst of the afternoon sun. Beneath the dappled sunlight the water was clear and inviting.

Meandering towards the water, she took careful notice of every tree trunk, until she reached the one she was looking for. And there it was, whittled deeply into the bark, a heart-melting moment etched in time. *Dylan loves Renee,* beside a heart with an arrow carved through it. She ran her fingertips over the lettering—her own heart aching with the beautiful memory of her and Dylan as they'd carved this together. They'd been so in love back then, so hopeful of their future together.

Removing her boots, she stepped into the coolness of the water, the slow-running stream only coming up to her ankles. In the wet season, in December and January especially, it was a different story, the creek deep enough to swim in. Bending over, she cupped her hands and splashed the water onto her face, drinking some at the same time, groaning at the delightful purity of the water upon her tongue. Above the surface, dragonflies fluttered, swooping up and down while making hairpin turns at breakneck speed, their multitude of vibrant colours radiant.

Renee beamed at the sight of the prehistoric insects, marvelling that they had been around for over two hundred and fifty million years. All around her, nature was demanding her attention. Sitting in the branches of a paperbark tree, a kookaburra called out to its mate, and bright-coloured rosellas fluttered from branch to branch of the towering natives. As if straight out of a fairytale, this place was a secluded haven. If she still lived here she would make an effort to revive it.

The thought made her belly tingle with excitement. How nice would it be, to have her very own slice of heaven amongst what was already an enchanting place? It was such a contrast to her city life, but inviting all the same. She smiled dreamily.

Maybe, one day, if I made Wildwood Acres my home again, I could do the little shack up...

She shook her head, surprised at her train of thought. This place, Wildwood Acres, her long-ago home, was growing roots within her once again. Or was it just that the seed she had buried deep down all those years ago had finally found the sunshine and the desire to spring forth from its dormant place?

On the banks of the creek, she lay back and rested her head in her hands, trying to not think any longer, but instead to enjoy the sounds of nature surrounding her—the calls of the birds, the whisper of the breeze through the leaves, the scuttle and scurry of the wildlife—and for the first time in as long as she could remember, she felt at peace. She closed her eyes, the image of Scarlet's smiling face the last thing she remembered before she drifted off into nirvana.

CHAPTER
12

With the sun slowly beginning to sink behind the distant Shadow Mountain, and sending a scattering of apricot and crimson hues across the horizon, Dylan worked faster, ignoring the deep ache in his back and the weariness in his bones. Dust covered his every inch and he could taste the grit in his mouth, the soft bellows of the cattle an ongoing soundtrack to his long day. He was still stewing with the fact that someone had tampered with his fencing and let his cattle out again, but at least Ralph had been able to go and sort it out for him, even taking the time to fix where the fence was cut. He didn't know what he'd do without his best mate. Dylan counted his lucky stars having him, and his mum, in his life.

Wanting to impress Stanley, he had volunteered to work through lunch, choosing to scoff a ham sandwich and scull a can of Coke while still drafting. Although he hadn't said much, he could tell that Stanley was grateful, the amount of work to complete before dusk not really leaving time for a lengthy lunch break. Allowing the last of the cattle that would be remaining on Wildwood Acres out the gates and back into the open pastures, Dylan gave Stanley a satisfied nod. The older man returned the gesture, his broad smile letting Dylan know he was happy with his efforts for the day. Relief filled Dylan. He'd strived to prove his worth, and Stanley had clearly noted it.

Riding from the other side of the holding yards, Stanley met him with a tip of his head. 'Well, that's this job done and dusted. We better head back to the homestead before sundown, hey?'

Dylan went to reply but the sounds of a four-wheeler coming up the dirt track diverted both their attention.

'Oh bugger me dead. What's that silly old fool trying to do?' Stanley said, shaking his head. 'He's going to break his other bloody leg if he's not careful.'

Dylan's jaw dropped at the sight of the bloke riding towards them, his broken leg resting on the front mudguard of the four-wheeler while he balanced unstably, his crutches resting over his lap and bouncing with every bump as he struggled to steer it. As he got closer, the look on his face told Dylan something was amiss, and that this wasn't a friendly visit.

Mick pulled to a sliding stop beside them, breathing heavily. He reached out to shake Dylan's hand. 'I'm Mick, good to finally meet you, mate.'

'What's up, Mick?' Stanley's tone was apprehensive.

'You really got to get yourself a bloody mobile, Stan. It's not the bloody nineteen hundreds anymore.' Mick sucked in a breath while trying to adjust his leg. 'It's Renee, she took off down to the caves and hunter's shack this morning… She promised me she'd be home over an hour ago and she's still not back.'

Stanley's face drained of colour. 'What! Why would she go all the way out there by herself, especially without telling me?'

Mick shrugged a little cautiously. 'She told me she just wanted to have a look about, and I reckon she was worried you'd stop her.'

'Damn straight I would have bloody stopped her.' Stanley pointed his finger at Mick. 'Why didn't *you* bloody stop her?'

'Oh come on now, Stan. We're talking about Renee here. You know there's no stopping her if she wants to do something.' Mick threw his hands up in the air. 'I woulda gone looking for her meself, but it's a bit difficult at the moment with my leg and all.'

'Anything could have happened to her out there,' Stanley retorted, trepidation lacing his every word. 'I have to go look for her before it's bloody dark—' he looked at his watch, '—which won't be too long, an hour at the most. Thankfully it's a full moon, so we'll at least have some moonlight to find her with if sundown beats us to it.'

Dylan's heart bolted like a wild horse—images of Renee lying hurt somewhere taunting him. And then in a sudden flashback, he was on the floor of his bathroom, holding Shelley in his arms as he sobbed, wishing with everything he had that he'd been home sooner and there was some way he could turn back time. No way in hell was he going to lose another woman he loved because he wasn't there for her. Realisation washed over him. He'd actually just admitted it to himself. He *loved* Renee, always had, and always would. It didn't mean he had to admit it out loud, though, to her or anyone else for that matter. It could remain his little secret—forever.

'I'll come help, Stan. You can't cover everywhere on your own. If you want to check out the caves, I'll head to the shack.' He gave Turbo the cue to go, calling out over his shoulder, 'I'll meet you back at the homestead if we don't cross paths out there, and if we haven't found her, we'll keep searching until we do.'

'You don't know where the shack is!' Stanley called after him as he enticed his own horse into a gallop.

'Yeah I do, I've been there before.'

'Oh, right. You have?'

The look on Stan's face was one of confusion, but Dylan didn't have time to explain, and he wasn't going to admit what had happened at the shack all those years ago. Going hell bent for leather, he headed towards the place where Renee had stolen his heart, hoping that it wasn't about to be shattered into a million tiny pieces once again. He'd only just started to glue the pieces back together after losing Shelley, he didn't think he'd be able to survive heartache like that again.

Please God, let her be okay.

***

Waking from her afternoon snooze, Renee sat bolt upright, instantly checking her watch. Holy heck! She'd been asleep for almost four hours. A quick glance towards the sky told her dusk was closing in. There was no way she was going to make it back before her pa got home. *Shit!*

Rushing to her feet, she pulled on her boots and then ran for the four-wheeler motorbike, jumping on it. She turned the key and then pressed the ignition button, startled when the bike did nothing. Checking the bike was in neutral, which it was, she pressed the start button again. Nothing. Shit! She got off the bike and walked around to the front, trying to figure out what was wrong with it. Hopefully it was nothing too serious. It was getting dark, so she went to turn the headlights on, to at least give her some light to work with, but they were already on. *Damn it.* Now she understood the problem.

She'd accidently had the headlights on and they'd drained the battery, and because she'd been riding in broad daylight, she hadn't even noticed. How in the hell was she meant to get back to the homestead now? It was way too far on foot. She regretted her decision not to ride Jackson out here now—he'd have got her home. Pulling her mobile phone from her pocket, her heart sank even further. She was near the border of the national park and there was no service out here. Bloody Telstra—so much for Australia-wide coverage! With darkness setting in, so did her panic. She had enough supplies to last her for the night, thankfully, but the thought of being out here all alone in the dark sent a chill through her bones.

Succumbing to the knowledge that she was going to have to wait here until help arrived, which it eventually would at some point—thank goodness she'd told Mick where she was heading today—she strode back into the shack with her torch. It felt slightly safer in here, partially out of the elements and away from the nocturnal wildlife. Her pa was going to kill her for not telling him where she was going.

Hands on hips, she stamped her foot in frustration, her boot breaking through the decaying floorboards and becoming wedged beneath one.

'Great, just fucking great,' she muttered, trying to pull her boot free. 'Could my day get any worse?' But it wouldn't budge. Sitting down, she tried to investigate what was stopping it. Her darn shoelace was caught on something. She pulled up the loose board and shone the torch down, and now with a clear view her eyes widened. The floorboard had been loose for a reason. Her shoelace was wrapped around a latch, a latch on what looked like a jewellery box. With shaking hands, she freed her shoelace, dug away at some dirt and then flicked the rusted latch open. It opened fairly easily, and inside, there was a diary that was identical to her own—it was Scarlet's diary.

Had her sister hidden it here? Breathless with exhilaration and with tears pouring down her face she lifted it from the box, being careful to not damage it. And then the scent hit her again. Frankincense.

Scarlet. She was here. She hugged the diary to her chest, just as the last of the sun sank behind the mountains, leaving her in shadowy muted light. 'Thank you sis, thank you.'

As her tears flowed freely Renee rested the diary in her lap. She sat staring at it, a mixture of excitement, intrigue and nervousness tumbling in her belly. What was she going to discover within the pages? Would Scarlet's written words finally reveal who had taken her darling sister? Her heart thudded so heavily with the thought she could feel it in her eardrums.

The torch threw a bright light across the room, the deep shadows retreating to the corners. Running her fingertips over the front of the diary, Renee traced her sister's perfectly curled handwriting, the ache in her heart immense.

Scarlet Wildwood. Private.

She couldn't believe how well-preserved it still was, the jewellery box having protected it from the elements. For whatever reason, Scarlet had chosen to hide it down here. Renee was eager to find out why. Slowly, cautiously, she opened the front cover and began to read the very first entry, which was surrounded by pink love hearts. The pages were a little yellowed with age but the writing was still very legible...

January 1st

Happy New Year! I reckon this year is going to be the year all my dreams come true, I can just feel it in my bones!

I had so much fun at the ball last night. Everyone was there, including him. I can't believe I've had a crush on him for an entire year

now and not told a living soul. It's my very own little secret. He kept
looking across the room at me, smiling at me in a way that made my
heart melt. I wish I had the courage to go straight up to him and kiss
him, but I can't, for so many different reasons. Especially considering
I'm with Billy. And I do love Billy, in a way, and I know Billy loves me,
so I don't want to hurt him.

And besides, she was there with him the whole time, and no-one else
can get near him when she's around. She hangs off him like a leech. I
seriously don't know what he sees in her, she's so boring and annoying.
And anyway, what if I told him I liked him and he rejected me? I'd
never be able to look him in his beautiful eyes again. It would be so
embarrassing.

I dream about him all the time, and I wish I could feel his hands
on my skin. Who knows if anything will ever happen between us, only
time will tell. A girl can only dream. For now, I have to be happy with
what I have, and that's Billy Burton. And I have to admit, he's lovely
too…most of the time.

Scarlet xx

Renee's mind was in a spin. Scarlet had feelings for someone other
than Billy. But who was he? And why did she choose not to tell her
about it? They'd always shared everything—or at least, *she* had. She
turned the page, praying Scarlet would mention his name, or give
more of a clue to who he was.

*January 12*th

I saw him in the street today; he was dressed for work and looked so
sexy. I almost forgot my name when he stopped and talked to me. I felt
like a complete idiot.

Being so close to him, being able to smell his aftershave, it made me
want him even more. He brushed my hand when he said goodbye, and

I swear I could feel electricity in his touch. I can tell he likes me, but he can't do anything about it because she has him wrapped around her little finger. I feel like I'm standing at the edge of the world when I'm near him. But if we are at the edge, where do we go from there? What would people think of me, and him for that matter, if they found out how we felt? And I can't do anything anyway because I'm with Billy. Damn it!

Maybe, one day, he'll just forget about her and take a chance on me, and then I can gently tell Billy we're not meant to be together anymore. Who knows?

All I know for sure is that I crave him, with every fibre of my being. He has me, hook, line and sinker. How can I ever like anyone else when I only have eyes for him? I just wish he only had eyes for me.

Poor Billy, I shouldn't keep stringing him along. I know it's wrong of me. But the hard thing is, I really like Billy too, just not in the same way.

Scarlet xx

What tangled webs—Renee's curiosity was piqued. Who was this mystery man? And who was the woman that Scarlet was so jealous of? Basically, the entire township went to the ball for New Year's back then, so it could be anyone's guess as to who the man was that Scarlet was clearly infatuated with.

Billy Burton would have been furious if he'd found out. Had he? Renee turned the pages, keen to learn more.

A few weeks passed, with a journal entry here and there, but no more mention of the man. Scarlet had never been one to religiously write an entry every day, and with the diary being hidden away down here it would have made it very difficult for her to write regular entries. Reading on, Renee got to an entry in late January that hooked her in once again.

January 28th

Grrrrr! I'm so confused! I've been trying to ignore the fact I'm falling for this man, but I can't! Even deciding not to write about him anymore isn't working, my attraction to him only getting stronger and stronger every day.

He secretly flirts with me whenever he sees me and I'm helpless to resist. But what would people think of me if they knew I liked him, and he liked me? All hell would break loose!

Not that he's told me out loud that he likes me, but I know he does. I wish I could tell Renee about him, but I don't want to yet because I know it's so wrong of me to even think about being with him, especially when I'm with Billy, and he's with her. But I can't help it. It's like he's a drug and I'm addicted to him. I see him almost every day, and I know he looks at me when I walk past him, I can feel his eyes all over me, undressing me.

I just wish he'd get rid of her and go out with me, and in some ways I wish Billy would drop me, because it would be much easier than me being the one to break up with him. Damn it, love can really suck sometimes!

Scarlet xx

So she saw him almost every day? That could mean so many different people—the bus driver, the newsagent, someone working at the school, another student, or even one of the casual workers they had on the farm at the time. If it was one of the guys at school, was he in the same year as her and Scarlet or was he older? But hang on, she'd mentioned seeing him in the street when he was dressed for work. Maybe he was older. But then it was January—he could have been a school kid with a summer job.

Renee was just about to turn another page when she heard the thunder of a galloping horse's hooves and her name being called out. It didn't sound like Pa, but it had to be, who else would be out searching for her? It couldn't be Mick—it would be impossible for him to get on a horse with his broken leg. But then again, he was a determined old bugger.

She quickly wrapped the diary up in a spare t-shirt and shoved it into her pack, not wanting Pa to see it. He would only want to give it to the authorities and she didn't want that just yet. She wanted the chance to read the entire thing herself, and draw her own conclusions before handing it into the police as evidence— which she knew she had to eventually do. After all, she was the one and only person who knew Scarlet inside out.

Standing up, she followed the beam of her torchlight outside, to where a horse came to a sliding stop. The full moon shone like a beacon in the velvety black sky, lighting up the landscape and her rescuer's features in the most enchanting of ways. Her heart leapt into her throat as she swallowed down hard. He. Was. So. Damn. Sexy.

Dylan Anderson, her knight in shining armour, had come to her rescue. But unlike in the movies, he didn't look one bit happy about it.

She gave him a wave. 'Um, hi.' She tried to muster her biggest smile, at the same time feeling like an incompetent dickhead for getting herself stuck out here. So much for the country girl resurfacing.

'Hey there.' Dylan leapt from his horse and was beside her in seconds, his frown remaining. 'What are you doing all the way out here by yourself? Are you okay? What's happened?'

There was no pause between his questions.

Renee half giggled while waving her hands nonchalantly in the air. 'Oh, yup, I'm fine and dandy.' Why was she acting like a frigging lovesick teenager? 'I came out here for a bit of a ride about and the bloody bike battery has gone flat. Sooooo, I was stuck here until someone came to my rescue. No biggie, really.'

Dylan blew out a breath as he tipped his head to the side, still scowling. 'No biggie, hey? We were worried sick, Renee!'

Renee had to stifle a smile. Dylan was obviously very annoyed he'd had to come looking for her and she didn't want to piss him off even more, but it moved her that he'd been worried about her. At least it showed he cared a *little* bit, much as she knew he'd hate to admit it. She gave him a heavy-lashed gaze, as though she was a damsel in distress and he had saved her from a life-and-death situation. 'I'm sorry. I didn't mean to worry you. I thought I'd be back well before dark. It's so kind of you to come looking for me.'

'Hmm, well, at least you're okay, that's the main thing.' Dylan pointed to the bike, the pulse in his neck prominent, the muscles in his jaw clenched. 'We'll leave this here and I'll come and grab it tomorrow.' He nodded towards his horse. 'Jump up with me so I can get you home. Your pa is worried shitless. He's out looking for you now at the caves. I said I'd meet him back at the homestead after I searched here, and we'd take it from there if we hadn't found you.'

Renee felt awful. Pa had enough to worry about at the moment without her adding to it. 'Okay, I'll just grab my backpack from inside the shack and we can head off. Won't be a sec.'

Dylan folded his arms, his mood sullen. 'Righto, but hurry up would you. I need to get home sometime soon you know. I have better things to be doing than standing out here all bloody night.' He chuckled sarcastically. 'You should've known better than to come out here on your own, especially considering you're a city chick now.'

That was it—enough was enough.

Renee reeled to face him, her eyes thunderous and fists scrunched at her sides. 'I'm so very sorry to inconvenience you, *Dylan*, but this was an accident. It's not like I chose for it to happen…and don't you dare have a go at me because I've had to live in the city for the past nine years, because it's not like I chose to do that either—as much as you obviously want to believe I did.' She crossed her arms, matching his stance while she glared at him. 'And believe me when I say this, I would rather be at home than stuck out here with you and your damn arrogance.'

She stormed off into the shack without waiting for his reply, her emotions on edge after her eventful day. This had just topped it all off.

***

Dylan watched her disappear into the darkness of the shack, kicking himself for being such an arse to her. He had to try and let his resentment go. She was right. It wasn't her fault, and he had no right to have a go at her for it. He'd just been so terrified on his way out here that he'd find her hurt badly—or worse—and it had made the emotions he'd felt on the night Shelley had died resurface with a vengeance. But that wasn't Renee's fault either, and he shouldn't be taking it out on her. Huffing, he swung down off Turbo's back and followed her into the shack, only to find her in tears. His heart dropped to the floor. He was officially an arsehole.

Placing his hand on her shoulder, he turned her around, the dappled moonlight making her already exquisite features even more beautiful. He reached out and wiped her tears away, his voice softening along with his heart. 'Renee. I'm sorry. I was just worried you were badly hurt, that's all. I shouldn't be taking it out on you.'

Renee sniffled, nodding her head. 'I understand. I've just had a really emotional few days. No, actually, come to think of it, I've had an emotional *nine years* since Scarlet died.' She rubbed her eyes, sighing wearily as she looked down at the floor. 'I'm sorry I'm being a sook. I think I just need to have a hot shower and go to bed, and then start the day afresh tomorrow.'

Dylan's soul ached. Seeing the woman he'd treasured for most of his life so vulnerable was heart-wrenching. He wished there was some way things could be different, that the words they'd so harshly spoken to each other all those years ago could be taken back, so he could take her into his arms and love the pain right out of her, but there wasn't. They'd crossed that bridge many years ago, and there was too much water under it now.

'You're not being a sook, Renee. You've been through a lot. More than most people go through in an entire lifetime.'

'Thanks for understanding, Dylan. I really appreciate it.' Renee smiled softly through her tears as she looked around the shack. 'Can you believe the last time we were in here at night we…' She shook her head as she bit in her bottom lip. 'Oh shit, I'm sorry, I shouldn't be bringing something like that up when you're married.'

Dylan instinctively touched his wedding ring and began spinning it on his finger. 'Oh, um, I'm not really married, Renee. Well, I mean, I am married, but… My wife, she um…' He couldn't bring himself to say it out loud. He was afraid he'd crumble into a million tiny fragments if he did, and he didn't want Renee to see him like that—it wasn't a pretty sight. He turned away, not wanting her to see his pain. 'I'll explain it to you another day. We better get you home.'

Renee walked to stand in front of him, gazing at him, her mouth slightly open as if she was about to say something, realisation in her eyes. She reached out and rested her hand on his heart, saying nothing. Dylan felt a pull on his heart and soul, like they were trying to interlace with hers, the connection between them what most only dreamt of. The energy shifted as the rest of the world faded away, the magic of the moment so intense it was as if time had stood still.

Succumbing to her magnetism, Dylan leant in, his lips only millimetres away from hers. Renee followed suit and melted into him, her body pressing against his as she wrapped her arms around the back of his neck. He could feel her warm breath on his cheek, and smell her sweet, familiar perfume—it reminded him of the beautiful scent left lingering after summer rain—and then he felt himself being transported back to that enchanted night, back to when Renee and he had made love for the very first, and very last, time.

It was like it had happened only yesterday, the passion, the hunger and the sensuality, all of it so poignantly real. Neither of them moved, their lips almost touching, their breathing getting heavier. He could feel Renee running her hands through his hair and feel the beating of her heart against his chest. Finally, unable to stop himself, he broke the last remaining distance between them and rested his lips against hers, just as a man's panicked voice carried into the shack, calling for Renee.

The sounds of a galloping horse brought him crashing back to reality. And then he recalled the argument they had had, the words Renee had spat at him. She had left him hanging on those words for nine long agonising years… Suddenly, the mystical moment shattered like a piece of glass, the dangerous shards lethal enough to slice through his skin and puncture his heart.

What was he thinking? Hadn't she already done enough damage to his heart, without taking it from him again? She had left without saying sorry, without even a goodbye, without giving him a chance to apologise for what he'd said in the heat of the moment—and it had ruined everything.

He stepped back from her. 'I can't do this, Renee. We can't do this. Not now. Not ever. I'm sorry.' Turning away, he headed outside just as Stanley pulled to a stop on his horse.

He cleared his throat, his emotions still high. 'I found her, Stan. She's just inside grabbing her backpack.' Dylan pointed to the four-wheeler. 'Apparently the battery's gone flat so she couldn't get home. Lucky we found her, really, otherwise she could have been stuck out here all bloody night.'

Stanley's expression was full of relief. 'Oh thank Christ.'

Dylan put his boot in the stirrup and got himself settled back in the saddle with one fluent movement. 'I'll head off, Stanley, if that's okay. Mum and Annie will be waiting for me for dinner. You'll be right to get her home from here, won't you?'

'Yup, sure will be. Thanks for all your help, Dylan, appreciate it. I owe you one.'

'You don't owe me anything,' Dylan said, giving Turbo the cue to head home. 'Catch you in the morning,' he called out over his shoulder.

CHAPTER

13

*February 14*th

I can't believe it! I'm over the moon! Of all the days, he chose today to finally admit he likes me, on Valentine's Day. How romantic!

I knew it! I knew he had the hots for me. A girl can just tell these things. This morning he surprised me behind the little shed at the back of the school, where he was waiting with a single red rose in his hands. He gave it to me and then he kissed me...tongue and all. I could have just died right then and there. He must have secretly been watching me for a while, because how else would he know I cut through the Bestmans' paddock to get to school? It's a bit freaky to know he's been spying on me, but exhilarating all the same...and it's so exciting to know he's interested enough to have been checking me out all this time.

He reckons he's going to leave her for me, and he even told me he couldn't imagine his life without me in it. Oh my God! He made me promise to keep it a secret for now, just until he leaves her, and I swore to him I would. Nobody can find out about us yet, nobody! I can't risk losing him. I love him too much to lose him.

Ohh, I'm so happy right now but then I'm kind of scared at the same time. I mean, how am I going to tell Billy? Maybe I'll just wait until he leaves her, and I can be with him, before I break it off with him. I don't want to raise anyone's suspicions. Decisions. Decisions. It's so frustrating!! I just don't know what the right thing is to do.

I don't want to upset Billy. He's got the worst temper. And I know he's going to be really mad with me when I tell him I don't want to be with him anymore. And just wait until he finds out who I left him for, when everyone finds out who I left him for… All the shit is going to hit the fan then!

I'm so worried Renee and Nan and Pa are going to be furious with me, but hopefully they will eventually understand and forgive me. Argh! Anyways, I can't think about the mess I'm in right now. I just want to think about the good things so I'm going to go to sleep now and dream about my sexy new man all night long. I hope he's dreaming about me too… I betcha he is!

Scarlet xx

Renee closed her eyes, and rested her head back on her pillow, shaking with anger. Her throat was tight with emotion and her thoughts were spiralling like a whirlwind. She needed to find a good head space to be able to filter everything she'd just read. Counting to ten, she took a few deep breaths, the conscious action calming her a little.

Who the hell was this mystery bloke? And why would it be such a problem if she and Nan and Pop found out who he was? For a second Dylan's face flashed before her eyes, but it couldn't have been him Scarlet was referring to. Dylan would never do such a thing. He had loved her too much to hurt her like that, by cheating with her sister. And Scarlet wouldn't stoop that low either. Renee reprimanded herself for even considering it. She clearly wasn't thinking straight—just like the day she had said those things to Dylan about his father. She knew she had to find a way to apologise to him for it, but she was afraid of opening an old wound he may have already healed. Or was it her own self-inflicted wound she was afraid of reopening?

Changing her train of thought before she drove herself mad, Renee went back to analysing the diary. Was Scarlet's intuition right—had Billy snapped and lashed out at her after finding out about her mystery man? Renee had seen him get into fights at high school a few times, and on a couple of occasions she'd overheard arguments between Scarlet and Billy, so she knew he had a bad temper when triggered. But was he capable of murder? Perhaps. The police had believed his alibi of being home all night with his parents. But she wasn't so trusting of him.

But there were so many different scenarios and her mind was painfully playing over each and every one. The words she'd just read chugged around and around in her head, taunting her, infuriating her. Whoever this bastard was had quite possibly killed her sister, or most certainly had something to do with her disappearance. Or was it his girlfriend? Had he left her for Scarlet and evoked a fit of jealous rage from this woman that Scarlet kept mentioning?

Or maybe it was none of them. Maybe it was someone she hadn't even considered. She groaned. There were so many possibilities, but no definite answers. And poor Scarlet. Her sister truly believed this mystery man loved her, and that she loved him. The very thought made Renee sick to the core.

Not wanting to read on, but knowing she had to, Renee opened her eyes, wiped away her tears and drew in a deep calming breath. She could do this. She *had* to do this. Grabbing the diary from her bedside table, she flicked open to where she was up to. Skimming over the now sparse entries, Renee was careful to take in every single minute detail as she tried to read between the lines. Scarlet kept mentioning her mystery man, but frustratingly, not once did she mention his name—not even an initial.

March 21st

I don't have time to write much today because I'm meeting him real soon but last night blew my mind. The way he kissed me all over and told me he loved me, and the way he cuddled me afterwards… It was like all my dreams had finally come true. I can't wait to spend the rest of my life with him.

Scarlet xx

Afterwards? That meant Scarlet had had sex with him. How could she not have known? How could Scarlet not have told her? Whoever it was had taken advantage of her sister and it made her furious. Who in the hell was he?

Finally she came to the last diary entry, the devastating day Scarlet had gone missing. Renee flicked past to make sure there was nothing towards the back of the book before reading it. She needed a few moments to come to terms with the fact that this was the last time her sister had written down her deepest feelings. Scarlet's life had been stolen from her on this very day. With her trembling hands calming, Renee turned back to the love-heart embellished page and read slowly, dissecting every word, every letter, every full stop.

May 11th

I'm so excited!! I cannot wait until tonight because we're going to go to our secret place to spend a few hours together, and I can tell him what I've been dying to tell him for days now. But first, I have to meet up with Billy and tell him it's finally over.

I can't keep pretending. I've tried a few times to gently tell him I don't think we should be together anymore, but Billy just laughs it off and tells me that I can't get rid of him that easily. He really thinks we're gonna be together forever, and I don't push the subject too much because there's something in his laugh that worries me, like Billy believes he owns me, but maybe it's just my imagination playing tricks with me. I know he's going to be really pissed off when I break up with him, but he's just going to have to deal with the fact I'm in love with somebody else. Not that I'm going to tell him that—not yet anyway.

Oh, my skin is tingling with the thought of making love to my secret man again. I really want to tell Renee about him, but I can't, not yet. She's going to be very mad and very disappointed in me when she finds out who he is, but I know she loves me enough to forgive me and eventually get over it.

I told him I hate keeping things from her but he told me to wait until we make it official, and then we can tell everyone. He still hasn't broken it off yet either. He's promised he's going to do that tonight, before he meets me, and then we can be together forever. Ah, I like the sound of that. Together forever.

Nan and Pa aren't going to be very happy about it either, but I'm sixteen and a half now, and they've got to let me make my own decisions in life sometime.

Anyways, I better sign off for now. I have to go get ready for tonight. Yay!

Scarlet x

Tucking the diary safely beneath her mattress, and then switching off the bedside lamp, Renee pulled the blanket up and over her head, enjoying the sensation of feeling cocooned. If only she could emerge as a beautiful butterfly in the morning—free and light and worry-free—wouldn't that be something. But with the way she was feeling—wretched, weighed down and drained—she'd be more likely to emerge as a slug. And after getting an hour-long lecture from Pa about taking off on her own today, loaded on top of everything else, she was utterly exhausted.

Looking at her watch, which was glowing in the dark, Renee grumbled to herself. It was just past one am—where had the hours gone? She had to be up in a little over six hours to get Mick to his doctor's appointment in town. Rolling over on her side, she flicked the blanket off her head and tried to get comfortable by hugging a pillow, her back sore after the bumpy double back with Pa on his horse, Gus.

She needed to get some sleep, especially considering she had an endless list of things to grab from Woollies and the agricultural store while in town—and her pa had warned her that it would be busy in town seeing as Thursday was pension day. Nan was coming home on Sunday afternoon and she wanted to have some baked goodies ready for her, along with loads of healthy food, and she also needed to get the homestead back in tiptop shape. She was nowhere near as good a housekeeper as Nan. The washing had piled up in the laundry, there was an overflowing basket of ironing to do, the timber furniture could use a dose of Mr Sheen, and the floors needed a good going over with the vacuum and mop. And with only a few days left to achieve everything, she definitely needed to get her act into gear.

Letting her heavy eyelids drop shut, Renee thought about how lucky she had been to find the diary, and for it to be in such good nick. She truly believed Scarlet had somehow led her to it, the scent of her frankincense not something to be ignored. There was clearly something in the diary that Scarlet wanted her to read. Although she was still at a loss as to who had taken her sister from them, she was now sure that it was someone she and her grandparents knew. If only Scarlet had given a name...

Beyond exhausted and trying to derail her train of thought so she could get a few hours of precious sleep, Renee traced her fingertips over her still tingling lips, sighing miserably. She and Dylan had come so close to a full passionate kiss, so close to stepping over the line and to pulling down that brick wall he'd built. And the look in his eyes when he had taken her into his arms was like he was diving into her and caressing her from the inside out. No man had ever had the ability to make her feel so protected, so cared for, so loved. But in the blink of an eye, he had pulled away from her like she was a poisonous snake about to bite him, and the way he had walked away, like nothing had happened, as though what she had just felt from him wasn't real, crushed her.

What had he meant when he'd said he wasn't really married? Had his wife left him? Or had she died? From the dark shadow that had passed over his eyes when he had spoken of her, she guessed that it was the latter. If her intuition was right, her heart broke for him. No wonder he was reluctant to allow anyone into his life again— especially her after the way she'd already hurt him so deeply in the past. She had intended to ask Pa about Dylan's wife over dinner, but she hadn't been able to get a word in as her pa lectured her about the dangers of being stranded in the bush.

Squeezing her eyes shut, Renee started to count backwards from one hundred—a technique she'd found helpful in the past to get to sleep. Counting made her mind focus on something other than all the jibber jabber. At forty-eight, her body began to feel heavier, and by twenty-two she started to forget where she was up to. Teetering on the edge of dreamland, she let herself fall into the abyss, her unconscious mind taking over as she slipped into a much-needed deep sleep.

***

The cry of a curlew echoed throughout the otherwise silent night, the unnerving sound making Dylan shudder beneath his doona. The Aborigines believed it was the call of death, and he wasn't the only one that thought that way. Craig and the other town copper, Jake, both laughed about the occasional calls from worried locals who thought someone was being murdered in their back paddock.

After not being able to get one wink of sleep despite having lain in bed for hours, Dylan kicked his doona off in a huff. There was too much spinning around in his overactive mind. Thankfully he was going back to see the shrink after work tomorrow—and the fact that he was actually looking forward to speaking with Theresa Wise again was comforting in itself. He couldn't wait to share the good news that the nightmares had stopped, hopefully for good.

Dragging himself from the bed, he walked over to his dresser and reluctantly popped a sleeping tablet from the blister pack. Hesitating for a few moments, he threw it in his mouth and then gulped a mouthful of water from the cup beside his bed. Flopping back down onto his mattress with a thump, he groaned again. He hated relying on drugs to sleep—he hated taking Panadol at the best of times—but drastic times called for drastic measures. He needed sleep if he was going to perform to the best of his abilities at work, and he was determined to try and impress Stanley enough to maybe score a more permanent position. There was something about being at Wildwood Acres that he loved. Maybe it was the sweeping landscape, maybe it was being able to work alongside such an experienced cattleman as Stanley Wildwood, he wasn't sure, but whatever it was, he liked it. He refused to believe it was because of Renee Wildwood.

Rolling over, he stared at his alarm clock like it was the archenemy, watching as minute after minute ticked over. He wished he could unplug the bastard, but he needed the alarm to wake him up—that was, if he ever fell asleep. Was a decent night's rest too much to ask? It was just past one in the morning, and he'd been lying here for exactly five hours since hitting the sack soon after he'd tucked Annie into bed. Yet again, insomnia was playing mind games with him, and it was winning.

He slapped his hand against the pillow in defeat. For fuck's sake, he had to be at work in less than six hours. Rolling onto his back, and then his side, and then his stomach, and then back onto his back again, he groaned. His mum had suggested a few times that he should try counting sheep. Yeah right! As if that was going to do anything. Knowing his Gemini mind, he'd probably just start imagining shearing them, or eating a juicy lamb chop—and then he'd make himself hungry and need to get up and have a midnight feast. Bless her for trying to help, though. Anyway, it was impossible to picture anything else when Renee Wildwood's beautiful face was hogging every millimetre of his mind—hadn't he already lost enough sleep over her throughout the years? When was enough going to be enough?

Throwing a pillow over his head, Dylan let his mind do whatever it wanted to, and gave up trying to alter its course. In seconds, he was back in the shack, standing in front of Renee, her full kissable lips so close to his he could almost taste her sweetness. It had taken every bit of his resolve not to tear her clothes off right then and there so he could feel the silky softness of her skin beneath his fingertips. He ached with the thought of pushing her up against the wall and sliding down to his knees so he could lick her sweet nectar. He wanted to tease her with his tongue, caress every inch of her, and push her to the brink just long enough to make him beg to be inside of her.

And oh, how he ached to be inside her, to be at one with her, to feel the entire world fade away as he made love to her once again, like they had when she was seventeen and he was eighteen. It was mind-blowing back then, and he could only imagine what it would feel like now. With his imagination wandering off behind closed doors, Dylan felt the grasp of sleep take his hand and walk him into the void of slumber, the heavy sensation of his body finally sinking into the mattress absolute heaven. And in a matter of seconds, he was in dreamland, along with Renee, her naked body pressed up against his as she took him to places he'd never been before.

***

The shrill beep-beep of the alarm clock dragged Renee from her deeply satisfying dream and for a few blissful seconds she hovered on the luxurious threshold between reality and fantasy. Allowing the ethereal feeling to capture her entirely, she refused to open her eyes and tried to ignore the alarm. She didn't want to wake up, ever. In her dream, Dylan and she were together, Scarlet and her parents were still alive, all of their lives perfectly entwined, and all of them without a care in the world. If only it could be true, if only her life could be so picture-perfect, but it was never that easy. Her parents and Scarlet were never coming back, there was no such thing as a life without worries, and Dylan Anderson clearly had deep-set issues with her—they were never getting back together.

Succumbing to the fact she was going to have to face the day, she reluctantly let the dream fade away. Bleary eyed, she rolled over and smacked her hand down on top of the offending clock, killing the sound instantly. Part of her wanted to throw the darn thing across the room. Groaning wearily, she dragged herself to sitting, her eyes still half shut, every inch of her dying to flop back down amongst her tussled sheets and go back to sleep. Her mind whirred like an engine with a failing battery, with her body chugging slowly behind it. Coffee, she needed coffee, and the stronger the better.

She rubbed her eyelids and willed herself to wake up. She'd only given herself half an hour to have a shower, get dressed and be at Mick's front door to take him to his check-up appointment at the Opals Ridge hospital, so she had to move her arse. Grabbing her towel from the floor where she'd dropped it last night, Renee threw it over her shoulder and then headed off down the hallway towards the bathroom.

She was looking forward to seeing her nan at the hospital today, seeing as she hadn't made her daily trip in to visit her yesterday. It would be the first time she had visited without her pa—her first drive into town without him as her chaperone. She was looking forward to the taste of freedom, the independence that she so greatly missed. The initial nerves were long gone. She was dying to venture into town on her own and act her twenty-six years.

CHAPTER
14

Feeling a little more human now that she was showered and had coffee and two golden syrup-soaked crumpets in her belly, Renee pulled into the last remaining car park of the small country hospital, thankful for the automatic parking assist in Nan's shiny black Holden Caprice. She was shocking at reverse parallel parking, quite often finding herself up the gutter and on the sidewalk or red-faced because she'd banged into something like a wheelie bin or lamp post.

Tia always refused to go anywhere in reverse with her, it being a long-standing joke between the two of them that Renee was only a good driver when going forward. Tia often got her kicks trying to get Renee to walk backwards after a few drinks, Renee just as clumsy on her feet in that situation as she was driving a car sober. On a few occasions she and Tia had found themselves upended, the pair of them in utter hysterics as they'd tried to get back on their feet, or high heels for that matter—a feat in itself after a few drinks.

The recollection made her giggle as she switched the car off and tugged the keys from the ignition, making another mental note to ring her friend tonight, not having had the chance last night after her eventful day out on the station. She missed her best mate, and had so much to tell her. If only they could catch up in person.

Mick sat in the back seat of Nan's going-to-town car, his broken leg resting up on the centre console, the cast covered in squiggles and signatures thanks to his good mates who popped in for a cold bevvy of an afternoon—an act that was helping him keep half sane with being confined to the house. Grabbing her handbag from where it had slipped down the side of the passenger seat when she had barely avoided hitting a frill-necked lizard on the way over, Renee jumped out and tried to help Mick from the back seat. But he refused to let her help him.

She respected his need to be self-sufficient and stood back, even though she had to bite her tongue as she watched him grapple with his crutches. It was painful to observe as he edged and slid himself in all types of crazy angles out of the car, looking and sounding as though he was re-birthing himself, it taking five *long* minutes of grunting and groaning before she was finally able to push the central locking button on the key.

Free of the confines of the car and basically upright, Mick tried to catch his breath as he shoved his crutches under his arms. 'I wish I was never stupid enough to become a smoker. Doesn't take much for me to lose me breath these days.' He gave her a lopsided grin. 'I reckon me and you should have some lunch at the pub today before we head back home, make the trek into town worth it. What do you reckon Reni?' If his eyebrows went any higher, they were going to disappear over the back of his bald head.

Renee gave him the thumbs up. 'Sounds like a plan—count me in.'

Mick's face lit up like a beacon as they headed in the direction of the front sliding doors. 'Great stuff. I'm hanging out for a cold one, or three, and a generous helping of Lorraine's famous reef and beef with her creamy garlic butter sauce.'

'Reef and beef smothered in garlic sauce… Oh my God, yum!' Renee's mouth watered with the thought of it. 'I normally wouldn't have a big lunch, but you've twisted my arm, methinks.'

'I promise you won't regret it. I get it every time I go into the joint, I can't resist.'

Stepping into the air-conditioned admissions area, Mick motioned towards a hallway that seemed to stretch on into the never-never. 'I got to head on down there for me appointment, and God knows how long I'll be waiting before I get to see the bloody doc. Hows about I just meet you up in your nan's room once I'm done, okay?'

Assessing how far Mick had to walk, and knowing how clumsy he could be at the best of times, Renee ummed and ahhed as she pointed towards the hallway. 'You sure you don't want me to—'

Mick cut her off. 'Positive. Quite capable of taking care of meself.'

'Okey-dokey then, that's sorted. Meet you up in Nan's room once you're done.'

Pressing the call button Renee waited for the lift as she watched Mick manoeuvre his way down the hallway, the determined bugger almost hitting the deck when his left crutch got stuck under a thankfully unoccupied gurney. With the gurney dragged halfway across the hall, a few swear words thrown in for good measure, and the crutch successfully retrieved from the floor after several attempts to bend over and grab it, Mick turned and gave her a feeble wave with a childish smile plastered across his face, letting her know he was okay. She shook her head, laughing along with him, just as the lift dinged its arrival.

Stepping in, she made sure to stick to elevator etiquette by staring at anything other than the few people that had stepped in beside her, the corny elevator music making her wonder why in the hell someone in the hierarchy didn't make an executive decision to ban all clichéd elevator music around the world. It did nothing to alleviate the uncomfortableness. If anything, it added to it. With everyone having selected their floors to get off on, and hers the top one, Renee closed her eyes and rested her head back against the wall, her mind starting to wander off on a weird tangent as she thought about all the times she'd had to sit and listen to similar mind-numbing music while waiting on hold on the phone. A tap on her shoulder brought her back to the present.

'Renee Wildwood. Holy snapping duckshit, is that you?'

The woman's voice was familiar, the slightly nasally tone unmistakable, and the use of colourful language in such an inappropriate place, well, it all added up to only one possible person. Spinning around, Renee was met with the distinctive toothy ear-to-ear grin of her childhood best mate, the face surrounding it a little older than she remembered, but recognisable all the same. 'Oh my God, Hayley Gregory? Of all people to run into in a lift! Hi!'

'Yup, that's me.' She swished her shiny black bob around her face, playfully pouting. 'A little older, I must say, but still just as classy,' she squealed, winking.

The two women threw their arms around one another, jiggling on the spot as Renee counted her blessings for not getting the same cold welcome home from Hayley as she had from Dylan. This was most definitely on the other end of the 'welcome-home' Richter scale. Joy filled her. It was nice to feel treasured by someone who'd played a major part in her life growing up. She pulled back, aware all eyes were on them in the lift, but she was so excited she didn't care. 'It's so great to see you, Hails!' She motioned up and down her friend's tall, yet perfectly curvaceous, figure. 'And I must say, you're still looking as good as ever.'

'Why thankya, matey.' Hayley cheerily slapped her on the arm. 'You're looking pretty sassy too, Reni. Loving the long black hair… noice.'

'Yep, long gone is the frizzy, bleached blonde hair,' Renee said, grinning.

'Good choice.' Hayley crossed her arms, her smile fading as her perfectly shaped eyebrows met in the middle. 'So tell me, where in the bloody hell have you been hiding all these years? Why didn't you tell me you were leaving? And why haven't you told me you were back?' Her eyebrows went in the opposite direction as she waited for Renee's reply.

And there it was, the interrogation. The lift seemed to shrink around Renee and she suddenly cared that the four other people left in there were watching them like hawks. Small towns were renowned for gossip spreading like wildfire, and she really didn't want to be the hot topic of conversation. It felt as though everyone was holding his or her breath for her answer. 'Oh, ah, umm.' With a ding the elevator announced its arrival to the top floor, saving her from having to explain everything in a darn lift as people bustled to get out.

Hayley strode out with her and placed her hand on her shoulder, the pair of them moving aside to let people past, Hayley thankfully waiting until they had a bit of privacy to begin talking again. 'I'm so sorry, Reni. Too many questions all at once, and not in the most private of places, but as you well know, I'm not backwards in coming forward.' She graced her with a caring smile. 'How about you save it until you come over to my pad for a cuppa?'

Renee smiled. 'I'd love that, Hails. When are you free for me to call over?'

'Coolio, we can do catch up later this arvy, after I do my wifey duties?' She held out the unmistakable McDonald's paper bag. 'I have to get this to the hubby before he chews his own arm off. He reckons this hospital food is going to make him fade away to a shadow.' Hayley rolled her eyes and laughed. 'No chance of that given his abs are well hidden under his love handles.'

Renee giggled, shaking her head. 'You still got the gift of the gab, Hails. What's he in for?'

Hayley leant in close to Renee's ear. 'A vasectomy.'

Renee's hands instinctively went to her crotch, a pained expression on her face. 'Ooh, ouch!'

Hayley nodded. 'Aha, apparently it feels as though his balls are about to explode, they're so swollen. Poor bloke. I offered to get my tubes tied but he told me that I had endured the pain of childbirth, twice, and now it was his turn to cop some of the pain.' Hayley smirked. 'I think he's kinda regretting his decision a bit now, but give him a few weeks and he'll be back to normal. Bless the bugger for doing it, he's always trying to do things to take the pressure off me. That's why I love him so much.'

'Wow, it sounds like you two are a match made in heaven. Who is the lucky bloke? Do I know him from school or anything?'

'Oh, nah, he moved here from the big smoke a few years after you'd left. His name's Greg. He grew up in Sydney but he's a countryman at heart. You'll have to meet him. I reckon you two will get on like a house on fire.' Hayley glanced at her watch. 'I hate to love you and leave you, but I gotta get a shift on, I have an appointment at the beautician's for a jay jay wax in an hour and then I've got a bit to do before I grab the anklebiters from day care.'

'A jay jay wax?'

'Yeah, you know, a Brazilian.' She dropped her voice as she pointed to her nether region. 'It's getting a bit like an Amazon jungle down there.'

Renee chuckled. 'Oh, now I'm with you. I just haven't heard it called a jay jay before.'

Hayley laughed, shaking her head. 'You gotta get with the times, girlfriend. So how's that cuppa sound for you this arvy? You can come and meet my rug rats.'

Hayley's lack of airs and graces made Renee giggle. Her childhood mate had never been one to stop and think about what came out of her mouth—and she clearly hadn't changed a bit. She'd got them both in trouble a number of times at school for chronic foot in mouth.

She was about to agree when an image of the messy state of the homestead flooded Renee's mind, and she sighed. 'I'd love to, Hails, but I have heaps to do before Nan comes back home on Sunday.'

'Oh yeah, Dad told me your nan was in hospital—a heart attack right? Old Shirley down at the post office reckons she's going to be okay though?'

'Sure was a heart attack, a pretty damn big one too. But she's on the mend, thankfully. The doc reckons she'll be right after a bit of bed rest.'

'Good luck keeping your nan in bed for any length of time. She's always been a feisty bugger.'

Renee rolled her eyes. 'Yeah, tell me about it, I'm going to have my work cut out for me, I'm guessing.'

'So when are we going to catch up then, if you can't come this arvo? I've got pretty full days tomorrow and Friday.' Hayley sucked in a breath, and then clapped her hands, not waiting for Renee's reply. 'I know, have you heard about the Studs and Fuds ball this weekend?'

'Yeah, Mick told me about it yesterday. Sounds fun. You going?'

'Bloody oath, I wouldn't be caught at home that night for quids! If last year's ball is anything to go by, it's going to be an absolute scream. I've already got the babysitter organised. Greg can't come this year because his knackers will be too sore. And guess who the band is going to be?'

Renee's eyes widened. 'Who?'

'The Overflow.'

'Oh my God, really? I love them!' If Renee's eyes got any wider her eyeballs were going to roll clean out of their sockets. She was finding it hard to believe a band as big as The Overflow would be coming to play up here in Far North Queensland.

Hayley grinned as she jiggled on the spot. 'I know, aren't they the best! And I love their song "I Want You". I'll be requesting it all bloody night.'

'Me too, I know every single word of it!' Renee's belly bubbled with anticipation, Hayley's excitement contagious. It was a relief to know she had a girlfriend to hang out with at the ball, and with Hayley, a good time was guaranteed. She'd been a bit worried she'd find herself feeling like a Nigel-no-friends while standing in some dark corner, but now she knew she'd be right. 'Excellent, we'll catch up there then—for something a little stronger than a coffee. Is Louise going along too? It'll be good to say hi to her.'

Hayley's older sister, Louise, was the polar opposite of Hayley—a little sheepish and very conservative. Being almost eight years older, Renee hadn't had a lot to do with Louise, other than the occasional times Louise had babysat them as kids, although she remembered her as a very kind and thoughtful soul.

Hayley shook her head. 'No, she left town about two years ago, after she split up with her husband. It was all very messy.'

'Oh shit, really? That sucks. Who was she married to?'

'She ended up with her high school sweetheart, Craig Campbell. You know, the town copper.'

'Oh that's right, I remember now. She was dating him before I left. He tried so hard to find out what had happened to Scarlet, bless him, but he was fairly new to the job at the time and didn't have much pull with the city detectives. He seemed like a really nice bloke.'

'Yeah, he is. Even so, Louise left him for another man, one she met on a holiday in Brisbane. I feel like the piggy in the middle at the moment because I'm good friends with Craig and of course I love my sister and want to support her too. They're still going through court for property settlement and to decide who's going to get full-time care of their son, Tom.'

'I'm sorry to hear that, Hails. It must be hard for you.'

'Yeah, it is, but such is life.' Hayley clapped her hands together. 'But enough of the sad stuff, let's focus on the fun stuff. It's going to be great to hang out again, it'll be just like the good old days.' Throwing her arms out, Hayley gave Renee a quick squeeze and a kiss on the cheek. 'Must run, see you Saturday night.' She pointed at Renee as she scuttled away. 'And no piking it. Make sure you come, or I'll come over to your place and drag you there myself.'

'Don't worry, I'll be there with bells on!' Renee called out after her.

Wandering into the private hospital room, Renee smiled when she saw Nan sitting up and doing a crossword puzzle, something she'd done for as long as Renee could remember—Pearl always saying it kept the brain perky. Beside her, a doctor was busily writing things down on a chart as he checked the monitors. He acknowledged Renee with a nod of his head and a small smile and Renee returned the gesture.

'Hey, Nan, you're looking pretty spritely today.' She flopped down on the end of the bed, placing her hand on the bump of the blanket where her nan's legs would be.

Pearl's face lit up at the sight of her granddaughter. 'Hi, love. I must say I'm feeling the best I've felt in days.' She reached out and patted Renee's hand. 'How are things at home? Is Pa behaving himself?'

'Pa always behaves himself. Unlike yourself.' Renee smiled cheekily.

'Now now,' Pearl said with a smile. 'I always behave myself.'

The doctor cut in on the conversation. 'And you will continue to behave yourself when you get home, Mrs Wildwood.' He turned to Renee. 'I can't stress enough how important it is that your nan takes it easy.'

'Don't you worry, Doc. I'll be making sure she rests up. If I have anything to do with it, she won't be lifting a finger.'

'Yeah, good luck with that,' said a voice from the doorway.

Renee and Pearl turned to watch Mick hobble through on his crutches. Both women smiled warmly in his direction.

'Gee whizz, that was quick,' Renee said.

Mick eased himself down on the chair beside the bed. 'Tell me about it. I'm usually there for ages.' He leant over and gave Pearl a peck on the cheek. 'How are you going, beautiful lady?'

'Pretty damn good, if I do say so myself,' Pearl replied with vigour, her eyes once again shining with her usual twinkle.

Renee was happy to see her sparkle back.

Mick looked to the doctor. 'Is she really as good as she says, Doc? Or is she just trying to fool us all so she can come home sooner.'

'This doctor's too clever for that. I've tried to pull the wool over his eyes a few times but the bugger has caught me out every time.' Pearl's eyes crinkled at the corners as she smiled.

The doctor chuckled. 'Yes, she's as good as she's saying, but that doesn't mean she can go home and start galloping around on horses again.'

'You're a party pooper, Doc,' Pearl said as she rolled her bottom lip.

Mick looked to his cast, and then to Pearl, smiling. 'Looks like both of us are banned from that for a while.'

Pearl chuckled.

Renee laughed along with her. 'God, what am I going to do with you pair?'

The doctor shoved his pen in his pocket and then hung the chart back at the end of the bed. 'Righto, I'm off to see the next patient. I'll be back in later today to check in on you, Pearl, okay?'

Pearl nodded. 'Okay, it's a date.'

With the doctor gone, the three of them sat and chatted about life at Wildwood Acres, the conversation making Renee feel all warm and fuzzy inside. She'd missed times like these—the simple times where you got to share cherished moments with loved ones.

Fleetwood Mac's song 'Little Lies' played as background music on the jukebox, the pub now filled to the brim with hungry lunchers. Thank goodness they'd come early. Shoving the last of the juicy tender rump steak into her mouth, Renee put her cutlery down and rested back against her chair, groaning pleasurably as she chewed her last forkful of the delicious counter meal. A few beer battered chips were still left on her plate, now scrumptiously soaked in the mouth-watering garlic sauce, and although she wished she could devour them, she couldn't fit another bite. She was so full her belly was aching, the button and zipper on her jeans now open after having to release the pressure halfway through her whopping-sized meal.

She'd forgotten how wholesome a good old-fashioned pub meal was after becoming accustomed to chic cafe food. She liked both, quinoa salad and smoked salmon one of her favs, but she had to admit she couldn't beat the warm and fuzzy feeling she got while eating a piece of fresh local meat cooked to her type of perfection—still mooing—along with a crisp garden salad and some crunchy chips.

Mick pointed at her with his fork, grinning. 'I told you it was to die for, didn't I?'

Renee nodded slightly, unable to move any other part of her body right now for fear of exploding. 'You bloody well did, and you weren't wrong. The reef and beef will defo be my pick whenever I come in here for a feed, that's for sure. Do Nan and Pa ever come in here for dinner?'

Mick shook his head. 'Your pa hasn't stepped foot in here since you left. To be honest, he's become a bit of a hermit over the years, only venturing out to collect supplies for the farm, or go to the doc's, or to do the banking and stuff. And your nan, well, she supports him by not going out much either, although she still goes to the quiz nights at the bowling club once a week and her scrapbooking group once a month. Sad really, they used to be so social before...' Mick met Renee's woeful eyes, swallowing hard. 'Well, 'nuff said really.'

Renee looked down at the floor, her heart sinking. 'Poor Nan and Pa.'

Heavy silence sat between them for a few moments—the noisy chatter around the lively pub a welcome distraction. Renee blinked back tears as she people-watched, at the same time wishing there was some way she could take her grandparents' heartache away and give them their lives back. She believed there was only one way she'd be able to possibly do that, but where to start, or how to do it, she honestly still had no idea.

She'd flicked through the old high school yearbook she'd found in her glory box over breakfast, but nothing or no-one had jumped out at her. Maybe Scarlet's mystery man wasn't a student, and hadn't even gone anywhere near the high school on a daily basis. There were so many possibilities, and it was driving her nuts. She just prayed the answers would come to her somehow, and held tightly onto the faith they would. It was a long shot, trying to dig up clues on a person who had been missing for nine long years, but she would never give up trying. She owed it to Scarlet to deliver justice.

Her gaze travelling down to the far end of the long timber bar, she spotted Freaky Frank—other than the few creases around his face he didn't appear to have aged a bit. She half laughed, half cringed to herself as she imagined him doing taxidermy on himself. Turning, he caught her looking at him and smiled, his crooked grin making him look extra creepy. She smiled nervously and then quickly looked away. No way in the world did she want to talk to him. A shiver ran up her spine and she shuddered. He still gave her the heebie-jeebies. Scarlet had been fascinated by his taxidermy, sometimes stopping off at his place after school to check out his collection of petrified reptiles, birds and fish, but Renee had never understood the appeal. She and Scarlet may have been identical twins, but they were certainly opposites when it came to some of their personality traits, and friends.

Mick took a swig from his icy cold beer. 'Your nan looked good today. It was a relief to finally see her sitting up and luring the doctor into some playful banter.'

Renee smiled. 'Yeah, apart from the fact she's lost an awful amount of weight, she's almost back to her normal chirpy self. She's even got some colour back in her cheeks. I don't know how we're going to keep her in bed for the next few weeks. "Just light activities" the doc said. Lord help me.'

Mick chuckled as he placed his knife and fork on his licked-clean plate. 'Yeah, good luck with that. Pearl isn't one to sit about. I'm sure that woman has had ants in the pants since the day she was born.'

'You can say that again, God love her,' Renee said, laughing. 'Speaking of visiting Nan at the hospital today, I ran into Hayley Gregory while I was there. We're going to catch up at the Studs and Fuds ball this weekend.'

'Bloody hell, I haven't seen Hayley since last year's ball. She's a nice girl.' Mick waved to someone he knew at the bar, then turned his attention back to Renee. 'You two will have fun together, that's for sure. I remember you both getting up to loads of mischief as kids.'

Renee laughed. 'Yeah, we sure did. What's Hayley's hubby like?'

Mick smiled broadly. 'Oh, Greg, he's a top bloke. I can't say a bad word about him. Hayley's definitely scored with him.'

'That's good. And I reckon he's scored with Hayley, too. She still looks as gorgeous as ever.'

'Yup, Hayley's certainly a looker. Those two make a great couple. They're always the life of the party. You'll have a ball with her on Saturday night.' Mick eyed her curiously. 'You mentioned to your pa you're going yet?'

'Um, not yet, but I will. After what happened yesterday I thought it'd be better to wait until he's in a calmer mood. I'm not in his good books right now.'

Mick pointed his almost empty schooner glass towards her. 'Good thinking ninety-nine.'

'Why thankya, Maxwell,' Renee replied cheekily. She glanced over at the clock on the wall above the bar. 'We better hit the road. Pa will be wondering where we got to and I've got stacks to do at the homestead before Nan comes home.'

'Ready to go when you are,' Mick said. 'I'll just go and give me regards to the chef.' He sculled the last of his beer, leaving a frothy moustache above his lips. Licking it off, he propped his crutches under his arms, and then headed over to the bar to say his goodbyes to Rex and Lorraine.

Renee stood, groaning as she did her zipper and button back up. 'Righto then, time for me to strap on the apron and get some housework done,' she mumbled to herself. Turning to head towards the front door of the dining room, she bumped into the last person she wanted to see: Billy Burton—Scarlet's boyfriend.

'Renee Wildwood, well I'll be damned. Other than the hair, you haven't changed a bit.' The brawny bloke eyed her up and down, and her belly flipped uncomfortably. 'Actually, I take that back, you've changed quite a lot…in a good way. You're looking very, how do I put it—' he stared at her breasts, '—womanly.'

Feeling exposed, even though she had a very conservative shirt on, Renee wrapped her arms around herself. Other than becoming older and rounder, his freckled face was exactly as she remembered it, and his roving eyes were as discourteous as ever. 'Billy, how are you?' She half smiled.

'I'm pretty good, thanks.' He crossed his arms across his broad chest, his stance wide. 'So when did you sneak back into town?'

'A few days ago.'

Mick joined her at her side, making her feel less intimidated. The men exchanged nods.

'G'day Billy.'

'G'day Mick.'

Renee stepped around Billy, half tripping over her feet in her haste to get out the door. 'Anyways, gotta run, heaps of things to do. Catch ya round sometime, Billy.'

'Yeah, okay, catch ya round, Renee,' Billy replied, waving her off as he shrugged at Mick, smirking. 'What's up with her? Anyone would think I stank.'

'Not sure. Catch ya, Billy.'

Stepping into the sunshine, Renee tried to calm her racing heartbeat as Mick placed his hand on her shoulder.

'What was that all about, Reni? You couldn't get away from the poor bloke fast enough.'

'I don't know about him Mick, I never have. Something just puts me on edge around him. And he's such a bloody perve—I can't stand it. No matter what the cops say, I still reckon he might have had something to do with Scarlet's disappearance.'

Mick eyed her apprehensively, his gaze softening. 'Oh, come on now, Reni. Just because the bloke was going out with Scarlet at the time, it doesn't mean he had anything to do with her disappearance. I can understand your suspicions, but he was questioned endlessly by the coppers and had a pretty tight alibi, so I reckon that takes him off the suspect list. Don't you?'

Renee gritted her teeth, not wanting to get mad at Mick. He didn't know what she had read in the diary and she had to remember he was only trying to help. 'Just because his mum and dad say he was home all night, doesn't mean he was. Most parents would protect their children no matter what. And I reckon if I looked hard enough, I might be able to find some sort of clue that will put him at the scene of the crime, wherever that is.' Renee put her hands on her hips, unexpectedly feeling very defensive of her opinion as Mick eyed her with exasperation. 'You got to be able to understand, Mick, I need to find Scarlet's body so we can finally lay her to rest. Surely you get that.'

Mick rubbed his face, sighing gently. 'I can completely understand your desire to do that, but one word of advice, Reni—and please don't take this the wrong way: Unless you have any hard evidence, please be careful of who you blame. A lot of people's lives were turned upside down during the investigation—and you were so desperate you yourself were pointing the finger at all sorts of innocent people. That was understandable at the time, but not so understandable now. It's taken many years for people to get past all the accusations and hearsay. You don't want to go opening up past wounds that might not have ever fully healed, if you get my drift. You might go treading on the wrong toes.'

Renee stared at him blankly, her mouth agape as she shook her head in disbelief. Did he know what she had said to Dylan all those years ago? There was no possible way. Surely Dylan wouldn't have repeated it. She shook the thought away. No, Mick just didn't understand, for her to try and heal the gaping wound in her heart, and in her grandparents' hearts, she had to try and find Scarlet's body and finally lay her to rest, no matter whose toes she trod on in the process. She'd honestly expected more understanding from him than this.

'Look, I'm sorry if I'm coming across as cold, but to put it bluntly, I don't want you putting your life in any danger, and pissing the wrong people off, because it might land you in pretty hot water. Your nan and pa couldn't handle it if something, anything, happened to you... And neither could I for that matter. We've all lost enough loved ones along the way. I think, as hard as it is, you should just leave it be, Reni. You getting my drift now?'

Renee folded her hands together as she stared down at the bitumen beneath her boots. 'Yeah, I get it. You want me to forget Scarlet ever existed.' Her tone was filled with sarcasm. 'Well it's not that fucking easy, Mick.'

Mick took her hands and unfolded them, placing them in his. He gave them a gentle squeeze as he met her tear-filled eyes. 'No, Reni,

I'm not saying that, and you know it, so stop being so difficult. I'm just begging you to let sleeping dogs lie. You're not experienced in criminology so you can't go starting your own murder investigation. And to be honest, the bastard that killed your sister is probably long gone. I don't believe for a second that any of the long-term locals had anything to do with her disappearance. And you've got to give Billy brownie points for trying to say hello—after you making it loud and clear you thought he was involved all those years ago.'

'I s'pose I do, even though I don't want to.' Tears fell from Renee's cheeks. Slumping forward, she wrapped her arms around Mick's shoulders. 'It just hurts so much to know that a killer is walking free, living their life, while Scarlet's life was stolen from her.'

Mick squeezed her back, wobbling a little on his crutches. 'I know, but for your own sake, and the sake of your grandparents, I reckon it's best if you leave it to the coppers to find out who it was. I truly believe that one day they will eventually catch the bastard.'

'Yeah, okay,' Renee mumbled into his shoulder, knowing full well it wasn't okay, and that she wasn't giving up, not until she unravelled the truth. She was positive Scarlet's spirit was still walking this earth for a reason, and as the saying went, only the truth was going to set them all free.

***

Dylan felt his mind begin to slowly refocus, his consciousness beginning to take over as Theresa counted him back to reality. His body still felt a little heavy in the reclined leather chair, the soft and calming office lighting aiding his relaxed state. He'd spent the last twenty-five minutes listening to Theresa with his eyes closed, his body relaxing more and more as she'd guided him with her calm and confident voice. Never one to believe in hypnotism before, he'd been amazed how quickly his mind had let go and turned inward while a mildly curious floating sensation had taken over his body. It had been an interesting, yet wonderful, experience. He drew in a deep breath, trying to will himself to full awareness.

'Take your time, Dylan. Just come back up to sitting when you're ready.'

Blinking his heavy eyes, Dylan slowly brought the recliner back to upright, his body and mind feeling somewhat cleansed, sort of like he'd been covered in mud and Theresa had just hosed it all off.

The psychologist smiled warmly at him. 'How do you feel, Dylan?'

He smiled. 'Really good—I honestly didn't think I'd like it so much.'

'Good, that's what I like to hear. How did you feel while you were going through the motions of it?'

'It was weird. It was like I wasn't really sitting in the chair anymore, like I was floating in the air instead. And your voice gradually became more and more distant, to the point where I sort of forgot you were there.'

'Uh-huh, and that's how it should feel. You were very easy to guide through the meditation—I really think you are going to benefit from the work we've done today.'

'That's good to know, because I could definitely use the help. I was worried you wouldn't even be able to hypnotise me. I kept imagining it would be like all the stuff you see on telly—you know, where they tap someone on the head and they pass out or start acting like a chicken because they've been told to—but it wasn't anything like that.'

Theresa chuckled. 'They make it all so theatrical on the television. No, it's more about you relaxing, your awareness of where you are, why you are here, and who is speaking to you, receding into the back of your mind until you're just content with effortlessly allowing my voice to act on you—which is when I really get the chance to reformat your mind, in a way, so you can think differently about certain situations and release the guilt and confusion you're experiencing about Renee and Shelley.'

'Amazing stuff.' Dylan smiled. 'And all without much effort from me—can't complain about that.'

'That's it, Dylan. Too many people think they have to fight their thoughts, and control everything going on around them before they are happy or at peace, when really, it's all about how you think and feel in situations. A simple change of the way we view things can make all the difference and put you back on the right track.'

'Sounds like good advice to me. Now I just have to put it to practice.'

'I don't think you'll have any problems at all doing that. You're progressing really well with each session. And not having nightmares anymore, that's a huge thing. You should be very proud of yourself.'

'Oh, thanks, that means a lot.' Dylan glanced over Theresa's shoulder at the clock on the wall. 'We've gone ten minutes over today. Sorry about that.'

Theresa waved her hand in the air. 'Not to worry, you needed it. I didn't want to stop the hypnosis when you were getting so much out of it.'

Theresa stood and so did Dylan as she opened her office door. 'See you next week?'

'Yup, with bells on,' Dylan said as he stepped through the door and headed towards the front desk, his eyes widening a little when he spotted Freaky Frank sitting in the waiting area. He quickly recomposed himself before Frank noticed his surprise.

'Hey, Dylan,' Frank said, avoiding Dylan's eyes.

'Hey, Frank,' Dylan replied, feeling equally uncomfortable. This wasn't really the place for small talk—not that he and Frank shared that at the best of times.

Theresa popped her head out. 'Hello Frank, come on through.'

Dylan breathed a sigh of relief, not wanting to seem rude but not knowing what else to say. He wondered what struggles had brought him to Theresa—maybe the recent death of his father? Whatever it was, it took a lot of guts to make the decision to come here, and good on Frank for taking that step.

CHAPTER

15

Pulling out of the rusty iron gates of Wildwood Acres, Renee skidded to avoid a massive roo as it bounded in front of her, the Land Cruiser coming to a halt as she missed it by mere inches.

'Crazy bastards, anyone would think they had a death wish,' Mick muttered as he tried to get comfortable, without much success, his cast-enclosed leg at a very unnatural angle while he sat sideways on the seat, the seatbelt twisted around him in a way that made him look half strangled. As Mick muttered and groaned beside her, Renee pointed the vehicle towards the other side of town, struggling not to put the pedal to the metal, not that the old girl had much horse power these days. She had been looking forward to the Fuds and Studs ball all week and couldn't wait to get there.

She hoped the outfit she'd bought at the local western shop was suitable—a short denim skirt, figure-hugging diamanté-studded red top and Ariat Terrace Acres cowgirl boots. Although comfortable, it wasn't the attire she was accustomed to now, Melbourne not really suitable for such clothing. But her love of western wear had never subsided in all the years she was away, and she had to silently admit she felt very sexy in it. She hoped Dylan would feel a twang of regret when he saw her all dressed up.

Outside the four-wheel drive, the hypnotic calls of frogmouths merged with the chirruping of crickets, the nocturnal calls drawing her into the deep stillness of the night. Up above, the ever-changing evening sky was faultless—trillions of stars twinkling brightly amongst equally glowing dust clouds, the Milky Way clear as day against the velvet-black backdrop of night. Renee felt a strong sense of belonging as she admired the dazzling show, the country sky so much brighter than what she'd become accustomed to in the city. She was going to miss this when she went back to her life in Melbourne, immensely.

Winding her window down further, her skin prickled with goosebumps, and the scent of the country—pure clean untainted air—invigorated her. The temperature had dropped significantly with the setting of the sun, from a balmy thirty degrees to just sixteen, the chill just enough to make standing by a crackling fire even more enjoyable. There was nothing more mesmerising for her than watching the flames dance, flicker and twirl upon the crackling logs. It helped erase her mind of all her worries, and she had plenty of them right now. And the scent of a campfire—smouldering earth mixed with charring wood—was powerful enough to wrap itself around her like a warm and fuzzy embrace. It was certainly a perfect night for a country shindig and she couldn't wait to see what adventures were to be had. Maybe she might be lucky enough to meet a man.

Fifteen minutes later they were on the main road through town, following the long convoy of beat-up and hotted-up utes, four-wheel drives and cars towards the Opals Ridge Showgrounds, her mind's eye flashing back to the times she and Scarlet used to attend similar get-togethers here with her grandparents as youngsters. They would enjoy a hearty communal meal—usually a pig or lamb on the spit with all the yummy trimmings—followed by a few hours of frivolity with the other local kids, the majority of the children ending up sleeping on blankets in a dedicated section of the hall while Mum and Dad and Nan and Pa, along with the other adults, bootscooted the night away. It was good old-fashioned country entertainment—and a great night had by all.

Sadly, all that stopped after her parents died. Life seemed to lose its magical lustre for all of them that dramatic day, and then Scarlet's disappearance was the final straw. She wished her pa had agreed to come along tonight, but even after her constant nagging, he had declined, saying he was too old for it all now and he would rather hit the sack early.

The country tune playing on the radio was one of her all-time favourites. Renee turned it up, smiling as Mick sang the words way out of tune beside her. Garth Brooks' 'Ain't Going Down 'Til The Sun Comes Up' reminded her of days gone by. It made her wonder if the Studs and Fuds ball was going to be anything like the B&S ball she and Scarlet had snuck off to a few months before Scarlet had gone missing, their antics that night enough to get them grounded for a year, if they'd been sprung.

By the end of the night they were both drunk as skunks from the potent punch someone had concocted in a few ten-gallon buckets—given that neither of them usually drank alcohol it had only taken a few glasses—and the pair of them were covered from head to toe in every shade of food dye known to mankind. Thank God they hadn't got themselves caught, making it back to the homestead just in time to sneak back through their bedroom windows before her pa got up at his usual time of five am.

The clothes they had been wearing that night, well, they kind of accidently-on-purpose went missing, the dye impossible to get out. Thinking back now, even though the evening had been a bit of a blur, she tried to piece together the fragments, wishing she could pick up a clue as to who Scarlet's mystery man was. But as usual, nothing clicked. Billy had hung around Scarlet like a bad smell all night, making sure no other man came near his prized girlfriend, so there was no way her secret lover would have come anywhere near them. That was, if he was even there in the first place.

Mick's throaty voice clutched her from the past and dragged her attention back to the present. 'It's good your pa agreed to letting you off the leash tonight, Reni. I'll be bloody honest—I didn't know whether he would. Even though he understands you're old enough to take care of yourself now, he's really worried about you being back here. Can't blame the poor bugger really.'

She reached out and turned the stereo back down. 'Yeah, I was a bit worried he was going to stress out too much about me coming along, but bless him for letting me. I think he knows I'm too old, and too stubborn, to be told what I can and can't do now anyway.'

'Don't know about the too old bit, but the too stubborn bit, most definitely,' Mick said, chuckling.

'Oi, you can't talk,' Renee said, lightheartedly digging Mick in the ribs.

It was a relief that Pa had allowed her to attend with Mick, but it had irritated her when he'd told her he'd also asked Dylan to keep an eye on her. She was twenty-six years old, for God's sake.

She didn't need to be babysat, especially by a man who would rather see the back of her—and at the moment, she'd rather see the back of him. After what had happened between them at the shack, and with how easily he had walked away, she didn't know how they were ever meant to be normal around each other again.

She had bitten her tongue, to the point of almost drawing blood, when her pa had told her, understanding his desire to protect her. But honestly, amongst so many people, it was very unlikely that anything untoward would happen.

Pulling the old Land Cruiser into the showground, Renee headed towards the camping area, which was surrounded in tall silvery gum trees, headlights illuminating an endless array of parked vehicles and swags already rolled out on the ground. Her belly filled with butterflies as the thump-thump of the popular country band greeted them along with hordes of partygoers and the bright red-and-orange glow of a few campfires. She wondered what familiar faces she was going to run into tonight, and most importantly of all, how people would react to her being back.

'Bloody hell, it's started already. Look at him!' Mick hollered in hysterics, pointing to where a bloke was standing on the roof of his ute, stark naked, his manhood flopping about for all to see as he danced like an elephant on rollerblades. His mates surrounded the ute, egging him on even more while a girl who appeared to be his girlfriend begged him to get down. 'Thankfully all the fuds will be in the hall, and that's where I'll be heading too, while all you young hoodlums have fun out here.' He wriggled his eyebrows. 'Segregation is essential at an event like this one, otherwise the young ones could find themselves getting in a fair bit of trouble from their elders.'

'Oh. My. God,' was all Renee could mutter in between her laughter as she drove a little further up the embankment and parked in a vacant spot, far enough away from the other vehicles to give her some privacy when she wanted to retire to her swag. She was looking forward to sleeping out under the stars, not having done it since she'd left Opals Ridge at seventeen—and she didn't want a group of larrikins taking away that privilege by yahooing into the early hours of the morning beside her. There wasn't really anywhere in Melbourne she could enjoy a night out under the stars, other than on the roof of her apartment block, and without the country night sky, it just hadn't been worth the effort.

After helping Mick from the passenger side—as much as he would let her help him—Renee grabbed her little rucksack, groaning as the bottom of her back pinched. After spending the entirety of the day cleaning the homestead from top to bottom, she wondered if she was going to need a wheelchair by the end of the night. A few bevvies would help her muscles relax.

'I'll go for a wander and see if I can find Hayley. I got a text from her just before I left home saying she was on her way.' She looked out over the crowd. 'Lord knows where she'll be—I reckon half the bloody town's here.' She pulled her mobile out from her rucksack. 'Maybe I'll try and call her.'

'Good luck with that, Reni, there's no phone service here. Knowing Hayley, though, my guess would be she's over at the bar near the stage.' Mick pointed to the hall. 'I'll be holding the bar up in there, if you need me. And I'll pop out here every now and then to check up on you too—your pa will shoot me if you get yourself into any trouble tonight.' Mick motioned to his crutches. 'Not that I'm any type of bodyguard with these bloody things—although I could wallop someone if the need arose,' Mick said with a wink.

'I promise there'll be no need for walloping anyone,' Renee said with a grin as she and Mick hugged quickly then went off in different directions.

'Not sure if I'll be needing it or not yet, but just leave my swag on the bonnet, Reni. You crash in the back,' Mick called after her.

She gave him a wave, letting him know she'd heard him.

Renee wandered through the gathering crowd, amazed at how many faces she didn't recognise and aware that a few of the blokes' eyes were on her, while some of the women eyed her warily, as if she was a threat to their marked territory. She understood. To most onlookers, she was a newbie, and anyone new to a country town always attracted plenty of attention—good and bad. It was different when she was a teenager here—back then, she knew everybody. Times had certainly changed as the picturesque township had increased tenfold in numbers.

With the attention making her a little uncomfortable, Renee desperately searched the sea of faces for a familiar one. A firm tap on her shoulder made her spin around. Expecting Hayley, she smiled broadly, her arms going out to pull her friend into a warm hug, her smile dissolving like quicksand and her arms quickly returning to her sides when she spotted who it really was. 'Oh, it's you. Hi.'

'Sorry to disappoint you,' Dylan said. 'But yes, it's me. Hi back.' He grinned as though amused by her moodiness.

And that annoyed her even more.

Then they stood there, unspeaking, pretending the band was of more interest.

Why, of all people to run into first, did it have to be him? And why did he have to look so damn hot in his black wide-brimmed going-out hat, butt-hugging jeans and blue button-up shirt, the top of it open just enough to show a sneak peek of his muscular chest. What she'd give to place her lips against its lusciousness or lay her head upon it so she could listen to his heartbeat just like she used to. She bit her bottom lip, at a loss for words, her heart bashing against her chest half because she was still mad at him and half because she always felt like this when he was near her—and that pissed her off even more. She didn't want Dylan to have this effect on her any longer. She had to move on and find another man to fall in love with, as hard as that was going to be.

Muteness hung heavily between them, the familiar song the band was belting out a slight reprieve in the uncomfortable silence. Renee hummed it to herself, needing to do something, standing still right now harder than ever. There were so many things that needed saying, so many questions that needed answering, but now wasn't the right time—but would there ever be a right time?

Dylan gazed sideways at her, his blue eyes hinting at mischievousness, a beer raised to his wisp-of-a-smile lips. He looked her up and down very fleetingly, and although he tried to hide it, the expression in his eyes let her know he liked what he saw. After leaving her high and dry only two days ago, his chivalry surprised her. Maybe the beer was helping. Either way, it made her feel good that he was covertly checking her out.

When the band announced an interval, Dylan took a swig from his beer, and then acknowledged her with a broad grin. 'Are you here alone? I thought you were coming with Mick?'

Renee grit her teeth as she returned his smile, mad at him for dragging her out onto a limb the other day, and then letting her fall flat on her face as he allowed it to snap. Wasn't any decent man supposed to catch you when you fell? 'He's gone inside. Have you seen Hayley Gregory around, by any chance?'

'I sure have, I was just yarning with her about half an hour ago. She's over thataway.' He motioned towards the bar. 'You want me to walk you over there? I could do with another beer anyway.'

Renee recalled her pa's words about Dylan keeping an eye on her and she felt her hackles go up. 'Why, because you want to, or because you feel you have to? I know Pa has asked you to keep an eye on me tonight, but believe you me, I really don't need to be babysat.'

Dylan threw both hands up in the air. 'Whoa down there, Miss Tetchy. Talk about having sand in your underpants.' He smiled again, his dimples prominent. 'I know you don't need to be babysat. Like I said, I just need another beer.'

Eyeing him cautiously for a few moments, Renee shrugged her shoulders. 'Alright then, if you're heading that way anyway, you may as well show me where she is.'

Dylan headed off. 'Righto then, follow me.'

Walking behind him, his bulky frame blocking her view ahead, Renee's eyes stayed glued to his jean-clad butt.

It. Was. Perfect.

Damn it! Oh well, she thought, a girl can dream. Tearing her eyes away before Dylan busted her perving, she looked across the sea of happy faces, her excitement building. It had been way too long since she'd enjoyed a country night out. 'Let the night begin,' she whispered to herself with a wicked grin.

A few fun-filled hours later, Renee was feeling carefree and footloose as she moved her body in time to the music, the five or so beers she'd had along with the four cock-sucking cowboy shooters she'd downed with Hayley at the bar giving her Dutch courage. She had met so many wonderful people, including a few hot blokes that had tickled her fancy—although none of them came anywhere close to Dylan. She hadn't felt this happy in ages.

Not normally being one to enjoy being a bit tanked, tonight her body felt like it was floating on air and in her mind she believed wholeheartedly that she was capable of anything. Maybe tonight she should apologise for what she said all those years ago and tell Dylan exactly what she thought of him—with no sugar coating, and see what he had to say. Or maybe she should just forget about him altogether and just enjoy the rest of her night?

The flash of a camera gripped her attention and blurred her vision for a few short moments, Hayley's laughter contagious as she encouraged Renee to pose for the camera still pointed at them.

Craig Campbell grinned back at the pair of them from behind the lens. 'Smile, ladies.'

He looked somewhat older—mind you, didn't they all?—but Renee recognised him instantly. She gave him a wave. 'Hey Craig, it's been years,' she called out over the music.

'Yeah, too long,' Craig replied with a smile as the flash illuminated the girls once more.

'We're gonna be in the local paper. Woohoo!' Hayley squealed, throwing her arms up in the air.

Renee flung her arms around Hayley, giggling, as the vivid flash owned the darkness for a split second. 'I thought he was the town copper, not the paparazzi!'

'Yeah, he is, but he does a bit of casual work for the paper too, has for years. So give him your best side, Reni.'

Renee struck a few lighthearted poses, making sure to pout in at least one of the shots—it was all the rage these days to have puffy lips in photos, not that she got the appeal. In her opinion it made most pouters look as though they'd been stung by a bee on the lips, several times. But tonight she didn't care if she looked ridiculous—it was all for a bit of fun.

The brief photo shoot over, Craig gave them the thumbs up as he went back through the shots on the camera. Renee and Hayley huddled around him, pointing and laughing at some of their poses.

'There are certainly some beauties in there—and a few I definitely won't be able to put in the paper,' Craig said, laughing along with them.

Renee feigned disappointment while fully appreciating that a couple of the snapshots were a little unfit for the conservative local paper. 'Oh bugger, really? Can I buy some of them off you, though?'

'Oh, for sure.' Craig pulled a business card from his top pocket. 'Here's my number. Just give me a call during the week and you can pop over to my place and pick which ones you'd like. I have my own studio and darkroom so I can print them once you know exactly which ones you want.'

'A darkroom? Isn't everything digital now?' Renee asked as she popped the business card in her skirt pocket.

'Most of it is, but I still like to delve a little into the old-fashioned way of doing things sometimes... Photos are amazing when you develop them yourself.'

'Righto, sounds great. Thanks, Craig.' Renee gave him a quick hug. 'Good to see you again, too, after all these years.'

'You too, Renee, and my pleasure—catch you two a bit later,' Craig said as he disappeared into the throng of partygoers, his camera at the ready for more shots.

Peeking across the crowd, Renee searched for Dylan's familiar hat, spotting it almost instantly. With his height and solid build it was hard to miss him. Ralph was standing beside him, his trademark smile on his face. It had been good catching up with him as well. He didn't seem to have aged a day, in his looks or with his exuberant personality. She'd always enjoyed Ralph's company as a teenager— he could make her laugh until her sides ached. He'd mentioned he was single, and had asked her if she had any nice girlfriends from the city she could introduce him to. Tia had instantly come to mind—shame there were thousands of miles putting a stop to that introduction.

As much as she tried, Renee couldn't take her eyes off Dylan, or the chick beside him for that matter. He was chatting intently to a very hot blonde, the same girl that had served her and Mick at the bar the other day at lunch at the Opals Ridge Hotel, and although she tried to ignore the unwelcome sensation, jealousy engulfed her.

Why couldn't he give her that kind of attention? She hadn't seen much of him since he'd walked her over to the bar at the beginning of the night, other than the occasional stolen glance from him across the dance floor—Dylan gracing her with a charming grin each and every time their eyes met before turning his attention back to whoever he was yarning to.

Mick had popped out once to check on her, and Hayley told him she would take excellent care of her. Satisfied with this, he had told Renee he would catch her on the flip side. That was when she had figured he'd had his fair share of beers—Mick was never one to use lingo like that. It had cracked her and Hayley up as they'd watched him wobble back towards the hall on his crutches, Mick almost finding himself upended in the garden along the way. But he had made it inside, much to Renee's relief. She didn't like the thought of having to go home to tell Pa that Mick had broken his other leg.

The lead singer of the band announced their next song in his renowned husky country drawl, an all-time favourite. Renee squealed excitedly along with the equally passionate swarm of partiers. Allowing Hayley to drag her up onto one of the three timber tables that had been pulled into the middle of the dance floor by a group of guys dressed in women's clothing, she grooved in time to the music. Hayley threw her head back and laughed while she bootscooted on the table, making it wobble precariously beneath them. All around them the crowd wolf-whistled and cheered them on, the atmosphere electric. Renee threw her hands up in the air, singing the words out loud and feeling the highest on life than she'd been in years.

A few songs later the band changed pace, as they announced their number one hit from years ago, still just as popular today: 'I Want You'. Not a song for dancing like billyo on the table, Renee and Hayley jumped off, Hayley being snapped up immediately by one of her male mates for a slow dance. Standing in the middle of the crowd of swaying lovers, Renee suddenly felt very out of place, until a pair of warm hands slid around her waist and she was spun around and pulled into Dylan's strong arms.

As much as she wanted to, she didn't resist, the magic of the moment taking her away with him. And how could she say no to the sexiest man in the entire place? She smiled coyly at him and he returned the gesture, the skin of his cheeks creasing as he flashed her his most inviting smile. Then, swaying her as though she were weightless in his arms, his lips mimed the words to the song, his eyes never leaving hers for a second.

I wanna touch, taste you, breathe you in.
I wanna see candlelight flickering over your sweet soft skin.
I wanna make slow sweet love to you until the sun comes up.
And then hold you close to me all day long…
It's just you baby, I can't get enough.

Come on, give in to me baby,
These feelings are too strong to ignore,
This deep soul loving I've never ever felt before.
Come on, give in to me baby,
And put those sweet lips on mine,
'Cause I know this deep soul loving
Has the power to stand the test of time.

I wanna fly off the edge of this cliff.
I wanna break down all the walls.
'Cause baby I'm gonna be right here
To catch you when you fall.
I wanna hear you whisper in my ear
Words that send shivers down my spine.
I wanna love you like you've never been loved,
Yeah baby, until the end of time.

Come on, give in to me baby.
These feelings are too strong to ignore,
This deep soul loving I've never ever felt before.
Come on, give in to me baby
And put those sweet lips on mine.
'Cause I know this deep soul loving
Is gonna stand the test of time.

I wanna turn on the slow songs,
And dance with you in my arms.
I wanna be a victim to your seduction,
And be magnetised by your charm.
I wanna climb the tallest mountain,
And tell the world that you are mine.
I wanna hold you in my arms forever,
Until the end of time.

Come on, give in to me baby…

Dylan whispered the words, his gorgeously kissable lips so close to Renee's she could smell the sweet alcohol on his breath. Was this really him, or was it the liquor doing all the talking? Unable to gaze into his eyes any longer, and with the power behind the poignant words making her want to burst into tears, Renee pulled out of his embrace and ran back through the crowd towards where she'd parked the Land Cruiser.

Little did Dylan know she had daydreamed about him every time she'd heard this song since it had hit the charts eight years ago. In her heart, this was their song, and never would she have believed that one day, this day, he would sing it to her. Sucking in deep breaths, she fought to keep her welling emotions at bay. She needed to be alone. Now. Right this second.

At the edge of the darkness, she stopped and briefly looked back over her shoulder to make sure Dylan wasn't following her, instantly wishing she hadn't. Billy Burton grinned back at her, his leering face mere inches from hers.

Stumbling a little to the left, he corrected his footing and he reached out for a tree to stop himself from falling flat on his face. 'Howdidoo, Renee. Why ya leaving so early—ya party pooper?' His words were slurred, and he was trying to stand up extra straight.

'Oh, I'm tired, so I'm going to hit the sack. Catch ya, Billy.' Renee went to spin around and make a break for it, but Billy stopped her, his grip on her arm too tight. She tried to pull away but he wouldn't let her.

'Let me go,' she snarled through gritted teeth.

'Nope, not until you tell me what your problem is. I thought you would have left the past where it was, but maybe not?'

'I don't have a problem with you,' she lied. Now wasn't the time.

He laughed cynically. 'Yeah right, and my mother's a nun and I'm an altar boy. Come on Renee, spit it out.'

Renee refused to answer him.

'All right then, play mute.' Billy swayed backwards, dragging her with him. 'Just for the record…I didn't have anything to do with your sister going missing.'

Yanking her arm free, Renee glared at him. 'Like I said, I don't have a problem with you, Billy. Now leave me the fuck alone.'

Billy threw his hands up in the air in defeat. 'Okay okay, whatever. I don't need your kind in my life anyway.'

Renee's eyes widened. 'My kind?'

'Yeah, your kind. You think it's okay to ruin other people's lives by pointing the finger, and then just waltz on outta town like you did, without even an apology?' Billy leant into her space once again, scowling. 'Well it's not, Renee Wildwood. You damn near ruined me by telling anyone and everyone that you thought it was my doing that Scarlet went missing… I stupidly thought that after all these years you would have seen sense, but clearly you haven't.' Turning away from her, Billy stumbled back into the crowd, not bothering to wait for a reply.

Renee stood mute, wanting to respond but the words a complete jumble in her mouth. Even though she still had her reservations about Billy, she had to begrudgingly admit that he had a fair point—the same point Mick had tried to make the other day. It was just so damn hard when all she wanted to do was discover who had taken Scarlet from them—desperation did tend to take away all logic. What if Billy was telling the truth and honestly had nothing to do with Scarlet's disappearance?

And he wasn't the only person she'd pointed the finger at—amongst others she'd also done it to the one person in this world she should never have doubted. Her heart sinking even further, she momentarily caught a glimpse of Dylan still standing on the dance floor and her heart wrenched out of her chest. He looked completely crushed. At least he wasn't following her. She hated running from him like this, but why stay and pretend there was something going on between them? Nothing was ever going to come of it. He'd made that perfectly clear the other day. For fuck's sake—one minute he didn't want her, the next minute he did. What did he want from her? Anger, frustration and confusion filled her as she escaped into the darkness, tears now falling down her cheeks like a dam that had burst its banks. Incredible how quickly a great night could turn to absolute shit.

With the music now more of a distant thump rather than a thunderous rumble, Renee tried to find her way through the darkness, being mindful to watch out for bodies in swags—especially ones that might be dancing beneath the covers. Away from all the commotion, she could suddenly feel every drink she'd had in her unsteady legs—she was officially well and truly wasted. Hayley was a bad influence—not that she was complaining—she had needed a night like tonight, one where she was free to let her hair down. And she'd been having a ball, but all that had changed in an instant. Sniffling, she wiped her teary eyes, determined to stop crying before she reached where she'd parked.

As her eyes adjusted to the blackness, she looked around, noticing there were very few people in the camping area. The ones that were here were either asleep in camp chairs or passed out on the ground. There was not a voice to be heard, making it ear-ringingly silent compared to where she'd just come from. She felt like a party pooper leaving Hayley when the party was just getting started, but she wasn't in the mood to dance the night away now. Hayley would understand when she explained it all to her tomorrow.

The sound of leaves being crushed underfoot drew her attention, and she suddenly got the eerie feeling that someone was following her. Stopping in her tracks, she turned warily, her heart in her throat, but she couldn't see anyone.

'Dylan, is that you?' she cautiously called out. 'Hello?'

There was no answer. She shook her head, annoyed at herself for getting the heebie-jeebies. Bloody hell, why had she drunk so much tonight? It was making her mind play horrible tricks on her. Wrapping her arms around herself, she picked up her pace, wanting to get to the Land Cruiser quick smart so she could jump in her swag. Trying to shake off the unnerving feeling, she thought of the positives. At least she'd have a little while to try to get to sleep before people started heading back this way, towards where they'd crash for the final few hours if they weren't pulling an all-nighter. And at least she wouldn't wake up in the morning with a smashing hangover if she stopped drinking now and got some decent sleep.

The sound of leaves being trodden on dragged her attention behind her once again, and this time, it wasn't just a feeling. She was sure of what she'd heard. Spinning around, she glared into the darkness, the deep throaty laughter of a man sending a chill down her spine.

'Billy, are you following me? Because if you are, rack off will you? I told you to leave me alone.'

There was no reply. Her pulse jacked up another notch.

'Dylan, Hayley, come on guys. Enough is enough. This isn't funny at all. You're freaking me out.'

But there was nothing. No response, no more noise, nothing. Frozen to the spot, Renee started to shake, all her fears and nightmares crashing down upon her like a tidal wave, and suddenly, she was drowning beneath it all. She wanted to run, but her legs wouldn't move. Nan and Pa were right. She wasn't safe here. She never would be safe until Scarlet's real killer was found.

And maybe, she was about to find out exactly who that was.

CHAPTER
16

Time stood still while everything around her moved in slow motion. Listening intently she tried to make out any sounds. Was someone hiding out there in the shadows, watching her? Or was she imagining it? Terror held her in a vice-grip as the shadows appeared to stretch like clawed hands across the ground, making the hairs stand up even further on the back of her neck. Finding it hard to breathe, she turned around slowly, assessing her surroundings. Other than the distant thump of the music, there was silence. Her heart hammered against her ribcage and the towering gum trees seemed to close in on her. The world felt as though it was spinning beneath her pretty rhinestone boots. Then there was a flash of light behind her, and she spun around. Was someone lighting a cigarette, or waving a torch about?

'Please,' she cried out. 'Whoever you are, stop it. You're scaring me.'

Intimidating masculine laughter broke the silence of the camping area once again. Whoever was hiding in the shadows was obviously enjoying taunting her. A loud crack of a stock whip from the far side of the showgrounds grabbed her attention for a millisecond. What she'd give to be back amongst everyone at the party rather than standing out here, all alone, in the dark. She knew she had to run. Now. And fast, before whoever it was got their hands on her.

Quickly assessing which way to go, Renee decided she had much more of a chance of making it to safety if she headed towards the Land Cruiser—there was too much shadowy ground to cross to get back to the party, and it also meant maybe running smack bang into the person that was trailing her. Turning on her heels, she bolted towards the ute, the terror that someone was about to harm her— or worse, kill her—almost rendering her motionless once again. But she pushed through the fear. She had to.

With everything blurring around her, Renee ran as fast as she could, all the while fumbling in her rucksack for the keys to the Toyota. Now she could hear the heavy footsteps of someone running at a distance behind her, matching her stride for stride, but she wasn't turning around. Making it to the passenger side she scrabbled with the keyhole, her hands shaking uncontrollably. The hurried footsteps were getting closer—someone's laboured breathing louder. Opening the door, she threw herself inside and slammed the lock down before lying down on the seat and sobbing her heart out. She had never felt fear like this before.

And then it occurred to her. *Call the cops. Craig is here already!*

Reaching into the rucksack once again, she found her mobile phone. Flipping it open she felt like smashing it against the dashboard when she spotted the lack of service and then remembered Mick saying it wouldn't work here. 'Fuck you,' she screamed as she threw it to the floor.

With her ears honed for any noises outside the four-wheel drive, Renee eased herself up and warily peered out the passenger side window, terrified she'd see a pair of malevolent eyes glaring back at her. But there was nothing, no-one. Was this some sick joke? Or was this real? Was she about to die or was she imagining things? Was this how Scarlet had felt before that son of a bitch had killed her? Closing her eyes, she prayed to God, begging him to save her. She was just starting to calm down when a knock at the window made her heart stop.

Holding her breath, she glanced towards the driver's side window. A flood of relief washed over her when she saw Dylan's kindly face smiling back at her. Gasping like a fish out of water, she fumbled for the lock, almost throwing Dylan backwards when she dived out of the Land Cruiser and into his arms. Sobbing breathlessly, she relayed the story, not even giving him a chance to speak. The alarm in his eyes melted her heart and made her see that he really did care about her. Deeply.

'Holy shit, Renee. Thank God you're okay.' Dylan hugged her closer, his solid arms enveloping her. He stroked the back of her hair to calm her. 'I really don't think you have anything to worry about when it comes to Billy, though. His bark is worse than his bite. The bloke's pretty harmless.'

'That's what people say, but I'm not so sure,' Renee replied, her voice still shaking.

'Well, whoever it is will be very sorry if they show their ugly face right now—the sick bastard trying to scare you like that,' Dylan said sternly, and loudly enough for anyone who may have been nearby to hear.

Renee pushed the hair from her face and wiped her tears. 'Do you really think this might just be some sick prank?'

Dylan shrugged, keeping her close to him. 'There's a big possibility. I reckon this would be the last place someone would try something serious. There's too many people about for that.'

'Maybe you're right,' Renee said as she huddled closer into his arms, still not sure what to believe. At least no-one would dare hurt her with Dylan here—he was known as a man not to mess with, thanks to his father's bad reputation. He wasn't as volatile as his father, but he definitely knew how to handle himself.

Pulling his mobile phone from his pocket, Dylan switched on the torch and shone the beam all around them. Renee stayed silent while he did so, her breath held once again as she rested her head against his chest. She was terrified they would see eyes staring back at them. But there was nobody there, nobody watching them.

She began to think a little more rationally. Wouldn't Dylan have seen whoever it was chasing her, seeing he arrived at the Land Cruiser less than a minute after her? The thought made her feel a little stupid. Maybe she *had* imagined it all. Maybe Billy had put the wind up her, and then some people were out getting it off in the bushes and she'd thought they were laughing at her, and maybe she'd imagined the footsteps. So many bloody maybes, she just couldn't be certain of anything right now.

'Are you sure someone was chasing you?' Dylan said as he tucked his mobile back in his jeans pocket.

Sniffling, Renee wiped her red-raw eyes. 'I don't know now—it felt so real at the time. I'm not that drunk that I would be imagining things, am I?'

Dylan smiled sadly. 'You are pretty drunk, sweetheart, but we better get you to the cop station so you can report it, hey. Just to be sure. You never know.'

Renee shook her head. 'Report what? I'm not even certain of what happened. I didn't see who it was, so what are the cops going to do about it? Besides, you and I are both over the limit—and I'm not going to annoy Craig on his night off.' She looked around them, staring into the darkness. 'And you were here less than a minute after whoever it was started chasing me, and you didn't see anyone.' She dropped her head in her hands, sobbing once again. 'I don't know, maybe I did imagine it.' She looked up at Dylan, completely devastated. 'Or maybe it was someone playing a horrible trick on me. After the way I was throwing accusations around after Scarlet's disappearance, I can understand there might be a few people out there that want to teach me a lesson…and I probably deserve it.' She looked into his eyes. 'I'm so deeply sorry I accused your father. I was way out of line saying that when you'd simply come to me for comfort after finding your mum in such a bad way.'

Dylan shook his head as he looked down at the ground, sighing. 'Renee, you were desperate at the time, and after what Dad did to Mum that night, I understand how you might have thought he was capable of hurting Scarlet too. My father is a bad man, but he's not capable of murder. It just hurt so much that you would think that, because in a way it tarred me with the same brush.'

Renee reached out and gently rested her hand on Dylan's arm, feeling completely ashamed. 'I'm so sorry I made you feel like that.'

Dylan touched her hand with his. 'Thanks. Your apology means the world to me. And I owe you one too, really. I didn't mean it when I said we were over and that I didn't love you anymore. I was just mad at the time, that's all.'

'I understand, Dylan. You had every right to feel like that.' Renee broke down, her emotions getting the better of her.

He cupped her cheeks, his thumbs wiping her tears as they continued to fall. 'It was so long ago, and we were both hurt, but can we just accept each other's apologies now and let it go—so we can stop being so narky with each other?'

Renee nodded. 'Okay, I'd like that.'

Dylan kissed her cheek, his lips catching her tears, and then he tucked a strand of hair behind her ear. 'And please know that if someone *was* following you tonight, and I find out who it was, I will make them pay for scaring you.'

Renee returned his kiss by placing one on his cheek. 'Thank you, Dylan. That means the world. I feel safe here with you.' She closed her eyes, drawing in a deep breath then letting it go slowly. 'Would you mind if we kept this to ourselves? I don't want to go worrying my grandparents over nothing, if that's what it was—and the entire town for that matter. News travels fast here, as you know.'

Dylan eyed her thoughtfully. 'I understand you not wanting to say anything, when you're so unsure. But please make sure you watch your back from now on, and don't go wandering around in the dark on your own, anywhere. Okay? I mean, I know you don't need a babysitter and all, but can you at least promise me that?'

'You have my word,' Renee said, smiling softly as she gazed into his beautiful blue eyes. In that moment, everything faded away, leaving just her and Dylan. Here. Now. Together. Alone. It was time to ask some of the questions she'd been dying to know the answers to.

'Dylan, please can you tell me what happened to your wife? I'm sorry, but I need to know.'

Pain flashed across Dylan's face, his easy smile fading as he looked downwards. 'She died, Renee, in an accident at home, and my beautiful little Annie was the one who found her.' Dylan's voice broke as he covered his face with his hands. 'I wasn't there to protect my two girls, like I should have been, and I beat myself up over that every single day.'

Renee's heart squeezed, the devastation Dylan had been through tearing her to shreds. 'Oh, Dylan, I'm so very sorry.' Tears filled her eyes and she tried to blink them away as she gently touched his cheek. 'I can't even begin to understand the heartache that would have caused you, and your daughter.'

Dylan looked up to meet her sympathetic eyes. 'That's not exactly true—I think you do understand, Renee, completely. You've lost your parents *and* your sister.' He reached out and slipped his hand behind her ear, stroking her cheek with his thumb. 'And that's just so typical of you, to always be thinking of everyone else before yourself. You've felt my agony, sweetheart, three times over. But thank you for caring as much as you do. Your beautiful kind heart is why I fell so deeply in love with you in the first place.'

As Dylan's words hit home, Renee felt a rush of mixed emotions, as though the floodgates had finally been opened with his profound understanding of her rocky life path. Compassion, devastation, sadness and loss swirled in her heart, and most of all, soul-deep love for this amazing man standing before her. She nodded. 'Now you put it that way I s'pose I can honestly say I do understand your pain. Completely.' She reached out and rested both her hands on his chest. 'Your big beautiful heart is why I fell in love with you so deeply, too, and it's also why I *still* love you as deeply as I do.'

'You still love me? But I thought...' Dylan said, his voice trailing off.

Renee smiled wispily. 'Of course I do, I've never stopped loving you. I've thought about you every single day since leaving here all those years ago, and no man has ever been able to come close to how you could make me feel with a single look, or a single touch.'

Dylan looked bewildered. 'Then why did you leave town, without even trying to sort things out between us?'

'Because my life was in danger, Dylan, and my grandparents wanted me to make a clean break and go somewhere I could be anonymous. After everything they'd been through, and done for me, I couldn't go against their word...as much as it killed me to leave you high and dry like that.'

Dylan took a few moments before answering, his eyes searching hers, as if trying to judge whether she was telling him the truth. 'I can appreciate you respecting their wishes, but how was your life in such grave danger?'

'I found a note under my windscreen wiper, Dylan, telling me I was next on the list to be—you know—killed.'

'Why didn't you tell me?' Dylan took a step back, shaking his head in disbelief. 'Holy shit, no wonder you skipped town. I never knew… I'm so sorry.' In four hurried steps Dylan stepped into her space once again and slid his hands around her waist, pulling her close to him. 'Over my dead body would anyone lay their hands on you, Renee, I can promise you that. I'd never let anything happen to you, ever.'

Her welling emotions making it impossible to speak, Renee placed her head against Dylan's chest, the sound of his beating heart the most beautiful sound in the world. It transported her back to the days when they would enjoy a picnic by the creek near the hunter's shack and then both lie back on a blanket in the sunshine, her head resting on his chest as they both drifted in and out of slumber. It was the simple things that had meant so much back then, to both of them. If only they could get those days back.

Tilting her head up, she warily placed her lips softly on his, waiting for him to respond, praying for him to give in to his feelings for her. And respond he did, as he lifted her from the ground and kissed her with so much passion she felt as light as a feather in his arms. Wrapping her legs around his waist and her arms tighter around his back, she melted into him as they kissed for what felt like forever. With their bodies pressed hard against one another's, and the passion and hunger building between them, Renee finally begged him to make love to her.

'Did you bring a swag?' Dylan whispered in her ear, sending pleasurable shivers all over her.

'Yeah, it's in the back of the Land Cruiser. I just got to roll it out,' she replied breathlessly, remembering that Mick had asked her to leave his swag on the bonnet. She was fairly certain he wouldn't need it until just before dawn, which gave her and Dylan a few more hours yet. She hoped to God she wasn't wrong with her hunch. It'd make for a very embarrassing situation, for all of them, if he suddenly rocked up now.

Without another word, Dylan carried her over to the back of the ute and placed her down so she was sitting at the end of the tray, her legs still wrapped tightly around his waist.

Capturing her eyes with his, Dylan slowly ran his hands up her sides, stopping to run his fingertips teasingly over her hard nipples that were pressing through her thin top. Renee's soft moans filled the silence as he brought his lips to hers once again, his tongue flicking over hers suggestively. Pulling back, he cupped her face. 'Are you sure we should be doing this? What if whoever was following you is watching us.'

'They'd be long gone now you're here. Please, just make love to me,' Renee said as she ravenously pulled him into another kiss.

Finally, she was going to get her wish. She was going to make love to Dylan Anderson once again. And this time, she knew, it would leave her wanting him more than ever before. She just hoped it did the same for him, because it would be devastating if it didn't. Dangerous ground for an already volatile relationship, but she didn't care. The rest, whatever that was, would just have to come later.

***

With her lash-framed gaze even more poignant in the moonlight, Dylan seized the moment and slipped the thin strap from Renee's shoulder, her silky smooth skin blooming with goosebumps beneath his fingertips. God, she was beyond beautiful—how on earth could he keep resisting such a gorgeous creature?

Looking into her chocolate brown eyes, her lips poised between silence and a whisper, he felt all his resentment drain away, only to be replaced by the soul-deep love that had always been there, lying dormant, until this very moment. He thought he'd rid himself of the hold Renee Wildwood had over him all those years ago, but clearly, a love like theirs could never be forgotten. She reached out and stroked the side of his cheek, her eyes filling with tears, her lips trembling. She went to speak, but he placed his hand gently over her mouth, shaking his head.

Instead, she spoke to him in silence, both her hands now caressing his face, down his neck and then over his chest. And at that very second he swore he could feel her soul surge towards him and join with his. This was love, in its purest of forms. This feeling within him, the fire within her eyes, needed no explanation. With their eyes locked onto one another's, the past and future seemed so unimportant, and this moment meant everything. Leaning into her, he let his kiss dissolve the silence, and he knew as her lips touched his once again that he wanted to be able to kiss this beautiful woman every day for the rest of his life. An overwhelming need to be at one with her filled him and he manoeuvred himself up and onto the back of the ute, so he was sitting beside her, their lips still united. As he ran his fingers through her silken hair, her hands fumbled with the buttons on his shirt, and with each one she opened, she would lean in and kiss his chest, her warm breath and lingering lips inducing a deep hunger from within him, a hunger he'd only ever experienced once before—with her.

What about Shelley? How would she feel if she saw me doing this?

Trying to ignore the voice in his head, Dylan immersed himself in the moment, his feelings for Renee now flooding him like warm whiskey sliding down his throat on a cold winter's night. His mind flashed back to the night they had first made love, in the swag at the hut. They'd torn each other's clothes off breathlessly, the passion between them unfathomable.

But as poignant as the recollection was, as tempting as it was to repeat, the memory unexpectedly sent him hurtling down a path filled with guilt and uncertainty. As much as he wanted to devour every inch of Renee right here, right now, and to feel them join on the most intimate of levels, hesitation filled him. This situation was a lot more serious than just two people having a bit of fun on a night out. He had a daughter to consider now, and the effect it might have on her if another woman came into their lives. He wasn't sure if it would be a good or bad thing, and until he was one hundred and ten per cent certain either way, this had to stop, right now.

Begrudgingly, he put the brakes on. He couldn't do this. *They* couldn't do this. It just didn't feel right. Renee deserved so much more from him than simply getting it off in the back of a ute. She also deserved his full commitment, and at the moment he couldn't give her that. It wasn't as simple as making love and then living happily ever after. Their lives were a lot more complicated now that they were adults—and adults with nine years of history that neither of them knew much about. They needed to spend a little more time together, as friends.

When he looked into Renee's eyes he saw a mixture of longing, love and fear. She looked so damned vulnerable. He took her hands in his and slowly shook his head. 'We can't do this. Not here, not like this, and especially after we've both had a bit to drink. We need to take things one very steady step at a time.'

Renee stared at him pleadingly. 'But Dylan, I want this, I want *you*.' Her voice was shaky. 'Please, I've waited so long…'

'I know. Believe me, I want you too. But you mean more to me than just a shag in the back of a ute, so I won't let our first time together again be like this. If it's destined to happen in the future, it needs to be special—memorable for all the right reasons. And we need to make absolutely certain this is what we both want, without any doubts whatsoever, and without alcohol clouding our judgement. I mean, you don't even live here anymore, so that's quite a big hurdle to get over if we decide to make a go of things again.'

Sighing, Renee looked away, as if searching for answers in the darkness. She dropped her head and closed her eyes. 'So what do we do now? Just pretend this didn't happen, like when we almost kissed the other day?'

'How about we just climb into your swag and hold each other while we fall asleep?'

Renee nodded, her smile now reaching from ear to ear. 'Now that sounds perfect.'

Dylan rolled the swag out in the back of the Land Cruiser while Renee grabbed Mick's swag and went to put it on the bonnet. Unable to keep his eyes off her, Dylan watched as Renee walked towards the front of the four-wheel drive, wishing they could both just give in to the moment with reckless abandon, like they had all those years ago.

But they couldn't. He still had to work on getting rid of the guilt he harboured at having feelings for a woman other than Shelley, and he also needed to introduce Annie to Renee, to see for himself how his darling daughter might react to her. Because as much as he wanted to have Renee back in his life as more than just a friend, Annie came first, and if the two didn't gel, then he couldn't see a future for them beyond friendship, no matter what he wanted. And on top of all that, a long-distance relationship was going to be extremely challenging.

When Renee jumped back up onto the tray of the Land Cruiser, they both took off their boots and then crawled into the swag still fully clothed. Cuddling into one another, their bodies melted into one, as if they were both made from the same mould.

Renee spoke first. 'As much as I hate to admit it, you were right in stopping us from making love. Not living here poses a big challenge, and we need to think of Annie too. We shouldn't be jumping into bed straight away. We have a lot of catching up to do before that, and a lot to consider.'

Dylan hugged her tighter. 'Trust me, I want nothing more than to make love to you, but yup, we need to take things slow. I've got a lot of stuff to deal with at the moment, and I don't want my stresses affecting us in any way.'

Renee stroked his hand with her fingertips. 'Is it something you can talk to me about?'

Sighing, Dylan took a few moments to respond. 'Some bastard is playing games with me. Cutting my fences almost every week and letting my cattle out, and on top of that they're tampering with my pumps that send water to the paddocks, so my livestock don't have enough water to drink. I have no idea who it is and they just keep getting away with it.'

'Oh Dylan, I'm so sorry. What bloody lowlifes. Do you reckon it could be bored teenagers, getting up to no good?'

'Quite possibly, I've got Craig on the case, but nothing seems to be happening. It's so bloody frustrating. And on top of all of this, the farm is struggling a bit financially, hence the reason I took the job with your pa.'

Renee turned her head to face him. 'I really wish there was something I could do.'

'Yeah, I know, me too.' He placed a lingering kiss on her lips, the sensation sending pleasurable warmth throughout him.

'There's something I need to talk about too.' Renee's voice was almost a whisper.

Dylan kissed her cheek. 'I'm all ears, what is it?'

'You know last week, when you found me at the hunter's shack?'

'Yeah.'

'Well, I stumbled across Scarlet's old diary in there, and in it she talks about this other man she was in love with—someone other than Billy. My instincts tell me whoever she's talking about was responsible for her disappearance.'

Dylan sat up, dragging Renee with him. 'Holy shit, Renee. That's a huge find. Have you taken it to Craig?'

Renee shook her head. 'No, not yet.'

'Why the heck not?'

'I haven't told anyone—not even Pa. I just wanted some time to mull over what I'd read, to come to my own conclusions, before I handed it into the police.'

'And have you had that time now?'

'Yeah, I suppose, but it's so frustrating that it hasn't really brought me any closer to figuring out who she was talking about.'

'Well then, I think you should definitely be giving it to Craig. You never know, he might see something in there you haven't picked up on.'

'I know. I just don't want to upset everyone by dragging the past up again, especially if the diary leads to nothing. Nan doesn't need the stress right now after her heart attack.'

'Fair enough. In that case, maybe ask Craig to keep it quiet for now, just until he looks it over.'

'Do you think he'd do that, keep it quiet from my grandparents?'

'I reckon he probably would. It's worth a try.'

'Yeah, you're right, it is worth a try.' Renee caught Dylan's eyes. 'I've missed you.'

Dylan grabbed hold of her hands. 'I've missed *us*.'

Renee smiled lovingly. 'Enough of my dramas. Have you got a photo of Annie? I want to see what your gorgeous girl looks like.'

Dylan reached into the pocket at the back of his jeans. 'I sure do.' He pulled a photo out of the little casing in his wallet. 'Here she is, the one and only Miss Annabel Anderson.'

'Oh my goodness, Dylan, she's beautiful.' Renee admired the photo for a few more seconds before handing it back.

'She certainly is.' Dylan glanced at the photo, smiling like only a doting father could, before placing it back in his wallet. 'But then again, I have a very biased opinion.'

'I look forward to meeting her.'

'You'll be meeting her soon, I'd say.'

The two of them eased themselves back down. Closing her eyes, Renee rested her head against Dylan's chest as Dylan wrapped his arms tighter around her. A comfortable silence settled between them, the touch of their bodies against one another speaking a thousand words. Above them, the night sky put on a dazzling show, the stars glittering against the black backdrop of night, the moon only hinting at its presence amongst it all.

Dylan sighed gratifyingly, as did Renee. In the morning, things might be different, but for now, just being able to *be* with one another, to be able to lie in each other's arms, if only for this beautiful breathtaking moment, was absolute heaven.

CHAPTER
17

Dylan stepped from the four-wheel drive and pulled on his jacket, making sure Annie did the same, before reaching back in and grabbing the flowers they'd picked from the garden at home from the dashboard. He looked skyward as he pressed the central locking button on his horsehair keychain. In every direction ominous dark grey clouds blanketed the blue sky and clung to the edges of the surrounding mountaintops, the sun only peeking out from behind as if it were teasing the earth beneath. The scent of rain was heavy in the air. It wasn't going to be too long before the sky opened up to a heavy downpour, and the darkening sky matched Dylan's increasingly gloomy mood. He just hoped the rain would hold off for the next hour or so. Was that too much to ask whoever was in charge above?

Upon arriving home from the Studs and Fuds ball that morning, his cattle had been let out again, the keys had been stolen from his tractor and four-wheeler motorbike—thank God he had spares—and the pump that sent the water up from the back creek had been switched off again, leaving his horses and cattle without sufficient water. He'd called into Craig's place and filled him in, but as usual, it was the same shit, different day, Craig saying he would investigate further and let him know if he came up with anything.

Dylan had felt like screaming blue bloody murder, but he'd held his tongue, the fact Craig was his neighbour and a man he considered his mate overruling his urge to lose it completely. What pissed Dylan off even more was that he'd woken so happy and optimistic just before dawn, with Renee still tucked up in his arms—and with Mick snoring like a trooper on the ground beside the four-wheel drive, the awkward position of his body on top of his swag letting Dylan know Mick had basically passed out before he'd even hit the ground—a feat in itself with a broken leg, but a huge relief because it meant he and Renee hadn't been sprung by his boss's right-hand man.

He hadn't wanted the night to end. It had felt so right to be holding Renee, and he'd wanted to stay with her like that forever, although fear of Mick seeing them together had forced them to part pretty speedily once the dawn light began to break. The way Renee had smiled when she'd first opened her eyes and seen him still beside her had melted his insides, and left him wanting her even more. She was just as beautiful first thing in the morning as she'd been when he'd first laid eyes on her at the ball. When he'd first spotted her in the crowd last night, with her long slender legs slipped perfectly into her cowgirl boots and that short denim skirt covering just enough to leave things to the imagination—wow! It had taken every bit of his reserve to not jump at the chance to make love to her in the swag. And thank God he hadn't, for he knew that he would have felt like the biggest arsehole on earth this morning.

Stepping off the pretty flower-lined pebble pathway, Dylan felt the all-too-familiar crunch of the pristine blades of grass beneath his boots. It was as if the entire lawn had been combed. Stopping, he bent over and picked two bright orange-and-yellow marigolds from the bordering flower garden for Annie, as he always did, one for behind each of her ears. It was one small way for him to bring a wisp of a smile to her face at a time like this. The flowers' pungent musky aroma filled the air—the scent halfway unpleasant and halfway alluring—bringing with it a flood of childhood memories for Dylan, some good, some not so good.

His dear late nanna, Edith—his mum's mum—had always planted marigolds, because they were the only flowers that never said die, no matter how hot it got—and up here in the North it got damn hot. His father had hated the smell of the blooms, and always took great pleasure in proving that as hardy as the flowers were, they couldn't beat him. Peter had gone out of his way to accidently-on-purpose step on Edith's garden whenever he got the chance. None of them ever said anything, though—him, his mum and his nanna—too afraid of the explosion it would cause.

Approaching the place where he and Annie had recently planted Shelley's favourite flowers, petunias, Dylan half tiptoed, feeling slightly bad for walking on the faultless lawn—the groundsman clearly proud of his job. All the trees and shrubs that provided much-needed shade and colour around the place were manicured to perfection, the scene almost too perfect for a place such as this. Yes, it needed to be made out to be heaven on earth, so people could visit loved ones and somehow feel at peace with them, but sometimes, especially at the beginning, he'd struggled with the *normalcy* of the place. His world had been turned upside down when Shelley had passed away, and after three long heartbreaking years he felt like he was only just spinning it the right way back up. It was getting easier each time he came here, but it was never a place he looked forward to visiting. This was where he could come and pay his respects to Shelley, and where her body would be for eternity, but he liked to believe that her spirit was with him and Annie always. It helped him, and Annie, get through.

Annie walked beside him, her face displaying the ache in her heart. Her tiny hand clutched his, the strength in her grasp beyond what you'd think a girl her size capable of. No matter how many times he came here, the lump in his throat never went away and his emotions quite often threatened to give way. And given way they had, on many occasions, but only when Annie wasn't with him. He would never let Annie see her father crumble. He was determined to be her rock, no matter what.

Reaching Shelley's final resting place, he and Annie stood motionless for a few moments, words unnecessary right now. The little flower garden they had planted around the marble grave was dotted with things Annie had wanted here for her mum, including a bright colourful wind catcher that spun in the breeze and two angel statues that sat either side of it. Kneeling down, Dylan placed the bunch of flowers into the sun motif vase in the ground. Annie knelt down beside him, her hand coming to rest upon her mother's headstone before she leant in and kissed the photo of Shelley. Tears welled in her eyes, but she blinked them away. 'I miss you, Mummy. I hope wherever you are you're having fun today.'

Dylan tried to swallow the lump in his throat as he sat on the grass and folded his legs. Then, gently pulling Annie onto his lap, his arms surrounded her protectively as he gave her a kiss on the head. 'I'm sure Mummy is having loads of fun up there in heaven, especially with your great-nanna Edith. And she'd want you to be having fun too.'

Annie fumbled with the bow on her pretty pink dress—she always wanted to dress up when coming to visit her mum. Her bottom lip quivered. 'I try and have fun but sometimes it's really hard when I'm missing her.'

'I know it's hard, sweetheart. I miss her a lot too. But when I get upset I imagine her standing in front of me telling me to put on a happy face. You know, like that song she used to sing to you all the time.'

Annie giggled, her wet eyes glistening. 'I love that song, even though Mummy sang it way out of tune.' She sighed, smiling softly. 'Daddy, do you really think Mummy can hear me when I talk to her? 'Cause I talk to her a lot…'

Dylan squeezed Annie's hands reassuringly. 'Of course she can, sweetheart. Even though we can't see her, Mummy is with us all the time now. She stays alive in our hearts, and our minds.'

'You always say that, Daddy. But how do I *really* know she is with me all the time, and you're not just saying that to make me feel better?'

Dylan drew in a breath as he stroked Annie's face, taking a few moments to gather the right words. 'Well, sometimes in life, we have to just believe in things we can't see, Annie.'

Annie tipped her head to the side, taking in Dylan's words, her brows furrowed. 'You mean, kind of like Santa, and the Easter bunny, and the tooth fairy?'

Dylan smiled at her uncomplicated comparison. 'Yup, that's exactly what I mean.'

Cuddling into Dylan, Annie looked up to the sky and smiled. 'I love you, Mummy.'

'Love you, Shell,' Dylan whispered before closing his eyes and lying back with Annie in his arms.

They usually spent an hour or so here, lying by Shelley's graveside, and as long as the weather held off, today would be no different. Sometimes, he and Annie would have a chat with Shelley about what they'd all been up to and the like, but today he needed to speak privately with her. There were things he needed to say that Annie shouldn't hear. So, silently, he asked Shelley to forgive him for having feelings for another woman, and begged her to somehow show him a sign that it was okay for him to move on with his life.

And it was at this instant that the black clouds parted for a few brief moments, allowing the sunlight to burst through in distinct golden beams right where he and Annie were lying, and at the edge of the cemetery a rainbow appeared in all its gloriousness. The sudden warmth brought goosebumps to his skin. He wanted to— *needed* to—believe this was a sign from his dear departed wife. And just as he'd told Annie only minutes ago, sometimes you just had to believe in things you couldn't see.

***

'I'll have to run in a minute, Tia. I think I can hear them coming up the driveway.' Renee pulled the curtains aside, watching as her pa's Land Cruiser came into view, followed by a cloud of dust. She'd tried to talk him into picking Nan up in the going-to-town car, but he refused to drive it, telling her his only means of transport were his feet, a horse or his Land Cruiser. 'Yup, they're back.'

'Okay, Reni, make sure you keep me updated on the lurve interest. It makes my boring life here a heck of a lot more interesting hearing all about yours. I still can't believe that your childhood sweetheart has simply walked back into your life. It must be fate, hey? Destiny and all that.'

Renee had told Tia about Dylan, but she wasn't going to mention the diary yet—not until she'd taken it to Craig and he'd looked it over. She didn't want to worry her friend unnecessarily. 'I know, mate. I can hardly believe it myself. Time will tell if it's meant to be, or not. As much as I'd love to dive in head first with him again there's a lot to work through before we know for sure, including the major factor that I don't live here anymore. I don't know how we're going to get around that. But I promise I'll keep you updated. At least I know he still has feelings for me—and that's a damn good start.'

'It sure is, Reni, so keep the faith that everything will work out how it's meant to, okay?'

'I will, honey, thanks.' Renee sighed. 'Far out, I miss you.'

'And I miss you—heaps! I'll try and visit you soon, before you come back home to Melbourne, if I can swing some time off work. I really want to meet this Dylan Anderson, especially seeing as I've heard all about him for the last decade. Who knows? I might just score myself a country boy while I'm there too and then we can both live happily ever after.'

Renee laughed. 'I'd love you to come and visit, and you never know—stranger things have happened.'

'Are there any potential hotties you can introduce me to?'

'There is this one guy, called Ralph. He's Dylan's best mate. I've known him since I was in nappies. He's a top bloke and good-looking to boot—he looks almost like Colin Farrell but with shaggy sun-bleached hair. I'd love to introduce you guys.'

'Ooh, really? I love Colin Farrell! He's one sexy beast. You'll have to send me a pic.'

'Next time I see him I'll sneak a photo and text it to you.'

'I'd love that. Thanks Reni, you little cupid you.'

'Yeah, well, you know me. I love love!' Out the window, Pa was trying to help her nan from the Toyota and Nan was defiantly shaking her head as she muttered indecipherable words. 'Shit, I gotta go, they're at it already… Thanks once again for looking after Kat, and my apartment.'

'Oh, I've trashed the place with all the parties I've been having, and Kat has turned feral and is pregnant with kittens, but my pleasure!' Tia replied, laughing.

'You smart-arse. I miss you!' Renee said, hopping on one leg and then the other as she pulled on her boots.

'Miss you too, mate. Say hi to your nan and pa for me. Bye,' Tia replied before hanging up.

Racing out and giving her nan a big hug, Renee had to stop herself from giggling as Pearl returned the embrace while still barking orders at Stanley to stop fussing. 'I told you, Stan, I'm not an invalid. I can very capably get out of the car and up the front steps. Yes, I had a heart attack, and I know you're worried about me, but my ticker is still ticking and that's all that matters in my eyes. I won't have you fussing all over me. It'll drive me darn batty!'

Looking over the bonnet of the Toyota, Pa rolled his eyes skyward, smiling cheekily. Renee certainly knew where she got her stubbornness from—the pair of them.

Stan sighed resignedly. 'Yes, dear, I know you believe you can take on the world and all, but—'

Pearl cut him off, her hands going to her hips. 'There will be no buts about it, Stanley Wildwood. You have enough to do around here without having to wait on me hand and foot. You'll end up giving *yourself* a bloody heart attack if you take on any more than what you're doing now. I know I'm no spring chicken, but I'm home and I'm going to get back to living my life just the way I used to. Any longer in that darn hospital bed and I would have grown roots into the mattress.'

'That's going to be my job, Nan—waiting on you hand and foot,' Renee piped in as she reached into the back of the Land Cruiser and grabbed Pearl's suitcase, the three of them heading up towards the front door of the homestead as the discussion continued.

Pearl's challenging gaze turned to Renee as they climbed the five front steps. 'Oh no it's not, love. Your job is to get back on that plane and get back to Melbourne, where I know you're safe.'

Renee placed the bag on the ground as she pushed open the front door and shook her head, mustering as much confidence as she could. 'Honestly, I feel safe here, Nan. No-one is going to hurt me.' *Thanks to Dylan protecting me,* she thought silently.

No way was she going to tell them about being followed at the ball last night. Hell, she wasn't even sure now that anyone had been following her—maybe her fears and a good dose of alcohol had conjured up something that wasn't even happening. Stepping into the dimness of the hallway, her eyes took a few seconds to adjust after standing outside in the sunlight—little white speckles floated like miniature fireflies in front of her.

'And I'm not going anywhere until I know you're back to a full bill of health. End of story.'

Although a little intimidated by her nan's defiant gaze, Renee matched her nan's stance and folded her arms too, just for good measure.

Pearl turned to Stanley, her eyebrows raised almost to her curly salt-and-pepper-coloured hairline. Her small frame did nothing to take away from the determination in her eyes. 'And what do you have to say about Renee staying here, Stanley?'

Renee noted the fact her nan had just called her pa by his full name. Things were getting serious. She stifled a smirk.

Stanley shrugged as he removed his boots and hung his tattered wide-brimmed hat on the hook at the doorway. 'Sorry, dear, but I tend to agree with Renee. I'm out working a lot of the time and I need to know there's someone at home with you—just for a little while. Mick, Dylan and me are making sure we keep a close eye on her, so there's nothing to worry yourself with.'

'I would like to say I'll take your word for that, Stan, but I still feel very uneasy about Renee being back here.' She huffed, shaking her head. 'And who's this Dylan anyway?'

'Dylan Anderson is my new right hand until Mick is fit enough to come back to work. And he's an old school friend of Renee's too, so that's a positive. I told you about him the other day at the hospital—I didn't think you were listening to me at the time, you were too busy reading your *Woman's Day*.'

'Did you? I *can* read and listen at the same time, and I do listen to everything you have to say, my dear. My memory has been a bit like a sieve lately, with everything that's happened, that's all. Dylan Anderson?' Pearl said out loud as she tipped her head to the side in thought and tapped her chin. 'Where do I know that name from?'

Stanley stepped inside, shutting the screen door behind him. 'He's Peter and Claire Anderson's son.'

Pearl sucked in a breath. 'I hope to God he is nothing like his hoodlum father? It was a blessing when that horrible man skipped town. I don't know Claire very well, but I've heard Peter left her in quite a state, the poor woman.'

'No, Pearl, Dylan's a good lad. I wouldn't have hired him if I had any doubts.'

Renee felt the urge to jump in. 'Pa's right, Nan. Dylan's nothing like Peter. He's actually a really charming guy. You'll love him when you meet him, I just know it,' she said a little too quickly, a stupid lovesick grin tugging at the corners of her lips. She bit her bottom lip to stop it spreading across her face. Nan knew her inside out and back to front, and she didn't want to give away her feelings for him. Not just yet.

Pearl's mouth dropped open a little as she regarded Renee, a knowingness flickering in the depths of her hazel eyes. Then she smiled ever so slightly, cheekily almost. 'Is that so, love? I hope to meet him soon, then—just to make sure he's trustworthy, even though I do trust your pa's judgement.'

Shit, too late. Her nan could read her like a book. 'He'll be here for work tomorrow, I think, so you can meet him then if you like.' Renee looked to her pa for confirmation.

'No, he's not here tomorrow, but he will be the day after—on Tuesday. We have some fences to fix and a few of the horses to shoe.'

'Goodo then, I'll be sure to pop my head out when he gets here. But regardless of all these men keeping an eye out for you, love, I'm still very uncomfortable with you staying here because of me. I'd rather you got back home to your apartment, and got on with your life there selling those stupidly expensive houses.'

Renee smiled lovingly. 'My life is here, too, Nan. This is also my home, my *real* home for that matter.'

'But what about your work? Surely your boss can't be happy with you taking so much time off.'

'It's all sorted, Nan, so no need to worry yourself. To be perfectly honest, I think I needed a break from work. It was pretty hectic and I was starting to feel burnt out.'

The two women stared at each other for a few seconds, as if in a Mexican stand-off, until Pearl threw her hands up in the air in defeat. 'Okay, okay, I know I'm not going to win. But as soon as the doctors give me the all clear—' she pointed to Renee, '—you, my love, are going back to your other home.' She brushed her hands together as if satisfied she'd had the last word. 'Now, let's all go have a cuppa on the back verandah. I've been dying to sit out in the sunshine. I feel like I've gone mouldy in that hospital.'

Renee got to helping her nan make a pot of tea in the only-for-special-occasions fine china while Stanley cut the red velvet chocolate cake she'd baked yesterday in preparation for Nan's return home. Cake cut, Stanley excused himself as he wandered out to the back verandah with the plate, licking chocolate icing off his fingers.

Watching her nan flutter around the kitchen like a butterfly that had just emerged from its cocoon, Renee had to silently admit that Pearl was looking ten times better already. Being out of the hospital and back in the fresh air was obviously giving her some of her legendary oomph back. And this home was where her nan's heart lived—just like her own heart, if she was completely honest with herself. There was something healing about being here, that fixed you from the inside out.

'It's so great to have you home, Nan. I've missed having a woman here to chat to. The blokes just don't get us sometimes, you know?'

'It does get a bit lonely not having a woman about the house, hey love,' Pearl said as she stopped pouring the milk into the pitcher, her eyes coming to rest on the photo on the windowsill of Renee and Scarlet with their mother.

Renee followed her nan's soulful gaze, her heart squeezing for not only what she had lost but for the insufferable loss her poor nan had endured, firstly her only son and daughter-in-law, and then her granddaughter too. Parents weren't supposed to bury their children, and especially not their grandchildren—not that they'd had the chance to do that with Scarlet—and that made it even worse. 'I miss Mum and Dad and Scarlet every day, too, Nan. I wish they were all still here with us.'

'I believe they still are, in their own way,' Pearl said softly. 'I especially still feel Scarlet around the house.'

The unique scent of frankincense suddenly filled the room and Pearl turned to Renee as she closed her eyes and breathed in deeply—her unspoken words loud and clear. And then as quick as the aroma had arrived, it was gone.

Renee stared back at her nan in shock. 'You can smell that too? So I'm not going insane?'

Pearl nodded slowly as she opened her eyes. 'I sure can. I only used to get a whiff of it occasionally, like once or twice a year, and so fleetingly I wondered if I was imagining things, but over the last six months I've been smelling it a lot more. I just wish I could take her in my arms and feel her close to me again.' Pearl drew in a deep breath, and then sighed. 'I haven't told your pa any of this either—he'd think I've lost my bloody marbles—so keep it between us, okay?'

'My lips are sealed. I thought I was losing my mind at first, too, but now the scent gives me a weird type of comfort. I feel so much better now I know you can smell it too, Nan. And like you, I just wish there was a way I could reach out and touch her.'

Stretching up on her tippy-toes, Pearl cupped Renee's face, her five-foot frame only coming up to Renee's chest. Her nan's lashes were heavy with unshed tears. 'It's a blessing her spirit is still with us, but it does make me wonder what she's trying to tell us. If only ghosts could talk, hey.' She smiled gratefully. 'Thank you for coming home to take care of me. I really do appreciate it from the bottom of my heart. I've missed having you around all these years, my love.'

Renee choked back tears. 'You don't have to thank me, Nan. You'd do exactly the same for me. It's just what family is meant to do.'

Pearl kissed Renee on the cheek before turning back to the sink. 'I just hope we find her body before I pass on, so we can give her the burial she deserves. The hardest part is not knowing where she is, even after all these years. And I hope the cops find the horrible person that took her from us so they can get the justice they deserve.'

Renee placed her hand lovingly on Pearl's back, resolve filling her. She had to get the diary to Craig as soon as possible—at least that way she would feel as though she was doing something to aid their plight. 'We will find her, Nan. I have no doubt in my mind.'

'I do hope you're right. I've prayed for justice for Scarlet every single night, and I will keep doing so until my prayers are answered. God has to hear my pleas for help sometime, surely.'

'When the time is right, he'll heed your prayers, Nan,' Renee said, her voice cracking with emotion.

Sniffling, Pearl wandered back over to the fridge to pop the milk bottle back in. 'Anyways, my love, that's enough moping. Let's join your pa out the back before the old bugger thinks we're missing in action. He's probably eaten all the cake by now, knowing him and his sweet tooth.'

'He better not have eaten it all. I've been looking forward to devouring a piece or two of that cake all day,' Renee said, chuckling as she placed the last of the cups onto the serving tray.

Following her nan out of the kitchen, Renee's gaze travelled out the large bay window and off into the distance, where the Opals Ridge National Park met with the edge of Wildwood Acres. There had to be a defining clue out there somewhere, but where? It was like trying to find a needle in a damn haystack, but she wasn't going to give up—she couldn't. Something was telling her she was close, closer than she or anyone else had ever been to unravelling the tangled truth. Scarlet was making her presence known for a reason, and Renee was determined to finally give her beautiful sister the justice she deserved.

That evening, Renee chuckled to herself when she caught herself yawning and looked at her watch to find it was only eight thirty. She was already bone tired and longing to hit the sack, and the gorgeous sound of rain hammering down on the roof of the homestead was aiding her lethargy. If she were back in Melbourne she would still have a few hours of life left in her—going to bed before midnight an absolute rarity. But she now loved getting up early in the morning, the change of routine suiting her and the surrounds she was in. There was something so very satisfying about rising just before daybreak and watching from the back verandah of the homestead as the earth came alive.

Much as she loved city life, this place was taking hold of her again. Going back would be harder than she'd expected. And if she and Dylan decided to make a go of things, how in the hell was she meant to walk away from the two things in the world that truly owned her heart? She just couldn't bear to think of it.

Making sure Scarlet's diary was still tucked safely under her mattress—she'd rung the police station and Craig had informed her he was on late shift tomorrow, so she was going to drop it off in the afternoon—Renee climbed beneath the feathery pleasure of her doona, turned on her side, and then snuggled into her boomerang pillow. Her ears rang from the beautiful silence, and the pitch black of her bedroom made her body sink even further into blissfulness. Country life could be so delightfully peaceful.

It had been lovely sitting around the dining room table with Pa and Nan and Mick, enjoying a Sunday roast like the good old days—the only difference being that Renee had cooked it herself. And her nan had been very impressed by her culinary skills, even going back for a small helping of seconds, while Pa and Mick had devoured every last drop of the luscious minty lamb gravy with thickly buttered bread. Then it had been onto the bread-and-butter pudding, which she'd made from Nan's CWA cookbook. It had been lip-smackingly delicious and was just what the doctor had ordered, the four of them enjoying the simple pleasures of life while catching up over humble home-cooked food.

Closing her eyes, Renee's thoughts turned to Dylan, and she wondered how he was feeling about spending last night with her at the ball. He had seemed smitten when they had awoken still wrapped in each other's arms, but they had quickly parted ways before anyone could spot them together, only briefly chatting to each other again over the barbecue breakfast. They had swapped mobile numbers before saying their goodbyes, and she had been checking her mobile every ten minutes just to make sure it was turned on, but she'd heard nothing from him all day. The silence was killing her, although she wasn't going to hound him. He had enough on his plate to deal with at the moment. And he'd been very firm about the need to spend some time together as friends. All in good time, she hoped.

Just as she was about to slip into a peaceful slumber, her mobile phone beeped, sending her flying from the covers and over to her dressing table. Her heart flopped around like a fish on the end of a line when she spotted it was a message from Dylan. *Hallelujah!*

Hi Renee. Hope your nan is doing ok. Was wondering if you'd like to come out to my place tomorrow arvo for a swim and a BBQ with Annie and me? No worries if you can't.

Renee jiggled on the spot, excitement filling her completely. A swim and dinner...*and* she'd be meeting Annie. She understood this was a huge step for Dylan, introducing her to his daughter, even as a friend—kids were clever little beings—and she was honoured.

She couldn't wait to meet Annie in person. She texted him back straight away.

Hi Dylan. Nan is doing ok. I reckon she'll be back to her feisty self in no time. And I'd love to. Pa said he's only got half a day of work tomorrow so he'll definitely be around the house with Nan—I don't want to leave her on her own just yet, even though she keeps telling me she's fine! I'll be there around 5ish, if that's okay? I'll even bring a six-pack and some dessert. ☺

While waiting for him to reply, Renee did a happy dance around her bedroom. The love of her life was finally *back* in her life, even if it was just as mates. She wasn't sure if he was ready to commit to a relationship—or if he ever would be after losing his wife so tragically—but at the moment she was happy to take whatever Dylan was offering, and a firm friendship was a very good start. One step at a time, she reminded herself. The phone buzzed once again.

Sounds great, whenever you can get here is fine. Text me when you're leaving so I know to look out for you. I've got a bit of work to catch up on around the place but I won't be far away from the house. Catch you tomorrow. Sweet dreams beautiful lady. Xoxo

Renee grinned, feeling like she was seventeen all over again as she wrote back to him.

Okay, catch you then. I look forward to seeing your place and meeting Annie. Night. Dream sweet. Xx

Freefalling backwards with her arms stretched out wide, Renee collapsed back onto her bed, grinning for all of Australia. Between having her nan back home and being invited to spend the afternoon with Dylan and Annie, life was looking brighter. Tomorrow was going to be a wonderful day.

CHAPTER
18

It had only just gone past six in the morning, but life on Ironbark Plains was, as usual, in full swing. Never one to be a night owl, Dylan loved the early morning starts that country living brought with it, his land stealing his heart each and every morning he watched it come to glorious sunshine-filled life.

Leaning against one of the timber railings, he watched as three of his mum's prized silky bantams went tearing past where he and Annie were standing in the shade of the stables, followed closely by Annie's two pet ducks, Funky and Groovy. Bossy raced behind the clucking birds in hot pursuit, her long gangly Great Dane legs making ground fast as she barked animatedly. Claire hurried behind the crazy mob, straw broom in hand, hair in curlers with a hairnet tied over the top and her pink terry towelling robe flapping out behind her like a cape as she shouted at Bossy to stop. It was a sight to behold.

Annie giggled as she brushed Rascal and the horse turned his head to watch the commotion, nickering as if laughing at the chaos. Dylan had to agree with Annie and Rascal—it was highly amusing, although very naughty on Bossy's part. Bossy ignored Claire's pleas to stop and she finally gave up the chase, huffing and puffing and shaking her broom out in front of her. Dylan shook his head and whistled to his mischievous canine friend, commanding Bossy come to his side immediately. He knew Bossy wouldn't hurt a fly—unless it was to defend Annie—but the terrified birds clearly weren't so sure. Bossy skidded to a stop, eyeing Dylan and then the absconders before doing as she was told. Panting heavily, she charged over, then leant her eighty kilograms against him, almost knocking him over in the process. Bossy was forever leaning against people. It was a well-known loving trait of the Great Dane.

Dylan gave her oversized head a loving rub. 'You've really got to stop scaring them like that, Bossy. Every time you do it they stop laying eggs for a few days.' He leant in to whisper in her massive upright ear. 'That really pisses Ma Anderson off, and you don't want to do that because then you won't be getting any treats off her in the near future.'

As if on cue, Claire came up beside them, out of breath and clearly not impressed. She wagged her finger and Bossy eyed her like a naughty child before dropping her head. 'Yes, you know you shouldn't be doing that, you cheeky thing. Stop chasing my chickens, and Annie's ducks, or I'll smack you on the backside with my broom.' Claire shook the broom for good measure and Bossy eased her way behind Dylan.

Dylan observed Bossy, smirking. 'Don't you hide behind me, you chicken.' He laughed out loud, winking at his mum. 'Get it? *Chicken*? You know… Bossy was chasing the chickens, and well, bad joke… Forget it.'

Easing herself down awkwardly, Bossy lay on the ground, both of her paws resting on Dylan's boots, as she appeared to sulk. He had to stifle a chuckle. She was a clever dog and knew she'd done wrong. She'd got into trouble countless times for chasing the chickens and ducks, so clearly the fun was well worth the stern talking to.

Claire rolled her eyes at Dylan, her frown disappearing as she giggled. She gave him a quick peck on his cheek. 'It's great to hear you joking about again, son. I think the psychologist is helping you a lot.'

Dylan smiled as he observed Annie and Rascal. 'Yup, she sure is. It's like magic. Even after two visits I'm already feeling a heck of a lot better than a few weeks ago—and I haven't had one nightmare since I spoke to her. I've got another appointment at the end of this week.' He turned to his mum. 'Thanks for keeping on my case about going to her, Mum. I reckon I'm actually ready to put Shelley's things away—' he touched his wedding ring tenderly, '—and maybe even take this off... *Maybe.*'

Claire reached out and squeezed Dylan's arm, her eyes full of compassion as she blinked quickly. 'That's so very wonderful to hear. I know it's going to be hard for you, but it really is time you let go, so you can move forward. I can help you pack up her things if you like.'

'No, I need to do it on my own, but thanks for the offer.'

'Okay then.' Claire smiled lovingly. 'I'm proud of you, Dylan, getting help like you have. It's a big step.'

'Thanks, Mum.'

Claire waved to Annie, who'd finished brushing Rascal and was now standing with her arms wrapped around the horse's neck in a loving embrace. 'Morning sweetheart.'

Annie waved, smiling her even more toothless grin after losing another baby tooth yesterday. 'Morning Grammy. I'm going to ride Rascal soon.'

'I know, how exciting. You be careful though, won't you.'

Annie rolled her eyes. 'Oh Grammy, I will be.'

'She'll be right, Mum,' Dylan piped in.

'I know, I know. I just worry, that's all.'

Dylan chuckled. 'I know you do, you're a professional worry wart.'

'Now now, you cheeky bugger,' Claire said, smiling. 'I'd love to stay and watch but you know I get too nervous watching Annie on a horse, and then I'll make her nervous. I'd better get back home anyway and get ready—it's bingo day at the community hall and I've offered to help with morning tea. What are you up to for the day, seeing you don't have to go over to Stanley's?'

'Ralph's coming over today to make a start on the dam.' Dylan paused, wondering whether to tell his mum Renee was coming over, or not. He didn't want to make a big deal of it, but in fact it *was* a big deal when he really thought about it. And as if his mum wasn't going to come over and say g'day when she spotted a woman wandering around the place with him—she wouldn't be able to help herself. 'Oh, and I've invited Stanley's granddaughter, Renee, over for a swim and an early dinner this arvo.'

Claire's eyebrows shot up. 'Renee Wildwood is back in town? Oh how wonderful.' She dropped her voice so Annie couldn't hear. 'I'm guessing that might be why you've got a bit of a spring in your step—you two used to date, didn't you?'

Dylan groaned silently. So much for playing it cool. Claire Anderson never missed a beat. He seriously believed she had eyes in the back of her head. 'Oh, yeah, we dated on and off before she left town. It was nothing too serious.' *A white lie never hurt anyone.*

Claire tutted. 'I wasn't born yesterday, Dylan Anderson. I remember how distraught you were when she left town so suddenly. But you were at that sensitive age where a boy didn't want his prying mother getting involved in affairs of the heart, and you were already going through so much with your father doing what he did to me and taking off the way he did, so I stayed out of it. You moped around for ages after she'd gone.'

A red-faced Dylan shook his head in amazement. She was as sharp as a tack. 'I can't hide anything from you, can I Mum? Yes, okay, I liked her a lot. But things have changed. She and I are adults now, with responsibilities, and we're just friends.'

Who am I trying to kid, Mum or myself?

Claire smirked cheekily, a glimmer in her eyes giving away her thought process. 'Just friends, hey? Well it's good you have a new *friend*. Am I allowed to meet her this afternoon?'

'Yes, Mum, you're more than welcome to meet her. It's not like I have any reason to hide her away from you, or anyone else for that matter. You can even join us for some grub tonight if you want.'

'Ooh, I'd love that. Are you sure that's okay? I won't be intruding?'

Dylan smirked. 'No, you won't be intruding. The more the merrier.'

'Great, I'll make a potato salad and some coleslaw. You just take care of the meat, and your *friend*.' Claire emphasised the last word once again.

'Haven't you got somewhere you need to be?' Dylan said lightheartedly.

'Okay, okay, I'm off,' Claire said, laughing. 'Bye Annie. See you this afternoon darling. Have a good day at school, won't you.'

'I will. Bye Grammy,' Annie called back, waving enthusiastically.

Spinning on her heels, Claire headed back towards her granny flat. 'See you tonight, Dylan. Looking forward to it,' she called over her shoulder as she waltzed away, stopping momentarily to do a very discreet, but still noticeable, happy jig.

Dylan found her enthusiasm for Renee endearing, and encouraging. It made him feel a hell of a lot better that his own mother thought it was okay for him to have a lady friend over. Claire had been very close to Shelley, and it gave him that little bit more of a shove to step forward into his future, rather than living in the shadows of his past. First things first, though, he wanted Annie to meet Renee, and see how they were around each other, before things went any further. Because as much as he'd love to just follow his heart and see where it led, Annie came first, no matter what. Then, they had the massive hurdle of the long-distance to deal with. It was a well-known fact that most long-distance relationships never lasted.

But one thing at a time. He hadn't told Annie about Renee yet— he would after she'd ridden Rascal. He was nervous about how she would react to having a woman as a guest in the house and he didn't want to risk upsetting her before her very first ride on Rascal.

By seven o'clock, the already intense sunshine was gradually creeping its way across the dusty ground of the round yard, its golden warmth gratifying. With Rascal now saddled up and lunged, Dylan motioned for Annie to join him. Jumping up from where she was cuddled into a sleeping Bossy, she raced towards him, only slowing down to enter the round yard so as to not scare Rascal. Pulling on her riding helmet, she buckled it up, her legs jiggling with excitement.

His little darling had been up well before dawn, racing to his bedside with her teddy in her arms as she'd begged him to wake up, gracing him with her broad gappy smile as soon as he'd opened his eyes. It felt damn good to know he could bring happiness to her life after all she'd been through. And it was also spirit-lifting to see today was going to be a famously beautiful Far North Queensland winter's day, especially after the rain yesterday. It meant that he, Annie and Renee would be able to enjoy a swim in the pool before cooking up a storm on the barbecue tonight. His belly backflipped with the thought of her visiting—in a very good way.

Dylan grinned as he adoringly cupped Annie's cheeks. 'Righto, sweetie, this is it. You're finally going to ride Rascal. How are you feeling?'

'Oh my goodness, Daddy. I'm so excited I could almost pee my pants!'

'Far out, Annie, the way you explain things sometimes is just priceless.' Dylan chuckled as he leant over and clasped his hands together, giving his little girl a leg up and onto the calmly waiting horse.

Getting comfortable in the saddle, Annie beamed like it was Christmas. 'I can't believe I have my very own horse now. All the girls at pony club are going to be so excited when I tell them.'

Dylan took hold of the lead rope. 'Yep, no more having to use Turbo. But remember that a lot of responsibility comes with owning a horse too. It's not just all fun and games.'

Annie huffed, but the smile never left her lips. 'I know, Dad. You've told me that a hundred billion trillion bazillion times already.'

'Just checking you remembered,' Dylan said, stifling a smirk as he enticed Rascal to follow him around the yard. 'I'll lead you around a couple of times, and then you can take control of the reins, okay?' Annie was a very confident rider thanks to almost three years at pony club, and the hundreds of hours he and Shelley had spent with her in the saddle at home. He just wanted to get Rascal used to having her on his back first.

'Okey-dokey,' Annie replied as she sat proudly.

After five steady laps, during which Rascal seemed to have no problem with her whatsoever, Dylan let Annie ride by herself.

Standing in the centre of the round yard with his arms folded, he watched her do her thing, her horseriding abilities something he was extremely proud of. A few times he nearly went to give her advice, but bit his tongue, understanding that she needed to find her own style and rhythm.

And Rascal listened to everything she asked him to do with her subtle cues and calm commands. Horseriding was definitely something Annie had in the blood, not just skills learnt from being taught. She was a natural at it, just like he was. It made him wonder if she would work with horses when she grew up. Looking at his watch, he noticed that half an hour had slipped by like it was merely five minutes. Dylan quickly motioned for Annie to stop. 'Time to get ready for school now, sweetie, otherwise you're going to miss your bus. You can have another ride this afternoon, as soon as you get home.'

'Okay Daddy,' Annie said, still beaming just as much as she'd been when she'd first got on Rascal.

Helping Annie down, Dylan then gave the horse a rub on the neck. 'Good boy. Thanks for taking care of her—I knew you had it in you.'

Rascal gave him a loving nudge with his muzzle before Dylan led him over into the shade of the stables. 'I'll be back to unsaddle you soon, buddy, and give you a bit of a bath. And I'll even bring you an apple to munch on for being such a champ.'

Annie stood in front of Rascal and he dropped his head. She giggled and gave him a kiss on the cheek. 'I love you, Rascal. You're my bestest friend ever.'

'I reckon you're Rascal's bestest friend ever, too, sweetheart,' Dylan said, smiling.

Annie grinned back at him, her eyes sparkling with happiness.

'Come on then, we better get a move on.' Dylan took her hand and led her out of the stables towards the homestead. No more procrastinating, it was time to tell her about Renee. His stomach did a cartwheel. 'I have a friend coming over to have dinner with us tonight.'

Annie looked up at him, her eyes widening. 'Yay! I hope it's Uncle Ralph. I haven't seen him for ages!'

Annie had always called Ralph her uncle, because even though they weren't tied by blood, Ralph was like a brother to Dylan.

'Um, no, it's not Uncle Ralph. It's actually someone you haven't met before. Her name is Renee. I used to be friends with her years ago, before she moved to the city. She's back in town for a little while so I thought it'd be nice for her to come over so you can meet her.'

Annie sat down on the verandah as she struggled to get her boots off, contemplation creasing her pretty little face. 'Oh, it's a girl. Will I like her?'

Dylan knelt down to help her. 'I reckon you will. She's very nice.'

Annie frowned for a second as she thought about that, and then smiled. 'Well that's good, because I wouldn't like her if she wasn't nice, and I hope she likes horses too, because I only really like people who like horses.' And with that she jumped up and skipped into the house without a care in the world.

Hands on hips, Dylan blew out the breath he'd been holding. He'd been so bloody nervous about telling Annie he'd given himself a stomach-ache. Now he wondered why he'd even concerned himself in the first place. Annie was clearly unperturbed by Renee having dinner with them—bless her beautiful little heart. He rolled his eyes at himself—as usual, he was clearly overthinking things. He just needed to take a deep breath, and relax, and also remind himself he wasn't doing anything wrong, by Annie or Shelley.

After removing his boots, he wandered into the house and towards the kitchen, hankering for his morning cuppa. Flicking on the jug, Annie's singing floating out from her bedroom made him break into humming himself. Life was looking up, and maybe the miracle he'd been begging for had arrived, in the form of Renee Wildwood. A bubble of anticipation filled his belly as he spooned a heaped teaspoon of Nescafé into his cup, followed by two heaped teaspoons of sugar. Looking down at his wedding ring, he felt a surge of emotions. It was time.

'I'm sorry, Shell,' he whispered. Carefully placing his fingers around the gold band, he slowly eased it over his knuckle and down the tip of his finger, the white mark left in its place proof of the fact he hadn't taken it off since the day Shelley had put it on him. He waited for a flood of guilt to pound his heart, but much to his surprise, it didn't. There was sadness, and a sense of loss, but no guilt. Holding the ring up, he kissed it—grateful he'd got to share a beautiful piece of Shelley's life. Then, clasping it in his hand, he carried his coffee into his bedroom and placed the ring back in its original box in his bedside drawer. He would give it to Annie one day—maybe for her twenty-first.

Tears threatened to fall, but he blinked them away, confident he was doing the right thing. After Annie had headed off to school he was going to pack up Shelley's things from the dresser. As Theresa Wise had said in their last session, he didn't need material things to remember Shelley, because her memory would forever live in his heart.

***

Stretching her arms high in the air, Renee sprung up on her tippy-toes and beamed at the awakening world outside the kitchen window. She'd had a brilliant sleep and was raring to go for the day. The glorious morning sunlight was beginning to creep its way beneath the back door, the handmade glass sun-catcher at the bay window propelling a spectrum of colours across the centre island bench and onto the walls. Perched up on the lower round yard rail, Rocket the rooster was making his presence known, his cock-a-doodle-doos boisterous and very macho indeed. In the horse paddock, Jackson was doing his morning ritual of prancing around the fence line as he tried to impress the mares in the paddock next to his. Renee smiled at her horsey mate—he was a character unto his own. She couldn't wait to get outside.

Giving her bright-looking nan a quick peck on the cheek, she excused herself from the kitchen. Pearl graced her with a smile before turning her attention back to the newspaper spread out in front of her on the dining table, her glasses perched so far down the end of her nose that Renee was very surprised they were staying put and not falling into her bowl of Weetbix. Stanley had just left for the day with his thermos and packed lunch, and with a firm promise he would be back by mid-afternoon. She'd told them both as soon as seeing them this morning that she was heading over to Dylan's for a swim and dinner, and she'd been met with wispy smiles and raised eyebrows, before both her nan and pa had said, 'That's wonderful, love,' at the exact same time.

Talk about being in tune with one another. It had shocked her a bit, as they'd never supported her when it had come to having close male friends before—but then a lot could change in nine years, especially considering she was a grown woman now and at an age where she should be getting married and having kids of her own.

Balancing her trusty MacBook Air in one hand and a steaming cup of coffee in the other, while also holding a piece of thickly smothered guava jelly toast between her teeth, Renee used her bare foot to push open the back screen door. It took a certain kind of pizzazz to get through the door before it closed again, with coffee un-spilt, computer still in hand and toast still between teeth, and making it through unscathed, Renee grinned at her dexterity. Although now her knickers had crept up her butt and she didn't have a hand free to fix the problem. She wriggled carefully on the spot, but it didn't help a bit.

Placing her coffee on the nearby side table, she readjusted her knickers and denim shorts before easing herself into the suspended swing chair. She crossed her legs and placed the computer in her lap, making herself comfortable, and then looked out over the sweeping countryside. Her eyes took a few moments to adjust to the brightness, and once they did, she let out a contented sigh. Wildwood Acres was such a breathtaking place—she felt blessed to have been waking up to it the last few weeks.

If only she didn't have her job to go back to in the city. She'd give almost anything to be waking up to this beautiful countryside for a while longer, especially now Dylan was back in her life. Talk about life throwing her a curve ball. She'd come home expecting it to be a challenge to be back here, but it was turning out to be quite the opposite. She was now finding it more of a challenge to think about going back to Melbourne—her heart aching more and more each time she thought about it. If only she could just go back and grab Kat, put her apartment on the market, entice Tia into moving to Opals Ridge too, and then return to live out the rest of her days happily ever after with Dylan. After discovering who Scarlet's abductor was first, of course—because until she did that, there would never ever truly be a happily ever after. Ah, dreams.

'Where are you, Scarlet?' she whispered as she blinked back tears. God, how she missed her. If Scarlet were here, she definitely knew what she'd have to say about her dilemma—her sister was forever telling her to believe in the power of fate.

Don't be such a stick in the mud, sis. Life is meant to be lived—not planned down to the very last second. Take a chance, jump off the cliff…

But if I don't plan anything, Scarlet, how am I ever going to get anywhere? You can't leave everything to chance and expect to get what you want.

Why the heck not, Reni? It's loads more fun that way. And who knows? You might get even more than you'd imagined.

Renee smiled softly at the recollection. Scarlet truly was a wise soul. Maybe she should, for once, follow her free-spirited sister's advice. Opening her laptop, Renee felt a massive bubble of anticipation. She had planned to scout for new properties in Melbourne that she could add to her growing portfolio but instead she typed in 'Properties for sale, Opals Ridge and surrounding areas', and was pleasantly surprised when eighty-seven listings popped up. The bubbles of anticipation turned into a rush of enthusiasm. She didn't need to live in the city to make the income she had grown very accustomed to, she could make a very comfortable income here in Opals Ridge too.

Where there's a will there's a way…

***

Pulling up beside where Ralph was hard at work in the dozer, Dylan held up the small esky and pointed to it. Inside he'd packed ham and salad sandwiches, chocolate chip muffins his mum and Annie had made yesterday, and a few cans of Coke. Ralph nodded and gave him the thumbs up. Dylan parked his Land Cruiser under a nearby jacaranda tree, so he and Ralph would have some shade, and then jumped out and sauntered over to the place his new dam would be, followed by Bossy, who'd been riding shotgun on the passenger seat.

The loud drone of the dozer suddenly ceased and Ralph leapt from the driver's seat. 'So how's it looking, buddy?' he called out.

'It's looking bloody excellent, Ralph. I can't believe it's already taking shape.'

In the six hours he'd been at work, Ralph had achieved a lot. He joined Dylan at the edge of the dam wall he'd been working on and gave Bossy a friendly pat on the head. 'Yup, I don't mess about.' He pointed down. 'I'm packing the soil up nice and tight to give you good firm foundations. We don't want the bugger to give way once the water's in there.'

Dylan used the toe of his boot to gently tap at the top of the dirt Ralph was compacting. It was almost like kicking cement. 'She's pretty solid.'

'Told you, I don't mess about,' Ralph said, chuckling. 'Come on, let's eat before I chew my own arm off. I'm starving.'

Dylan shook his head and laughed. 'You're always bloody starving. You must have hollow legs or something because I don't know where you put it all.'

Sitting down in the shade, the men unpacked the esky and began devouring the goodies inside. Dylan had even brought Bossy her own sandwich. This she inhaled in three seconds flat, and then lay down beside them, minding her own business other than the very occasional sneaky look to the side, knowing full well it was bad manners to bother humans while they ate.

Not much more was said while Dylan and Ralph filled their bellies. After a minute, the hum of an approaching diesel engine made Bossy look up. The noise was coming from the fence line that separated the property from Craig's.

Spotting his neighbour, Dylan gave a wave. Craig waved back as he pulled up in the shade of a tree.

'Was he all right about you doing this?' Ralph said quietly, smiling in Craig's direction as he stepped out of his vehicle. 'He looks a little pissed off. And we don't want to be pissing off the town copper, no siree.'

Dylan grinned. 'Craig always looks pissed off. Comes with the territory of being a copper I think, and everything else he's dealing with too—you know about the separation? He seemed fine about the dam when I asked him about it the other day. Said as long as I wasn't taking his water allocation it didn't bother him.'

'Hey boys, how's it going?' Craig called out. He jumped the fence and stopped to inspect the beginnings of the dam in typical investigative copper style—eyebrows scrunched, hands on hips, eyes taking everything in.

'Yeah, good.' Dylan held up a can of soft drink. 'Wanna join us for a drink? Only got Coke though.'

Craig nodded, leaving the dam behind him, and strolled over. He took the can from Dylan's outstretched hand, remaining standing as Dylan and Ralph sat. 'Thanks, mate.' Bossy jumped up from where she was lying, went over to Craig and leant on him, almost bowling him over with her eighty or so kilos. Craig chuckled as he gave her a few taps on the head. 'You look ferocious, don't ya Bossy, but you're just a big teddy bear to those that know you.'

'Day off?' Dylan said, smiling at the way Bossy was lapping up Craig's attention.

'Nah, I'm on late shift today.' Craig took a swig from his Coke and then pointed back to the massive hole in the ground. 'Did you check with the council before doing this, to make sure there were no approvals you needed first?'

'Sure did. They were very supportive of it, actually. Said it's a good way to save on water usage.'

Craig nodded. 'Just don't want either of you getting into any trouble. The council's so bloody fussy with their rules and regulations.'

'It's all good, Craig,' Ralph said lightheartedly. 'I've built plenty of dams before. I know the rules and Dylan's following the council's guidelines.'

'Well, it's good you're the man on the job then.' Craig was squinting, but it was hard to know whether it was from the sun, or because he was just in a bad mood. 'You don't want a half-arsed job, hey Dylan.'

'Definitely not. But Ralph's a pro at jobs like this so no worries about that.'

'That's good to hear.' Craig sculled the last of his can, burping loudly at the end of it. 'I better be off, got a bit to do before I head into the station. Just wanted to check in to see how it was looking—' he smirked playfully, '—and to make sure you weren't doing anything against the rules.'

'It's all above board, Officer,' Ralph piped in, chuckling.

'Good lads,' Craig said, smiling for the first time. Turning, he crushed the now-empty can and tossed it into the back of Dylan's ute with a clutter. 'Catch you both later, and don't be doing anything I wouldn't do.'

'Any further luck finding out who's cutting my fences?' Dylan called after him—slightly annoyed that Craig had taken it upon himself to use the back of his ute as a bin.

'Nope, but I'll be sure to let you know as soon as I have anything substantial. You just do your job, Dylan, and let me do mine, and it'll all pan out just the way I expect it to,' Craig replied, not bothering to turn around as he headed for his four-wheel drive.

'Right, okay, thanks,' Dylan said a little curtly. 'For nothing,' he mumbled under his breath.

Ralph leant into his space. 'Shit man, was that a little bit of attitude I could hear? What's up?'

Dylan grunted. 'No idea. I'm just tired of feeling like my problems here don't matter. Some bastard is trying to ruin my livelihood—and getting away with it—while Craig takes his own sweet time to find out who it is. It's like he's lost all interest in the job he used to take so seriously. I reckon he needs a holiday or something.'

'Yeah, the poor bastard, can't help but feel sorry for him. It'd be hard losing your wife and kid to another bloke,' Ralph said before shoving the last of his sandwich in his mouth.

'I've tried to talk to him about it, but he clams up and just says he's better off without her…but that's just the bitterness talking I reckon.'

'Understandable. He's been a different man since Louise left. But what do you do? The bloke's obviously heartbroken. Anyways, with the amount of bloody cameras you've put up around the place, I'm sure you'll catch whoever's responsible soon,' Ralph said while pointing to a camera perched high up in the jacaranda tree above them. 'How in the hell did you get that one up there?'

Dylan's frown broke as he grinned. 'With great difficulty. I almost fell out of the bastard of a thing trying to get the camera attached—haven't climbed a tree in years.'

Ralph looked impressed. 'Well, hurrah to you for not breaking a leg, mate. What are you up to tonight anyway? Wanna come down the pub for a couple?'

'Nope, and I've got a good reason why I can't, too.' Dylan tried not to smile like an idiot as he pretended to clean an imaginary smudge off his sunnies.

'And what's that? You got a hot date?' Ralph replied, lightheartedly shoving Dylan as he laughed out loud.

'Kinda sorta something like that,' Dylan said, grinning.

'Holy shit! Really? Who?'

'Renee Wildwood.' Her name felt so good rolling off his tongue.

'No! Really? She's turned into an absolute stunner. I almost didn't recognise her at the Studs and Fuds the other night!' Ralph poked Dylan in the ribs. 'I wondered if there was anything going on between you two at the ball—especially when you disappeared around midnight. Go you good thang!'

Dylan recoiled from the jab in the ribs, laughing. 'She's only coming over for a barbecue and a swim, nothing serious. And Mum and Annie are going to be there too. So it's not like anything's gonna happen.'

Ralph wriggled his eyebrows. 'There's always afterwards, when your mum and Annie have gone to bed.'

'Oh lay off, Ralph, it's not like that. She's a mate, and that's that,' Dylan lied.

'Oh come on, stop trying to play it down. Remember, I know you. Any chick coming to your pad is pretty serious, Dylan. I don't think you've had another woman in the house since Shell, have you? And you can't include your mum in this either.'

Dylan shook his head, his smile fading. 'Nope, I haven't. You don't think it's wrong of me, do you? Like I'm disrespecting Shelley in some way?'

Ralph put his arm around Dylan's shoulder and gave him a manly squeeze. 'Mate, in no way are you disrespecting Shelley. I reckon it's great you've got a new lady friend. It'll be good for you, and for Annie. As much as it hurts sometimes, the world keeps on spinning after people pass away. It's a fact of life.'

'You really reckon I'm doing the right thing?'

'I sure do. It's about time you got on with your life, buddy.' Ralph gave Dylan a few hearty slaps on the back. Stepping back, he smiled, his eyes full of mischievousness. 'Has she said any more about introducing me to that friend of hers she told me about? Tia, I think her name was?'

Dylan laughed. 'I'm not sure yet—it's only been a couple of days—but don't worry. I'll be sure to let you know.'

Ralph gave him the thumbs up. 'Great stuff, thanks mate. It can get a bit lonely playing the bachelor all the time. Believe it or not, I want to find me a good woman to settle down with soon. This single life is getting old.' He pointed over towards the bulldozer. 'Anyhoos, I better get back to it.'

'Okay mate. Thanks for the pep talk.'

'Any time,' Ralph said. 'That's what mates are for.'

Dylan watched him wander back to work as he packed up the esky. It was good to know both his mum and Ralph thought it was time to move on with his life. He just hoped Annie felt the same.

CHAPTER
19

Pulling up out the front of the police station, Renee felt as though she could quite easily throw up. She took a deep breath and exhaled it slowly, trying her best to calm down. So many emotions were churning inside her right now—fear, anxiety, uncertainty—and somewhere within all that there was also hope that what she was about to do would lead them to Scarlet's killer, that somehow Craig would see something hidden within the words that she hadn't.

She turned the ignition off and grabbed the diary out of her handbag, but didn't open the door yet. For a minute she sat with it in her lap, tears starting to make her vision blurry. Blinking them away, she traced her fingers over the writing on the front, her heart aching. Was she doing the right thing by handing it in? She knew she should, that there might be some evidence inside, but part of her didn't want to let it go—it was the very last piece of Scarlet's thoughts and feelings she had left.

Before she could change her mind, Renee carefully placed it back in her handbag before tugging the strap over her shoulder. Then, determinedly, she opened her door and stepped from the car, making sure to blip it locked before she strode towards the station's front doors. They automatically slid open and she stepped through them. Craig was standing at the counter, sorting through paperwork. He looked up and smiled.

'Hi, Renee, I was wondering if you were going to make it today.'

'Hi, Craig, yeah, sorry, got waylaid at home helping Nan with a few things.'

Craig leant on the counter with his forearms. 'So what is it I can help you with?'

Renee stepped forward on shaky legs as she reached into her handbag. 'Well, I found this the other day—' she placed the diary on the counter in front of him, '—and I was wondering if you could have a read through it for me, see if maybe you can pick up on any clues.'

Craig placed his hand on top of it and slid it towards him, his eyes widening as he read the words on the front. 'Is this—?'

'Yup, sure is. It's Scarlet's diary.'

Craig picked it up. 'Have you read it?'

Renee nodded. 'I have.'

Craig remained staring at the diary in his hands, his expression stern as he slowly shook his head as if in shock. 'Stupid question really.' He cleared his throat. 'Anything you want to talk to me about?'

'Sadly, nothing substantial, but I did find out she was in love with a man other than Billy Burton…'

Craig glanced up at her, his eyes wide. 'Go on…'

'…Frustratingly, she didn't name him.'

Craig groaned. 'That's a bugger. I wonder why she was being so secretive.' He went quiet for a few brief moments before he sighed and spoke again. 'Have you told anyone about finding it?'

'Only Dylan.'

Craig's eyebrows scrunched together. 'Dylan Anderson?'

Renee nodded. 'He's the one who talked me into bringing it to you.'

'Well, he's certainly correct in telling you to. This could contain the evidence we've been looking for.' He leafed through the first few pages. 'I'm gathering your grandparents know you've found it?'

'Um, no, and I'd prefer it if they didn't know, just until you've had a read through it and seen if there is anything worth investigating. After Nan's recent heart attack I don't want to burden her with any more stress, unless it's completely necessary.'

'Completely understandable.' Craig turned it over in his hands. 'We searched everywhere for this thing back when she first went missing.' He placed it on the desk beside him. 'Where'd you find it?'

'I was out exploring Wildwood Acres the other day and I found it hidden under the floorboards of the old hunter's shack.'

Craig's eyebrows shot up. 'Lucky find.'

Renee half laughed. 'It certainly was.'

The door behind Craig opened and a young copper walked through. 'Hey boss, sorry I'm a bit late. The missus needed me to drop her at some Tupperware party thingy.'

Craig turned. 'Hi Jake, no worries mate.'

Turning back to Renee, Craig glanced at his watch. 'Sorry to cut this short, but I have to be at an appointment. I'll be sure to let you know if anything grabs my interest when I read through it, okay?'

'Okay, thanks Craig, I really appreciate it.'

'Don't thank me, it's my job to make sure the bad guys are caught.' He gave her a hurried smile as he gathered his keys from the desk. 'And don't forget to give me a shout about those photos too.'

'I certainly will, when I get a spare minute.' Renee gave him a quick wave as she headed back through the sliding doors and into the late-afternoon sunshine.

There, she'd done it, and it felt good to know the diary was now in the hands of the law. Back when it had all happened, Craig had been very diligent in trying to find out who was responsible for Scarlet's disappearance, so she knew he'd do his very best to gather any sort of clues he could from the diary.

The intense glare of the setting sun made it hard to see the unfamiliar road ahead. On either side of the bitumen, endless fields of sugar cane swayed in the late-afternoon breeze, the fluffy pink flowers at the top of each cane reminding Renee of fairy floss.

Her mouth watered with the recollection of sucking on a piece of the cut cane stalk, the delicious raw vanilla flavour that is unique unto its own. She and Scarlet had loved the taste as kids, often riding their pushbikes to a nearby cane farm to nick a piece, and she wondered if she'd still love it just as much now. Only one real way to find out, but not right this minute. She had herself a date with one very sexy man.

And his daughter and mother—considering she lived next door Renee gathered his mum would join them for the barbecue. Butterflies swarmed her stomach. Holy crap. She had tried not to think about this fact all day, but now she was on her way to Dylan's, it was terrifying. What if the two most important women in his life didn't like her? Her belly did cartwheels with the thought. All she could do was be herself and hope for the best—and hope the little gifts she had brought along for Claire and Annie would help to break the ice.

Not far up ahead the winding blacktop ended, the asphalt appearing to dissolve into red dust. Remembering Dylan's warning to be very careful of the roos at this time of the day—apparently the long dirt road to his place was full of the unpredictable marsupials—Renee slowed down to seventy, even though she was still officially in a hundred zone.

Sitting up at the steering wheel like an old person with bad eyesight, all the while trying to find some shade from the sun visor, she kept a keen eye out for the turn-off to Ironbark Plains. Holding up her hand in a bid to give herself a bit more vision—it would be awful to have to call and cancel because she'd driven into a bloody cane field—she slowed even further as she hit the dirt. Just as she left the asphalt behind, a B-double truck that had been following her made use of the wide unlined road and overtook her, the truckie taking great pleasure in perving at her as he passed. She gave him a friendly wave, understanding it would get quite lonely being out on the roads day in day out with just the radio for company. He tooted his horn as he thundered past, Renee slowing down even further as she was almost swallowed up by the truck's trail of swirling red dust.

Approaching a T-intersection, the GPS she had borrowed from her nan spoke to her in its annoyingly fake accent: *Turn left, then make a sharp right, and then you have reached your destination.*

'Really?' Renee muttered, remaining stationary while glancing about and seeing nothing but a picturesque endless landscape devoid of any houses. After being told to make three U-turns in the middle of town only to end up heading in the original direction she was going before making the U-turns, she had a very strong urge to tell the computerised woman where she could shove her directions. But having become accustomed to using a GPS after living in Melbourne for so many years, she was afraid she'd get completely lost. She'd never been over this side of Opals Ridge before. She'd never had a reason to, until now. She took a gamble and switched it off—how hard could it be to find a couple-of-thousand-acre property?

Turning left, she stole a quick glance at the pecan pie beside her, extremely proud of her efforts. It had turned out beautifully, with the perfect balance of creamy, crunchy, nutty, sweet and sticky. She had wanted to try making one ever since tasting it in Las Vegas at a real estate conference and finding herself completely addicted to the mouth-watering pie with her very first bite, but today had been the first time she'd had a good enough reason. Living alone, she didn't often have the motivation to cook such elaborate things— salads and takeaway were her usual in Melbourne. She'd have to try her hand at making her other American favourite, clam chowder, now she had the cooking bug again. She adored being back in the kitchen, and being able to create culinary delights for those she loved. Living back at Wildwood Acres was giving her so much more time to do the things she adored, the kind of time that made life seem so much more gratifying.

Unexpectedly spotting the landmark Dylan had told her about—a mammoth anthill that would make a six-foot man appear to be a midget—Renee slowed the four-wheel drive down and took a sharp right turn, the beers she'd grabbed from the drive-through in town spilling from the box and rolling across the seat. She reached out to stop them falling onto the floor just as two kangaroos shot out from the scrub and bounded across the road in front of her. Slamming on the brakes, the Land Cruiser slid to a shuddering stop, and, as the irritating woman on the GPS had stated only minutes ago, Renee had reached her destination. As the dust cleared, Ironbark Plains sprawled out before her like a pair of welcoming arms, the countryside green and lush and inviting.

Her pulse rate returning to some form of normalcy after her near miss with two of Australia's icons, she drove through the open front gate and across the teeth-jittering cattle grid. Heading down the long drive, she admired the paddocks peppered with horses and cattle along the way. A windmill spun slowly in the distance as if in tune with the unhurried vibe of the countryside, and just over the rise she could spot the metal roof of the cottage aglow in sunshine. She smiled from within. Just like at Wildwood Acres, something about this vast, rugged, ancient landscape drew her like nothing else. Space, freedom and silence, pleasures she couldn't obtain easily in the city, were in abundance. This, right here, was her kind of paradise—the country girl inside of her now outshining the city girl she thought she had become.

With the charming cottage now in full view, Renee pulled off the drive and parked up beside Dylan's Land Cruiser. A little girl was playing in the front yard with a dog large enough to pass as a pony, her smile as wide as the woman's beside her. It was obviously Dylan's daughter and mother. Annie and Claire acknowledged her arrival with a wave. She waved back, her hand shaking a little. Now she was here, she was shitting herself.

Just calm down, she whispered to herself as she turned off the ignition and bent down to gather her handbag from the floor, her eyes coming back up to meet Dylan's baby blues as he suddenly appeared beside the driver's window. She fought to stop herself drooling. Wearing a half buttoned up flannelette and butt-hugging denim jeans, along with bare feet and a dazzling smile, he looked smoking hot.

'Howdy, Renee. Find the place okay?' His smile accentuated his striking dimples.

She wasn't about to own up to the fact she had used a GPS. How embarrassment! 'Hi, Dylan, sure did, was a cinch…thanks for the great directions. I stopped along the way and dropped the diary off to Craig, too.'

'That's great. I reckon that was the right thing to do.'

'Yeah, me too.' She dragged her eyes from where his chest peeked out from his button-up shirt and clambered down from the four-wheel drive. He reached out and touched her arm, sending what felt like lightning reverberating throughout her. She could almost swear her heart stopped for a second from the shock of it.

'You need a hand with anything?'

His voice was so husky, and God he smelt good. 'Um, yes please.' She reached back across the seat and grabbed the dessert, acutely aware of his eyes upon her as she did so. She turned and passed it to him, pleased with his reaction as he caught sight of the pie.

'This looks bloody amazing, Renee.' He licked his lips. 'What is it?'

'An American classic—pecan pie. One bite and you'll be addicted.'

'I already am.' With a quirked brow, he smiled charmingly. 'Hmm. You're a woman of many talents, Miss Wildwood.'

'Why thankya, but you haven't tasted it yet.'

'If it tastes as good as it looks, I'll have died and gone to heaven.'

The way his eyes were drinking her in as he said that made Renee wonder whether he was referring to her or the pie. God, how she wanted to reach out and rip his clothes off right now, to make love to him with reckless abandon. The thought made her feel flushed and she hoped her cheeks weren't as red as they felt. 'Well, the proof of the pudding is in the eating, as they say.' She rolled her eyes at her stupid choice of words as she reached across the seat once more to retrieve the beers and the shopping bag, relieved to be able to look somewhere other than in his deeply hypnotising eyes. Turning back to him she held up the beer. 'And I've also brought cold beverages.'

He grinned. 'You've thought of everything. Thanks.' He pointed to the bag she was now holding. 'And what goodies are hidden in there?'

'Oh, just a little something for your mum and Annie. I thought it might help break the ice between us.'

'Thanks Renee, but you didn't have to do that.' Hidden from any prying eyes by the Land Cruiser, Dylan balanced the pie in one hand and pulled her in by the waist with the other, giving her a kiss on the cheek. 'Thanks for coming. I hope I haven't thrown you in the deep end by inviting Mum to join us.'

Taken aback by his gesture, but tingling pleasurably from his touch, Renee smiled shyly. 'To be honest, I'm nervous as hell, but I'll be right.'

'If it makes you feel any better, I'm a little nervous too.' Dylan chuckled, his deep throaty laughter very sexy. 'God, look at us. Anyone would think we're bloody teenagers again.'

'I know, crazy huh?'

'Yeah, crazy, but in a good way.'

Silence fell between them. Renee's eyes were briefly drawn to Dylan's hand, where the gold wedding band he'd been wearing was replaced by a white suntan mark. He'd taken it off. As much as it broke her heart, knowing how hard it must have been for him to do that, it also filled her with hope and joy.

Oblivious to Renee's observation, Dylan smiled and motioned towards the house with a nod of his head. 'We should head on over and say g'day, and then we can jump in the pool before dinner if you like. Annie's hanging out for a swim.'

'Sounds like a plan.'

'Follow me. I promise my mum won't bite. She'll probably love you to death if anything.'

Dylan headed off towards the cottage, and Renee walked beside him, his easy-going nature helping to relax her. She wouldn't have guessed he was feeling nervous—he looked so cool, calm and collected. Claire met them at the gate while Annie remained playing with Bossy.

'Mum, this is Renee. Renee, this is my mum, Claire.'

'It's so lovely to meet you,' Claire said as she reached out and pulled Renee into a hug.

Renee hugged her back, feeling instantly at ease in her company. 'It's lovely to meet you, too, Claire.' She grabbed the bottle of local mango wine she had brought along for Claire from the bag and passed it to her. 'This is for you. I hope you like white wine.'

'I don't drink much, but when I do, white wine is my favourite, and I still haven't had a chance to try this one. Thank you, love, that's very kind of you.'

Renee breathed a sigh of relief. She shouldn't have been so worried. 'You're welcome.'

'While you settle in, love, I've just got to go over home and check on the potato bake. I was going to make potato salad but changed my mind at the last minute. We don't want to be eating charcoaled potatoes. Back in a jiffy,' Claire said as she toddled off towards her granny flat.

'Annie, come and say hello,' Dylan said, placing the pie and beers down on the outdoor table.

Happily obeying her dad, Annie jumped up from where she was rolling around on the ground with the giant dog, and skipped over towards them. Renee knelt down to greet her. 'Hi, Annie, I'm Renee.' She held out her hand. 'Nice to meet you.'

Annie smiled in a way that melted Renee's heart, the little girl's eyes full of vibrant life as she enthusiastically shook her hand. 'Hi Renee, it's nice to meet you too.'

The dog came skidding in beside Annie, clearly eager to meet their new guest.

'And who is this?'

'She's my dog, Bossy.' Renee reached out and gave her a rub on the head. Bossy responded by trying to lick Renee on the cheek, but she warded the doggy love off just in time, giggling.

Annie giggled too. 'Looks like she likes you.'

Renee stood, smiling. 'I reckon she might.' She reached into the shopping bag and pulled out a small box. 'I thought you might like this. It's a loom-band kit. You can make bracelets and necklaces, and even rings.'

Annie gasped with delight as she took the box from Renee's outstretched hand. 'Oh wow, I've seen these on telly.' She smiled gratefully. 'Thank you so much, I love it.'

'My pleasure. I can show you how to make them later, if you like.'

'I'd love that,' Annie said as she sat down on the ground and eagerly opened the lid, grinning as she began sorting through the multicoloured little elastic bands.

Dylan smiled appreciatively. 'That's so kind of you, Renee. Thanks.'

'That's okay, I'm glad she likes it.'

'So who's up for a swim?' Dylan raised his eyebrows at Annie, but the little girl was in a world of her own. 'Earth to Annie,' he added, chuckling, as he gently tapped her on the head.

Annie looked up at him, beaming from ear to ear. 'Yes, Daddy?'

'You still want to go for a swim, sweetheart?'

'Oh, yes please!'

'Well, you run inside and get changed into your togs then, okay?'

'Okay, Daddy.'

Watching Annie skip off inside the cottage with her loom-band kit tucked safely under her arm, Dylan turned to Renee and smiled.

'Looks like you've won a little girl's heart, and simply by just being your thoughtful self.'

'She's so beautiful, Dylan,' Renee said, returning his smile. 'No wonder she's your everything.'

'Yep, she sure is.' He stopped, searching her eyes. 'And so are you.' He reached out and tenderly stroked her cheek with his fingers. 'In a matter of minutes you've just made me feel like everything's going to be okay.'

His tone was so deep and rich Renee felt as though she was going to gain weight just by talking to him. 'I hope so, Dylan. I really do.' She placed her hand over his and the two of them stood staring into each other's eyes, words evading both of them.

'You need to get changed into your swimmers?' he said vaguely, his penetrating gaze making her feel giddy.

There was so much Renee wanted to say right now but instead she just nodded. 'Uh-huh.'

'Well, we better head inside and get changed then.'

'Uh-huh,' she said again, biting her bottom lip.

Turning around, Dylan made sure the coast was clear before bringing his lips hard up against Renee's, and with a quick swirl of his tongue he had her feeling as though her legs were going to give way yet again.

A few hours later, refreshed from a few fun dips in the pool and their bellies full from the delicious food, Renee and Annie sat together at the end of the alfresco table, an assortment of colourful bracelets and necklaces in front of them. Renee, Claire and Dylan also sported quite a few around their necks and arms and fingers.

Annie was beside herself with excitement as she gabbled on about all the friends she was going to give her newly made treasures to. Dylan watched on with a huge smile on his lips, conscious that it was half an hour past her bedtime but not wanting to break the magic between Annie and Renee. He would put her to bed soon. Claire sat beside him with a now almost-empty glass of wine in her hands, an equally happy smile lighting up her face.

'They're getting on like a house on fire,' Claire whispered.

'They surely are. It's like they've been best buddies for years,' Dylan said softly before taking a casual sip from his beer.

'It's beautiful to watch,' Claire said before she hiccupped. 'Oh dear, I think I've had my share of wine for the evening. Two glasses and I'm ready for bed. Talk about a wild party girl, hey.' She chuckled heartily as she stood, padding over to lay a kiss on Annie's head. 'Night my darling. I'll see you in the morning.'

'Night Grammy. Love you to the moon and back,' Annie said, blowing Claire a kiss.

'Love you 'til the cows come home,' Claire said fondly as she caught Annie's kiss and placed it upon her heart. She gave Renee a peck on the cheek. 'It's been really lovely meeting you, Renee. I hope to see you again soon.'

Renee stood and gave Claire a tight hug. 'Thank you for making me feel so very welcome tonight, and thank you for that yummy potato bake that I ate *way* too much of.'

'It's been my absolute pleasure. And thank you for my very first taste of pecan pie. You'll have to give me the recipe.'

'I'm so relieved you all liked it. It was the first time I've ever made it.'

'It's the best dessert I've ever tasted,' Claire said sincerely.

'I'll be sure to give you the recipe next time I see you.'

'That'd be lovely, Renee, thanks.'

'Night then,' Renee said as she went back to work with Annie on a necklace for her teacher.

'Night, son.' Claire leant in and gave Dylan a hug, making sure to keep her voice to a whisper. 'She's a keeper. Don't let her get away, will you?'

Dylan choked back emotions, his mother's observation meaning the world to him. 'I'll try my best not to.'

'Nighty night, then,' Claire said a little too loudly as she wobbled off in the direction of her granny flat, with Bossy close beside her. Bossy always walked her home before returning to her bed on the back verandah—forever the protective dog.

Dylan stood, tossing his empty beer bottle in the nearby bin. 'I've just got to duck to the loo, you two, and when I get back, it's time for bed, Annie.'

'Okay Daddy,' Annie replied sadly.

***

Bossy returned from walking Claire home just as Dylan disappeared into the cottage.

'Can I ask you something?' Annie said, expertly twisting a loom band onto another to form a chain.

'Sure, shoot,' Renee replied casually.

'Are you Daddy's girlfriend?'

'Um.' Renee's heart pounded. How in the hell was she meant to answer this? Honestly, she supposed, because really, she and Dylan weren't officially girlfriend and boyfriend. She relaxed, knowing she wasn't lying. 'Your daddy and me are just really good friends.'

'Well, you're really pretty and very nice so I think you would make a wonderful girlfriend for Daddy one day. He needs somebody other than Grammy and me to love him, so will you please have a think about being his girlfriend?'

Annie smiled at her with so much innocence that Renee wanted to just take her into her arms and hold her. This poor little girl had suffered immeasurable loss and heartache, and yet here she was, at only six years old, thinking of her daddy and what would be nice for him. And also welcoming Renee into their lives with open arms, and even more importantly, an open heart.

Blinking back tears, she reached out and gave Annie's little hands a gentle squeeze. 'Thank you, Annie, that means a lot. And I promise, I'll think long and hard about it.'

Annie thought for a few seconds and then tipped her head to the side. 'Do you like my daddy?'

'I think your daddy is a very lovely man, and I like him a lot.'

'Good, that's settled then. You have to be his girlfriend,' Annie said, beaming.

After Renee read her two books and then looked on as she used her nebuliser and explained how cool her locator watch was, Annie turned over and was now sleeping soundly in her bed.

Renee said her goodnights to Dylan in the darkness of the front verandah, wishing the night didn't have to end. She was enjoying the sensation of his arms around her waist, and the feel of his breath on her cheek as they stood staring out at the beautiful starlit night. Turning to face him, she clasped her hands around the back of his neck, her full lips curling into a smile as she admired his rugged features. 'You're one sexy man, Dylan Anderson, still just as damn hot as the first day I laid eyes on you. No, actually, I reckon you're even hotter now.'

Dylan rolled his eyes. 'Yeah right, whatever. You're the sexy one here. I haven't been able to keep my eyes off you all night.'

Renee felt her cheeks go warm with his compliment. 'Ditto.'

They were silent for a few moments as they contemplated one another, neither knowing what to do next. Dylan broke the silence.

'Thanks so much for coming over tonight. I'm really happy it all went so well. Mum and Annie absolutely adore you.'

'And I adore them. I feel like I've known them both forever already. It's a very comforting feeling.' Renee tucked her long hair behind her ears. 'I have to tell you something, though. Annie asked me if I was your girlfriend when you went to the loo.'

Stepping back, Dylan blew air through his lips as he ran his hands through his hair. 'Oh shit, really? She's too switched on for her own good, my little girl.' His eyebrows shot up in question, but his tone was still soft and gentle. 'What did you say to her?'

'Don't worry, I just told her we were really good friends, but then she told me I'd make a wonderful girlfriend for you and that I should think about being your girlfriend one day—' Renee chuckled softly, '—and then when I told her I'd think about it she said "Well that's settled then," and went back to making her loom bracelet like it wasn't a big thing.'

Dylan sank down on the edge of the well-used rattan chair, blinking wet eyes but refusing to let his tears fall. His emotions almost getting the better of him, he sucked in a deep breath and smiled. 'Oh bless her beautiful little heart. She's an old soul, Annie is. I swear to God she's been on this earth many times before.'

'I know, she's wise beyond her years. I just wanted to hug her so tight, Dylan.' Renee sniffled, her throat tightening with sentiment. 'She's just so damn loveable, it's beyond ridiculous.'

Dylan stood and wrapped both arms around Renee again, pulling her in until there was not an inch of space left between them. 'Tonight has gone even better than I could have ever imagined. The fact that you and Annie get on so well means the world to me. Thank you, Renee, just for being you.'

Renee sighed softly as her body melted into Dylan's. 'Thank you for trusting me enough to invite me...' She pulled her head back and gripped Dylan's gaze with hers, the soft moonlight illuminating his chiselled jaw in the most erotic of ways. 'I love you, Dylan Anderson. I always have, and no matter where this road we are on leads us, I will never stop loving you until the day I die.'

Dylan's smile spoke a thousand words. 'And I love you, Renee Wildwood, more than I ever have before, and tomorrow, I know I'm going to wake up loving you even more than I do now.' He let his hands drop from her waist and then he tenderly cupped her cheeks. 'I know you have a life back in the city, and I know I still have a few inner demons to deal with, and I know we have to take things slow for Annie's sake, but I'm willing to work through everything to be with you. Are you?'

Renee nodded, tears now pouring down her cheeks. 'Yes, yes I am. I want to give us a go with all my heart and soul.'

Dylan smiled, the depth in his eyes unfathomable. 'You've just made me a very happy man.'

Leaning in, Renee feathered her lips over Dylan's, teasing him until he pressed his lips hard against hers. Using his strong arms, he picked her up from the ground and she wrapped her legs around his waist. As their passion increased, so did the intensity of their kisses—their tongues exploring and tasting one another with hunger, their lips wet and breathing heavy.

Renee's body trembled with raw desire. She was hungry for him, and she could feel he was insatiably hungry for her, but she wasn't going to spend the night with him with Annie in the house—not yet—and she knew he'd feel the same way. Reluctantly pulling away, the taste of him still on her lips, she slowly let her legs fall from around his waist, the sensation of his hardness pressing into her as she did so making her ache even more for him. 'I better head home.' Her voice was faint.

Dylan said nothing as he slid his hands beneath her top and caressed the bare skin of her back before sliding his hands around to her stomach and working his way tantalisingly up to her breasts. His fingers expertly traced around her erect nipples, the sheerness of her lacy bra only increasing her sensitivity.

Tingling from head to toe, she arched herself into him.

'I really should go,' she said breathlessly, her hands travelling beneath his shirt, her body aching for his as she ran her hands over his firm chest and through the fine hairs on his belly.

'Soon…you can go soon. I need to make love to you first. I can't go another day without devouring every inch of you.' His voice was exquisitely husky as he kissed down the side of her throat, only stopping to gently lick the place where her pulse flickered. Then he nibbled on her earlobe as he breathed sensuous heat into her ear, making goosebumps flood her skin. The intense sensation stole her breath and she fought to control herself, resisting her animal instincts to tear his clothes off right here and now and taste every glorious, pulsing inch of him.

Unable to stop herself, she let her fingers travel down to where his hardness was pressing into the denim of his jeans. The material was so strained, she was surprised his zipper hadn't burst. She groaned as his lips came to meet with hers once again and he pulsed beneath her hand.

Dylan let his lips glide down her chin, his hands sliding beneath her hair as he gently tugged her head back and kissed the front of her throat. 'I want you, Renee, now. I can't wait any longer to be at one with you.'

Renee fought to answer him, her breathing heavy. 'But where? We can't in the house, not yet.'

Picking her up in his arms, he carried her into the darkness. 'I've already thought about that, and just in case this happened, I made us up a bed somewhere private, close enough to the house but where we can make as much noise as we like.'

Renee grinned wickedly. 'Hmm, wishful thinking on your behalf, hey.'

Dylan returned her cheekiness with a grin mischievous enough to make a she-devil fall to her knees. 'Well, hooray for me because I'm getting my wish, aren't I?'

'Yes, you are, and so am I.'

Carrying her across the driveway and up a few stairs that led to a loft above the barn-style stables, Dylan carefully placed Renee back down on her feet. Renee gasped with delight when she saw the mattress on the rustic timber floor, the sheets on top of it crisp and white and scattered with red rose petals. A large window opened up to reveal the star-studded night sky above and a kerosene lantern flickered in the corner of the room, spilling soft light over the romantic country setting. A stereo sat on a little old table, George Strait's classic country love song, 'I Cross My Heart', playing softly. The words were so fitting for this magical moment.

Renee could see the verandah from here, the cottage not even ten metres away, but far enough away for privacy. Her hand fluttered to her chest, her heart melting. 'When did you do this?' she said tenderly.

'When I said I was going to the loo. I thought you'd wonder why I took so long but I think you and Annie were having so much fun together you didn't even notice I was gone for almost twenty-five minutes.' Dylan sat down on the end of the mattress and lay back. Propping himself up on his elbow, he patted the spot next to him. 'Come here so I can kiss you all over.'

Renee wandered over to join him, her eyelashes heavy with unshed tears. 'This is the most beautiful and romantic thing I've ever seen… And the most amazing thing is, it's all for me. Thank you, Dylan.' She pulled her t-shirt over her head and let it drop to the floor, and pulled her jeans down and over her feet. Then, she slowly removed her bra, her full round breasts falling free, her eyes never leaving Dylan's the whole time. Leaving only her black lacy G-string on, she eased herself down beside him, and lay so she was facing him, his gaze drinking all of her in.

Dylan gently pushed her hair back from her face and then let his fingers trace down her neck and over her breasts, his touch gentle and tender. Her nipples responded, growing even harder.

'You deserve to be spoilt,' he whispered before leaning in and licking her nipples so softly she wanted to scream out his name and beg him to ravage her.

But instead, she grabbed his flannelette shirt and tore it open, the buttons popping off as she did. Pulling it from his shoulders, she threw it behind her and then began unbuttoning his jeans, Dylan's mouth never leaving her, his tongue now trailing tantalisingly down her stomach. Before he reached her throbbing wetness, the one place she was truly aching for him to lick, he stopped and stood, removing his jeans, and then his underpants, his erection tempting her to her knees.

She eyed the eagle tattoo that began at the side of his throat, and followed its path down his chest, over his abs and to his groin. It was so damn sexy. She motioned for him to stay standing as she knelt before him. He slipped his hands into her hair, his fingers pressing into the back of her head. Slowly, she licked the end of his cock—tasting him, tracing the ridge and then running the tip of her tongue ever so slowly down his shaft, and then back up it again. Dylan was breathing heavily, gasping and moaning in pleasure. Lightly, she wrapped her lips around the tip, then millimetre by millimetre, wanting to savour the sensation of him easing into her, she ran her wet mouth downwards, taking all of him in. Not in a hurry, she repeated the movements, enjoying every stroke, every lick, and every drop of his wetness.

Dylan pulled himself from her mouth and slid down to his knees so he was facing her. 'I want to feel you drift inside me,' he said. 'So when I place my lips on yours, just breathe out into me and I'll draw you in.'

Renee nodded as she leant in and opened her mouth and Dylan did the same until their lips were pressed up hard against one another's, as well as their bodies. Renee breathed out and the sensation of Dylan breathing her deep inside him was out of this world. Then, reversing the roles, she breathed him in, the motion making her feel a connection with him beyond anything she'd ever felt before. This was all-encompassing love.

Without saying a word, Dylan eased her backwards until he was lying on top of her. He kissed her parted lips, her eyelids, her face and then her neck, making his way downwards until he was at her breasts. With hard strokes of his tongue he flicked her nipples and then took them one by one into his mouth, biting down until she was verging on the brink of pleasure and pain. She arched into him, her nails digging into his back. Then, he continued his journey down her trembling, tingling body, his lips, tongue, mouth and hands exploring her every inch with mind-blowing skill.

When he reached her place of pure indulgence and began circling it with the tip of his tongue, she cried out in complete pleasure, the sensation bringing her closer to climax by the second. Her hands gripping the back of his head, she pushed his face into her. Dylan followed her cue as he plunged his tongue inside her, taking his own sweet time to drag it up the sides of her before licking the length of her wetness on the outside. Unable to take any more, and wanting to reach the height of absolute pleasure with him deep inside her, Renee pulled him back up so she could kiss him.

Dylan rested the tip of his manhood against her sweet heaven, and very, very slowly slid himself inside her, kissing her deeply all the while. Once he was all the way in, Renee tilted her head back in sheer bliss, her breath escaping her in short sharp gasps. She moved her hips in union with his, Dylan's moans of pleasure matching her own. Gripping one another, they positioned themselves so he could be as deep inside her as possible. With the thrusting getting faster, and more and more hungry, their bodies began to shudder, and then balancing on the edge of euphoria, they fell into a world of ecstasy together, calling out as they came together. Then, completely spent, they lay in each other's arms, enjoying the paradise they were still floating in as they tried to catch their breath.

'I love you, baby,' Dylan said, feathering a kiss on her cheek.

'And I love you, my gorgeous man,' Renee said as she closed her eyes and rested her head against his chest, enjoying the feeling of his heart beating against her cheek. She smiled from within. Her fantasies of the past nine years had finally become her reality.

***

Dylan waited until Renee's taillights had completely disappeared before he headed inside the cottage. From her rug on the verandah, Bossy regarded him with droopy eyelids—her job of guarding the cottage over now that her master was back. Her eyes dropped shut and she was instantly asleep. Glancing at his watch, Dylan shook his head, still smiling. It was one in the morning, which meant he only had about six hours before he had to be back up and on his way to Wildwood Acres for work.

Not that he cared. He was so damn high on Renee he felt like he didn't need any sleep at all. Making love to her again after all these years had been even more beautiful than he'd imagined, and now he'd allowed himself to fall off the cliff he'd been balancing on, he felt more in love with her than he'd ever been. He wished she didn't have to go home, and that they could have slept wrapped around each other all night, but she didn't want her grandparents to worry—and he had Annie to think about too.

Soundlessly he crept into Annie's bedroom to check on her, her night-light throwing an assortment of multicoloured stars onto her ceiling. Smiling, he looked down at her angelic face. He was so very blessed to have a daughter like her. He blew her a kiss—imagining it landing in her kind loving heart—before sneaking back out of the room on his tiptoes.

Wandering down the hallway and towards his bedroom he stopped as he passed his office. His laptop was aglow in the dark; he must have forgotten to turn it off this afternoon. Shrugging, he padded over to shut it down, the screen coming to life as he tapped the space bar. The page popped up that showed him the areas he had on camera around the property. Curious to see if the cameras had captured anything untoward after he and Ralph had left this afternoon, he decided to skim through the last few hours of recordings on speed rewind. And as he did, something made him pause.

He pressed play, his anger building by the second. He couldn't make out who it was—the moonlight only hinting at the shadowy figure—but there was definitely someone wandering around his half-built dam. He looked to be examining the earthworks, but after almost ten minutes he disappeared into the scrubland that bordered the national park.

What the hell had they been doing? It was too late to go out there now, so he made the reluctant decision to check it all out before he headed off to work in the morning. He wasn't about to leave Annie alone in the house while he went driving around the property tonight—especially not with the possibility of whoever it was being anywhere near the house. This was all getting beyond a joke—it had to stop.

CHAPTER

20

'You got in late last night,' Pearl said, a twinkle in her eyes as she buttered a piece of fruit toast.

'Yeah, I heard you coming up the drive well after midnight. Time flies when you're having fun, hey,' Mick said from the dining room table, a cheeky smile on his lips as he enjoyed his morning cuppa. 'Oh, to be young again, Reni.'

Feeling her face beginning to colour, Renee quickly turned all her attention to the cup of coffee she was making, her spoon clanking noisily as she stirred for all of Australia. She'd tried to be extra quiet when she'd got home, even rolling the Land Cruiser in neutral down the last bit of the drive and slinking down the hallway like a teenager that had snuck out the bedroom window, but obviously she couldn't pull the wool over anyone's eyes here. Thank goodness her pa wasn't home to hear this conversation, she'd be even more embarrassed than she was now. But he and Dylan had already headed off to work before she'd got out of bed.

'Oh, I didn't think it was that late. Dylan and I were talking and I lost track of time, that's all.'

Pearl began spreading her toast with some homemade passionfruit-and-lemon butter that a neighbour had dropped off the day before. 'Oh, come on, love. I wasn't born yesterday. And believe it or not, I was young like you were once.'

'You were young once? I never would have guessed,' Renee replied lightheartedly as she gave Pearl a wink, praying to God that her humour would divert the conversation somewhere else. She levered herself up on the counter, swinging her legs, feigning casualness.

Pearl smiled perceptively as she pointed at Renee with her butter knife. 'I know what love looks like, and you, my girl, have got love in your eyes.' She plopped the knife into the sink full of hot soapy water.

Renee stared back at her with her mouth slightly ajar, words completely evading her. What the hell was she meant to say to that? It's not like she could deny it.

Chuckling softly, Pearl picked up her plate and wandered over to the dining table, her terry towelling robe emphasising her tiny waist. 'You know, you're not a teenager anymore, love. You *are* allowed to date boys.' She sat down, smiling wistfully. 'And you don't have to hide it from your pa and me. After meeting Dylan this morning, I must say he seems like a really nice young man.'

'*Okay*,' Renee replied cautiously, not knowing where this conversation was going to lead. She'd been put on the spot and had no idea what to say. She tried to remain cool, calm and collected on the outside, but on the inside she was running around like a mad woman with her hands up in the air. She took a sip from her coffee, trying to buy some time as she thought about whether to tell the truth, or divert her nan's correct assumption altogether, her legs now swinging nervously and bumping against the kitchen cupboard. Upon opening her eyes this morning, she had made the decision she'd been contemplating before falling asleep, and she couldn't wait to let Dylan know. First, though, she wanted to tell her grandparents—it being the respectful thing to do.

'Just remember, though,' Pearl continued, 'you don't live in Opals Ridge anymore. It's going to break your heart, and his, if you get in too deep before you return back to Melbourne—which you are going to be doing in the very near future, I might add.'

Honesty is the best policy. Tell her the truth, while she's left the gate open.

'Nan, we need to have a little chat about that,' Renee said as she hopped down from the counter and wandered over to sit at the table.

Her nan was right, she was old enough to date, which meant that she was also old enough to make her own decisions, whether her grandparents agreed or not. No, she didn't want to upset them, but she couldn't go on leading a life she wasn't happy with either, and if she was going to be completely honest with herself she was far from happy in Melbourne. And now she'd been given a precious second chance with Dylan, there was no way in hell she was going to rush back to the city and blow it like she did all those years ago.

Mick must have felt the deep and meaningful coming on, as he quickly excused himself from the table. 'Well, I better get going. I've got thingamajigs that need tending to.' Grabbing his crutches, he hobbled out. 'Catch you two later.' And he was gone in a flash, his coffee only half drunk.

'Go on then love. What would you like to talk about?' Eyeing Renee, Pearl took a bite of her toast, the anxious look on her face letting Renee know she knew exactly what she wanted to talk about.

Renee reached out and took Nan's hand. 'Yes, Nan, you're right. I do have feelings for Dylan and he has feelings for me. The truth is, we are deeply, head over heels in love. I want to give it a go with him, which means I will have to be living here to do that.'

Pearl's eyebrows knitted close together. 'But you've only just started dating. How can you be so deeply in love so quickly?'

'Dylan and I started dating when I was sixteen, and we were still dating when you and Pa got me to skip town. We loved each other and I left him behind, Nan, without an explanation. I broke his heart, and mine, in the process.' Renee shook her head as she blinked back tears. 'I'm not going to do that to him again, or me for that matter. I've pined for him for nine long years, and by some miracle I have him back in my life. Fate has brought us back together and I'm going to do my damned best to keep it that way—not that I've told Dylan I'm seriously thinking about moving home. I wanted to sleep on it, and I'm glad I did because I've woken up this morning feeling more determined about it than ever, so nobody's going to be able to talk me out of it—not even you, Nan.'

Pearl's eyes widened and she opened her mouth to speak but then snapped it shut again.

'I'm sorry, Nan. I know you and Pa would prefer me to go back to Melbourne, but honestly, we can't go on living our lives around what happened nine years ago. Well, I can't anyway. I need to move forward and follow my heart, and my heart is here, in Opals Ridge, with you and Pa, and Dylan. Especially now Aunty Fay is gone—I don't feel I have much keeping me in Melbourne. I want to move home, Nan, and I just hope you and Pa can give me your blessing to do so.'

'Oh, I see,' was all Pearl could muster. She sucked in a breath and then let it out slowly, the whole time looking towards the ceiling and blinking her eyes furiously. Somewhat recomposed, she looked back at Renee and smiled sadly. 'I had a feeling this day might come, love, when you wanted to move home, and so did your pa. We can't stop you doing what you want to do. We're just terribly worried about something happening to you, too, that's all.' She gave Renee's hand a tight squeeze. 'I'm very happy that you've found love. You deserve to fall in love and be loved for the wonderful woman you are. And I know from when I fell hard for your pa all those years ago, nothing stands in the way of true love.' Tears began to roll down her cheeks.

Emotion overwhelming her, Renee stood up and wrapped her arms around her nan. 'I know you and Pa worry about me, and I love you both dearly for it, but I can't spend the rest of my life running away.'

Pearl hugged her back tightly. 'I know, love. And it's wrong of us to expect you to.' Reaching across the table, she pulled a bunch of tissues from the box and then handed some to Renee. 'As much as I worry about you, you have my blessing. I'm not going to stand in the way of your love for Dylan again and I'm deeply sorry we stole that from you when you were seventeen, but we had no other choice back then. Now we do, but we'll just have to work on your pa a bit before he gives you his blessing, I think.'

'Yes, that's going to be a bit of a tricky one, I'm guessing. I'll broach the subject over the next few days, when the time feels right. Just please keep this between you and me until I speak to him,' Renee said, smiling through her tears as she gave her nan a kiss on the cheek.

'I promise I will, love. That conversation should be between you and him, and it's not my place to say anything beforehand.'

'Thank you, Nan, I appreciate it, and your blessing means the world to me, too.'

Pearl cupped Renee's face. 'I love you, very much, and I just have to trust that you're doing the right thing. Your happiness means everything to me.'

Renee sniffled. 'Thanks, Nan, I love you too, with all my heart.'

Picking up her now-empty plate, Pearl padded towards the sink and began washing up. 'Are you still okay to drop me and Pa at Shirl's house this afternoon? Your pa always likes to have a few beers with Tom and I'm not allowed to drive until the doctor gives me the all clear.'

'Sure, Nan, that's no problem at all. Hayley has invited me to her place for a catch up tonight anyways. Apparently there's a school reunion on next weekend and she has some old school stuff we could go dressed in for a bit of fun, if any of it fits. She's only a couple of blocks away from Shirley's, so that works in well. You and Pa can just give me a call when you are ready and I'll come and pick you up.'

'That sounds lovely. It'll be nice for you to have some female company, other than an old fuddy-duddy like me, that is.'

'Oh, Nan, I love your company,' Renee said as she joined her nan at the sink with a tea towel. She looked out the window at the cloudless blue sky stretching to the horizon. 'I think I'll go and read a book out on the back verandah this morning.'

'Sounds like a plan, love. It's a beautiful day to be outside. I'm going to potter around in the garden a bit myself, and get rid of all those weeds that have snuck up while I was in hospital.'

Renee instantly worried about her nan overdoing it. 'Do you want a hand?'

'No, you take some time out for you, love. I'm not going to overwork myself, if that's what you're worried about.' Pulling the plug from the sink, Pearl wiped her hands on the tea towel Renee was holding. 'So what are you going to do about work back here? It's such a shame you're going to have to give up that wonderful job you have in Melbourne.'

'Yeah, I have to admit I'm sad about having to give up my job but I'm thinking about maybe becoming a realtor here. I've looked into the market and Opals Ridge is a very happening place. I don't think I'll have any trouble finding places I could sell, especially to some of the big business contacts I have in Melbourne who are looking for investment properties, or holiday homes in the country.'

Pearl smiled. 'Always the go-getter, Renee. I'm proud of you, love.'

'Thanks, Nan.'

'Anyways, I'm off to get dressed in my gardening gear before the morning gets away from me.'

'Okay, see you outside.' Renee watched her nan disappear through the kitchen archway, the weight she'd been carrying about moving back here eased a lot now she had her blessing. Fingers crossed her pa would be as understanding as her nan—not only about moving back, but with the fact that she was madly in love with his new right-hand man.

Standing at the edge of the dam wall Dylan huffed as he ran his hands over his head. This was getting way beyond a joke. He'd been wandering around for the past two hours, trying to find something, anything, to give him a clue as to who it was that had been sneaking around last night. But as usual, there was nothing. A tropical shower had fallen during the night, washing away any footprints. If it weren't for the video footage he'd put onto a USB stick, he'd have nothing to show Craig. Pulling his mobile from his jeans pocket he dialled the police station, hoping he was on shift. After four rings Craig answered.

'Hi Craig, it's Dylan. Are you going to be there for a while? I have something I want to show you.'

'Hey Dylan, yup, I'm here for another two hours, or so. Can it wait until I get home, though, to save you driving into town?'

'Not really, I put some cameras up around the place and I caught someone sneaking around on them last night…but I can't see their face, only their silhouette. I thought that maybe you might see something I haven't picked up on.'

'You didn't tell me you were putting cameras up.'

'I hadn't really thought to mention it to you, Craig. Sorry.'

'Not to worry, but can you try and keep me in the loop from now on?'

Craig sounded a little pissed off, and that pissed Dylan off too. He had kept him in the loop up until the cameras, not that that had done him any good anyway—they were still no closer to finding out who was behind all this. 'Like I said, it slipped my mind. But I'll do my best to let you know my movements in future.'

'Good, because we need to be able to work together on this, Dylan.' Craig sighed. 'Sorry if I'm a bit snappy… I've had a long day. Just bring it in and I'll have a look.'

'I'll be there in halfa, or thereabouts.'

'See you then, Dylan.'

***

Sitting on the floor of Hayley's loft with old school uniforms and photos strewn around her, Renee laughed as she unrolled a poster of Aerosmith with red lipstick kisses all over Steven Tyler's face, now smudged after the years but still very visible. She held it up to Hayley who was busy sorting through a box beside her. 'Had a bit of a teenage crush on Stevie, I see?'

'Hey, don't judge. I honestly believed I was going to make him my husband one day.' Hayley burst out laughing as she grabbed the poster from Renee's clutches, almost ripping it in half in the process. 'His loss,' she said through her giggles as she scrunched it up and threw it over her shoulder. 'I did much better scoring Greg anyways. He's *way* sexier than Steven Tyler.'

'You sure have scored with him, Hayley. He seems like a really lovely guy. I'm glad I got to meet him this afternoon before he left with the kids.'

'Yup, he sure is—and bloody great in the sack too. Even after seven years of marriage I still want to rip his clothes off him all the time.'

'Oh my God, too much information,' Renee said lightheartedly as she screwed her face up.

'Yeah, well, you know me. Never one to hold any info back,' Hayley said, grinning. 'I still can't believe you and Dylan are getting back together after all this time. I'm so happy for you guys.'

'Trust me, I'm still pinching myself too. But Hayley, please keep it to yourself for now. I don't want the whole town talking about it just yet. I want some time to ourselves before everyone starts having their say about it.'

Hayley zipped her lips shut. 'Your secret is safe with me, my dear friend.'

'Thanks mate, I've always been able to rely on you.'

Hayley held up a fawn-coloured school skirt. 'So who's going to be the guinea pig, you or me?'

Renee eyed the teeny skirt. 'My God, Hayley, how did you cover anything in that?'

Hayley wriggled her eyebrows. 'That was the whole point, Reni, so I could show off a bit of leg.'

'A *bit* of leg? I reckon you better try it on first, I'm scared that if I'm able to get it on I won't be able to get it off!'

'All righty then,' Hayley said as she stood and pulled her denim shorts off and then began tugging the skirt on with grunts and groans.

While Hayley was struggling to pull the thing up, Renee went back to sorting through the boxes of her friend's teenage memorabilia, finding herself almost at the bottom of the box and still no closer to discovering anything suitable, or size-worthy, to wear to the reunion next month. Oh well, it was a good excuse to just go in her favourites, a pair of jeans and a nice top. Then, something familiar caught her eye. A maroon scarf. Her throat tightened as her heart took off in a wild gallop.

It couldn't be, could it? Lots of people had them...

Slowly, as though reaching out to touch a flame, she placed her hand on the scarf, making sure to keep it within the confines of the box as she investigated it further. And there it was; her and Scarlet's little thing, the tassels at the end of the State of Origin scarf plaited by her very own hands. The last time she'd seen this it had been loosely hanging around her sister's neck, on the very day she had gone missing. She held her breath as the room began to close in on her, Hayley's laughter behind her now sounding sinister and mocking.

With a rush of adrenaline, she yanked the scarf from the box and held it up in front of Hayley, her body trembling. 'Where did you get this, Hayley? And the truth would be a great start.'

Hayley's face drained of colour and she took a step back. 'Why, what in the hell's wrong with you, Renee? It's just a footy scarf. What's the big deal?'

Renee's cheeks flushed as the blood inside her hit boiling point, but she tried hard to keep herself calm on the outside. 'Just please answer my question, honestly.'

Hayley avoided Renee's eyes as she took yet another step back, glancing towards the closed loft door and looking like she was about to make a run for it—or was Renee just imagining things?

'Umm, just let me think for a minute.' Hayley threw her hands up in the air, smiling. 'That's right, I got it from the op shop in town years ago. Is it yours? Is that why you are so upset? You can have it back, you know. It doesn't bother me.'

Remaining silent, Renee tried to read Hayley's now unruffled expression. She'd gone from looking like she'd seen a ghost, to completely composed again in less than a minute. Alarm bells were ringing. Something wasn't right. Hayley wasn't telling her the truth. Was *Hayley* the person behind Scarlet's disappearance? Was the real killer standing in front of her? *Holy fuck*, she had to get out of here.

A suffocating feeling came over her as she ran for the door, flung it open and scrambled down the small flight of steps. She hadn't had a panic attack in years, but it felt as though she was about to have one any second. Her throat was constricting and she was struggling to take a breath. Her fight-or-flight had definitely kicked into gear.

Hayley ran after her. 'Renee, where are you going? Come back. What's wrong?'

Fear filling her and with her mind in a spin, Renee raced out the front door of the house and towards where she had parked her nan's car on the street. But suddenly she stopped in her tracks, remembering she had left her handbag inside with the car keys and her mobile phone in it. Damn it! Uncertain of what to do next, she turned to see Hayley coming through the front door. Her feet felt like they were frozen to the spot as she contemplated going back inside to retrieve her bag. It wasn't worth it.

Hayley ran towards her. 'Renee, wait, what's going on? Have you lost your fucking mind?'

Making a snap decision, Renee took off down the street, her thudding heart matching her pounding strides as she kept stealing terrified glances behind her. Hayley had stopped running after her, and now stood in the middle of the street, her arms folded in front of her, the streetlight casting deep shadows across her face. Renee was glad to turn the corner, knowing she was now out of Hayley's sight.

Being cautious and staying in the shadows of the dimly lit streets, she clutched the scarf to her pounding chest as she kept her ears and eyes open for any movements or sounds, every one of her senses on high alert. She had stopped running now, her anxiety making it difficult to draw a decent breath, but she was still taking quick strides, not able to get to her destination quick enough.

She kept feeling as though she was being followed, but glances stolen behind her proved otherwise. *But am I looking hard enough?* A dog barked at her from behind one of the fences and her hand flew to her mouth as she stifled a scream. Her heart hammered a frenzied drumbeat in her chest as she fought to hold it together. Twice cars drove past her and she scrambled behind nearby trees until they were gone, not knowing if she'd been seen or not.

It was only nine o'clock but the suburban streets of Opals Ridge were basically deserted, not like in the city, which would be a hub of activity no matter what time of the day or night it was. She drew in a deep breath and tried to calm herself. Only a few more blocks and she would be at Shirley's house, where she would find her grandparents, and then they could all go down to the police station and report what she had found—more evidence that could lead them to the answer to her sister's disappearance. If only she had her mobile phone she could call them.

Her hands tightly holding the scarf, she felt a wave of hope laced in amongst her fear. This precious item was the clue she had been praying to find, but it broke her heart and shocked her beyond belief that she had discovered it in her *apparent* friend's house. Was there any way that Hayley could have been telling her the truth? Judging by her body language, she doubted it.

Renee was kicking herself now for not telling Nan and Pa about the diary, but then what good would it have done? She would have to tell them about it now, though, and she hoped they understood why she had wanted to keep it from them. Although there weren't any concrete clues in the diary—none she could see anyway— this very unexpected breakthrough would surely kickstart a full investigation. The police couldn't ignore a piece of evidence like this. The very thought brought with it the faith that they would finally be able to uncover what had happened to Scarlet and lay her to rest.

Turning the corner that led down to Tom and Shirley's house, she spotted the familiar driveway and Shirley's jeep parked on it. She let out the breath she'd been holding. Thank God. Her safety zone— twenty more metres and she was there. Just as she was focusing on what was ahead, she heard the crunch of tyres behind her. Looking back, she recognised the car, and immediately relaxed. She stopped walking, relief flooding her as she waited for it to pull up. Thank goodness for small miracles.

'Hey there, Renee. What are you doing walking around in the dark—especially so far from home? Are you okay?'

'Oh thank God it's you.' She held the scarf up in front of her as she peered through the window. 'Look at this. I've found Scarlet's scarf, the one that I told you she would have been wearing when she went missing. You won't believe who had it.'

CHAPTER
21

The first thing Renee felt as she tried to blink open her lead-heavy eyes was the intense throbbing in her head. A piercing pain was shooting behind her eyes and almost to the point of making her want to throw up. She was enveloped in darkness, unable to see even an inch in front of her. The world felt as though it was spinning around her, the wooziness adding to her nausea, and her thoughts tumbled around in her mind like objects being tossed about in a cyclone, the combination of everything making it impossible to think at all.

Trying to lick her dry lips, she instinctively went to place her hand on her head but something stopped her. Her wrists were bound. And then her state of unconsciousness gave way and her reality came crashing down upon her. He'd invited her into the car and then once he'd locked the doors he'd hit her so hard she must have blacked out. Where had he taken her? What was he going to do to her? Never in her wildest dreams would she have thought he was capable of this.

Renee pictured his face, his evil eyes leering at her seconds after he'd pressed the central locking and then grabbed her by the throat. Terror gripping her once more, she started to hyperventilate as she tried to forcefully yank her arms free from her restraints. Chains jangled and clinked as she fruitlessly struggled, the agony she was inflicting upon herself as she tried to free her wrists from whatever was wrapped around them bordering on unbearable.

Along with her innate instinct for survival, every one of her senses snapped to attention, sight, smell, taste, hearing, and touch. She was extremely relieved to still feel the press of her clothes against her skin. She couldn't see past whatever was over her head but she could hear water dripping and smell strong chemicals. She was sitting up and her back was pressed up against a wall that was icy cold. Utilising the little give she had from the chains around her wrists and ankles, she clambered onto her knees and used her hands to feel around the floor. It was cold and felt like tiles. Something scurried past her and she froze, her breath catching in her throat. A barrage of questions engulfed her, making fear consume her even more as she rolled herself into a ball on the floor and wept. Was he going to rape her? Kill her? Was this the place where Scarlet had taken her last breath? That thought chilled her to the very core.

A new sound made her stop crying and instead hold her breath. She heard a key sliding into a lock, and then a door squeaking open before being slammed closed again, followed by heavy footfalls coming down a flight of creaky steps. At least now she knew she was underneath something—not that it helped with the state she was in right now, but if she somehow broke free…

Shaking with fear, she silently counted each chilling step. There were nine—nine steps between her imminent death and possible life. As he got closer, her skin grew colder. She could hear his laboured breath now, his sheer presence weighing so heavily down upon her that she felt as though she was going to suffocate. Then she heard the most heart-wrenching sound—the whimper of a child. A flicking sound was followed by light blazing through the bag over her head. She strained to see through the fabric but all she could make out was a moving form.

'I've brought you some company. Being the extremely considerate man I am I thought you might like some. From what I've heard, you two know each other quite well already.' The sardonic laughter at the end of his proclamation was spine-chilling.

Chains jangled as the child began to weep. 'Please don't tie me up. I want to go home to my daddy.' The child's sobs grew louder. 'Please don't hurt me.'

Renee's heart froze. *Oh dear Lord, please no, it can't be.*

'Shut up with your whining, you annoying little shit! Or I'll give you something worthwhile to whine about.' The man spat vehemently. 'And it's your daddy's fault you're here, so have a hard think about that before you go saying you want to go home to him. If I were you, I'd hate his guts!' He sniggered. 'Come to think of it, I do hate his guts, have ever since he stole her from me… He always gets everything he wants.'

Not caring about her own wellbeing anymore, Renee blindly turned towards where the voices were coming from as she tried to reach out. 'Annie, is that you, sweetheart? It's me, Renee.'

'Renee?' Annie's voice was trembling, and sounded so tiny. 'I'm so scared.'

A forceful smack across the face slammed Renee's entire body into the wall behind her, sending Annie into a screaming fit beside her.

'I'll tell you when you can speak, you bitch,' his voice boomed. 'And if I were you, Annie, I'd stop your bloody screaming. This is your last warning. Shut the fuck up or I'll gladly make you.'

Annie's screams became stifled whimpers before she broke into a bout of chesty coughing. Footsteps moved away from Renee and she heard a tap being turned on.

Using the small reprieve without him, Renee snuck her hand along the floor as far as the chains around her wrists would allow her to, trying to feel for Annie's. A tiny hand finally found hers and they entwined their fingers tightly. Annie's hand was so cold. She was desperate to take her into her arms, but frozen with fear she remained huddled against the wall, her inability to see what was going on rendering her motionless. She didn't want to do anything to piss the bastard off even more.

The heavy footsteps were heading back towards them. 'Here, Annie, drink this,' the voice demanded. 'I hate coughing, it drives me up the fucking wall.'

Annie must have disobeyed.

'Now!' His voice was thunderous. 'Don't make me hurt you.'

Renee could hear Annie taking glugs of water in between her coughing. 'Please, she has nothing to do with this. Let her go. Please, I'm begging you.'

His hands went around Renee's throat, the pressure increasing as he crouched down and pressed himself up against her. 'Oh, trust me, she has everything to do with this. What better way to hurt him than to take away the one person he loves most in this world.' Dropping his hands from around her throat, he grabbed both her breasts through her top and squeezed them forcefully, making Renee cry out in pain as he laughed. 'Your tits feel just like your sister's did all those years ago. It was a bloody shame I had to kill her, but when she told me she was pregnant, what was I meant to do?'

Renee's jaw dropped. Her beautiful sister was pregnant? 'You sadistic bastard. It's horrific enough you killed my sister, but you killed her unborn child too... *Your* unborn child?'

'I had no choice. It would have ruined me if she'd kept it. I wasn't going to let her keep a child that she could hold over me for the rest of my life.' He sniggered. 'And how ironic is it that the whole time, she thought I was in love with her, when it was actually *you* I was infatuated with, Renee. But you never showed any interest in me, whereas Scarlet did. So handy for me with you being twins, I could just imagine it was you when I was touching her.'

Renee's stomach heaved as Scarlet's beautiful face swam to her mind's eye—her poor darling sister, and her unborn child—her niece or nephew—had died at the hands of this evil man. What she must have gone through was unbearable to even think about. 'Fuck you, you sick son of a bitch. I hope you rot in hell,' she snarled through gritted teeth. 'You'll be going to hell because karma's going to make you pay for what you've done. And if karma doesn't, I fucking will.'

He laughed menacingly once again. 'Oh, you will, will you? Well, we'll see about that, won't we.' He tutted. 'I was going to let the fact you'd found the diary go, seeing as there was nothing concrete in there pointing to me. But it's such a shame you found the scarf really. Otherwise I might have left you to get on with your pathetic life with your equally pathetic boyfriend.'

How in the hell does he know I have a boyfriend?

There was a pause as he mumbled something to himself and then chuckled.

'Actually, who am I kidding, no I wouldn't have. I've had my eyes on you since you were ten years old, and I was patiently waiting until you turned sixteen, so you were legal.' He chuckled cynically. 'I know what they do to child molesters in prison. But when you were sixteen I couldn't have been charged with anything if you blabbed.' He huffed. 'I'd waited six long years…but then Dylan got to you first and ruined my chances, the selfish bastard. The only reason you've lived this long is because you fucked off outta town after I put that note telling you that you were next on my list under your windscreen wiper...but now I got ya.' He grunted, as if pleased with himself. 'I can't wait to have my way with you. I've fantasised about this for close to sixteen years now.'

Annie was sobbing beside her as the bag was ripped from Renee's head. It took a few seconds for her eyes to adjust to the sudden brightness before they finally came to meet with the sadistic eyes of her sister's killer once again.

She would never have believed for a second that the man standing before her was capable of murder.

Jumping from the shower, Dylan grabbed his mobile phone that was now ringing for the second time in a row. He was going to wait until he was finished and ring whoever it was back once he was done but it was clearly important, especially seeing it was almost ten o'clock and most people would be in bed by now. He checked to see what the number was but it was a private.

'Hello.'

'Dylan, it's Stanley. Are you with Renee at all?'

Stanley's voice was uneasy, almost desperate.

'Oh, hi Stan. Nope, I'm at home. Why? Is everything okay?'

'I've been trying to call her mobile for the past half an hour and I can't get a hold of her. She was supposed to pick me and Pearl up from Shirley and Tom's place. She was meant to be at Hayley Gregory's tonight, and I've tried ringing there too but it keeps giving me the engaged signal. I just thought there might have been a chance that she'd finished at Hayley's and headed out to your place.'

An extremely bad feeling settled in the pit of Dylan's stomach. 'No, she's not here, Stan. Have you tried Hayley's mobile number?'

He tried to keep his voice casual, not wanting to alarm Stanley any more than he already sounded.

'I don't have it. Do you?' Worry laced Stanley's every word.

'Yup, I've got it. How about I give her a quick ring and see what's going on?'

'I'd appreciate it, Dylan. Thanks.'

'Righto, I'll call you back as soon as I've spoken to her.'

'Please be quick, Dylan. Pearl and I are getting extremely worried.'

Hurriedly, Dylan searched for Hayley's number in his contacts list. Finding it he pressed call, his hands clammy. Something wasn't right. It rang out and he called it again. After several rings he was diverted to her message bank. A sense of desperation washed over him. *Fuck it.* He was going to keep ringing until Hayley answered. It went to message bank yet again. He left a message.

'Hayley, it's Dylan. I want to know where Renee is. Answer your goddamn phone or I'm driving over there.'

He tried Greg's mobile number, but it, too, went to message bank.

Dylan tugged a pair of jeans and a t-shirt on, readying himself to drive over to Hayley's. He was going to have to ask his mum to come over and watch Annie. But in less than a minute, Hayley was calling him back, bawling uncontrollably. Dread filled him. 'Hayley, what's happened? Where's Renee?'

'I don't… She ran off…after she…found…the scarf.' Hayley was hysterical, her words fractured between her sobs.

'What scarf? Ran off where?'

Hayley was crying so hard she couldn't speak.

Dylan fought to control his own panic as he tried desperately to calm her. 'Hayley, take a deep breath. You have to calm down so you can talk to me. I can't help you, or Renee, if you don't tell me what happened.' He could hear Hayley trying to breathe at the other end of the phone.

After a few moments, Hayley began explaining, her voice trembling. 'He told me not to tell anyone until he'd sorted it out, but if I don't tell someone I'm going to lose my fucking mind. He went looking for her, but it was hours ago and I haven't heard from him since, and now his mobile is switched off. I don't know what to do.'

'Who told you not to tell anyone, and about what? Who's gone looking for her?' Dylan demanded, his patience wearing thin as he began to seriously worry about Renee's safety.

Hayley began rambling hysterically. 'I had a Maroons scarf in the box upstairs. When Renee saw it she flew into a panic and went running out my front door like I was a murderer or something.'

'I don't understand. Whose scarf was it?'

'Craig Campbell's. It was out of the boot of his car.'

Dylan fought to keep his voice calm, needing Hayley to try to do the same. 'I'm really confused. Hayley, what in the fuck is going on?'

'Craig and I slept together years ago, when he and Louise broke up once for a few weeks. I'd had too much to drink one night and one thing led to another, and it shouldn't have. It makes me so bloody sick just thinking about it. I took the scarf at the time to remind me of the night we spent together, but apparently it wasn't his and by the look on Renee's face it might have belonged to her... or someone she knows very well.' Hayley gasped as though she'd been drowning and just resurfaced. 'Oh my God, Dylan. It's just come to me. I think that scarf must have been Scarlet's. That's why she was so terrified when she found it here.'

Ignoring the million questions in his head, Dylan asked the most important one, everything dangerously making sense now. 'Is Craig the one out looking for her?'

'Yes, I rang him as soon as Renee ran off. I wanted to find out why the scarf had upset her so much. Craig told me he had no idea, but to leave it to him to sort it out. He told me not to say anything. Oh my God, Dylan, what have I done?'

'Hayley, lock all your doors and don't let Craig anywhere near you. Okay? I'll call Jake at the cop station in town and let them know what's going on.'

'Okay, Dylan, please let me know as soon as you know anything. I'm so sorry—'

But Dylan was already hanging up and dialling the local police station. As he spoke to Jake, he instinctively dashed down the hallway to check on Annie. Halfway through explaining the dire situation, the phone dropped from his hands and crashed to the floor. Annie's bedroom window was wide open, and his little girl was gone, her favourite teddy bear the only thing left lying in her ruffled bed.

His entire world caved in on him. Wherever Craig had taken Renee, he intuitively knew Annie was there too. Everything was adding up now, all the things going wrong around his place and Craig so conveniently unable to find out who was responsible. Dylan had found it a bit odd that Craig hadn't wanted to watch the video footage when he'd turned up at the station earlier today, instead saying he'd rather watch it without distraction and then he'd let him know his findings. He'd put it down to it just being the way Craig liked to work…but it was because it had been him all along. He obviously had it in for him, for fuck knows what reason, not that it mattered right now. Bossy would never have let a stranger near the house, especially near Annie's window, Craig only got away with it because Bossy trusted him, like they all did. He was a cop. You were supposed to trust him.

Falling to his knees, Dylan pulled the teddy bear to his lips and cried out Annie's name, over and over, the tinny voice calling out to him from the phone not registering with him at all. And in that moment of utter despair and horror he remembered Craig's words at the dam only days ago: *You just do your job, Dylan, and let me do mine, and it'll all pan out just the way I expect it to.*

His blood ran cold as he snapped out of his shell-shocked daze, fortitude now storming to the forefront. Craig was the one man the Opals Ridge township should be able to trust, the person responsible for upholding the law and catching the bad guys, and somehow he had fooled them all. Everything now pointed to the fact that he was behind Scarlet's disappearance, because why else would her scarf be in the boot of his very own car?

It made Dylan sick to the core to think that he now had Renee and Annie holed up somewhere, doing God knows what to them. Was he planning on making them disappear, like Scarlet? A flood of pure rage engulfed him. He felt like killing him with his bare hands, but he wouldn't let the bastard get off that easy. Dylan was going to find his two girls, now, before it was too late, and make sure Craig went to prison for life for what he had done.

Grabbing his mobile phone from where he'd dropped it, Dylan raised it to his ear and hurriedly explained to the copper the situation as he raced to his desk to grab the keys to his gun cabinet. Jake told him he was calling for backup from the neighbouring town and then heading straight over to the Campbell property. Knowing that would take at least twenty minutes, Dylan said he was heading out to start searching now, and hung up before the copper could oppose his decision to take matters into his own hands.

Where the hell would Craig have taken them? And then his phone vibrated—a text notifying him that Annie had pressed the alert button on her locator watch. He opened the GPS locator's map application, and a beeping red dot on the map showed that Annie, and hopefully Renee, were only a short distance away— somewhere on Craig's property to be exact.

Her puffer... Dylan took off to Annie's bedroom to grab it from her bedside table, his heart wrenching out of his chest as he imagined her having an asthma attack without her medication—it would kill her. 'Hang in there—I'm coming...' he whispered. *Lord, I beg you, please keep my little angel safe.*

Swallowing the lump in his throat and blinking back tears, Dylan reprimanded himself for wanting to crumble. He had to keep it together. He'd be no good to either Annie or Renee if he fell in an emotional heap right now.

Racing to his gun cabinet, he retrieved his shotgun. Then, sprinting out his front door and towards the back bushlands of his property, he dialled the number Stanley had given him—Shirley and Tom's house number. He dreaded making this call, but he had to.

Stanley answered the phone in one ring. 'Dylan, Shirl has you on loudspeaker...any news?'

Dylan's throat squeezed tighter. 'Yeah, Stan, and I'm afraid it's not good.'

He kept running as he explained the dire situation, adrenaline filling him. He could hear Pearl screaming in the background and Shirley trying to console her. Stanley was crying too, the man's wracking sobs tearing at Dylan's heart. 'Stan, I promise, I'm going to get your girl back. The cops are on their way. I'm sorry, but I gotta go...I'm almost at Craig's boundary now.'

'I'll see you out there, Dylan. I'll borrow Shirl's car and be on my way.'

Stanley was gone before Dylan had time to tell him to stay put. He didn't want anyone else's life put in danger. But then again, what did he expect? Renee was Stanley's little girl, as Annie was his, and fathers protected their children with their lives.

What a fucking nightmare—his two most precious girls, in the hands of a murderer. He knew he had to get to them fast, because with a man as callous and coldblooded as Craig clearly was, time wasn't going to be on his side. It would take him about ten minutes on foot to get to where the screen was blipping, and the clock was ticking...

Pavarotti's 'Nessun Dorma' pounded the walls of the underground cellar. Renee had worked out that this was the darkroom Craig had mentioned at the Studs and Fuds. It gave her some relief to know they weren't in the middle of nowhere, but instead right next door to Ironbark Plains, to Dylan. The famous song was so very out of place in the dank, cobweb filled space. Opera was meant to be glitzy and glamorous, but here a single blazing bulb hung from the low ceiling, illuminating the blackened walls and giving Renee a good view of where Craig was holding her and Annie captive.

A multitude of photos hung from wooden pegs, the ones of her and Hayley from the other night pegged to a thin rail above her, the smile on her face in such sharp contrast to the sheer terror she was experiencing now. There were also shots she hadn't been aware of Craig taking while she and Hayley had been dancing on the table, all of them from very compromising angles. It was repulsive to think he'd taken advantage of their personal space without them even knowing. Looking beyond the recent snapshots, she muffled a gasp as she spotted the back wall, photos plastering every single inch of it.

She slowly scanned the pictures, her disbelief growing by the second. There were recent shots of her outside the pub with Mick, walking into the hospital to visit her nan, coming out of the post office and the local grocery store. There were old photos of her and Scarlet swimming in the dam as teenagers, others of them playing at the hunter's shack, and a series of her running in the dark towards the Land Cruiser at the ball. So there had been someone following her—and the light she had caught a very fleeting glimpse of was no lighter, or torch, it had been the flash of Craig's camera. What would have happened to her if Dylan hadn't come to her rescue? And then her eyes came upon the most disturbing photos of all—she and Dylan making love at the hunter's shack as teenagers. The images were a little blurry, their naked flesh lit only by the many candles flickering within the shack, but it was unmistakably them. She felt utterly violated, one of her most precious moments now tainted by this monster who now held her and Annie captive. Anger surged throughout her. How dare he... And then everything about the note being left on her windscreen the following day made sense. Craig had lashed out in a jealous rage.

A snort-filled chuckle dragged her attention back to in front of her.

'That back wall is a work of art, wouldn't you agree, Renee?'

She said nothing, her gaze steely.

Craig snickered, then began mouthing the words to the song with exaggerated movements, his right leg bouncing, a baseball bat in one hand and a smouldering cigarette in the other. The drifting smoke made the room even more claustrophobic. On the floor sat an almost empty bottle of whiskey, the rest of it now pumping through his veins. Other than his occasional melodic attempts, he'd been silent for the past half an hour, instead smiling at Renee and Annie in a way that suggested so many morbid things, his fingers occasionally tapping the gun in the holster on his hip suggestively.

Renee clutched a shivering Annie to her, the chains around Annie's wrists and ankles with just enough give to allow the girl to partly sit on her lap. As the minutes ticked by, Annie's breathing was becoming more and more laboured, the dampness and cigarette smoke triggering her asthma. Renee stroked her hair and part of her back, trying her best to calm her. Her hand travelling down Annie's petite arm, her fingers found her watch—the tracking watch Dylan had bought her for her birthday. She felt a jolt of hope.

Renee tried to raise her voice above the music. 'Please, Craig, she needs her asthma puffer.' Her breath trailed in front of her for a few seconds, the temperature of the room icy.

Craig just shrugged and then took another swig of whiskey.

Wishing she could gouge Craig's cold heart out of his chest with her fingernails, Renee turned her attention back to Annie. 'Are you doing okay, sweetheart?' she whispered.

Annie remained silent—her body now heavy and limp. Her head was pressed to Renee's shoulder and her eyes were closed. 'I feel a bit weird,' she mumbled, almost inaudible. Her breath was becoming more of a wheeze.

There was something very wrong, Annie looking and feeling like she had been given a sedative. Renee recalled the drink Craig had given her and her heart dropped. 'What did you give her?' she cried over the music.

'Nothing too serious. Don't worry that pretty little head of yours,' Craig said, smirking.

Trying not to panic, Renee gave her a kiss on the cheek. 'Don't worry, Annie. Your daddy will be here soon.'

Annie didn't respond as her body relaxed completely in Renee's arms. Filled with dread, Renee moved her face to try and feel any sign of Annie's breath, the rhythmic warmth on her cheek worth more than all the gold in the world. Annie was obviously drugged, but at least sleep was stealing her away from this terrifying nightmare.

'What the fuck are you telling her!' Craig boomed as he stood, throwing his chair backwards in the process. The crash echoed around the room, but it didn't wake Annie. He stumbled over to Renee and placed the end of the baseball bat against her cheek. 'I told you before, don't open your fucking mouth unless I tell you to.' He pushed the bat in harder. 'Or I'll smash this into the back of your head, just like I did to Shelley. Got it?'

Biting her bottom lip to stop it quivering, Renee nodded—mortified by the revelation. All this time Dylan had believed Shelley had died from an accident, and yet she'd been taken from him just like Scarlet had been taken from her. And all because Craig was jealous that so many of them loved Dylan so very deeply. This was going to break his big beautiful heart even more.

'Good, and don't push me, because I'll take great pleasure in doing it if I have to,' he roared over the music. He stood in front of her, using the bat to push her chin upwards so she was looking at him. 'So this is what Scarlet would have looked like if she'd lived long enough. Damn shame I had to kill her really. You're a fucking doozy.' He pulled the bat away and waved it around in the air as he continued, smacking it into his hand as he did. 'Just think, if you'd fallen for me instead of Dylan, none of this would have happened. Your sister would still be alive, and so would Shelley.' He grunted while laughing at the same time. 'And do you know what the funniest fucking thing is?' He swayed a little to the right, the whiskey taking away his sense of balance. 'Scarlet's buried at your boyfriend's place, right under all your fucking noses, and you still haven't found her. I thought he and Ralph were going to find her body the other day, when they were digging that great big fucking hole for the dam. Then I could have pinned the murder on Dylan, like I'd planned to all along. But they didn't...the useless pair of fucking idiots.'

Renee fought to keep the horror from her face, not wanting to give Craig the satisfaction of seeing it—it had just been one shocking revelation after another. Instead she screamed on the inside, silently crying for her beloved sister and her unborn baby, and for Shelley. The snapped pendant resting against her heart felt like a heavy weight on her chest. At least now she knew where Scarlet's body was, so if she got out of here alive, she could finally give her the burial she deserved. How she wished she could break free from these chains and make this evil excuse for a human being pay for what he had done.

Unexpectedly and very abruptly, Craig slumped down beside her as though the wind had been beaten out of him, and every muscle in her tensed, her breathing shallow. And then he dropped his head in his hands and began to cry, loud wracking sobs that echoed around the room.

'All I ever wanted was for you to love me, like I love you, but you never even noticed I existed. And then I got stuck with Louise, so I thought I would make a go of it with her, but then she couldn't love me either. She kept going on and on about how much of a good man Dylan was and why couldn't I be more of a family man like him, and then she left me and took my boy with her.' He blew his nose on the sleeve of his copper's uniform then glared at Renee. 'All you women are the fucking same...never fucking happy. And Scarlet was no different. I was quite happy to just fuck her, but then she wanted more and more and more. I reckon she fell pregnant on purpose to try and trap me. Never fucking happy.' He leant in and kissed her on the cheek, then rested his head on her shoulder. She shuddered with terror and repulsion. 'I wish things could have been different, Renee. Our lives could have been so great if we'd ended up together.'

Renee closed her eyes, begging herself not to vomit as she fought the urge to turn her face away. She knew if she did, he would quite possibly kill her on the spot. This man was beyond unstable—he was a bomb on the verge of exploding. She needed to somehow get him on side, to buy her and Annie some time so Dylan had more of a chance of finding them. Needing to remove herself from the reality of the situation, Renee mentally separated herself from her body. 'I never knew you had feelings for me… I'm so sorry I made you feel as though you never mattered.'

But Craig didn't respond, his body now heavy against her as he began to snore. Renee spotted his gun, and her hopes soared. If she could manoeuvre herself without waking him, she might be able to grab it…

***

Racing through the darkness, Dylan held his shotgun in one hand and his phone in the other, with the map open on the screen. He was close now, so very close. He could see the outline of Craig's machinery shed just ahead, the GPS indicating that it was the exact point Annie, and most certainly Renee, were. Dashing towards the entrance, he then dropped to his hands and knees on the dusty floor, making sure to stick close to the corrugated iron walls.

The GPS was now showing a huge red wave. It was saying he should be right on top of Annie, but she was nowhere to be seen. He pocketed the phone and crawled about, straining to see anything in the dark, to hear anything near him. There was no movement, but there was a muffled sound. Putting his ear down to the ground he swore he could hear music. Where the hell was it coming from? The distant wail of a siren stole the silence, making it harder to work out the source. Damn it! He'd told the copper to sneak in here, not with all guns blazing—the damn rookie was trying to be a hero. If Craig heard the siren, the girls would most certainly be plunged into a grimmer situation. Ripping his phone from his pocket, he dialled the cop station's number, praying to God it would divert to the copper's mobile number. Jake answered in one ring.

Dylan dropped his voice to a whisper. 'What the fuck are you doing with your sirens on, Jake? I can hear you from here, God damn it, turn it off.'

'From where, Dylan?'

'I'm in Craig's machinery shed, the bastard has the girls in here somewhere.'

'How do you know they're in there if you can't bloody see them?' The copper's voice was tinged with annoyance.

'It's called a GPS. I'll explain later.' Dylan hung up the phone, leaving Jake to find his way here. He didn't have time for this. It wouldn't take them long, the road only a few kilometres from where he was.

Lying down on his stomach, Dylan peered beneath the machinery parked in there, a flicker of light capturing his attention from the far side of the shed. Something slithered in front of him and he recoiled. A python about two metres long moved past him, unperturbed by his presence.

Clambering over to where the tiny beam of light shot up from the ground, he discovered a metre-by-metre trapdoor behind a stack of hay bales. He began to shake with a mixture of hopeful anticipation and sheer terror at what he was about to find. Carefully, he grabbed the handle. Easing open one half of the double door, the music and light hit him in the face, followed by the smell of strong chemicals. With his frantic heartbeat pulsing in his ears he carefully positioned himself to climb down. He began to creep down the flight of steps, halting in a panic each time the step creaked beneath his weight, the music thankfully drowning out his arrival. He held his shotgun to his shoulder, ready to shoot, and swallowed down hard. What was he about to see?

Time seemed to move in slow motion. Five steps down he could just make out Craig's legs sprawled out along the floor. Six steps down he could see Renee huddled beside him with Annie in her lap, but Annie wasn't moving. Was she hurt? Worse? A furious rage coursed through Dylan as his finger began to lightly press against the trigger. Seven steps down, Renee's fear-filled eyes finally met with his and the unspoken pleading within them made him feel as though his chest was about to explode. She mouthed, *Annie's alive*, and he almost collapsed then and there. It was then he saw that Craig was asleep. Eight steps down he spotted the chains wrapped around Renee's and Annie's wrists and ankles, and a storm of red flashed before him as he lost all sense of morality. His finger began to press a little harder against the trigger. He wanted to shoot Craig right this second, but was stopped short by the fear that shrapnel might hit Renee or Annie. Nine steps down and three cautious steps forward, he bumped into a shelf and something went crashing to the floor.

Craig jolted to life and within a split second he'd spun sideways and had his revolver pointed at Renee's head. 'Come any closer, Anderson, and I'll pull the fucking trigger.'

Renee hugged Annie closer, her body wracking with the sobs she refused to allow to escape her lips.

Dylan halted in his tracks, his shotgun still pointed at Craig. 'Get away from them you sick son of a bitch,' he roared.

Craig's eyes turned to slits, the smile on his lips repulsive. 'What are you going to do, Anderson? Shoot me? Surely you aren't that fucking stupid… Or are you?'

He shrugged while fighting the compulsion to run to Renee and Annie's aid. 'Maybe I am, maybe I'm not—you wanna try me?'

'I ain't gonna give you the satisfaction. By the way, just for the record, before I kill you, I killed Shelley too…'

For a few brief seconds, the shock of the revelation blurred everything around Dylan, and before he had time to react, Craig's gun fired, the noise in the small room deafening. Renee screamed, her voice reverberating along with the gunshot. A searing pain shot through Dylan's left arm as he fell to the floor. He'd been hit, but how bad? He didn't have time to find out—the only thing he could focus on right now was saving Annie and Renee. Still down on his knees, he raised his gun and began to press the trigger, anger ridding him of any rationality.

'I won't let you take my life, and I ain't fucking going to jail either,' Craig spat, still grinning, before turning the gun on himself and pulling the trigger.

Renee screamed out once more as the thunderous sound ricocheted around the small room. Craig slumped to the floor, lifeless, the gun still clutched in his hands, a pool of blood seeping out around him. Dylan stood, his shotgun now at his side.

Annie stirred in Renee's lap. Time sped up, and Dylan's heart slammed against his chest with every second passing. This evil man had stolen his beautiful wife from him? His poor darling Shelley— and all this time he'd thought it was an accident. With the shocking news, his brain flicked to autopilot—they weren't out of the woods yet. The pain in his arm was excruciating but he couldn't worry about himself right now. On his knees in seconds beside Renee and Annie, he called for an ambulance as he gathered Annie to him and checked her pulse. It was faint, but there. He wrapped his spare arm around Renee, huddling her to him, as he continued to assess Annie.

Renee checked his arm. 'There's so much blood,' she cried. But Dylan was so focused on Annie he didn't hear her. Tearing at her shirt, she pulled off a piece of material and then tied it around where blood was oozing from the wound.

Annie began to stir.

'The bad man is gone, sweetheart. You're safe now,' he said, his voice breaking as he rocked her back and forth.

Annie mumbled something in reply and Dylan put his ear near her mouth so he could hear her. 'I knew you'd come, Daddy. I love you.'

'I love you too, sweetheart. You rest now, the ambulance is coming.' He pushed her matted hair from her face, kissing her cheek over and over as he said her name. She was cold, so damn cold. Renee grasped an old painter's blanket from beside them, wrapping it around herself, Dylan and Annie. Pulling the puffer from his pocket, Dylan asked Annie if she could take it. Annie nodded ever so faintly. He pumped it for her and Annie breathed it in as best she could. Then, having done all he could do, Dylan embraced Annie and Renee, hugging them both into him so there was barely an inch of space left between them all.

His reserve broke, and he sobbed from his heart and soul, for the life Shelley had lost, the two lives he could have lost, and for the pain and torture they had been through. 'I'm so sorry I wasn't there to protect you both.'

With her eyes still closed, a wisp of a smile tugged at Annie's lips. 'You saved us, Daddy. You're my hero.'

Renee shook her head, capturing his eyes with hers, tears pouring down her cheeks. 'You *were* there to protect us, Dylan. If it wasn't for you, I don't think we would have survived the night.'

Voices were heard in the shed above, and then heavy footsteps clambered down the stairs behind them. 'They're down here.' Two paramedics ran towards Dylan, Renee and Annie as blue uniforms filled the room, and close behind them all was Stanley.

On seeing Renee huddled in Dylan's arms, Stanley ran to them and fell to his knees, sobbing as he took Renee into his arms. 'Oh Missy-Moo, thank God you're okay. I love you.'

Renee hugged him even tighter. 'I love you too, Pa.'

Dylan looked past Stanley to where Craig Campbell lay dead on the floor, relieved that nobody had to fear his evil ever again. Nothing could bring back Scarlet or Shelley, but at least Renee and Annie would be able to live out the rest of their lives without forever looking over their shoulders—which Renee had done for long enough. Looking from Annie to Renee, Dylan felt his heart reach out for the two of them. They were his world, his everything, and he was going to do his damn best to never let anyone hurt either of them ever again.

EPILOGUE

Twelve months and one week later…

It was exactly a year to the day that Scarlet had been laid to rest, although it still only felt like yesterday that the Opals Ridge Catholic church had been overflowing with mourners—most of the town there to pay their respects to a young woman who was taken well before her time. Louise had also attended, the poor woman hiding beneath her black veil, and having to be carried from the church when she had collapsed. Finding out that her ex-husband had been a murderer had taken a massive toll on her. How unfair it was that Craig didn't have to repent his sins, leaving his family to feel as though they had to do it for him.

Standing at the now lawn-covered grave, Renee wiped the tears from her cheeks. Pa and Nan stood beside her, Pearl equally as emotional as she was. Stanley's face was solemn, his emotions in check on the outside, although Renee knew he suffered in silence while trying to remain outwardly strong. Forever the rock of the family, he liked them to believe. He and Dylan were so alike in so many ways, which was probably another reason she loved him as much as she did.

Without the two of them to hold her up through her darkest of days, she didn't know how she would have made it through. Between the horrific ordeal Craig had put her and Annie through, and the aftermath—coming to terms with the knowledge that Scarlet and Shelley had been taken from them by such an animal— it had been an extremely tough year for them all. But by loving each other through it, they'd survived, and had also found many things to be grateful for along the way, including the fact the sale of her apartment had saved Ironbark Plains from the grips of the bank, giving Dylan back the freedom to work day in, day out on their now-lucrative property. She still hadn't had the heart to sell Fay's cottage in Hawksburn—all in good time.

After placing the sunflowers she was carrying into the vase— Scarlet's favourites—Renee's hands fluttered to the split heart pendant around her neck. The other half was now buried with Scarlet's remains that had been discovered exactly where Craig had said they were, on Dylan's property. No longer did Renee or Pearl catch the scent of frankincense within the homestead, but neither of them begrudged the fact, the knowledge that Scarlet was now at peace meaning everything to them. Placing a kiss to her fingertips, Renee then pressed it against the headstone. 'I love you, sis.' Turning, the three of them embraced. A family, with so much loss and heartache to deal with, but with so much to also look forward to.

Sitting on the cowskin rug in the middle of the lounge room, Renee folded the last corner of the gold wrapping paper, smiling as Annie passed her another piece of sticky tape. 'Thanks, sweetheart. Do you want to put the pretty pink bow on top now?'

Annie clapped her hands, her eyes wide with excitement. 'Oh, yes please!'

Renee pushed the box towards her, avoiding Kat and Bossy in the process—the two of them snuggled up together beside her as they slept. Kat had taken a shine to the Great Dane from the get-go, and when Bossy was in the cottage the two were inseparable. 'Do you think Uncle Ralph and Aunty Tia are going to like what we've picked for their housewarming?'

'I reckon they will. How can anyone not love an ice-cream maker?'

Renee nodded and gave her the thumbs up. 'Too right, Annie, ice-cream is the best! It was a good choice of yours, sweetheart.'

Dylan admired his two girls from the lounge chair, balancing his plate on his lap as he forked another mouthful of his lunch in. 'This is the yummiest caesar salad I've ever tasted,' he mumbled between pleasurable groans. 'I'm one lucky man, I tell ya.'

'Renee is the bestest cook ever!' Annie said, busying herself with positioning the bow in exactly the right spot.

'She sure is,' Dylan replied, smiling at Renee in the most loving of ways as he did.

'Thanks guys. The secret is the salad dressing I made with the fresh eggs Annie collected from our chooks this morning.' Renee struggled to get up from the floor, her aching back and generously curved stomach making it a challenge. She edged around onto her hands and knees, thinking that might be easier, but instead she felt like a beached whale. Rolling onto her back, she giggled. 'Oh Lord, talk about being absolutely useless at the moment.'

Dylan jumped to her aid, making sure she didn't strain herself as he grabbed both her hands and slowly helped her to her feet. 'You got to stop sitting on the floor, beautiful, otherwise you might just find yourself stuck down there one day if one of us isn't around to help you up.'

'I know, I know. I got stuck in the darn recliner chair the other day, too. It took me a good part of ten minutes just to get the leg rest down.'

Now that she was on her feet, Dylan pulled Renee in as close as he could, laying a quick kiss on her lips as his hands went lovingly to her belly. 'Not long now until we meet our new addition to the family. I wonder if my guess is right about it being a boy?'

Renee placed her hands over Dylan's. 'We'll soon find out, only six weeks to go.'

'No way, Daddy,' Annie said from the floor. 'I keep telling you it's going to be a girl, I just know it.'

'I reckon that might just be wishful thinking, Annie,' Dylan said, laughing.

'Whatever, Daddy, I know I'm right,' Annie said, jumping up. She smiled from ear to ear. 'I'm going to get dressed for the party, I can't wait to see everyone.'

Racing off down the hall, Annie's footsteps faded into her bedroom.

Renee wrapped her arms around Dylan's shoulders, her eyes capturing his. 'I love you so much, Dylan, more and more every single day. I can't wait to be Mrs Anderson next year.'

Dylan smiled from his heart. 'And I love you, my beautiful fiancée. I'm going to keep on loving you for the rest of my life, and into the next.'

ACKNOWLEDGMENTS

A grateful group hug to my wonderful team at Harlequin headquarters—my publisher Sue Brockhoff, my editors Annabel Blay and Lachlan Jobbins, and the rest of the extremely devoted team who've enthusiastically helped make *The Wildwood Sisters* the very best it can be. I honestly can't thank you all enough. The faith you've shown in my work, and the inspiration you've given me with your suggestions and guidance have been immeasurable. I feel so very blessed to be a part of such a devoted, caring and tremendously talented bunch of people.

To my best friend, soulmate and spunky hunk of a hubby, Clancy. Thank you for always believing in me, loving me with all you have and filling my life with so much positivity. I love that we can create storylines together, dream together, laugh together and live our every day together. You're the reason I believe in true soul-deep love, and the way you love me inspires my written word.

I look forward to every single second I spend with you. Love you more and more every day, beautiful.

To my gorgeous little girl Chloe Rose. You're the most beautiful soul, with a spirit that makes all around you smile, and a heart bigger than the ocean. To see the world through your innocent eyes is a blessing. I'm so very proud to see your love of reading and how you like to sit and write stories that melt my heart. You mean everything to me sweetheart, and I love you a million bazillion gazillion.

To my dedicated dad John. You're such a kind, caring, wise and loving soul. I'm so very lucky to have a father like you and Chloe is equally blessed to have such a loving grandad (who spoils her rotten!). Thank you for always being there for me—be it to give me a much-needed hug, some fatherly advice or just to share special moments with. Love you.

To my step-dad Trevor. We've shared so many happy times, and you've also been there to help me through the rough times too. Your positive outlook on life has taught me to believe in myself and to approach each day with an open heart and mind. Thank you for being the best step-dad ever! Love you.

Wayne and Pam, I thank my lucky stars for having such kind and thoughtful in-laws. And you're wonderful grandparents too. Thank you, Pam, for always being more than happy to read through my manuscripts and give me a constructive critique. I feel very blessed to have you both in my life.

To Taylor, thank you for being the best stepsister anyone could wish for—Chloe adores you, and so do I. You're a beautiful soul, inside and out.

To my beautiful crazy-in-a-good-way mates, Tia, Kirsty and Fi, I'm one very lucky chickie to have girlfriends like you! You make me laugh until my sides ache, are always there to wipe my tears, even if it's from afar, and give me a gentle shove in the right direction when I'm feeling a little lost in life and also with my writing. I couldn't imagine my life without you all in it. Love yas!

To my sisters Mia, Karla, Rochelle and Hayley, what a wonderful bunch you are! Each of you has a uniqueness I love and I feel so very blessed to have you all in my life. And you rock as aunties too! Love you all with all my heart.

To my beautiful Aunty Kulsoom, thank you for loving me for who I am and for always being extra keen to help edit my books—your teacher's eye is invaluable. Love you heaps.

To my newfound New South Wales mates, Kristie, Kelly, Rowie and Kristen, thank you for welcoming Chloe and me into the Grenfell community with open arms. It means the world that I have friends like you nearby.

To my author buddy Rachael Johns, thank you for always being there to answer my many questions, and to just have an authorly chinwag with. I really appreciate it. You're honestly just the loveliest!

And last, but certainly not least, a massive squeezy hug to YOU, the reader. Without you my dream of writing wouldn't be my reality. I'm honoured and humbled that you've chosen to pick up my book to discover the story within...it truly means the world to me. I'm passionate about this great big beautiful country down under and I hope my storytelling takes you to the very heart and soul of country life, and of course, true love.

Until my next book keep smiling and dreaming,

Country cheers,
Mandy ☺

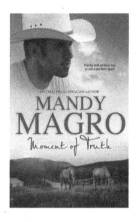

Turn over for a sneak peek.

Moment of Truth

by

MANDY
MAGRO

OUT NOW

mira

CHAPTER

1

Diamond Acres Horse Sanctuary, Blue Ridge,
North Queensland

A resounding boom echoed throughout the cottage, sending a black wave of fruit bats soaring from the surrounding mango trees in search of safer perches. Kicking off the bed sheets, thirteen-year-old Alexis Brown stirred from a dream where she was travelling through a magical world. For a split-second she fought not to return to reality, the wonderful feeling of her horse, Wild Thing, galloping beneath her as they rode across a luminous rainbow arch was enticing her to stay in dreamland a little longer. If only she could get to the end of it and finally see what treasures lay at the foot of the band of colours that arched across the bright blue sky – her mum was always telling her about the pot of gold and she wanted to know if it was true. But to her disappointment she tumbled back into the real world, her nightie stuck to her sweaty skin and her heart still racing from the invigorating ride. Resting her hands on her chest she took a few deep breaths, slow and steady, the rhythm returning to normal as she opened her eyes.

A deafening crash of thunder made her start and then a bright flash of lightning briefly lit up the room as if someone had just switched a light on. The wet season was finally upon them. The much-needed rain was here, the thirsty ground desperate for it. She almost clapped her hands in delight, but refrained so she didn't wake her younger sister. Her mother's many wind chimes jingled from the front verandah, the clangs melodious. The sheer white curtains flapped in the breeze, allowing the full moon to cast its silver–grey light through the window, illuminating the entire bedroom like the colours in an otherworldly dream. The big old fig tree she liked to climb so she could read her books in peace scraped its branches along the side of the house as the wind blew noisily through its leaves. The scent of the balmy summer night, of the jasmine blossoms and the freshly mowed grass, mixed with the scent of imminent rain floated in through the open window, all of it tantalising her senses – she truly felt alive when she was outside and she felt drawn there now. Her mother was always trying to get her to hang out in the kitchen, wanting her to learn boring things like baking; but she much preferred to be with her dad (if she wasn't reading) – not because she didn't love her mum, she loved her to bits – it's just that her father worked outdoors and did much more exciting stuff, like fixing tractors and fences, and her most favourite job of all, helping Mister King take care of the wild horses that he and her dad brought here when they rescued them. Her father was the best horse trainer around, or that's what the people at the local agriculture shop always said to her, and she liked to believe it was so.

Heavy raindrops suddenly hit the tin roof in a roar, making it almost impossible to hear anything else. Unperturbed by the noise,

Alexis breathed in deeply – she loved the smell of rain. It was so new and pure, and made her feel super alive. She thought about how her Grandpa Bob had once told her that the rain was God watering his garden. But if it were the case, God had been a bit slack in that department, because they hadn't had a drop for almost a month now.

Turning away from the window she gazed at the stars and moon that appeared to be dancing across the ceiling, projected by the revolving bedside lamp – her favourite gift from her favourite Nanny Fay. She couldn't wait to see her again, and Grandpa Bob, in a few months time; it was going to be so much fun spending the Easter school holidays at their place in Townsville. She just hoped her mum came along because she didn't seem too keen on the idea.

Wide awake now and with her mind wandering, she thought about going for a ride on Wild Thing at first light, if the rain stopped, when loud voices caught her attention. Trying hard to hear over the storm Alexis caught words from a heated conversation. It was coming from the kitchen at the other end of the cottage. She could hear her father's distinctive deep voice, but as much it made her feel happy to know he'd arrived home a day early from visiting her grandparents, his angry tone worried her. He rarely got mad. And her mum sounded like she was crying as she said things Alexis couldn't quite comprehend. Instantly blaming herself for the argument, because her dad had gone to her great grandad's funeral on his own, Alexis choked back a sob. She chewed on her bottom lip to try to stop it quivering. Although they sometimes grumbled at each other, she'd never heard her parents argue like this. Thinking back to the tension that had hung over the dinner table when her mother had said they wouldn't be able to come along to the funeral because Alexis had to go to school made her feel as though this was all her fault. Luckily she'd had what looked like a billion peas on her dinner plate at the time, because she could focus on moving them around with her fork rather than thinking about the glare her father had given her mother.

Rolling on to her side so her back was now to the window she looked at the strip of light under the closed bedroom door, the pale moonlight shining on her Polaroid camera, which hung on the doorknob. Her heart jumped up to her throat as she tugged the doona in closer. She and her younger sister Katie never slept with their door closed. Her parents both knew how much it scared them. So who had closed it? The voices grew louder. Fear stabbed at her belly as she squeezed her eyes shut. Something wasn't right. Part of her wanted to fix whatever it was, but another big part of her wanted to stay right here, where she felt safe. Katie was asleep beside her. She had crawled in with Alexis after having yet another bad dream, and being the big sister Alexis felt it was her job to make sure her sister was safe too.

Staying right here was the best thing to do.

But then the rain eased and her father's voice got even louder, and all the more angry.

Clutching her favourite blue teddy bear, scruffy as it was after thirteen years of cuddles, Alexis shot up to sitting when she heard him. She was so unsure of what she should do – go out and stop her parents arguing, or protect her sister? Rubbing the bear's fluffy ears in the same place she always did when she was sad or worried, she looked down at Katie; her sister's petite features were even more adorable as she slept but also made her seem even more vulnerable. And that made Alexis feel even more protective. She huffed. Renewed determination filled her. Her parents should quieten down, and maybe she'd better go out there and tell them so. Perhaps, with all the noise from the storm, they didn't realise just how loudly they were talking.

Her father's voice became harsher, his bad language not something Alexis was used to. Her stomach tightened and hot tears stung her eyes. Her mum was saying sorry over and over again while begging him to understand. Understand what? Alexis felt like her heart was going to bang its way out of her chest, it was beating so fast now. She wanted to go and comfort her mother, and tell her dad to stop being so nasty, but then something smashed, maybe a glass hitting the floor. Twirling a strand of her long blonde hair tightly around her finger she held her breath, terrified of what might happen next as her eyes darted back and forth from the open window to the closed door.

Warily slipping from the bed she tiptoed towards the slither of light and pressed her ear up against the plywood door.

'I can't take any more of this, Peggy,' her father's voice boomed.

'Please, stop yelling, Jason, the girls are asleep.' Her mum's sobs got louder.

'And so they should be at three in the morning, just like you should be, too. I can't believe you've done this to me, to us. We're a family. I thought we were happy. I thought we were going to live out our days together, side by side.'

'I'm so sorry, Jason. I don't know what to say.'

'Then don't say anything, Peggy, because there's really nothing more to say. I've seen it for myself, you can't talk your way out of it now.'

Hearing the rustle of sheets Alexis turned around as Katie stirred and her eyes flickered open. Alexis's sisterly instincts kicked into full force – she didn't want Katie to hear any of this. She dashed over to her as quietly as she could, placing her hand on her arm. 'Hi there, Pebbles, did the rain wake you?'

'I don't know.' Katie looked past her to the door and her eyes grew misty. She hugged her knees to her chest. Her lips quivered as she sucked in a shaky breath, then the welling tears rolled down her cheeks. 'Sissy, why's the door shut?'

Before Alexis could answer a strong draught of wind blew through the open window, lifting the curtains, and gave her the perfect answer. 'I think the wind might have shut it, Pebbles. I was just going to open it when you woke up.'

'Okay, can you open it now?'

Alexis wished she could but was too terrified to do so. 'In a sec, I want a cuddle first.' Climbing back onto the bed she cradled Katie, making sure to subtly cover her little sister's ears as Katie wrapped her arms around her neck.

Just as things seemed to quieten, her parents' voices no longer loud and the rain now more of a soft pitter patter on the roof, Jack, their bits-of-everything-dog (well that's what her father had called him when they saved him from the pound a few months ago) began to bark from where he was locked away in his kennel out the back. Her dad roared for Jack to *Shut the hell up.* Instead, the barking became more insistent. Alexis silently prayed for her newest best furry buddy to do as he was told, while she pressed her hands in harder against Katie's ears.

Heavy footfalls stomped down the hallway, past the bedroom, and moments later whoever it was pounded back past again. A gunshot followed, so close to the cottage it seemed to echo through the walls. Katie jumped, her eyes filled with fear and a wail escaped her. Rocking Katie, Alexis swallowed down hard as she squeezed back tears. She needed to be strong for Katie, no matter how terrified she felt. As her dad always said, it was a big sister's job to be the strong one, to lead by giving a good example.

'It's all right, Pebbles, I think Dad might have been shooting at one of those pesky dingoes again.' It seemed to calm Katie but

Alexis knew better – her dad must be real mad, shooting his gun like that to warn Jack. It had worked, though; Jack was silent now.

But then the voices got louder, more urgent, and Alexis was sure she heard a third voice, but she couldn't be certain with Katie's wailing filling her ears. Her already racing heart beat faster. The hair stood up at the back of her neck. Maybe it was time to think about hiding under the bed? Or in the cupboard, like ET had with all those toys? But that would scare Katie even more – she hated the dark. With her mind in a spin Alexis tried to think quickly. Their favourite place, that's where she should take Katie until her parents stopped fighting, and they could get to it by climbing out of their bedroom window. They often climbed out through the window to avoid walking all the way down the hall and out the back door, much to her mother's annoyance.

'Come on, Katie, let's go and have a tea party in the cubby house.'

Katie smiled through her tears. 'Now?'

Alexis tried to fake calmness by shrugging. 'Why not?'

Katie looked to the open window. 'Because it's dark outside and the boogieman might get us.'

'Don't be silly, Katie, like I always tell you, there's no such thing as the boogieman. We still have Daddy's big torch in there, remember, so it won't be dark once we turn that on.'

'But aren't we going to get wet?'

'When have you ever been afraid of the rain, Pebbles?'

'Okay then, Sissy.' Katie didn't sound so sure as she climbed from the bed, her comforter blanket clutched tightly in her small hands. 'Why are Mummy and Daddy yelling?'

'I don't know, Pebbles.' Springing from the bed, she gathered Katie into her arms. 'Sometimes people just get mad at each other, like you and I do, I suppose.'

'Yeah,' Katie said with a giggle. 'You get mad at me a lot.'

'I do not.'

'Yes you do, all the time.'

'Okay, I do, but only because you're a little ratbag and you drive me nuts.'

'Am not.'

'Are too.'

Katie giggled.

Alexis tried to keep the mood light as she walked over to the window. She helped Katie to climb out first and then it was her turn, her feet hitting the sodden ground before she had even let go of the windowsill. Hand in hand, the two girls then dashed the few metres to the cubby house, both of them drenched through to the skin when they got there. The small backyard of the worker's cottage didn't allow for much, but her dad had built the finest cubby house Alexis had ever seen. If she had her way, she would turn it into her bedroom.

Just as she switched on the torch, igniting the cubby in so much light that she and Katie both squinted, another gunshot rang out, its boom piercing the quiet countryside and ricocheting off the surrounding mountains. Heart-wrenching screams from her mother were immediately followed by her father's cries. Katie burst into uncontrollable tears, her sobs only quietened when she needed to draw a breath. Although wanting to comfort her sister Alexis stood frozen to the spot, her breathing ragged as she felt a part of her snap in two. She'd never been so terrified in all her life. What was she meant to do? Go inside and make sure her parents were all right, or do everything she could to protect her sister and herself? Was that selfish, to want to protect herself?

She grabbed Katie's hand. Hurrying out of the cubby house she tugged her towards the scrub at the side of the cottage. Like she always did, Katie followed in her footsteps without complaint, and within seconds they were standing at the edge of the paddock that led down to Mister and Missus King's house – their neighbours and also their father's bosses. She had no idea what was going on but she instinctively knew she had to get down there, fast, to get Katie to safety and to ask for help for her parents.

The wind blew wet tresses of her long hair across her face as more gunshots rang out, her mother's blood-curdling screams driving Alexis into a wild run. No longer hand-in-hand with Katie, she could hear her sobbing so she knew Katie was beside her, even though it seemed as if her sister were a million miles away, all of Alexis's senses feeling as if they'd short-circuited. With her chest burning from the exertion and her breath hard to catch, she reached the driveway that led to the big homestead. If only Wild Thing wasn't all the way up the other end she would have run to him for comfort. Mud splashed up her leg as Katie tripped and fell into a puddle, her little body heaving with angst-ridden sobs, and she rolled into a ball, her knees cuddled to her chest.

Crouching down Alexis tried to help Katie back up, but her sister refused to move.

'Come on, Pebbles, please, we have to go and get help.' Taking her wrist she gave it a tug.

Katie yanked her arm free and slowly sat up, her bottom lip trembling. 'I want to go home to Mummy.'

'I know, Katie, me too,' Alexis said softly as she placed her hand on her sister's shoulders. 'We will soon.' Using the corner of Katie's blanket, she wiped her sister's face and nose before tucking the loose dark curls behind her ears. 'Don't worry, as long as you and I stick together everything's going to be all right, okay?'

'You promise?' Katie mumbled, her fingers in her mouth.

'I promise, Pebbles.' Alexis's throat was so tight with emotion she was finding it hard to speak.

'I don't want to go to the big house. I don't like Missus King. She's grumpy and she scares me.'

Alexis gently wiped the hair back from Katie's forehead. 'I know, she scares me too, but hopefully Mister King will answer the door. He's never grumpy, is he?'

'No, he's really nice.'

'Yes, he is, and he always gives us those yummy butterscotch lollies when Mrs King isn't looking, doesn't he?'

A hint of a smile shone through Katie's tear-stained face. 'He does, naughty Mister King.'

'Will we go and see if he has any left?'

Nodding, Katie got up. Her powder-pink singlet was now mud spattered, as too was her beloved cuddle blanket. Moving into more of a jog, Alexis breathed a sigh of relief when Katie did the same. She couldn't go shouting at Katie to hurry up, she was upset enough. Not long and they would be able to knock on the front door and ask for help. She wondered if Ethan was staying at his grandparents' place this weekend – he was always so calm, even when she'd fallen off Wild Thing and broken her arm, he knew what to do. Being three years older than her, he was smarter about certain things. How she wished he were with her right now, so she didn't have to be the adult.

The rambling homestead finally came into view and with her galloping heart feeling as though it was about to explode she slowed, as did Katie. Stealing a second glance back up at the only home she'd ever known, Alexis gritted her teeth to stop from crying. Something very bad had happened and she didn't dare think what it was right now for fear of crumbling into a million tiny pieces. She had to believe her mum and dad were okay and, most importantly, alive.

Hurrying through a white picket fence they took a short cut and headed across the front lawn instead of following the winding garden path. The wet grass was cold on Alexis's bare feet. Casper, the Kings' pet Border Collie, still only a pup, barked incessantly from his kennel at the side of the house. As they climbed the five front steps a floodlight fired to life. Alexis held her free hand up to shield her eyes, the other still holding tightly to Katie's. The front door swung open and Mister King appeared. When he heard Casper barking, he must have raced down to the door to get there so fast. Pulling his robe in tighter he stepped towards them, concern twisting his already wrinkly features.

'Oh my goodness, Alexis, Katie ... ' He looked from one to the other. 'What are you two girls doing up and about at this time of the night, and in this horrible weather? Is everything okay?'

Katie burst into inconsolable tears. Momentarily unable to speak for the growing lump in her throat Alexis shook her head as she peered down at her mud-covered toes. 'Mum and Dad were fighting ... ' she choked out. 'And then there were gunshots, and now I don't know if they're okay.' She brought her eyes back up to meet Mister King's. 'Please, we have to go and help them.'

'Oh my goodness, you poor darling girls.' Mister King knelt down and took them into his arms. Alexis crumpled into him; the comfort he gave with such a simple gesture was overwhelming.

The flyscreen door creaked open. Alexis peered over Mister King's shoulder to see Missus King standing at the doorway, her hair in rollers and her arms folded across her fluffy pink robe. The frown creasing her thick black brows was even bigger than it usually was. 'For goodness sake, what's happened at the Browns' place now, Charlie? Can't they give us a rest from their incessant dramas?'

Dramas? Alexis felt confused.

Mister King turned, his arms still enfolding the two sisters. 'Go and call an ambulance, Mavis.' His tone was firmer than Alexis had heard it before, especially when speaking to Missus King. Usually it was the other way around.

Missus King rolled her eyes and clucked her tongue. 'Surely we don't need an ambulance, Charles, whatever it is it can't be that bad, hmmm?'

'Oh, for goodness sake, woman, can't you just do as you're asked one time without damn well questioning me?' Mister King dropped his arms and stood, his well-built, six-foot-tall frame seeming to tower over them. 'There have been shots fired at the cottage and the girls have no idea what's happened or if their parents are all right.'

Shock stole Missus King's frown as she raced back inside without another word.

Mister King placed a hand on each of the girls' shoulders. 'Now, you two, come on inside and wait with Missus King while I go up to the cottage to find out what's going on, all right?'

'Okay,' they said in union. Mister King ushered them inside, ran upstairs to get dressed and then quickly strode over to his ute, parked beneath a paperbark tree near the house.

Now standing on the other side of the flyscreen door, her hands and face pressed up against it, Alexis watched Mister King speed off down the driveway. The back of his ute was sliding this way and that. She couldn't help but wonder what he would find when he got there, and she prayed with everything she had that this was just some misunderstanding and soon she and Katie could give their mum and dad a great big cuddle.

With the taillights finally disappearing she turned to find Katie nowhere in sight and neither was Missus King. She called out to them, but there was no answer. Strange. Katie never left her side when they had visited the Kings' place before. She called out again as she wandered around, going from room to room. Walking towards the staircase, she looked up. She didn't want to go up there. It was so very dark and, besides, she and Katie were never allowed upstairs. Missus King had made that very clear over the years. She heard a muffled cry and knew it was Katie's. Why was she upstairs, and where was Missus King? Sighing, she did what she knew she shouldn't and climbed the steps. Missus King would be very angry if she found Katie wandering around up there, so she needed to find her little sister and bring her back down before they both got into trouble.

More great titles
from bestselling Australian author

MANDY
MAGRO

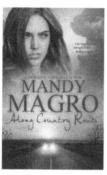 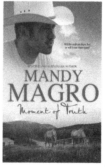

AVAILABLE NOW